Praise for *Blood and Iron*...

"Bear works out her background with the detail orientation of a science fiction writer, spins her prose like a veil-dancing fantasist, and never forgets to keep an iron fist in that velvet glove."   —The Agony Column

"Complex and nuanced. . . . Bear does a fantastic job with integrating these centuries-old elements into a thoroughly modern tale of transformation, love, and courage."   —*Romantic Times*

"Bear overturns the usual vision of Faerie, revealing the compelling beauty and darkness only glimpsed in old ballads and stories like 'Tam Lin.' "
                    —*Publishers Weekly*

. . . and the novels of Elizabeth Bear

"A gritty and painstakingly well-informed peek inside a future world we'd all better hope we don't get, liberally seasoned with VR delights and enigmatically weird alien artifacts. . . . Elizabeth Bear builds her future nightmare tale with style and conviction and a constant return to the twists of the human heart."
                    —Richard Morgan, author of *Altered Carbon*

"Very exciting, very polished, very impressive."
                    —Mike Resnick, author of *Starship: Mutiny*

"Gritty, insightful, and daring."
                    —David Brin, author of the *Uplift* novels and *Kiln People*

"A glorious hybrid: hard science, dystopian geopolitics, and wide-eyed sense of wonder seamlessly blended into a single book."
                    —Peter Watts, author of *Starfish* and *Maelstrom*

"Elizabeth Bear has carved herself out a fantastic little world. . . . It's rare to find a book with so many characters you genuinely care about. It's a roller coaster of a good thriller, too."   —SF Crowsnest

"What Bear has done . . . is create a world that is all too plausible, one wracked by environmental devastation and political chaos. . . . She conducts a tour of this society's darker corners, offering an unnerving peek into a future humankind would be wise to avoid."   —SciFi.com

"An enthralling roller-coaster ride through a dark and possible near future."
                    —*Starlog*

Whiskey and Water

A Novel of the Promethean Age

 Elizabeth Bear

RoC

A ROC BOOK

ROC
Published by New American Library, a division of
Penguin Group (USA) Inc., 375 Hudson Street,
New York, New York 10014, USA
Penguin Group (Canada), 90 Eglinton Avenue East, Suite 700, Toronto,
Ontario M4P 2Y3, Canada (a division of Pearson Penguin Canada Inc.)
Penguin Books Ltd., 80 Strand, London WC2R 0RL, England
Penguin Ireland, 25 St. Stephen's Green, Dublin 2,
Ireland (a division of Penguin Books Ltd.)
Penguin Group (Australia), 250 Camberwell Road, Camberwell, Victoria 3124,
Australia (a division of Pearson Australia Group Pty. Ltd.)
Penguin Books India Pvt. Ltd., 11 Community Centre, Panchsheel Park,
New Delhi - 110 017, India
Penguin Group (NZ), 67 Apollo Drive, Rosedale, North Shore 0745,
Auckland, New Zealand (a division of Pearson New Zealand Ltd.)
Penguin Books (South Africa) (Pty.) Ltd., 24 Sturdee Avenue,
Rosebank, Johannesburg 2196, South Africa

Penguin Books Ltd., Registered Offices:
80 Strand, London WC2R 0RL, England

First published by Roc, an imprint of New American Library,
a division of Penguin Group (USA) Inc.

First Printing, July 2007
1   3   5   7   9   10   8   6   4   2

Scripture quotation on pp. 279–80 taken from the New American Standard Bible®, copyright © 1960, 1962,
1963, 1968, 1971, 1972, 1973, 1975, 1977, 1995 by The Lockman Foundation. Used by permission.
(www.Lockman.org)

LIBRARY OF CONGRESS CATALOGING-IN-PUBLICATION DATA
Bear, Elizabeth.
Whiskey & water : a novel of the Promethean Age / Elizabeth Bear.
p. cm.
"A ROC book."
ISBN: 978-0-451-46149-0
I. Title. II. Title: Whiskey and water.
PS3602.E2475W47 2007
813'.6—dc22   2006035124

Set in Cochin
Designed by Ginger Legato

Printed in the United States of America

PUBLISHER'S NOTE
This is a work of fiction. Names, characters, places, and incidents either are the product of the author's imagina-
tion or are used fictitiously, and any resemblance to actual persons, living or dead, business establishments,
events, or locales is entirely coincidental.
    The publisher does not have any control over and does not assume any responsibility for author or third-
party Web sites or their content.

This book is for Hannah Wolf Bowen,
Whiskey's wicked stepmother.

Acknowledgments

I would very much like to thank everyone who helped out, fielded questions, or listened to me complain about this book. Especially but not exclusively, thanks go to Karen Junker for authenticity checks on body modification practices; to Tobias Buckell and Chantal McGee for assistance with Caribbean dialect; to Sherwood Smith for master's classes in omniscient POV; to Lt. Ed Finizie, NLVPD, for vetting my police procedures; to Abigail Ackland, the maintainer of www.tam-lin.org (an invaluable resource for would-be balladeer-deconstructionists); to the talented answerers-of-silly-questions—Amanda Downum, Hannah Wolf Bowen, Jaime Voss, Nick Mamatas, Jenni Smith Gaynor, Nalo Hopkinson, Kathryn Allen, Lis Riba, Chelsea Polk, and Sarah Monette—who helped keep me looking smarter than I am; to Kit Kindred and to my agent, Jennifer Jackson, for service above and beyond the call; to Stella Evans, MD, for helping me manage the massive amounts of medical background necessary for this narrative; to my copyeditor, Cherilyn Johnson, for fixing my mistakes; and to my editor, Liz Scheier, the unflaggingly meticulous—and encouraging.

⟋ Contents

Whiskey and Water

Chapter One
Fairytale of New York

Once upon a time in New York City, there lived a Mage with a crippled right hand. Once he wore ten iron rings upon his fingers. Once he had a brother. Once he had a calling. Twice, he touched a unicorn.

Once upon a time.

Streetlights might burn out in Matthew Szczegielniak's presence, or dim and flutter dark for as long as it took him to pass. Car alarms and stereos might deploy unexpectedly, computers crash, neon signs flicker messages they were never meant to spell.

He knew they were trying to say something, to play the oracle. But he understood only a fragment of what they told: that a powerful shadow hung over him, that a powerful shadow lay cupped in the scarred hollow of his claw-hooked hand. Beyond that, the signs were too wild for him to read as he would have, once. Or to control.

It was a frustration so intense that the only response he could manage was to kick it away, kick it aside, and carry on as if nothing was wrong. You could learn to run on an amputated limb. If you were stubborn enough. Adaptable enough. And didn't mind a little pain.

He wasn't mad, Matthew Szczegielniak. He had been lucky to venture into Faerie and return sane—more or less—and lacking only his good right hand. He taught his classes at Hunter College—British Literature (one section general, one section Elizabethan Drama, one section Elizabethan Drama and Poetry Other Than Shakespeare)—and he stayed away from the students' laptops, and he practiced until the chalk and dry-erase scrawls he wrought with his left hand formed words.

Matthew kept a magnetized iron knife in his left front pocket and he wore a ring carved of rowan wood on his right thumb. Ink in dark unsettling labyrinths marked his back and arms, and his nape under the clean blond ponytail. He wore steel-rimmed spectacles that twinkled compassionately when he tilted his head. He lived alone in a half-remodeled apartment; someone else paid his bills.

The someone's name was Jane Andraste. She was the former lieutenant governor of New York, and the only other Mage Matthew knew of, anymore. All the rest were dead, and whether that was Matthew's fault or Jane's, Matthew did not take her calls.

He ran in Central Park like a wild thing and lifted iron weights as he always had—although it took some cleverness to lash them into his right hand—but he no longer wore the iron rings on his fingers and in his ear that once had drawn him to oppose anything Fae that set foot on Manhattan. Iron and copper and bronze were anathema to Faerie. Matthew would not permit himself to be enslaved to his tools again.

Once upon a time, he *had* permitted. It had cost him his duty, his honor, his brother, his heart's blood, half his soul, control of his magic, and whatever faith he'd managed to preserve through thirty-odd years of service. It had cost him the use of his good right hand.

Once upon a time.

Somewhere in Hell, a poet was packing his bags. He wasn't particularly circumspect about it; the master of the house would know of his actions, as Lucifer tended to know what concerned him, and so the poet rehearsed arguments as he folded shirts and found his rapier and a notebook. He didn't expect to be permitted to leave without some sort of confrontation.

All the same, he packed only what he'd need for a day or two. He could send for the rest, once—*if*—he got settled somewhere. And if the Devil proved recalcitrant, well. It wouldn't be the first time the poet had lost everything.

Things were only that.

He was pulling the drawstrings of his rucksack taut when a rustle of feathers by the door caught his attention, as it was meant to. He swung the bag onto the neatly made bed and turned, flipping his layered patchwork cloak over his shoulders in a practiced gesture. He crossed his arms over his chest and set his heels, and said, quietly, "Morningstar."

Lucifer's beauty was not the sort to which one could grow accustomed. It was composed of small imperfections—the long nose, the too-lush mouth—that amounted to a breathtaking gestalt, so every shift of expression revealed some new facet of the Devil's charm.

He framed himself in the poet's bedroom doorway as if standing for a portrait. His wheat-colored hair dragged in disorder over the black velvet shoulders of his jacket, and even in the dim light of the gas lamps his eyes were sharply blue. His white wings rustled as he folded them against his back to step into the room, and rustled further when he let them fan wide. :I wondered when thou wouldst make thy mind up to go.:

"I made my mind up some time ago," the poet said. "I've no reason to stay, with Murchaud gone."

:Thy old Devil beguiles thee not, Kitten?:

The poet's smile felt tight across his teeth as he chose not to answer the question. "You know I hate that nickname."

:Then perhaps thou shouldst have kept thine own name. What wouldst barter me, to have it back?:

The poet picked up his bag and slung it over one shoulder, and stepped wide around the Devil on his way to the door.

He was almost there when the flagstones shuddered under his feet, in time with an enormous hollow thumping. He sidestepped, almost tripping, and Lucifer steadied him with an outstretched wing. "Were you expecting a visitor?"

:I know that knock,: Lucifer answered. He swept the poet forward with the leading edge of his wing, and followed him through the door.

The poet's footfalls were hushed on long silk carpets, but the vast emptiness of Hell's corridors gave the sense that they *should* echo. The poet shivered, gathering his cloak tighter in his left hand, tugging it over the rapier he wore on that hip. You could feel the loneliness here, the constant awareness of exile. It had the weight of oppression: whatever was in Hell was forgotten, shunned by the larger world.

"What would bring him here?" the poet asked, as much to fill up the silence as because he cared to know.

Lucifer's shrug lifted his wings. He gestured with one long hand as if brushing a curtain aside. :Perhaps he's come to see thee off. Or to invite me to a ball. It is All Hallow's Eve—:

Someone stepped into the corridor before them: a big man, bearded, his red hair twisted into a club at the nape of his neck. The freckles across the bridge of his nose made a striking discontinuity with his glower. "There's a Devil on your doorstep," he said.

:Thank you, Keith,: Lucifer said. :I had noticed. You will accompany me to greet him.:

Keith MacNeill, the Dragon Prince—and so in a metaphysical manner the heir to Arthur Pendragon and Vlad Dracula—shook his head. "You can hold me captive by my oath, but I won't be compelled to fight your wars, Morningstar."

Lucifer smiled through his curls. :Shall it come to fisticuffs?:

"You're on your own if it does."

The poet chuckled, but Lucifer took no notice. Instead, he strode into the lead, leaving Keith and the poet to spin in his wake, hurrying to keep pace.

The great doors to Lucifer's palace stood open and unguarded, and beyond them, in the courtyard, waited Satan. Another poet's Devil, that one, a batwinged horror with his upswept horns and smoke rising in coils from wings that radiated sooty heat like fire-charred stone. Lucifer stopped the poet and the Dragon Prince in the doorway with a sweep of his hand, and stepped outside to meet his brother.

The poet folded his arms again and leaned against the doorframe to watch. Beside him, Keith stood squarely, frowning, shoulders tense. They didn't spare each other a word, but Keith did offer the poet's rucksack a raised eyebrow. The poet answered with a shrug.

In the courtyard, the devils circled like tomcats. The poet could imagine their mantling wings—Satan's stone-black and membranous, Lucifer's shining white under the sunless sky—transformed to lashing tails and flattened ears.

:Satan,: Lucifer said, with all his exquisite mocking politeness intact. :You haven't the look of one who comes seeking society.:

"I heard a rumor," Satan answered. His voice sifted dust from the stones, and the poet flinched from it, covering his ears with his hands. Keith winced, but held his ground. "I came to find the truth in it."

:You presume I know of which rumor you speak.:

Satan paused. He held out one black, knobby fist, the talon on his thumb projecting between his fingers. He loosed them, and a wad of paper slipped free, smoking slightly from his touch.

With a swift, careless gesture, Lucifer swept it up in the curve of a wing and flicked it into his own hand. He uncrumpled it, the paper weighty and soft, and smoothed it between his fingers. After studying whatever was written there for a moment, he looked up, tilting his head back to meet the other Devil's sullen stare. Satan seemed a monolith beside him, though Lucifer was both well-made and tall. :It is a letter by my hand, requesting conversation with Him who exiled us. What of it?:

"Morningstar," Satan said, his voice low and reasonable, "see you who stands in yonder doorway, watching you? You have a Dragon Prince, my brother. You hold in your hand a weapon even God must respect. But wield it, and all the devils in all the Hells will stand beside you."

Lucifer turned and looked, as if Satan's words could indeed come as a revelation to him. Kit knew him well enough to read irony, however, and even Satan could not have missed it when Lucifer turned back with an elaborate shrug.

Satan curled a lip off his fanged teeth and snarled, "Do you expect the rest of us to bear idle witness while you crawl to *Him*, begging forgiveness? I will not have it."

Lucifer tossed the slip of paper over his shoulder. An unseen servant, swift and mindless as a gust of wind, swept it aside to be disposed of. The Morningstar tilted his head and smiled. :Darling,: he murmured, :that is but a request for an audience. Do I seem to you the sort that crawls?:

For a moment, the poet thought Lucifer might actually get away with it. And then Satan moved, his right arm straightening on a swinging blow that caught the other angel across the stomach. Lucifer doubled around the blow. The second one smashed him to his knees, while the stones of the courtyard groaned under Satan's moving weight.

So fast. The poet realized that he had started forward only when Keith's hand locked on his right biceps and dragged him back into the door arch. "That's not your fight," Keith said, but the poet noticed that Keith's other hand had dropped to the pommel of his sword.

Keith asked, reluctantly, "Will they kill each other?" He wasn't over-fond of the poet, or vice versa.

"No more than Fae are likely to, outside a field of war or honorable combat," the poet muttered in reply. "If Michael would not strike them down, but only hurl them from Heaven, they'll not destroy each other so easily. There are"—he grimaced—"*forms* for these things."

The pause was brief, and then both men winced when Satan kicked Lucifer, a swinging blow that sent him sprawling on the courtyard flags. He strode after, the earth groaning under his feet, and caught Lucifer a sweeping kick under the ribs that lifted the fallen angel into the air.

"Exile's a possibility, though," the poet continued. "Or imprisonment. And seizure of chattels."

"Meaning us."

"Meaning you," the poet said. "I'm a free man."

"Hah," Keith answered. "You think *he'd* care about that?"

Both re-covered their ears as Satan raised his stinging voice again. "That seems a creditable approximation of crawling to me." Lucifer pushed himself to his knees, his wings sagging on either side of his shoulders, his velvet jacket torn at the elbow. Satan stepped forward, foot swinging—

Lucifer got one foot under him, knee bent as if making obeisance, and the poet flinched. But then Lucifer rocked aside, dodging the kick, and rose to his feet with a bar of light flickering in his left hand like a tongue of flame. He extended his arm en garde.

:So draw your sword.:

Satan folded his arms over his stony chest. "You won't meet me with fists, Morningstar?"

Lucifer smiled. Right-handed, he wiped blood from the corner of his mouth, and flicked it sizzling on the stones. :It's easy to forget that I stood against Michael too, isn't it, brother mine?:

"Stood," Satan said. "And fell."

:A flaw we both endure. Come. I'll show you the door.:

"Don't bother," the poet said, stepping forward, his cloak swirling heavily against his calves. "I'm headed that way myself. I'll see the Devil out."

The year Matthew Magus turned forty, Halloween fell on a Sunday. He'd canceled his classes for Monday and Tuesday, and now he stood before an antique silver-backed mirror in a wrought-iron frame and made ready for a duty more sacred than teaching. First he bound his bobbed hair into a stubby ponytail, the end twisted with copper wire. Once, he would have worn a camouflage jacket, buttons buttoned and zippers zipped. But he had no intention of blending into *this* night, even if he still could; sympathetic camouflage did not suit his purpose now.

Instead he wore a patchwork tailcoat, red velvet and copper brocade sewn with bugle beads, fringes, droplets of amber, silver and steel bells and chips of mirror, a phoenix embroidered on the left lapel and a unicorn on the right. Matthew wouldn't wear a shirt under the talisman on Hallow's Eve, so the skin from his collarbone to his belt shone bare, revealing the black edges of the spells etched into his skin. The coat smelled of nag champa and dragonsblood incense; he kept it with his aromatics so the odor wouldn't fade.

The owner of the vintage shop he'd bought it from—without haggling, as was right for a ritual tool—had claimed it had belonged to Jim Morrison. This was a lie. Joey Ramone had tried it on once but hadn't bought it, but the real magic of the coat lay in salvaged fabric and beads: a skirt panel from the original Broadway production of *Kiss Me Kate*; a harness bell from Andrew Carnegie's carriage horses; a fragment of a busted bathroom mirror from The Bitter End; enough baubles to buy Manhattan twice over (purple and white wampum sawn from the shells of quahog clams, a handful of love beads thrown away by Robert Crumb, a tourist's charm shaped like the Empire State Building which somebody had given to Gregory Corso, once); a steel jingle made from a valve cover off Peter Beagle's motor scooter; a horseshoe nail lost when the nag bolted in the Five Corners; a penny John Coltrane picked off the floor of Birdland—heads—and ran through a press at Coney Island in 1963. . .

Matthew brushed the gold fringe on the epaulets until it fell properly.

He double-knotted his steel-toed boots and stared at the man in the mirror one more time: a little more gray in the hair, a few more lines beside the eyes, the ink in his tattoos starting to fade and blur a little, here and there.

His jeans had a steel zipper and copper rivets. He wore a black leather glove on his clawed right hand. The healed scar where a unicorn's horn had pierced his heart shone white and crescent-shaped among the black lines on his skin.

He slapped his hands together, the strong one and the shattered one, and let himself out through dead bolts, chains, and the police lock to see what Hallow's Eve would bring.

Sunset gave the illusion of warmth to a city whose nights were already chilling into winter. New York had never been one of those cities where Halloween became a ritual, a citywide block party and an excuse to riot all rolled into one. San Francisco claimed Halloween; New York's saint's day was New Year's Eve.

But Halloween was Halloween, and New York also wasn't a city that missed an excuse to throw a party. Or a parade. So Matthew armed and armored himself, and went out like Gawain—or perhaps like Don Quixote—to defend the innocent. Or the best approximation he could find, in New York City.

He walked south through the Upper West Side under the watchful eyes of gargoyles: leering faces and twisted animals bent in manners foreign to their anatomy. A green man watched him pass; a beaked creature something like a wingless hippogriff twisted in its skin of stone to follow him with a weathered granite regard. In the bright eyes of buildings only sleepily alert to the mayfly existences of their creators, Manhattan's last Mage burned with iridescence, a dragonfly catching sunlight through lazy summer air.

His city knew him still.

Matthew headed for Greenwich Village. The noise of the city followed like a lover's whispers. He jingled with every step. The Fae were in the city tonight, this night of all nights, though they usually gave New York the respect due a graveyard.

Matthew couldn't keep them out, not alone, and he was too tired to try.

He couldn't keep them out. But he could try to make sure they stayed out of trouble. And they knew his name, both the Daoine Sidhe and the Unseelie, even if the residents of his city did not. They remembered a bridge of iron and Matthew's own heart's blood that had carried a war into Faerie.

New York remembered a woman on a white horse and a dragon with black iron wings that had carried that same war back to the heart of the city. And Matthew preferred it that way. He could walk through New York unheralded, the new gray streaks twisted into the blond of his hair, wearing the city's essence like a hermit crab's home on his back, and play its warden in the dark, with no one but the gargoyles the wiser. It was a lonely existence.

But it would serve.

The buzz of his cell phone pulled him from his reverie, but when he read the display, he saw the name Jane Andraste. His right hand ached when he thought about it, so he stuffed the phone back into his pocket and rubbed the scarred palm with his opposite thumb, trying to chafe some comfort into the old wound.

He settled against a brick wall, his shoulder to the traffic, and fussed with his glove for a minute. A car alarm buzzed across the street, the flashing lights attracting his attention. He dropped his hands to his sides and turned, scanning the crowds moving along the sidewalk, faster pedestrians wending between slower clumps.

Matthew spotted the follower before he quite caught up. The man was easy to pick out of the crowd, not because his head was bowed over a PDA, his lips moving in concentration, but because Matthew could not have failed to notice the twisted, dark-colored rings encircling his thumb and forefinger.

Matthew didn't know this apprentice. But Matthew knew what he was and also knew why his phone had rung just then.

Matthew had it in his hand already when it rang again. He didn't bother answering, because at the sound of his phone, the apprentice's head came up. He turned until he faced Matthew directly. He was good-looking, Irish or Swedish extraction, with freckles scattered across his cheekbones and the bridge of his nose, and wavy dark red hair. The young man's face rearranged itself around a positively dazzling smile as he slipped up to Matthew, who found himself ridiculously at bay with his back against a brownstone wall.

"Matthew Magus?" the apprentice asked, and stuck out the hand that didn't have the PDA in it: his right hand, and Matthew didn't reach to take it. He didn't care to offer his crippled paw to shake like a well-trained golden retriever.

"I am," he said. "What does Jane want?"

Matthew should have asked the man's name; his eyebrows drew together at the sting of that slight. He recovered, though, and lowered his hand. "I'm Christian Magus," he said, smoothly. "I'm here on behalf of Jane."

"Christian *Magus*," Matthew repeated. "She's recruiting. It figures. How did she find you?"

The young Mage wore a copper-colored brocade blazer over a black turtleneck. He dropped his hands into his pockets and drew the brocade around himself, fist balled around the PDA. There was a bit of Mage-craft on it, Matthew could guess, a spell to help find Matthew through the link established when Jane called his phone, whether he chose to answer or not. Simple enough magic. The sort he would have worked without thinking, himself, once upon a time.

Christian didn't answer his question. "Jane wants to talk to you. Just talk."

Matthew stared through his eyeglasses. The apprentice didn't drop his gaze, but met him glower for glower. He wondered how long Jane had been recruiting apprentices, how many new Magi she'd col-lected . . . whether she was planning on moving against Faerie again.

"Jane needs everybody," Christian said. He held out a granite-colored business card; when Matthew didn't take it, he tucked it into the breast pocket of his gaudy coat with a sort of charming insolence. "She needs as many of us as she can get. She just wants to talk to you."

"How many of you are there now?"

"About twenty," Christian said. "And growing. I've been with her five years, and I know she's sincere."

Matthew put his phone away again and smoothed his left hand over his hair. "You know why she doesn't have any Magi left, Christian?" he asked. "Why she's starting over from scratch?"

Christian bit his lip, frowning. "The Faerie War."

"Because she got the last batch all *killed*," Matthew told him. "And she'll get you killed too. No."

"Matthew?"

He turned away, showing Christian the back of his hand. "No," he said. "I won't talk to Jane. I have a city to take care of. Leave me alone."

Two young women and a man in their early twenties hesitated on the platform, bewildered by the rumble of trains, the reek of grease and the arch of yellow metal against swallowing darkness. The train had breathed them into Penn Station like a dragon breathing particles of soot onto the air. The chambered heart of a vast beast echoed around them, sound ringing off granite blocks laid with a master's precision. The three exchanged glances, their own hearts thundering in their chests as New York's thundered in their ears.

They ascended the narrow escalator single file, passing through a gap in a dull, corrugated walkway suspended above the platform like a vast air-conditioning duct. Inside, grimy cement was punctuated in long rows by the alien luxuriance of cobalt tiles, blue as a madonna's robes against char.

The city noticed their coming.

The train watched them climb, calm in its long steel body, and the sidewalks took their weight in knowing silence when they ascended into the indirect brightness of a New York morning.

The eldest of the three was Althea Benning, who bought a white T-shirt from a vendor. It was marked in black and red and blue with a map of the New York subway system that stretched across her breasts when she pulled it over her tank top.

The boy was named Geoffrey Bertelli; his mouth twitched sideways when he was amused. It was twitching now, as he raked bony, beautiful hands through his matted, matte-black-dyed red hair and said, "Everyone will know you're a tourist."

"Everyone will know I'm a tourist anyway, and this way, if we get lost, all you have to do is stare at my tits." Althea checked her reflection in the shopwindow; Geoff laughed at her, shifted his knapsack, and dropped an arm around the third companion's shoulders.

She only smiled.

She was the one who might have seemed most Fae, at least to someone who had never seen the Fair Folk. She was called Juliet Gorman, known as Jewels, and she was scarred and tattooed and pierced through fair freckled skin, her ears altered to points and a terrible homesickness in her flinching gestures.

She wasn't Fae. She was Otherkin, a peasant child dreaming she was a stolen princess . . . who knew that her real parents—who loved her—would be along any moment to reclaim her from unkind but temporary mundane bondage.

Jewels slid from under Geoff's arm and stood atop a subway grate, the warm wind swirling her skirt around her ankles. She'd braided her hair and pinned it so it covered her ears, mostly at Geoff's insistence.

"Look at me," Althea said, spinning in place, colliding with a hurried pedestrian whose fluffy lemon-yellow skirt hung low on her hips, two sunflowers with gnarled stems wrapped in a plastic supermarket bag dangling head down from her left hand.

Althea skipped aside and laughed. "Sorry."

The city girl tossed her a look like acid, and the city breathed in hope and breathed out dreams, and the dragons rumbled under their feet in the long darkness of Penn, jointed snakes in oil-slick squalor.

"Where to first?" Althea asked, dropping her chin to stare down at the map across her chest.

"I don't care as long as we're in the Village by six to see the parade," Geoff answered.

He glanced at Jewels, who cocked her head and pursed her lips. "Times Square. I want to see where the war started."

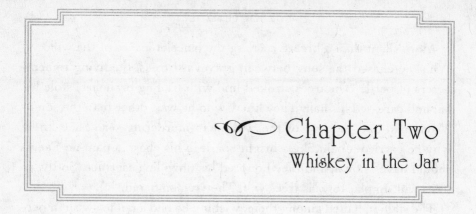

Chapter Two
Whiskey in the Jar

Warmth slid from the stallion's withers as he entered the shade of willows. His coat gleamed white over stout muscles; black streaked his mane and spotted his face and his richly feathered feet. A rivulet of water as silver as his moon-shaped shoes led him deeper into the wood and higher upon the hills; he wrote in hoofprints on its verdant bank, a line that would tell any who cared to look, *The Kelpie was here.*

He could have passed without a mark. But this was hallowed ground, sacred enough that when he came to the place where low hills tangled the willows' roots, he cantered to a halt and stood for a moment, tail stinging his flanks as he swiveled an ear at *something* borne on that breeze.

Singing.

A song.

He'd come to air his pain, his un-Fae sorrow and the low, slow, un-Fae ache in his belly. To stomp, and paw, and kick things under the grieving willows. To let his anger at his beloved Queen and on his beloved Queen's behalf fly. To *feel,* as he was not yet accustomed to feel, having been Fae for millennia and having borne a mortal soul but seven years.

Irritating to have his grief interrupted. The stallion drew a great bellows breath and *folded* into the angular form of a man, tugging his silk suit into place and reaching up to tip a hat at the right rakish angle. He was barefoot. Silver rings glinted on his thumbs and each great toe, pale against skin dark as loch water.

More silent than a breeze rustling the lancelet leaves of the willows, Whiskey chased the song between graveyard trees, the living remem-berers of battle. The trees stroked him with trailing branches, stole his hat and caressed his hair. They knew who he was, other than the son of Manannan and the god of the wide man-murdering sea. They knew why he carried a pain like a bright spark in his chest, a pain no Faerie should have known, and they honored his unwilling sacrifice. Softly, as trees will. Implacably, as trees will. They remembered.

The stallion halted among them, wishing he had a tail to swish in per-plexity. A small slight man sat beside the spring halfway up the hill, wrapped in a bard's patchwork cloak of colors, leaning against a tree as he half sang an old rhyme. " 'Ellum do grieve, and Oak he do hate, and Willow he walk if you travels late.' Good afternoon, traveler."

"Good meeting, Sir Bard. I do not know you." The stallion stepped from the shelter of laurel and scrub oak.

The singer gestured, the layers of his ragged cloak falling from his shoulders. Underneath he wore black, a silk shirt with silver buttons tucked into narrow trousers. "It's changed."

"The hillside?"

"That too." He had fine golden-brown hair in well-brushed waves, a neat beard, and dark, deep-set eyes, whoever he was, and as he leaned forward between bent, spread knees his bootheels furrowed the earth. The stallion saw nails wink in their soles and tossed his forelock from his eyes. Iron nails, and not silver.

The bard was a mortal man.

"What manner of creature are you?"

"Kelpie," the stallion answered.

"You're a servant of the new Queen."

"I am."

"Bound servant?"

"This Queen makes no bindings." The stallion came uphill, relaxing into his own shape now that he need not fear startling the singer. In horse-shape, his eyes would not sting with unshed pain. He stamped and snorted, shaking his mane over his ears. It didn't help. "But I have a soul."

"I as well," the bard said. "I am sorry."

"One grows accustomed."

The man had an accent the stallion knew of old, although time had faded it. "You're English," Whiskey said.

"I was. Of Canterbury, and then London."

"Ah. Have you a name, mortal man?"

Which netted him a strange sort of smile in return. The bard stepped from the shadow of the trees, sunlight gilding his dull hair auburn. "In fact I do not. But I will come to what you call me. Given a little warning, of course, what that may be—Thomas will do if you are not otherwise inclined. Does Morgan le Fey still roam these hills?"

"*Roam* is perhaps not the proper word—"

"I beg your pardon. Dwell here, then? And the new Mebd, the new Queen—"

"—whom I serve."

"To whom you owe service, yes. She is Morgan's granddaughter."

"By Morgan's son, Murchaud. Got on a mortal Mage."

"Ah, I see. And Murchaud is buried here." Thomas glanced aside, his voice losing its trained fluency.

The stallion lowered his head and cropped a bite of grass, releasing its rich green scent. It tasted of nothing, of straw. There was no blood in it. "Yes. As are many. Murchaud, Duke of Hell, Prince-Consort to the previous Queen of Faerie, son of Morgan and Lancelot. He is buried here."

"I brought flowers," the bard said, producing a bundle of iris and eglantine from his cloak. "Show me where?"

"Were you friends?"

"In Hell."

"Ah." The stallion cropped grass again, tail swishing. "I know your name."

"I haven't got one—"

"I know who you were. You wish to see the grave."

"Yes."

"Yes," the stallion answered. "And I shan't even bid you climb upon my back."

The bard paused, and then grinned up at him. "Just as well, pony," he said, his voice ringing empty as a tin cup when you drop a penny in it. "You wouldn't like my spurs."

"Doubting Thomas." The stallion arched his neck to hide unease, flirting with the poet from under long lashes. "Call me Whiskey. For that is also not *my* name."

The poet who wasn't named Thomas knelt by the grave of a Prince of Faerie and didn't shed a tear. It wasn't precisely unmarked, that grave, bowered as it was by branches and cradled between roots, beribboned with sunlight trailing through leaves. Thomas dug his inkstained finger-tips into the greensward and uprooted a tuft of grass, turning it over in his hands. Two waxy grubs shone. He touched one idly and closed his eyes to feel it writhe against his skin.

The grief pressed like a stone on his breast and would not be moved. He said, "Your Queen's mother is a mortal woman."

"Our Queen's mother is a Mage," Whiskey answered. "High in the counsels of their Promethean Society, so-called, who were the other side of this war—you've heard of the Prometheans?"

"Known with some intimacy," the bard replied, in a tone that suggested it hadn't been a pleasant knowing. He'd been in Faerie long enough to learn Fae ways: never show soft emotion, should you feel it. Never sorrow, nor affection, nor fear. No matter that the grief came up from his belly like wine sickness, painful and sharp, stinging his eyes and burning his sinuses. He kept his face placid, his voice mellifluous and mocking.

Unlike Whiskey, ruined by the soul he'd been tricked into accepting, the Fae did not admit pain.

The bard turned the turf in his hands, careful not to shake the grubs loose, and tucked it back into the wound he had made over Murchaud's grave. He scrubbed earth-stained fingers on his trousers, and then rubbed them across his face. His fury came out in the softness of his tone. "What is her name, this Maga?"

"Jane Andraste, Sir Thomas." Whiskey didn't mind saying. Didn't mind at all, when he felt the wind blow across his ribs and lift his mane, and smelled the sunlight of Faerie on it.

"I'm only a knight in Faerie," the bard said, standing, and tugging his cloak about him as if the warm air carried a chill. "That honor was never conferred for all my service to mortal queens." When he angled his head in the sunlight, it caught more coppery sparks from his sand-colored hair, and his right eye was brighter than his left.

"You're in Faerie now, Sir Thomas."

"Whiskey, that I am." The bard glanced down at the grave, and then shook his head at the earth between his shoes. "And your Queen, who knows all names but has none of her own—"

"Aye?"

"Does she know her mother killed her father?"

"The Dragon killed her father, Thomas. He died in the rubble of Times Square, these seven years since, on Hallow's Eve. 'When the Faerie court do ride.' "

"I know that song."

"Too well, I judge."

A spark of pain as bright as Whiskey's infected the bard's voice. "But her mother started the war."

"The war is older than the Queen. And older than her mother too."

"It's not older than I am . . ." The bard sighed, and came and stood beside the stallion, staring down at one grave among a row of graves that stretched until the trunks of the willow grove occluded sight. "Is there a tree for every fallen Fae, Master Whiskey? And one for every Promethean Mage who laid down his life in this battle?"

"There are not so many trees as that. Or the wood would go on very far indeed. Murchaud was more than your friend."

"He was the breath in my lungs and the marrow in my bones."

Whiskey sidestepped closer, and the bard took that invitation and leaned a shoulder on horsey solidity. The stallion smelled of sweat and tide pools, brackish, salt, fertile rot. His warmth eased the ache that threatened to close the bard's throat, and after a moment he could speak again.

His fingers curled as if they cradled a dagger hilt. There was always revenge.

Contrary to myth, it really could help one feel better.

The poet glanced sideways, meeting the stallion's ice-blue eye. "I went to Hell to be with him, and I had been in Hell before. I did not go twice blindly. A question for a question, stud. Do you prefer your new Queen to your old?"

"I had no Queen before this one," Whiskey answered, the trickle of pain in his unwanted soul like the trickle of water that spread under his hooves. The warmth of the day chilled on his neck, now, too, and the bard threw an arm over his shoulders. Whiskey endured it, and felt the better after all. "I was a Wild Fae, and unbridled. Now I am tamed."

"And?"

"—and?"

"She who tamed you. Is she a good Queen?"

"I would see her unQueened, Sir Thomas. Because I love her. Because I carry her soul, and her soul makes me to love her, and were she to abdicate I would no longer be bound to that burden—I would see her unQueened."

Silence, until the poet stepped away. "I understand."

Whiskey shook his mane and pawed lightly. His black-marked forehoof left a gouge in wet greensward, and the scent of fresh-turned earth almost covered the scent of sympathy. Worse, that he was cold enough that the sympathy warmed him. Worse, that he had a soul to see kinship, where he should have seen the weakness the bard let slip, just a little, and thought, *Prey*.

"Yes," he said. "I think you do." He tossed his forelock and snorted. "My Queen forgave her mother the war."

"Did she." Not a question, as the poet sank into a crouch with his cloak spreading on the ground around him, a puddle of a thousand colors. The patch that gleamed at his right shoulder was some sort of silk, blue as watered steel and catching the light and shadows when it moved, like the sea.

"Someone could *find* this Jane Andraste, Promethean and Mage. Someone could do something about redress. For these crimes. For this war," the poet said. He dug his fingers into the earth again, as if unwilling to ever let go. As if he wanted to pull the turf over his shoulders like a blanket and lie down under it, warm and still.

"Get on my back," Whiskey said, before the words could freeze in his throat and choke him. "Climb on my back and ride."

Times Square had not become a monument, other than the monument to the gods of capitalism that it had always been. There had been very

few killed here: a Fae girl pregnant with a royal child, a television re-
porter, a Duke of Hell, a rookie cop. The damage had been for show—
though how much show is necessary to bring home a point is
questionable, when a dragon the size of a jetliner unfolds basalt wings
across a city sky.

There's a certain admirable fierceness in the way New York mythol-
ogizes its trauma, and the dragon of Times Square was no different.
Two years later, a smaller, somewhat pudgier replica of that dragon
made its debut in the Macy's Thanksgiving Day Parade. The LCD
screens had been rebuilt, the shimmering marquees repaired. Old stone
facades still lurked behind the frameworks of advertising displays,
dowager creases and age spots concealed under gaudy paint. Worker-
ant traffic crept nose to tail in red- and white-lit profusion, and the
TKTS booth had a line around the block.

The city had left the knife-cut claw marks along the rooftops alone,
and tourists with telephoto lenses clotted beside the police substation,
peering up and snapping pictures, couples handing cameras and binoc-
ulars back and forth.

Geoff and Althea and Jewels stood shoulder to shoulder in the
chill, Geoff's arm around Althea's shoulder, holding his coat open for
her to crowd inside because she was shivering in the gaudy tourist
T-shirt. She trapped a layer of warm air and cloth between them, her
arms wrapped tight across her belly although she was not *quite* shivering. Her head was craned back, and the delicate rings of her larynx
pressed her skin from the inside, revealing pale highlights and blood-
blue shadows.

It was Jewels who spoke, eyes bright and streaked brown hair
pulling free of braids to twine in the rising wind. "What wouldn't you
give to have seen that?" Her voice throbbed with wistful envy.

"Funny," Geoff answered. "I was just thinking I was glad I'd missed
it." He glanced at his watch. "We should go if we're going to eat before
the parade."

They wound up in a steel-countered deli on Fifth Avenue, eating overstuffed pastrami sandwiches and salty kosher pickles. Althea ate her
own, and Geoff's too. They were too hurried for much conversation,

and by the time they left, the sky had darkened and the streetlights were on.

Althea found herself falling into Geoff's and Jewels' slipstream. Jewels walked hurriedly, cold in her thin skirt, and Geoff kept positioning himself to break the wind for her. Jewels endured his attention with a kind of annoyed stoicism, but at least she didn't say anything about it.

Although maybe it would have been better if she did. Althea had time to think about it, following his black coat and her gray sweater through the increasing crowds, shivering a little bit in her own thin shirt. Her jacket was in Geoff's knapsack, though, and she'd have to catch up with him and make him stop to put it on, and they were in a hurry.

She'd stay warm enough with the walking until they made it to the parade. And she was keeping up all right. Geoff turned to look over his shoulder once in a while to make sure of her, and she was never more than three steps behind.

Which was why she couldn't explain how she lost him. She hadn't taken her eyes off his jacket, or his back, and Jewels' braided hair was hard to miss, as was her laugh. But one moment they were there, and the next Althea realized she was following another couple entirely.

She blinked and her eyes blurred. For a moment, she saw Geoff and Jewels again, getting farther away through the crowd. And then, as if a slide had been pulled from a projector, they were gone again, and she saw only a red-haired man in a black leather jacket and a girl with dark hair, not Geoff and Jewels at all.

Althea stopped and turned, rocking on her heels. She hadn't accidentally walked past them, either. She hesitated, oscillating, and tried not to meet the eyes of the passersby who snuck quick glances at her and then looked down.

"Dammit," she muttered. And then she heard Jewels laugh. A side street. They must have turned, just there, and she'd missed them. A shortcut. They'd notice she was gone in a second, and turn back, and she'd meet them coming to look for her. Skipping, hugging herself with relief, she hurried down the alley.

The last thing she heard was the tremendous whirring rush of wings.

❈　　❈　　❈

Halloween fell on a Sunday that year, and so did the end of daylight savings time. The coppery warmth gilding the green men and gargoyles had dimmed to quicksilver by the time Matthew reached the Village, and the blue hour of twilight held the city in the cool, lingering embrace extended by building shadows. The parade wouldn't start until seven, and Matthew intended to watch the spectators as much as the participants. He wandered along Fourteenth Street, flotsam in a stream of humanity, alert for the messages flickering in neon or reflected in storefronts.

Several bars of "The Lady Is a Tramp" slid from a basement doorway along with a coil of smoke. Matthew walked through the scent of cigarettes and unwashed bodies; they clung to his skin along with prophecy, and like prophecy broke and slid away before the force of his talismans and a survived destiny.

Cars slid past, stop and go, one stereo blaring a Don Henley song. Matthew had heard that one before, the morning the towers fell; New York's Magus hadn't been able to take that bullet for his city either. *Maybe it's time we make it a ceremonial position*, he thought, but understood the portent and read his directions in the flickering light of a Dos Equis sign.

He turned his face away but the sign persevered, heartbeat of electricity stuttering its neon, and another across the alley took up the plaint. They were coy, long-lashed things, never quite forthright, but transparent enough in their intentions. He sighed and turned left between buildings, picked past bundled newspapers and a green plastic trash barrel, and walked through a puddle of floodlight, glancing up once to make sure the human-seeming shadow at its edge was the outline of another gargoyle. It was: one he didn't remember having seen before, a squat birdlike silhouette whose gorgeously fluted antlers must have been the chef d'oeuvre of a master stonemason, imported from Europe along with all those boatloads of marble.

He sought after it, but no trace of magic hung nearby—just the thinking chill of stone worked fine enough to hold an ageless, patient soul. A hungry soul, and he pulled back.

The coat was not keeping him warm. But now he was close enough to smell what hung in the air, and he frowned. It was an old, wild musk, harsh and deep—the scent of weathered bones at the maw of a preda-tor's lair. It was a thickness as deep and sweet as the Kelpie's, but with-out the tang of sea-rot and sea-change that kept the Kelpie's trace unique. He walked on, an ache in his scarred hand. The fear was alive in him, a wild cold coiling thing, but he would not honor it. No matter how it made his hands shake and the bile rise in his throat.

The girl was already dead when he found her, her tourist's subway-map T-shirt ripped from breast to belly. Matthew crouched beside the body and pulled his cell from his pocket. He checked for a pulse—cursorily: her blood was a banner spread ragged on the stones around her, along with her entrails—thumbed 911 with his ruined hand, and raised his head to search the shadows, taking comfort in a child's lie: that he did not fear the dark.

The reek of raw meat and spilled bowels made him gag. There were no footprints in the blood and the foot*steps* echoing behind him came too soon and too lightly for the police. He turned just his head over his shoulder, spectacles flashing in the light, blood drying on the first two fingers of his left hand. The runners held hands as if one of them meant to pull the other up from drowning. The leader was a cautious, coltish boy in black leather, black denim, black-dyed hair and steel-grommeted boots. The flowered chiffon skirt of the sandaled girl beside him blew about thin ankles, and a charcoal sweater that fell to the top of her thighs was rolled up three times at the sleeves, draping off her reedlike wrists in fat doughnuts.

"Don't—" he said, and stood.

At the far edge of the puddled light, Jewels dragged Geoff to a stop as the red-coated man spread his arms helplessly. The movement pulled the cuff of the coat away from his glove and let the fine hairs on his arm be limned. He stood foolishly, shaking, as if he could block their vision of Althea. He wasn't tall, but he looked dangerous, strong.

A snaky breeze scarfed Jewels' skirt between her thighs and locks of wavy tea-brown hair across her eyes. She pushed the latter aside with a nail-bitten finger and sucked her lower lip into her mouth, her stomach tangled around her ankles. She stepped from artificial light into a shadow, shielding her eyes, and felt no chill; the meaty reek of

the alley fevered her. Not cold at all, though she was shivering.
"Al . . . ?"

"Don't look," the man said. "Just don't look. I called the police." He
twisted his wide-held hand to show the green lights of the phone; the
911 operator's voice was still audible, and he moved slowly to bring it
back to his ear. "Sir? Some other bystanders just arrived—"

"Althea," Jewels said, and took a step forward, almost tripping out of
her sandals. She caught herself and shook free of Geoff's clenched hand.
She couldn't feel herself breathing. "Oh, God. Al."

Matthew saw her distress and came to her, still holding the phone to
his ear, ready to catch her if she rushed forward or went down. Beside
her, the boy swayed, pressed both hands to his mouth. His head dipped
as he gagged and shuddered; his knees folded like a foal's and he went
straight down, curled forward, kneeling. The girl turned and tripped
again; this time she didn't catch herself. She collapsed against the boy,
her hands on his wrist and the nape of his neck, holding him up while
he gagged, her face nearly in his hair. "Geoff?"

Matthew moved a step closer, still pressing the phone to his ringless
ear. *Today is the naming of names*, he thought. Patently unfair, considering
that it seemed to be her friend on the ground, but he recognized his own
distanced chill as shock. He almost put his hand in the girl's hair to comfort her, but saw the blood on his fingers and winced, and scrubbed
them on his jeans first, shuddering. *Jesus.* "Yes sir," he said. "I'm right
here. I won't hang up. Somebody just fainted."

A banshee wailed—a siren, only a siren, after all. The girl's hair was
soft and faintly greasy. She leaned into the touch silently, suffering,
holding her friend, smelling of patchouli. The scent reminded him of a
woman he hadn't seen in seven years, and almost covered the tang of
blood. "Miss?"

"Jewels," she said, without lifting her lips from her friend's spiked,
matted hair. The word struck music in his breast—her name, and her
true name too. A breath caught in his throat; he stroked her hair out of
her face and stopped, shocked by what his fingers brushed. A fine
braided tracery of raised scar tissue ran along her hairline, leading his
fingers to an ear tipped to a delicate point.

At the mouth of the alley, light flashed, blue and red and gold and white. *Fae,* he almost said, but no, she wasn't. She was as human as he, mortal blood and mortal bone. "Otherkin."

She looked up at him and grimaced. The brackets on her braces were fashion colors, fuchsia and violet between the wires. A titanium hoop glimmered in her nostril.

"Holy fuck," he said, the phone in his hand forgotten as the first policemen hustled down the alleyway, paramedics right behind. "Otherkin. Sweetheart, what the *hell* were you kids doing in New York City if you're playing at being Otherkin? Don't you know your kind aren't welcome here?"

For the ten millionth time, Jewels said, "We came to New York for the Halloween parade," and for the ten millionth time Detective Peese shook his head.

"Three Otherkin kids? Pull the other one."

"Geoff's not Otherkin." She dropped her head into her palms, knotting wisps of hair between her fingers. She itched and stank and her butt hurt from the hard wooden chair, and she wanted to go home. The steel-edged Formica table was worn in two patches under her elbows, and she imagined how many other people had leaned forward in this interview room just as she was leaning now, hopelessness a bubble under their breastbones. That was the worst part. She hadn't even cried for Althea yet. Couldn't cry, as if her fear for herself had stopped the tears or soaked them up. "He's just a friend."

The cop braced his hands on the other edge of the table, looming over her. He smelled sharply of Irish Spring and Old Leather, an infelicitous combination. "You had to know you were taking a risk coming to New York, with your ears tipped like that and those scars hanging out there."

They rasped the heels of her palms: her own work. Her own design, a fragile Celtic braid, pale stains of aqua and lime overworking the white lines. Her hair mostly covered it, most of the time. She took a breath and spoke more sullenly than she'd intended. "It's still a free country."

The cop wasn't much bigger than Geoff, and definitely not any bigger than the guy with the ponytail and the red velvet tuxedo jacket who'd hovered over her until the police separated the three of them into different rooms. His hair was cropped close to the skull, the short dull brown fuzz showing pale lines of scars sparser and less intentional than Jewels', and he was wearing a suit instead of a uniform. A badge hung on a cord around his neck like he'd forgotten to take it off.

He sighed tiredly and leaned back, thumbs hooked through a creaking leather belt. "That doesn't mean you weren't asking for trouble coming here, Halloween or not. You're lucky whoever got your friend didn't get you too. Tell me the truth, Julia. You were looking for fairies, weren't you? Come to New York, go look at the claw marks on top of the Times Building, wander around and see fairies and try to talk them into taking you to the Otherlands, right? The only way we're going to find your friend's killer is if you level with us about where you went and what you did."

"There aren't any Fae in New York City." She shifted her bottom against the chair and didn't correct him regarding her name. "Everybody knows they never came back after the fight in Times Square. I wouldn't come to New York for Fae. And we went to Times Square, but only for a few minutes. It was just for the parade. I swear . . ." She trailed off as someone tapped on the door of the interview room, then lifted her head out of her hands, meeting Detective Peese's flat hostile stare.

"Christ, if you were my kid, I'd haul your ass right back to the plastic surgeon who put those ears on you and get them cut right off." He turned away and opened the door.

This man *was* enormous. His skin was a few shades darker than his cocoa-colored sportcoat, which was a few shades darker than his sherry-colored eyes, and his right paw almost enveloped a two-liter bottle of Poland Spring, condensation running between his fingers and dripping on the floor. "You about done in here, Ernie?"

Peese raked him with a glance, a frown hardening the corners of his mouth. "Oh, look. It's the good cop." He shot a searing look over his shoulder at Jewels, who lost her battle not to clench her hands on the table. She gasped, but Peese had already turned back to her rescuer. "Yeah," Peese said. "I'll go see how they're doing in the other room."

Jewels bit her lip and pulled cold fingers inside the sleeves of her sweater as the white cop brushed stiff-shouldered past the black one. The newcomer held the door open with his elbow, then let it ease gently into place.

"Shit," Jewels said, leaning back against the painful wooden chair, "if that's Detective Peace, I'd hate to meet Detective War."

The big man laughed as he set the bottle of water in front of her and retrieved the pilled navy blanket he'd tucked under his other arm. "I'm Detective Smith. Will that do?"

"Are you really?" She watched him as he shook the blanket out. She wasn't cold enough to shiver, but the warmth when he swung the rough cloth over her shoulders was enough to make her sigh. "I think I'd like to see some ID."

He laughed and held out his hand. "Donall Smith." A faint flavor of a fluid island accent underlay his speech: Jamaican, she thought. She shook the hand, but didn't get up. "Peese gets a little—"

"Yeah. So you *are* the good cop, I take it?"

"Nah. I'm the cop who came to run Ernie off so you can make your train home. It's tomorrow."

"You're not going to keep us in the city?"

"What purpose would that serve? You're not suspects, no matter what he would have liked you to believe. We've got your info. Drink your water"—he jerked his chin at the bottle—"go home to Hartford, and for Christ's sake don't go wandering around New York City looking like you just stepped out of *The Brown Fairy Book* if you know what's good for you, okay?"

She opened the water. It was cold, and the plastic ring cracked when she unscrewed the top. Her lip split and the blanket slipped down her shoulders when she tilted her head back and drank, holding the bottle in both hands, shaking with weariness.

Her eyes closed, short dense lashes interweaving like the fringe on a Venus flytrap, and she swallowed once, twice, a third time—so thin each gulp showed as it bobbed down her throat. She set the bottle aside and wiped her mouth on the back of her hand. "I'm not leaving without Geoff."

Donall leaned against the doorpost. The edge dug into his spine through shirt and sportcoat. He crossed his arms. "He's waiting for you in the lobby."

"The lobby?" She looked up, startled, a flush under the pale olive of her skin. Attenuated hands fumbled the blanket closed over the ridges of her collarbones. "I thought he'd be—"

"Getting the Peese treatment? No, I made sure both he and Szczegielniak were out of harm's way before I came to rescue you. Look, kid"—as kindly as he could manage—"we've got your information. Your friend's parents are en route to pick up her body. I know you don't believe it at your age, but there's no shame in needing a shoulder to lean on once in a while. Do yourself a favor and call your mom, have her come get you."

The girl hesitated. She reached for the water again and tipped it to her mouth. Smaller swallows this time. "I can't call my mom," she said when she was done.

"I'll let you use my phone."

"My mom's dead," she said.

Donall grimaced in self-reproach. Stupidity. "Your boyfriend's mom?"

"Geoff's?" She stood, gawky and awkward, staggering briefly with exhaustion. "We'll get home okay. We have money." She widened bright eyes the color of agates and smiled faintly. "Thank you, Detective Smith."

"I'm sorry," he said. Her smile blew away. She took his hand between hers, dwarfing both of her own, and slipped out the door and was gone.

Seven years after the Dragon, Whiskey returned to New York.

He had risen dry from the filthy ocean earlier on that All Hallow's evening, the bard not named Thomas on his back, and in the shadow of a ferry he changed from steed to man. His hooves didn't clip-clop on asphalt, because he made his silver horseshoes into boots with silver nails, but he felt the cold burn of the city threading his body anyway. Iron and steel, bronze and copper under the stone, her poisoned bones themselves were ward and pain. But she was wrapped in water and born of the sea, Manhattan, and though she was built on bedrock, all her bridges, all her tunnels could not chain him away.

The crossroads of the world.

Beyond his bitterness, beyond the cold obsessive weight of emotion he could not lay aside, it still amused him that he fit in better than the half-mortal knight beside him, who struggled not to gape as they walked the length of the docks. Even on a Sabbath night, the streets bustled. Whiskey felt the bard wrap glamourie around them, pass-unseen and pass-unheard, and they slipped between pedestrians and police without notice. "You've never been in New York?"

"Never," Thomas answered. He shrugged under the weight of his cloak, turning to watch a woman dressed as a fantasy warrior in chain mail and leather stride past. "London, and then Faerie, and then Hell. Why is she dressed like that?"

"Samhain. The Americans celebrate it with a masque. Are there no cities in Hell?" An honest question, if perhaps a little sharper than Whiskey had intended it. The magic shoes and mortal soul were some help, but the weight of all that metal shortened a temper that had never been legendary for its length.

The poet tilted his head back, watching a shadow bigger than a bat row across the sky with the *otherwise* sight of his right eye. Something antlered, with broad hard wings. "Yes, Whiskey. There are cities in Hell. But they are empty."

The stallion shoved his hands into his pockets. The reek of oily water carried over the tang of smoke and stone, diesel and grease. Someone slipped past him, wrapped in Fae glamourie that hid flat serpent's eyes and hands webbed and sequin-scaled. She eyed him incuriously, flicked blood from her wide lipless mouth with a fork-tipped tongue, and slid toward the estuary they'd left behind. Whiskey shrugged at her dismissal.

The smell of blood made him sick with hunger, an empty twist in his belly he couldn't crop enough grass to fill. Seven years tamed, seven years named.

No one respects a king without fangs.

"Mermaid?" Thomas asked, turning to watch her go. Whiskey noticed that he saw through the glamourie.

"Undine. Jenny Greenteeth, I think, all the way from Yorkshire—if it's not one of her sisters. Rusalka, lorelei . . . one's much another. They came with the ships across my back, a hundred, two hundred years gone."

"Your back?"

"Each-Uisge," Whiskey said, and tapped his forehead with his knuckle. He brushed the back of a long-fingered hand across the buildings and the night-black water behind. "Water of all water in the world. The Atlantic and the North Sea, the channels and the inlets and the rivers and the lochs. The beat of the tides up the Stour and the Thames—and the East River too—is the beat of my heart."

"Who's the poet here?"

Thomas smiled when Whiskey snorted and shook his head, water flying from spring-curled hair, and said, "You are, poet."

"So if you're all the water in the world, what are they?"

"They're water too. Lakes and springs, creeks and billabongs, seas and storms. Greater or lesser. Rusalka, lorelei, merrow, selkie, mermaid, nixie, naiad, kappa, undine, samebito, the golden carp, and brother frog. Hapi, Masacouraman, Tocouyaha, Melusine—"

"Nuckelavee. Orkney's Devil from the Sea. The black horse and the skinless rider."

"You know of him." Not a surprising tidbit, from one who wore a bard's patched cloak, but it was easy to forget that when Thomas was trying not to gawp like a child at his first court.

"I was to Scotland once. And the Devil bears many names. So you're all those things and all those creatures at once? Isn't this city forbidden to the Fae?"

"Not forbidden," Whiskey answered. "But respected."

"Then what was your subject doing, hunting here?"

Whiskey answered with a snort and glower. The sidewalks grew crowded, and Thomas let the pass-unseen lapse so they wouldn't be trampled. There was music and laughter, sirens and lights. The bard had developed a tendency to veer a bit from side to side as one thing or another caught his attention, and he seemed not to notice the admiring glances he received, not all of them drawn by the splendid cloak.

Whiskey laced long fingers through the crook of Thomas' arm, slightly surprised that the bard let him. In fact, he scarcely seemed to notice the touch, but drew his cloak closer about himself with his free hand.

Even the slow dreams of the city stirred when Whiskey walked her stones. She knew him. She remembered the wild ring of hooves and a tail flying like a banner, a charge down Broadway and the groaning weight of the world come to rest on her stones.

Whiskey led the poet faster.

"The seas have been strange of late, wild where they should be tame, tame where they should be wild." The poet made his observation quietly, but he was waiting to see how Whiskey would react. The stallion didn't, not even a flexing of fingers on the poet's arm — which was as revealing as anything else. "And before you ask, yes. There are seas in Hell."

"*Nor is it circumscribed in one self place,*" Whiskey answered, and smiled at Thomas' sideways glance. "I hear the Devil is fond of your work."

Thomas' smile went tight. "Rather."

"Unfortunately so?"

Something was following them. Thomas hadn't noticed yet, but Whiskey could smell it, sweet brackish water and mud rich with rot, the taint of methane and the sweetness of blood. Maybe all the *otherwise* world had come to New York for Samhain and the fat orange moon.

Or for feasting. Whiskey scented something else. Blood — not the thin blood on Greenteeth's lips, but sweet blood spilled hot and fresh. They were bumped and jostled, moving against the flow of humanity now. The stallion drew himself up taller under the tilt of his white hat and let the nails in his heels ring on the pavement. Mortals fell back like the tide washing down the beach, without seeming to notice they had stepped aside.

"His fondness has served me well," Thomas said. His sigh went almost unnoticed as Whiskey leaned into the wind. Mud on one side, blood on the other: a poet's grief was no more than a passing concern. The scent of raw meat made his stomach rumble. "How do we find the Maga, Jane Andraste?"

"I hope to catch her scent," Whiskey answered. Lights flashing blue and red down the block drew his attention. The press of Thomas' cloak against his side was soothing. There were spells of ward and guard wound into it, powerful enough even to ease the ache of all that metal.

Something in his tension communicated itself to the poet, who followed his gaze. Two men and a woman stood within the radius of the lights, surrounded by uniformed peace officers.

Whiskey snorted and stopped, outside a streetlamp puddle of light. The blond man, he knew.

Thomas disengaged and stepped aside as Whiskey melted against stone. It was foolish to hide; Matthew would feel him in a moment if he hadn't already.

"And did you just?"

"Just?"

"Catch her scent?"

"Yes," Whiskey answered, as Matthew turned, looking over his shoulder, a flash of bare patterned skin and the glint of light off bullion. "After a manner of speaking, I did."

The Devil makes house calls. Often when he's neither summoned nor desired; often when a debt is owed; often where he has called before. Any two of three are as good as a guarantee that he'll venture the threshold, though he may not be well-recognized.

Fionnghuala the cursed, swanmay, princess, sister of Manannan, daughter of Llyr, straightened from her oven. She had a baking tray of ginger biscuits in her mitted hands, a smudge of golden syrup drying itchy alongside her nose, and she turned to confront the rustle of wings.

"Out of my kitchen, Nick," she said, her hands too full to swat at him when he stole a cookie from the tray.

Lucifer ducked under the low beams of her kitchen and smiled at her, wearing his most beautiful of guises. His coat was gray velvet, tailed and worn over a snowy shirt and boot-cut jeans in indigo. His boots had a heel, and blue eyes glittered mischief under the curve of his golden brows. If she hadn't heard the wings, she never would have seen them, pale glints of light in the shadows as they flicked closed and were gone.

:I understood I was invited,: he said, and put the biscuit in his mouth.

He smelled of good tobacco and better whiskey, a heady blend that mingled with the scents of spice and sugar. She stepped forward and thrust the searing tray into his naked hands; he received it gracefully, balancing it on an open palm. While she stripped off her mitts, he took another biscuit.

:If thou hast asked me here to petition for a job in Hell's kitchen,: he said, :thou hast it.: He reached a spatula off the counter with his free hand and set about transferring biscuits to cooling-racks, his rows very tidy although she would have thought the biscuits still so warm they'd break.

"No," she said. She tossed her mitts on the counter as he placed the tray atop the old bottled-gas stove, and stretched past him to douse the oven. Her heart shuddered behind her ribs, the pulse so fast her hands trembled like hummingbird wings. "I asked you here to bargain. Come on, you, out of the kitchen before you curdle the milk."

Pale eyebrows lifted under the flickering shadows crowning his curling locks. :Nuala,: he purred, and brushed her cheek with the back of his hand, sweeping a thread of wire-gray hair from skin the texture of parchment, soft and worn. She shivered and closed her eyes, to feel the warmth as he enfolded her in his wings. :After all thy service, lass? What's mine is thine for the asking.:

He leaned against the hot stove as if it were nothing and ducked his head to kiss her, his breath like fading roses across her mouth. She let his lips brush hers before she stepped out of his grasp—but not out of reach—and smirked at his petulance. "What, got a twisted wing, old Swan? Out of my kitchen, I said."

:Ever at the lady's bidding,: he said, and followed her into the sitting room.

There were only two rooms in the cottage, a thatched stone tumble on the bluff over a rocky strand. A slanted ladder led to a dark loft over the warmth of the kitchen, where a bed made up neatly under a patchwork eiderdown peered from the shadows.

Fionnghuala lit the lamps by a nine-paned window overlooking the sea, then crouched to poke up the fire, adding another brick of peat while Lucifer folded himself into the settle, one leg drawn up and bent at an angle so he sat on his heel. She dusted her hands on a rag so her apron stayed clean. "Tea or whiskey?"

He smiled, as he was often smiling, and stretched his arms along the scrolled wooden back of Fionnghuala's tapestry love seat. :I require only my lady's company.:

"Right," she said, and poured whiskey for both of them before she sat on the chair beside, letting her fingers brush his palm as she pressed the glass on him. He might sense her fear, and her desperation. And he might admire her strength, for walking on.

He swirled the glass under his nose and breathed in the fumes. The color was pale in the lamplight, more like brook water than water rich with peat, and he inhaled deeply before flicking out a snake-forked tongue to taste a drop. :No water?:

Silently, she passed him the decanter and waited while he doctored the drink. "So measured in our vices," she said, and watched him taste again. His hands were like the ivory sticks of a fan. He sighed, and closed his eyes, relaxing into the embrace of the settle. Fionnghuala, watching, felt an ache in her own vanished wings, and wondered if even the Morningstar grew tired.

:So bargain,: he said, without opening his eyes. :One swan to another. What dost thou want, Nuala, if it's not love or money, or God's old Devil in thy bed?:

"Who says I don't want any of that?"

One blue eye cracked open and his mouth curved on one side. :Don't lie to the Devil, love.:

"I want Keith MacNeill," she said, naming someone who had been as much foster-son as friend. "The Dragon Prince, the Wolf of Scotland. I want him back from the teind."

:For thy very own? For a pet? For a toy?:

She sipped her drink, and shook her head. The fire glowed warm along her thigh and hip, and she turned to absorb its heat. The cottage was cozy, but the nights were raw. "For the world," she said, and waited. "For friendship. For himself and for his son. For my nephew the sea."

:He went to pay a debt. As thou shouldst know, my lady of the white shoulders. Where's thy swan-cloak now?:

"The debt is paid." She went and perched beside him, turned side-ways, one hip on the edge of the couch. He straightened his leg to make room and cupped a warm wing around her shoulders, rasping feathers through her wild gray hair. "How you dispense with the payment is your choice, old Swan."

:Ah, and if I need him? I've a brother devil or two brewing a renewed war with Heaven, Nuala. A Dragon Prince might be just the thing, if it comes down to a fight. He might even slow Michael down a little.: He raised his glass and toasted her, waiting until she clinked rim to rim, and then turned it to cover with his mouth the place where her glass had touched. She felt a cool shiver at the gesture, the touch of his wing, the brush of his eyes. *He is the Devil*, she told herself. *He could tempt the swan from her nest, the foam from the sea.*

She tasted her drink, and waited to be denied.

:And what dost offer in return?:

Her heart skipped in her chest. The whiskey caught in her throat like a stone. "Old thief," she whispered. "What is it that you want?"

:Love,: he said. And did the Devil ache? Perhaps, or he counterfeited it well, a sad flicker of his mouth, a moist gleam in his eye. He set his glass on the window ledge between the hurricane lamps and leaned forward to kiss her mouth.

This time, she permitted it, permitted it and kissed him back, the tapping of his tongue-tips like ribbons flicking in the wind. The taste of the Scotch was warmer on his lips. "Not *my* love." His mouth smiled on her own.

:No,: he admitted. :But thine will serve today, little Swan, if mine will serve for thee. Art lonely, lady?:

He knew she was. He was the Devil, after all. But she pushed against his shoulder, and he shifted back, and it was her turn to smile. "What of your renewed war with Heaven?"

:I never said it was *my* war, lady.:

And how audacious was it, for the Devil to seek redemption? Courage, or the same hubris that had damned him in the first place? Fionnghuala sighed, and found comfort in her religion: love the sinner; hate the sin. "And if I win you your lover's heart, then?" *Old serpent, old Swan.*

:The wolf goes free. I vow it.:

There's no promise on earth to equal the Devil's. She kissed him, to seal it, and barely noticed when he lowered her to the knotted rag rug and plucked the glass out of her hand.

Across the water, she heard the black horse neigh.

Jane Andraste watched the sun rise over New York with a bone china cup of Jamaican coffee cradled between her hands. She leaned over the granite wall of her penthouse balcony and breathed in steam. The iron inlay was colder than the stone. The coffee cup was uncomfortably warm, and the rings on Jane's fingers should have picked up that warmth, concentrated and contained it. Iron is a notoriously poor conductor of heat, but it retains it beautifully, and the heavy intricate filigree rings she wore on both hands were base metal plated with platinum so they would not irritate her skin. On her left wrist was a folksy toggle bracelet, peridot and onyx with a marcasite clasp, and silver beads set with the glittering lead-black iron sulfide. She slept in the bracelet, even now.

It looked a bit odd with her white Egyptian-cotton robe and fuzzy slippers, but that was a widow's privilege, as was her sleep-tousled hair and her lack of makeup. There had been a time when she rose before dawn every morning to make up her face, first for a man and then for the cameras.

Now she rose alone, and greeted the sun.

She had to live high up, in New York City, to see it. She had a house near Albany, one with a sloping lawn over the river that gave her sunrises almost in her lap. But it wasn't the same. She would live out the end of her life here, in this city she had fought for and lost, mourning the daughter she had also fought for and lost and the grandchild she had never seen. Atop a high, lonely tower, as befitted an aging sorceress. Like a pope without cardinals, like a king without barons, Jane Andraste was an archmage with no adepts, only apprentices.

She would dream her dreams, and watch the sun rise and watch the sun set, and prune her roses in their heavy stone planters, and watch her protégé pretend he had not sold a whole world with his treachery. Pretend he had not betrayed his brother's death, and his comrades, her Magi.

Or so she had believed. And so she had intended.

And now her rings were cold on her fingers, and the scent of blood hung heavy on the wind.

And Jane Andraste, who had half expected to be the last Promethean archmage, watched the sun rise over New York City, and knew a bright pale sort of hope as she smiled and contemplated war.

She turned away from the wall and the sunrise, balancing her coffee cup on her palm, and headed for the shower. Christian would be arriving soon with news, and she needed to be presentable.

Later, when the rising elevator chimed, she greeted it with more coffee and the pastry that was delivered every morning. Jane rarely left her tower now. The caution and dignity befitted an archmage, and if a still, small voice sometimes whispered in her ear of cowardice, wasn't everyone prone to self-doubt?

Christian still wore the turtleneck and blazer she'd seen him in the night before, and he accepted the breakfast she pressed on him with the appetite of the young. Matthew had eaten like that too, and it delighted Jane to watch them. All that energy and vitality.

"What did you find out?" she asked, when Christian had consumed his second cup of coffee and was halfway through a bear claw, frosting sticky on his fingertips.

"Matthew doesn't want help," he said, brow furrowing. "Categorically. The body was very messy, and I'd say it's definitely a Fae murder. You can't talk to the mayor's office and try to get the turnover expedited?"

"The mayor's a Republican," she said. "He doesn't owe me any favors. He'll want to solve the crime in this jurisdiction if he can—"

"Can't we use that?" Christian finished the pastry in a few more bites and licked his fingers clean. "A Faerie crime and a cover-up . . . if we wanted to start turning public opinion against them again, it could be useful."

"We have to be careful," she answered. She poured more coffee and fussed with it, but didn't drink. "Fear gives them strength. Any kind of belief and awareness makes them . . . more."

"Then how do we fight them?"

Jane said, "Last time, we starved them out. And they are still weak from that, but we haven't another four hundred years to spare. The Dragon unchained is a problem, but we've still warded our cities well enough to make them very uncomfortable. And we *can* exact a price for their arrogance." She shook her head. "If it was a Fae murder. If Elaine does not deal with it herself."

"Jane," Christian said softly, "she's not your daughter anymore. You can't expect—"

"Oh, what do you know about it?" She was on her feet before she realized it. Still spry for an old lady. "What the hell do you know about it, Christie?"

He shrugged, and reached for another pastry. "Not enough, it seems."

Chapter Four
This Free Will

The man who'd found Althea's body sat on the back of a horseshoe-shaped chair, a cell phone pressed to his ear, watching Geoff over the tops of wire-rimmed spectacles and nibbling on the nail of his left thumb. He was bare-chested under the gaudy coat, patterns of ink stark on his pale skin, but Geoff didn't think it was a costume, exactly. Nor did he think the appraising glances were a proposition. So he looked back calmly and waited for the call to end, eavesdropping shamelessly. "Christian," the man said, and then something Geoff didn't quite catch. "No, I don't need help. Or bail. Please tell Jane her assistance isn't required. I'll handle it myself—no, I do not care to speak with her."

The tattooed man flipped the cell closed, something awkward about the method that Geoff didn't understand until he took the phone from his right hand with his left and the right one stayed curved into a claw. He stuffed the gray metal phone into the pocket of his jeans and stood, just waiting, dark eyes incongruous under all that fair hair, as if he expected Geoffrey to come to him. He didn't say anything. He held out his hand, the right one, crooked inside his black glove.

Geoffrey got up from the mustard-colored chair and went. He blinked, surprised to find his feet had carried him all the way across the checkerboard floor. The blond man's eyes *were* dark, brown as bottles behind glare-proof glasses, with a sharp kind of knowing gleaming at the bottom of them—a very long way down, as if light shone sideways through the irises. "I'm Matthew," he said. "You're—Geoffrey? And you don't like blood—"

"You're one of them," Geoff said, swallowing hard enough to sting his throat.

"No," Matthew said. "I'm one of *us*."

Geoffrey stepped back, fighting now, magic drawing tight around him: the strands of a spider's web on a struggling fly. Geoffrey's power was ignorant—reflexive—but it was real. It flickered up the strings of Matthew's control, trembling and ineffectual, the strength under it un-leveraged. Matthew used a touch of mesmerism, put his soul and his power into his eyes and waited for the boy to stop struggling.

The girl had died on Matthew's watch. Had died due to his negligence. She was his failure. Crippled magic and a crippled hand were not excuses.

He was angry.

Furious, with a kind of cold rational wrath that left him in a limpid state of focus. He'd come to rely on Faerie's gratitude, he realized. He'd pulled off his rings and turned his back on his responsibilities, and it had been stupid, *stupid*.

Unforgivably so. Because the conscience of a Faerie was as reliable as the conscience of a shark.

Althea Benning had paid the price for his arrogance. For his complacency.

And he had a long, long way to go to atone for that.

"I'm not Otherkin," Geoff said, his voice shivering. He raised both hands. Matthew did not move. "That's Jewels. And Althea. They're the ones who want to be kissed by Faeries—"

"Nobody wants to be kissed by Faeries," Matthew said—a painful lie, a falsehood that chipped away at his strength. Faerie magic, like Faerie gold, was based on glamourie and bindings, half-truths and misrepresentations and outright skullduggery. Matthew's magic was opportunistic, but it relied for its power on the naming of names and the knowledge of essences. To tell a knowing lie was to undermine the fabric, warp and weft of his power. And he had known one person who very much had wanted to be kissed by Faeries. Matthew had paid more than passing consideration to it himself, when it came to one Fae in particular.

"You don't have to tell *me* that, man." Geoff shivered harder, dropping his hands to tug his zipper edges together. He hugged his elbows to his sides. The gesture pressed skin-warmed air away from the coat, spreading the scent of leather. "There's nothing Faerie's got I want, you know? But they've got their fantasies."

Matthew knew. "But you're with Jewels."

"Yeah," he said, and turned his head, because Matthew's power held his body. "I'm with Jewels. I don't like blood either, you're right. But I'm with Jewels."

A cryptic statement, and Matthew would have ferreted after it, but he caught a hitch in his new acquaintance's breathing, and followed the direction of his gaze. The girl in the gray sweater had paused in a slip of light between the door and the doorframe; illuminated, she was positively translucent. Pale-colored markings followed the scars along her hairline: a tiara of knots, wrought in dye and pain. "Jewels," Matthew said, tasting it, and let the young man go to her.

He'd seen a body like Althea's before. Seven years before, when he hadn't stopped Elaine Andraste, Seeker of the Daoine Sidhe and the daughter of his archmage, Jane Andraste, from carrying off a part-Fae whore. The Seeker's familiar had killed and partially eaten a man in the process.

But there hadn't been a Seeker in New York in seven years, and Elaine wasn't Elaine anymore; she was the Queen of the Faeries. Matthew wiped the sweat from his left hand onto his jeans, feeling the stiffness of dried blood in the fabric, and followed Geoffrey across the room.

Geoffrey pulled Jewels into his arms. She made it look like he was comforting her, but his hands shook, one on her hip and one in her hair. She leaned close, pressed against warmth, sliding her hands under his jacket and the untucked tail of his shirt. His breath ruffled her hair. His skin was firm and warm.

"They're letting us go," she said, when his grip eased and she could speak. "We can go home. You have your train ticket?"

He nodded and gave her one last squeeze and stepped back, breathing carefully. "Who's going to call Althea's mom?"

"They already did," Matthew supplied, when Jewels hesitated. "The police. They had somebody sent to her house."

Neither one thought to ask how he knew it. Geoffrey looked down at his knuckles and cleared his throat once. "We should—"

"God, her mom will . . ." They shared a look that was meant to exclude Matthew and failed.

Matthew stepped forward, placing the pressure of his presence on the conversation. Jewels glanced at him first. "Look," he said. "I've got to drive up to UConn anyway. Why don't I drop you? It'll be faster than the train, and I'll buy you both breakfast."

It would be stupid to accept, of course.

Jewels looked him in the eyes, her own cool as topaz, and nodded. "What are you doing at UConn?"

"I'm going to talk to Merlin the Magician about what killed your friend. Do you want to come along?"

Morgan le Fey, once-Queen of Gore and Cornwall, stood in the grand entry to the court of the Daoine Sidhe with her wolfhounds at her side. The three of them made a splash of brightness—crimson, silver, indigo—against checkerboard flagstones, and the red dog and the silver bitch crouched low, unworried to be waiting.

Morgan wasn't worried, either, or impatient. She was as calm as the golden stones rising story on story overhead, the high echoing spaces of the reception hall, the ancient shoe-worn flags scattered with sweet rushes underfoot.

She was old enough to know how to wait.

And truthfully, she hadn't been waiting long. She slid flat hands into the hip pockets of her jeans and leaned back on the heels of her boots, tilting her head to stretch out her neck and shoulders. Sunlight tumbled in spectral fragments through the vaulted crystal overhead, a brilliance the Mebd would never have permitted, in her later, sadder days.

But the Mebd was Queen here no longer, and had not been for seven mortal years, which could be a day or a lifetime in Faerie. And the new Queen crossing to Morgan wore ivory and silver, a gown beaded from collar to hem in flashing crystal. Around her neck like a fur collar, a warm shadow furled and unfurled immaterial wings. The creature, named Gharne, was lithe and skittish, and he raised his barbed head to greet Morgan.

Rushes slid under the Queen's train, dragged into chevrons like a wake behind a ship, and the herbs and flower petals strewn among them fluttered up and drifted aside: pansy, rose, and rue.

Morgan crossed her feet and made a curtsey. Graceless in jeans, but she was past caring for such things, and she had come as she was bid. The Queen wouldn't care if she wore a glamourie.

"Grandmother," the Queen said, and pushed Morgan's wind-tangled hair behind her ear to kiss her cheek.

"Elaine," Morgan said. The Queen smiled slightly. It wasn't her name any longer, but that didn't stop Morgan using it. The witch had known some others who made the same bargain—a fact that was much on her mind today—and selling the power in a name didn't remove the need to have something with which to turn a person's head in a crowded room. "I come as I am bid."

"Then sit to tea."

The Mebd would have had courtiers on all sides, except on those occasions when she roamed the halls of her palace by night and alone, and no one dared come to her. This Queen was a solitary soul, a thing that both grieved Morgan and eased her.

But then Morgan caught a glimpse of the page Wolvesbane, almost out of sight and just within hearing of the clap of Elaine's hands, and hid her grin behind the fall of hair that was tangled strands of red and gray and gold. Her dogs paced them, compact feet rustling on herbs and nails clicking on stone. "What did you wish to know?"

The Queen beckoned her to a side table, and with her own hands lifted fistfuls of flowers from a shallow silver tray, leaving the water behind. She blew across it, and the rippled surface smoothed. "Watch," she said, and passed her hand over.

A white horse splotched with black appeared, a blond man in a bard's cloak on his back. Morgan recognized them both.

The Queen turned from her improvised mirror, her arms held wide so the embroidered ivory silk of her sleeves would swing clear, pearls and diamonds whispering among the dark strands of her hair. The locks caught and cobwebbed across her shoulders as she raised a hand and made a loose fist. She wore no braids and no bindings, just the jewels and the chains. "You know him?"

"Intimately," Morgan said. "His name was Christopher Marlowe."

"Yes."

Then Morgan fell silent as the Queen brought her onto a broad patio over the garden. She stood for a moment and watched her granddaughter fuss with the tea things, her dark head bent, nearly black hair netting in soft locks all around her face. The Queen of the Daoine Sidhe was not a pretty woman, with her peaked handsome nose and her hollow cheeks, but her gray-green eyes were bright as river rocks when she glanced up. "The author of *Dr. Faustus*. The same one, I take it?"

"The Fae have a love for poets." Morgan shrugged. She folded her arms over her chest, pressing shirt buttons into her skin, and looked out over the gardens. The dogs flopped on the marble steps, soaking in the sun, the old bitch grunting a little as she found a comfortable hollow. "How is Ian, Elaine?"

"Well enough. He's with Cairbre often now. He still mourns Hope." The Queen seated herself without waiting for assistance, and gestured Morgan into a chair opposite. She was the scandal of the court, pouring tea and passing cookies with her own long brown hands. "You don't want to talk about this Marlowe."

Morgan shrugged. "It's old history. He went to Hell, not as the tithe but adjunct to it. He was my lover—"

"Who hasn't been?" Arch, but not disapproving. A cup rattled on the saucer as she handed them to Morgan.

Morgan took the tea and set it down, and gave her attention to selecting a slice of lemon. The sharp scent overwhelmed the heady sweetness of sunlit flowers. Behind a row of yews, someone's foot crunched on a gravel path. "—and Murchaud's."

"I gathered."

"You've met him?" Morgan glanced up sharply, and Elaine permitted herself a smile.

"Not precisely." She took her time with the sugar tongs. It was always a minor victory to know something in advance of Morgan—an advantage best used quickly, because Morgan inevitably found out. "He's snuck off with Whiskey to New York."

Morgan stirred, and set the spoon aside, and glanced up through her hair. Her eyes were like the Queen's, gray that was green or green that was gray, a changeling's lichen-colored irises catching sun on copper shimmers buried deep. The little hitch in her breath said she knew already, but she played the line the Queen gave her. "Toward what outcome?"

"The death of Jane Andraste. Whiskey seeks what he always seeks, and your Marlowe wants revenge."

"That's Kit for you." The witch sipped her tea, holding her hair out of her face with the back of a freckled hand. The tendons stood out across it, taut as the strings of a lute over the bones. "What do you plan to do about it? Would you like me to intervene?"

"Other than wish them luck? I sent Kadiska to keep an eye on them. And I can truthfully say I had nothing to do with the arranging of it, if they succeed."

"Cold words, for the death of your mother."

The Queen shrugged, her eyes shadowed. "Someone told me once that if I were to be Fae, I should learn ruthlessness."

"And if it fails, and Jane comes back with another war?"

"With what forces?"

Morgan soaked a biscuit in her teacup, borrowing time. "She's had seven years. And I heard Arthur say something similar once."

"Let's not hear from Dragon Princes, just this once, shall we?" The Queen drank her tea quickly, as if she wished she were tossing back liquor, and set the cup down with a click. "You've a look in your eyes, grandmother."

Morgan smiled. "Your Marlowe?"

"Not mine. But out with it."

"You said you did not wish to speak of Dragon Princes."

"Aye, and he was born between Vlad and Keith, was he not? One Prince in five hundred years, thank what there is to thank for it. And Marlowe a century too late—"

"Aye," Morgan said, and finished her tea with a bit more decorum than Elaine had shown. "But you need to know that his return precipitates a situation I'm not sure has ever occurred before. He was born between Princes, aye. And his tenancy was complicated by other factors—the rise of the Prometheans, a captive angel, the heavy hand of the Morningstar—"

The Queen leaned her elbows on the table like a child, not a queen, and rested her chin on steepled fingers. A shadow caught in the furrow between her brows. "But."

"But he was a sorcerer and a poet both, Elaine. And there were some who wrote his name as *Merlin*, even then."

Merlin the Magician taught Geology 102 at a public university in northeastern Connecticut. Weekend nights, she played keyboards in a prog-rock bar band. Her name was Carel Bierce, and her office was on the third floor of a sprawling, subdivided, slate-roofed academic building. The office was shaped in an unequal trapezoid, the result of decades of temporary dividers that had turned the enormous old brownstone into a rabbit warren for academics: musty, fusty, stuffy, and difficult to navigate. The office was cluttered, overcrowded, inefficiently wired and four floors from the mass spectrometer, but the wide, heavy, old-fashioned casement window overlooked the sweep of the chemistry building lawn and the long smooth curve of Horsebarn Hill, and the play of sugar maple tawny and vermilion over that backdrop ensured that the Merlin clung to her space ferociously every time her colleagues provoked the administration into shuffling office assignments.

All Saint's Morn, a Monday, had dawned cold and crisp with pale curls of frost delineating those dag-edged maple leaves and every blade of grass. It had melted into Indian-summer heat by nine o'clock, when Carel left her office, bounced down the stairs amid a cataract of students with her skirt swirling heavily around her ankles, trotted through Beach Hall's partially enclosed rear courtyard, and headed up the walk toward the nearest roach coach for a second large cup of coffee better than the stuff in the lounge. She hurried back ten minutes later, gravel crunching under slouchy boots, shoulders pulled back and head held high under the weight of beaded braids.

The beads rattled around her shoulders when she jerked to a halt, scalding coffee—white, no sugar—spattering her knuckles. Matthew Szczegielniak stood before the door, gaudy in a white T-shirt, jeans, and a red patchwork tailcoat that *gleamed* with power. Two nondescript young persons huddled behind him and off to one side; Carel spared them barely a glance.

"I haven't seen you in a long time, Matthew Magus," she said quietly. She transferred her paper cup to her left hand and shook her fingers. They stung, still wet under her rings. She sucked the remaining coffee off her skin. "What brings you to my humble place of work?"

"I brought some friends to meet you."

They didn't look like Matthew's friends. They looked like a couple of Carel's students, slightly Gothier than the norm, and scared out of their wits. They huddled together with a hunched-in self-effacing aspect that Carel associated with abuse survivors. "I see that." She sipped her coffee. "You're a ways from New York City, Matthew."

"I know," he said, and tossed a glance over his shoulder at the heavy wooden door. It had been a long drive, nursing his dowager Volkswagen — the only car he could drive anymore, old enough that it had no trace of a computer and warded to the spark plugs against his erratic magic — up the Merritt Parkway to 91. "It's important, Carel. Aren't you going to invite us in?"

More than a polite request: it was an offer of trust, and one he'd refused before. Stepping into a wizard's tower meant stepping into her *power*, and it wasn't the sort of thing one did lightly. Carel cocked her head so her braids splayed over her shoulder, tasting confusion and bittersweet and blood, sensing a lance of white strength and pure light that hadn't pierced him before, the way it did now. A lot can happen in seven years.

"Something happened last night."

"Someone died," he said.

"In New York? On Halloween? Someone died? And you come to me for that?"

"I come to you for this," he said, and reached out slowly, with a right hand that hadn't been twisted in such an ugly fashion the last time they met. A lot can happen in seven years.

Apparently.

His hand brushed the hair of the girl in the dirty gray sweater. The girl didn't flinch as he tucked strands behind her ear, but Carel did. Flinched, then stepped forward, frowning at the delicate curve of the ear. "She's not Fae. Otherkin?"

"Yes." Then his voice took on a singsong formality, though he tilted his head so his eyes caught the light. "Dr. Bierce, this is Juliet Gorman, called Jewels, and Geoffrey Bertelli. Jewels, Geoff, this is Carel Bierce. Merlin the Magician, for the uninitiated."

The children gaped. Carel sighed and pursed her mouth, studying the girl's startled pale eyes behind fair lashes.

Carel propped her free hand on her hip and shook her head. Authority figures could be comforting, in a crisis, and she knew how to cock that hat. "Girl, what were you—no, never mind. We'll talk about that later. Matthew Magus, a girl who wants to be a Faerie when she grows up is *not* enough to drive all the way up here to see me."

"No." He pulled a manila envelope from the inside front pocket of his vulgar morning coat, left-handed. "This was."

She knew what she would see before she opened the flap. She knew it from the bruised light around Matthew's fingertips where they touched the envelope, from the black-clad boy's quick breaths and the way he looked down at the gravel, one hand on the girl and one hand on the brownstone wall. She opened the flap anyway, juggling her coffee, and fanned the contents like a hand of cards.

She'd seen worse, but not recently. "You think it's Fae."

"We don't have wolverines in New York City," he said.

She thumbed the amber ring on the second finger of her right hand and considered the way the light fell through it, looked past the photos in her hand as much as at them.

She stuffed the photos into the envelope. He took them, expressionless, and she met his eyes through the clear glaze of his spectacles. "Come up to my office."

They followed her up the stairs in silence. In the middle of the class period the old stairwell—dingy despite a few dozen coats of interior latex—was empty except for the four who climbed, two women and two men. The Merlin's hand was on the door to her office before she spoke again. "It's cramped."

"We'll manage." Matthew took the door from Carel and held it open for Geoff and Jewels while she preceded them.

She paused before her desk, dropped off the cup, and fussed papers, then scrubbed her hands together as if the photographs had left a stain.

Matthew shut the door, the atmosphere creaking with the pressure change, and their eyes met over Jewels' head, adults deciding on safe conversation in front of the children.

Carel went to prop the ancient window open on a piece of board. "You think it was Gharne."

"There weren't footprints in the blood." He shrugged. His red coat jingled. "And the Kelpie was in the city last night, not far from the scene. So I don't know what to think. But *you* don't think it was Her Majesty's familiar demon, do you?"

Slowly, Jewels looked from face to face, and then moved from between them. She licked her lips and stood by the wall. Geoffrey fell back beside her, took her hand, and clung.

"What purpose would Elaine have to hunt your city, Magus?"

"I thought you might know."

The Merlin laughed, low in her throat, and put her back to the window. The morning light gilded her high serene cheekbones and burnished her fine-grained skin. She flicked her beads behind her shoulder and examined his impassive face, the tiny lines pulled taut against the corners of his mouth, and wondered if he even knew how much hurt he was sheltering, or if his denial was complete.

Hell of a thing to have happen to a Mage. Lying to yourself was still lying, and their magic wasn't the sort that liked self-deception. "Who was the girl?" she asked.

"Ask these." His gesture included Geoff, who flinched, and Jewels, who stared back. "I don't know, myself."

The Mage's eyes met the Merlin's, a brief contest of wills. Matthew pushed his spectacles up his nose with one forefinger, and pretended a calm compassion he didn't feel. *Fake it till you make it.* Or until you forget how an honest reaction looks.

Carel glanced at the young couple. "Not yet. But I will."

"You could ask the stones what they remember . . . Merlin."

"Matthew."

The irritation in her voice was genuine enough to bring him up short. "I don't know." This time she heard the honest worry and pain that underlay challenge and sarcasm. "I don't know. What you saw, gutted and eaten, the soft parts first—"

Geoff whimpered. Jewels took his arm with a rustle of cloth and leaned against him, warmth comforting warmth, but the Dragon could smell the fear and grief that rose from her pores, and what the Dragon could smell, so could Carel.

"—Jane's going to flip. Jane's going to start the whole damned war all over again. She's already had one of her watchdogs calling me."

Carel closed her eyes and let her head fall back against the window frame with a sound like a thumped melon. Autumn filled the room, cold and crisp, rich with the smell of leaf mold like the musk of serpents. For a moment, it seemed a shadow fell over Carel, like the overhang of an enormous head, a head too vast to fit in her tiny office. The children stopped breathing. Matthew felt his own heart clench, icelocked, at the Presence who came among them.

The Merlin extended her hand, silver bangles clashing. "Let me see the photos again."

Matthew handed her the envelope without comment and crossed his arms, keeping his eyes on her face as she swept the glossies across her blotter in an arc. "What could it be besides Gharne?"

"Werewolves," Matthew supplied promptly.

"You know better than that." Carel tapped the top photo. "Could it have been done with a knife?"

"There aren't any Fae in New York," Jewels said, lifting her head from Geoff's shoulder. "The city is warded against them. No Fae, and we are mostly scared to go there."

Matthew laughed, a flat unresonant sound. "You can't hang iron and rowan over an entire city, Jewels."

"There aren't any wards?"

"There are thousands of wards. They just don't work."

"At all?" A vein of excitement gleamed in her voice.

"Enough." He shrugged, disgusted, and kept his eyes on Carel as she selected one photo out of the half-dozen or so and carried it to the window and daylight. "If you had any idea what Faerie was, what it's done, you wouldn't be so eager to get down on the ground and roll in it, kid."

"You have *your* magic, Matthew Magus," the Merlin said. "It's easy for us to forget mundanity. And there are worse things than Faerie in the world."

There was no shadow over her this time, no scorch and hiss of the Dragon underlying her words. It didn't mean the Dragon wasn't there; the Dragon was always there. That was what it meant to be the Merlin: to comprehend the Dragon Whose Pearl Was the Heart of the World, to understand the counsel of the selfish and violent mother of everything as the spoken word rather than a mere savage trickle of instinct.

Matthew never let himself forget it. "What do we do?"

She glanced from him to the children and tilted her head. A braid slipped over her ear. "Are you expected home?"

Jewels glanced at Geoff. "We haven't got anybody," she said. "Why?"

Carel showed her teeth. "Then no one will miss you if you come with us to Faerie," she said, and a shock of joy went through Jewels as hot and cold as liquor.

"Morgan?" Matthew asked.

Carel's senses weren't any more acute than a normal woman's. But the Dragon smelled the fear rising cold and bittersweet and appetizing through his coat, although it never showed in his expression. "Scared of a little fire, Scarecrow?"

"I wasn't planning on a day trip to Annwn."

The Merlin's lips pulled tighter. "Not Morgan. Elaine." She reached for the phone. "But first, *I* have to call home and tell my girlfriend I'm missing dinner."

Chapter Five
The Ballad of Thomas the Rhymer

He was a gray cat with one white rear foot, Rumpelstiltskin by name. A twenty-pounder, cougar-bodied, lean and soft, and that one foot glimmered like a moth's wings in the half-dark as he picked his way across a red and ivory carpet, intent on a single morning sunbeam that had slipped between the drapes. He stalked the bright patch as he would have stalked a mouse, not deigning to notice the three women and three men already seated in or standing around the room.

Only two of them noticed him. One was Christian, splendid and silent with his curled red hair and his eyes like a cat's, green and hazel and tawny all at once, who leaned in the shadows beside the fireplace. The second was Autumn, whose house and whose cat it was, and who watched Rumpelstiltskin's stately progression as she closed her cell phone and sighed.

Christian noticed that too, but Christian noticed everything. He smiled at her with only the corners of his mouth and eyes, shy commiseration. He cupped fine-boned hands around a steaming pottery mug, and didn't speak a word.

"Carel?" Moira asked, her voice bright with sympathy, and Autumn nodded. "That woman does not appreciate you."

"Oh," Autumn said, "she does."

"If she came to circle we'd be eight. One more makes nine. It would be nice to have nine."

"If Lily showed up once in a while." Jason, the high priest, crouched over a glass-topped coffee table teaching tarot to a young woman by the decreasingly unusual name of Michael. He placed another card, completing the cross, commencing the tower.

"Carel's busy supporting me in the style to which I'd like to become accustomed." Autumn folded the phone and replaced it in its pouch on the outside of her leather daypack. Her skirt slid between her knees and as she tugged the layers of gold and violet cotton gauze smooth she smiled around the irony of being unable to tell a house full of pagans that her lover was *busy* because she was the Merlin.

"Wish I could find one of those." Gary—*Gypsy*, he'd tell you—looked up from his seat behind a card table in the corner. He'd laid silk scarves across its surface and was methodically dipping crystals in springwater and wiping them dry before laying each one on a scarf and winding it in two turns of insulating silk. He usually wore flannel, ragged jeans, and unlaced boots, a red-piped navy down jacket zipped over his belly and barrel chest when things grew cooler. But today, in honor of the holiday, his grizzled beard decorated a silver silk shirt and neat black jeans tapered over black Frye boots.

A few strands of cut grass had dried onto the heels; Autumn's house had a deep, sloped, narrow backyard with a grove of white pine at the bottom. They'd raked the earth between the trees bare for the bonfire— legal as long as it was "primarily a cooking fire," so they'd roasted marshmallows, and apples and onions in tinfoil with maple syrup, and the sharp garlic sausages that Gyp made himself—and held circle until sunrise.

There were smudges under Gyp's eyes, blue-black as bruises. Staying up all night wasn't as easy as it used to be, although he comforted himself that they were all tired. Tired, but anticipating a Denny's breakfast once the ritual tools were packed away. Enough grease could make up for a sleepless night. And Autumn made very good coffee.

"First," Jason said to Gypsy, without looking up from his cards, "become a lesbian." He rode the chuckles with a half-hidden smile, black ponytail sliding over his shoulder as full of rainbows as a raven's wing. He had a Jewish nose in a Grecian profile, and wore his hair pulled back sharply because strangers asked if he was American Indian when he did.

He was using the Thoth deck, bladed lines and smoky colors, and Michael leaned forward to see the cards better. Straight dark locks drifted in feathers across her cheek, but she kept her hands folded behind her back, and her hair clipped clean at the nape of her neck revealed shoulder blades moving like wings under her Trogdor the Burninator T-shirt. "What's this one?" she said, with a bob of her pointed chin.

"The Ace of Wands." Jason touched and straightened a corner of the card. "It represents you in this case, and indicates a fiery youth, full of spirit and passion. A generative, creative force. Also, you have a lot of court cards and Major Arcana."

She watched his hands as he caressed the cards. "Is that unusual? It's handy how they have the names or the little . . . summaries on the bottom."

"One of the many nice things about this deck." He touched an antelope-faced card, slick and webbed with vein-blue symbols on a background the color of flesh. Ponderous horns spiraled from the animal's head to the upper corners of the card. "The Devil," Jason said. "And here's the Queen of Swords, the Queen of Cups, the Empress, the Universe . . ." He grinned and looked up, catching her eye. "The Lovers."

Moira chuckled. "Going to bring him by sometime, Michael?"

Michael blushed and leaned back, and Rumpelstiltskin leaped up on the coffee table, scattering the cards. "And sometimes the spirits of the house demand their due," Jason said wryly, and stroked the cat's big wedge-shaped head before bending to pick a bent card off the rug. It was the Magus, and he smoothed it before he swept the deck together again. "Gyp, you hungry yet?"

Gypsy tied the last bundle of cloth and crystals, and slipped it into his pouch. "Ready to eat," he admitted, and pushed his chair back from the card table as he stood. "Pity Lily couldn't make it."

"Halloween is a high Goth holiday too," Michael said. "She does have other friends." She scrambled up, crossed legs untangling with coltish speed, and turned to grab her Windbreaker from the corner by the radiator.

Moira kicked Jason lightly on the thigh with a green suede boot, and said to Michael. "Don't let him get under your skin. He just likes to get a rise out of people."

Michael put her back in the corner and slid her hand down the silky Thinsulate-lined tunnel of her sleeve. She shrugged it across her shoulders and slipped her left hand into the other sleeve. When she looked up, Christian was staring at her directly, silently, sharing one of his half-grown smiles. It looked like an invitation, and so did the lean angle of his body as he propped one elbow on the mantel, long legs crossed in dark blue jeans. "You don't think she's avoiding you, Michael?"

Michael met his look frowning, with a lifted chin, and held on until he glanced away. She zipped her jacket, the long smooth sound of nylon teeth meshing like a paper slicer. Autumn, crouching to spare her back when she swung her pack over her shoulder, saw the exchange, and wondered why it left her uneasy, her palms clammy and cold.

The stare held no mysteries for Michael. She stepped forward, her footsteps swinging like the stride of a big, angry man, and headed for the door. "See you there," she called.

Christian at her heels, she left the rest behind.

The house was a ramshackle old creature with a shabby front porch, three concrete steps descending to a graveled walk before the drive. Crisp air surrounded them, filled Michael's lungs as she breathed deep, stepping to one side.

As the screen door banged shut behind Christian, she turned and kneed him in the groin. He doubled and she swept his legs out from under him, a hard well-placed kick that sent him sprawling off the stoop. He fell silently but grunted when he hit, and rolled onto his back, hands raised in front of him, bits of grass and gravel clinging to indented palms.

"Michael—" he said, warningly.

She paused on the second step, her broad blade shining in her hand. "Stand up and fight," she said, the words curling from her lips on wisps of breath. The grimace on her face was almost a rictus. "Stand *up*, damn you."

"Too late," he said, and scrambled backward into a crouch. "Don't you think you'd better put your sword away before somebody notices?"

She snorted. "Nobody notices an angel unless he wants to be noticed. *Christian.*"

"*He* notices." A short jerk of his thumb upward, and then a wince, as he looked down and brushed sharp pebbles off the heel of his hand. "Sparrows falling and blades of grass. And He doesn't like you getting involved the way you used to anymore, does He?"

Michael descended the last two steps as if sliding on a track, her blade glaring savage green-white as she cut air. The hiss of collapsing vacuum followed the slash; the sword annihilated what it touched.

"It might be worth it." She leveled the blade at Christian. "Just this once. To make sure you leave that girl alone, instead of twisting her around your devil's finger."

Christian blinked at the weapon, and stood, dusting himself with careful palms, as casually as if Michael were aiming a feather duster at him and not a blade composed of primal entropy. "Lily *likes* me," he said. "And you know what? That's your problem, Michael. Nobody *likes* you. Nobody ever has. And I can teach Lily to use her power. You wouldn't even permit her that."

"I have love," Michael said. "And that's all I need. Or Lily needs."

"Just like your God." He stepped back. She didn't follow, though the sword remained trained on him, unwavering. "Just like Him to give potential and desire, and make the fulfillment a sin. Bit of a practical joker, isn't He?"

"Leave Lily Wakeman *alone*."

Christian kissed the palm of his hand at the angel. "Make me."

From the moment Matthew Magus emerged from the police station with the two human children under his care, the stallion had known he would not serve the purpose. He and the poet retreated to the green and relative comfort of Central Park to seek another angle. Thomas—his cloak folded now into his rucksack along with his flute—threw popcorn purchased with vanishing Faerie silver to a motley crowd of pigeons while Whiskey stood, hands in the pockets of his trousers, and watched the children and the carriages and the pretty girls. The carriage horses knew him, and shied or nodded as their natures indicated when they creaked and clopped past. The mortal men were less aware, although more than one of the young women turned to look and flirt and smile.

"Could we not make haste, Whiskey?" the poet said, when he couldn't stay silent another second. He cast a sidelong glance at Whiskey, biting his lip to hide impatience that Murchaud would have seen through. Murchaud would have brushed his hair off his brow and said, *'Tis only time, and hast that to spare.*

It wasn't the first time he'd known this pain. But familiarity did not breed comfort now. *You will live,* he told himself sternly. *You will live, and someday you will breathe again without pain.*

If it were a lie, he would have hated it less. But blood would pay for a good deal of truth. And were he revenged on Murchaud's killer, the eventual easing might not seem like such a betrayal, when it came. Besides, they said, when you plot revenge, dig two graves. He might not have to heal, if he was lucky.

The poet hurled another handful of corn violently, and the wind sheered it aside on concentric arcs. Pigeons scrambled, skewbald and charcoal and gray with rainbow throats, and one that was white as Lucifer's wings and lame in one malformed foot. The poet threw it a piece in particular. His aim was good.

Whiskey let his head droop, sun warming his nape. If he could but shrug on his stallion-shape for a moment and stand in the sun, the wind lifting his mane, the light warm on his white hide and scorching against his black—"Make haste to where?"

Whiskey turned to stare as the poet crumpled the popcorn bag and twisted his hands around the paper as if to throttle it. The poet frowned across the water as another carriage rustled past. "If I had something of Jane's, I could trace her with it."

"You were Cairbre's student. And Morgan's."

"And Raleigh's, and Baines', and Dee's. Not all at once." The poet dismissed them familiarly, the names of acquaintances not recently seen.

"That spell you used this morning?"

"The pass-unseen? A bardic trick."

"You learned nothing in Hell?"

Thomas hesitated, and glanced down between his knees, slim scarred fingers whitening on the paper. "You know, I'm not that other Thomas. It was more than seven years in the service of the Queen of the Faeries. And I am not constrained to the truth."

"You learned witchcraft."

Thomas nodded. "I was Lucifer's student as well, though I no longer use those spells. But any magicker can trace someone with a bit of hair or blood; you needn't be a witch for that."

"Something of Jane Maga's?"

"Some rag or scrap that belonged to her—as, for example, that pretty little bastard in the bloodred coat, if he is her liegeman—I could find her with it."

"He's left the city."

"Yes, and hang me for an imbecile, I've no better ideas."

Whiskey considered. "I can think of nothing," he said at last, and tossed his head.

Thomas picked bits off the bag and rolled them between his fingers before flicking them away. Pigeons scrambled, but were disappointed. "We should be doomed that she'd be the first to venture Faerie's gates and leave not a scrap of herself in the otherworld. Most of us, it tears strips off."

"She never was to Faerie. Or not so I knew of it. She sent her Magi, and stayed safe in the iron world herself."

"Sorcerers and towers," Thomas said, disgusted.

Whiskey kicked earth. Less satisfying than pawing at it, and Thomas' impatience was wearing at him, raising the hair at the nape of his neck. He wished the poet paced. Anything would be better than this stagnant fury, like scowling thunderheads. "Very like. We have got a scent of the policemen who came for the murder."

"You have a scent, mayhap. I did get a look at the two who liked each other least, the ones who were not in uniform, but deferred to. Lord protectors of some sort, or commanders of the militia, I wot?"

"More or less." Whiskey had better things to do than explain the organization of a modern police force to an Elizabethan poet, even if he himself were certain he knew how it worked. His hands ached so badly they tingled, and the pain was creeping up his wrists, and starting to infest his knees and hips. "I thought if we found the police, since Jane's man was at the scene, then they might lead us to her."

"It's not an impossible thought."

"Oh." Whiskey blinked. Even his eyes itched with mortals and their doings. "I lie."

"That's what devils are for," Thomas said unpleasantly. "Tell me more."

"I have something that belongs to Jane Andraste," Whiskey said, and grinned wide enough to show his worn yellow pegs to the root. "Or something close enough for sympathy. I have her daughter's name and soul."

"Then why are we limed to this park bench?"

"Stand up, Sir Thomas," Whiskey said. "Suddenly, I feel the urge to be afoot."

"You and mischief," Thomas answered. But he stood and cast the remains of the bag into the chained can, which sighed a few particles of dust. "We'll need a private place."

"I know one. Unless it's changed since I hunted here."

The poet fell in alongside Whiskey. He cleared his throat. "Do I detect a hint that the Fae avoid this place?"

"The Daoine do, and the Unseelie mostly fear the Queen."

"And the undine we saw wasn't Unseelie?"

"Oh," Whiskey said. "Unseelie enough. If she slips in and sups the blood of rats and tomcats, who's to know? If she took a human life, things might be different. But this is Matthew Magus' home. And Matthew Magus—your pretty bastard in the pretty coat, Sir Thomas— does not care to see Fae in his city."

"They stay away out of respect?"

"They'd respect better, if he enforced the rules as he should."

The brief walking silence that followed was broken by a lower tone. "Have you noticed, Whiskey, that we are observed?"

Whiskey smiled, bent over Thomas, and murmured in his ear, "Which one?"

"Across the pond. A dapper but otherwise rather nondescript fellow in a gray suit of clothes. Slim, with dark hair. Don't these Americans wear anything with color in it? It's all black and brown and gray, unless it's laborer's clothes. And the cuts are very plain."

"I see *you've* adopted trousers."

Thomas shrugged. "They're comfortable. But these people dress like Puritans."

"They're American. What do you expect?" Whiskey straightened up as if stretching his back and flared his nostrils wide. Warm morning air and women's perfume, the savor of horses and human sweat, asphalt and oil and vomit and dried leaves rustling under trees. And a thick, cold thread like iron on a winter's night, like the raw red metal in rust and blood weathering from balcony railings down the gray faces of buildings, tearstains etched by acid rain. "Magus," he said without hesitation, louder than he had intended.

"Promethean?"

"Aye," Whiskey answered. "I can smell his ring. It seems Jane Maga has found us."

"Then we don't have to find Jane. Where's your other observer, Master Whiskey?"

"By the boat launch."

The poet turned casually, as if they were setting out to complete a walk delayed by their conversation. "The Moor in the hat, with the newspaper?"

"The same." Whiskey laid his hand on Thomas' sleeve. "He's no more a mortal man than I am."

Thomas examined Whiskey's objective as carefully as he could without seeming to stare, but saw only a wiry man, dark-skinned and light-haired, with sun creases thick across his cheeks despite the broad-brimmed hat shading his eyes. A mortal man, to all appearances, with no foxlight of feyness around him. "You're going to ignore the Promethean?"

"On the contrary," Whiskey answered. "I plan to lure him into a dark corner, terrorize him, question him, hold him under until he stops kicking, and possibly consume him afterward." He shrugged, and started forward again. "But first, we have to deal with this fellow, don't we?"

The poet cast a longing look at the Mage. "Dammit," he said. "You'd better hurry."

"Don't worry, Sir Thomas. There's nothing I am looking forward to more than dragging Jane Maga's head home to my mistress like a cat with a most particularly juicy rat. But it's unwise to go into battle with an unconsidered element on your flank." He paused, and blinked long-lashed eyes at the poet. "Now come along. I thought you were in a hurry."

* * *

Jewels laced her fingers through Geoff's and followed Matthew and the Merlin down broad dished steps and across a richly green slope to a pedestrian crossing. A rural highway sliced the easternmost edge of campus off the main sprawl, and behind the row of redbrick dormitories a steeper slope down to the river was forested and laced with deer trails and poison ivy. They veered left, across a tributary brook in the bottom of a willow-verged gully, the last branches fluttering their length on a breeze that was chill in the shade.

When they emerged, the sun was warmer by contrast. Jewels and Geoff looked across a road and up the hill that had been visible from the Merlin's office window. Jewels tightened her grip on Geoff's hand and settled on her heels to look up. Mown grass settled long shadows in the slanted morning light, and the wind freshened. A horse whinnied, high and quavering, and the sound of hoofbeats echoed off the bank and rolled back.

Althea would have loved it, and Jewels flexed her fingers tight against Geoff's to stop herself from thinking about it.

They rounded a curve in the road; there were barns and paddocks above and a pasture below, and a dirt road split off from the asphalt, tending upward. Mobiles of iron horseshoes hung over the barn's tractor doors to ward off the Fae, and Jewels smoothed her hair over her ears.

Geoff wondered how a cultivated hill bound in by barns and dormitories, crowned with a knot of trees and houses, could seem so high and lonely. And Jewels thought of Watership Down, which she'd never seen but had read about, and when she glanced down found herself watching Merlin the Magician and thinking, *She has beautiful skin. I wonder if she would let me cut her, sometime.*

The Merlin glanced over her shoulder and met Jewels' eyes. "Sometime, I might."

Jewels kept walking, a cold sensation creeping from the cleft of her buttocks to the base of her skull. The Merlin turned away again. Bracelets slid and caught on the hairs of her wrist and on her bones and skin, jangling as she waved up the dirt road toward the crown of the hill. "The way is closed," she said. "Prometheans one, thorn trees zero."

"I'm the one who closed it." Matthew slipped his coat off. He folded it over his arm, a flash of color against the autumn brown of the hillside that turned the head of a red-tailed hawk floating on the thermal off the slope. The hawk sheered off when Matthew started up the side road; this was game too big for its talons. "I guess I can get it open again."

"That blood of yours has more than one binding in it. I wonder what else you've got that somebody might be willing to kill for."

Matthew paused, sun warm on the shoulders of his T-shirt, one boot on the blacktop and the other on the badly graveled drive. The freshening wind was unpicking his ponytail, and pale strands snagged in the corners of his eyeglass frames. The glass twinkled flatly and sand gritted under his boots when he turned to glare at Carel. "You think Althea died because of me?"

Carel shrugged, and caught his arm when she walked past him. Reluctantly, he allowed himself to be tugged into motion, the gaze of the others scorching his back. "I think it's possible. You or Jane. She died in your city, and her death brought you out of it—sorry, kids." She glanced over her shoulder, swirl of braids and clatter of stones, and shrugged her apology.

"And she died of my neglect," Matthew said. "Don't forget to mention that."

Jewels swallowed. Geoff stiffened against her grip. She squeezed his hand again, twice to calm him, and three times for the charm, and waited for the sigh and the sideways glance. It came. "She wasn't meat," Geoff said, though he kept walking. His matted black hair was dull in the light, but glimmers of color like fire, highlights of copper and amber, sparkled off the roots. "You shouldn't talk about her—"

"She was meat," Matthew said over his shoulder, without turning. Jewels' flinch didn't keep her from noticing that the Merlin winced too. "To the Fae. Mortal meat, blood and bone. And if there was something they wanted that her death or torment would pay for, no more than meat to appease the dogs."

"They'd kill her just to get you to come to them?"

Matthew laughed like it scratched his throat. "She's lucky all they did was kill her," he said, and shut up, hard, but Geoff saw his broken hand writhe inside the glove, a cringe.

Carel's fingers paled as she clung to Matthew's elbow. "If you can't handle the truth, Matthew Magus, it's no surprise you can't handle your magic, either."

He didn't answer, just jerked his arm away. Jewels rose up on her toes and looked like she was about to press, but she must have caught something of Geoff's understanding, because she settled back with a sigh. Her lips flattened and she shoved her hair irritably behind her ears, where it stuck in greasy elflocks. Her face was shiny and unwashed.

They climbed for a few minutes until they came to the little grove, and the houses warded with hex signs and rowan clustered among it. A black dog barked in a wire run; Matthew didn't meet its eyes.

By one tree in particular, he crouched and pushed the leaves aside. "White oak," he said, and drew his fingers back as if something had stabbed the tips. An electric shiver wrenched up his arm. "There it is."

An iron railroad spike was rusted into the root, crusted ochre-red and driven deep.

"I didn't bring a crowbar," Carel said. She crouched beside him, a hand on his shoulder, and Matthew felt her breath on his neck and her breast against his arm. Her warmth and her shifting aroma—now oranges, now vanilla, now peppermint and sandalwood—were tickles of distraction that were far more welcome than he would have wished to admit.

You're not her type, he told himself sternly, and was then bizarrely flattered that she would forget herself enough to treat him like a person, and not a man. They had been almost friends, once, with the porcupine friendship that was the best two wizards could manage, and he'd mourned that more than he expected once things fell apart.

Or maybe it was simply that she couldn't think of him as a threat because he wasn't exactly a man by her standards. *She* knew about the unicorn. There was what she'd said, about blood and whatever—

Oh, Matthew thought, his left hand hesitating over the spike. *What do you suppose that's worth, Matthew Magus? Not to Carel: her idiom is raw power, earth and flame, not symbols. But to a witch, or to a Mage? What do you suppose the virginity of a unicorn's chosen would be worth?*

More than he could easily calculate. He knew what his blood and his brother's death had bought.

He handed Carel the coat. She held it tightly folded over her knees, her charms and bangles rattling. Geoff and Jewels stood breathing behind her, pressed together like owlets in the nest, eyes huge and wild. Matthew flexed his fist, kneaded the fingers together convulsively, and reached out to lay his hand on the spike that, seven years before, closed a door into Faerie.

The jolt raced up his arm again, locking his fingers, clenching his shoulder muscle, and flashing across his heart. Oversensitive, overtuned. The same rawness that kept him from understanding half of what his city said to him, in the broken babble of its multitudinous voices, and the same undirected power that crippled his magic. Magician's Tourette's.

The problem wasn't denial. Unless that was denial too. He found it, found the magic under the shock, the wit under the pain, found the rust and the blood and the binding. The power was there, but the craft was naive, unpracticed.

He teased the snarl apart like a child's badly tied shoelace and the spike slid into his hand, leaving a smooth-walled, rust-stained wound. He looked up, gasped, and rose on the balls of his feet to stand, his left arm numb and tingling. He transferred the spike to his right hand, slipping it into the curve of withered fingers, and shook his left arm.

Wordlessly, Carel offered the topcoat back. He took it and held the spike out to Geoff. "Hold on to this," he said. "You might want to slip it into your pack or something. Oh, and don't drink or eat anything in Faerie, unless you get a promise first, or you won't be able to leave."

Jewels nodded, knotting her hands to hide the trembling. *This is happening. This is happening.* "We should stay with you?"

"If you can." He patted her shoulder, absently. "You'll see a lot of magic. Manifest magic, not like what you're used to seeing in our world."

"I've seen Fae," Jewels felt bound to insist, but Geoff's question rolled over the end.

"Not like what you just did?"

"Child," the Merlin said, with a sigh and the settle of her palms on generous hips, "what he did was barely magic at all."

"Thanks for the vote of confidence."

She flashed him a grin. "It was Magery, sure, but their work is all bound up in symbols and material things. It's magic for the iron world, and you see the results, maybe, but not the magic itself. A Promethean spell—no, you don't know what a Promethean is, either, do you?"

"Fire from the gods," Jewels snapped.

Matthew laughed. He knew all this, rote and drill, and it was easy to recite in ways that actually talking about what the Prometheus Club had done for him—and to him—before he destroyed it could never be. "More than that. *Taking* fire from the gods, and bending it to the service of man. My order was founded in the sixteenth century, and its original members numbered among them some very . . . notable folk. Sir Francis Walsingham, for example, who was Queen Elizabeth's spymaster. And William Shakespeare too."

"You're kidding." That was Carel, her brows beetled over flashing eyes. "You just made that up."

"Cross my heart," Matthew said, and the gesture he made with his ruined hand was so amused and full of self-mockery that she believed him, or believed he believed it. "His plays are Promethean artifacts, and the transcontinental railroads are ours too. Leland Stanford—" He stopped himself, and shrugged. "I'm making it sound like the Skull and Bones with magic wands."

"Isn't it?"

He ignored her, and Carel grinned. *I should have looked him up years ago.*

"Originally, the Prometheans wished to protect England and Elizabeth from Spain and the Catholics, but Elizabeth did not live forever, and when she died, we needed another purpose. We opposed the Wild Hunt. We brought Faerie and wild magic under control. We would have destroyed it for good, but—" He stopped, restarted. "It was a long war, and in the end we lost."

Jewels stood with her arms folded, absorbing, the sunlight flickering through the bare oak branches to dapple her shoulders and her hair. Geoff leaned on her, feeling her taut attention, the near-craving she felt for every hint and tidbit Matthew offered. He said, "So. That's the kind of magic we're not going to see."

"It is." He shrugged. "One of the seven categories. Magic of symbol, to which almost anyone can be trained. Magic by gift, which is to say, there are some who are born special in some way. And then there is magic by initiation, where the power is earned by sacrifice. That's bought and paid for."

Matthew's right hand rubbed the white cotton cloth over his heart for a moment before he covered the gesture by shrugging into his coat. Geoff remembered the scar there, amid the black patterns of ink, and didn't ask—but he caught Jewels looking too, and knew she was wondering the same thing.

"What about witchcraft?" Jewels asked, leaning forward, oblivious to her own shivers. The wind cut through her coarse-knit sweater. Geoff opened his coat and tucked her inside it, under his arm.

"Wicca," Matthew asked, "or witchcraft?"

"There's a difference?"

The Mage smoothed stray strands of hair behind his ears. "Yes. One, Wicca—modern Paganism—you exercise through the manipulation of symbols. It's not so different from High Ritual Magick, the Golden Dawn sort. Both Wicca and Magick are . . . sort of hedge counterparts to Magecraft. Although those who follow those paths wouldn't be pleased to hear me say it.

"Also, it helps to be stubborn. That's a fourth kind of magic"—he checked on his fingers—"fourth. Willmagic, power claimed through sheer force of personality; exactly what the name implies. One imposes one's will on the universe, or on another creature, simply by being . . . stronger than it is. Willmagic, you'll run across in Faerie. It's what's behind the magic of bindings and namings, and if you weren't both human creatures, I'd caution you to keep your true names private. Names are tricky things."

Jewels nodded, face paler now, as if she was listening and believing and—finally—a little scared.

"What about the changelings?" Geoff said, balling a knobby fist against the nylon lining of his pocket, steel zipper teeth scratching his wrist.

"Magic by blood." Carel twisted her bangles, listening as they chimed. "Magic by birth. Werewolves, Fae, spirits of the wood and vale. Nothing any of us can touch; it's yours, or it's not."

"And glamourie," Matthew said. "The art of illusion."

Geoff said, "So those are the rules? Stay with you, and don't tell anybody my name, and don't eat or drink?"

"Stay on the path." Matthew buttoned one button on his topcoat and turned away from them, toward the white oak and the wild rose and bramble tangled around and behind it. "Stay on the path. Don't look back. Never trust the guardian. That's all there is to know."

"That," Carel said, amid a flash of teeth, "and nothing that walks into Faerie emerges unscathed, or unchanged."

Matthew just nodded.

"Grab my hand," the Merlin said, and Jewels did, holding on to Geoff with an arm around his waist. He wrapped his hand around hers through the pocket lining. The wind lifted her dirty hair, and when he looked down at her, some light seemed to sparkle and fill the shadows on her throat and the hollow under her chin, as if she wore a dress sewn with sequins or leaned out over water on a sunshiny day.

The Merlin held out her left hand and laced it into Matthew's right, her touch so delicate and warm it didn't even hurt. "Open sesame," she said. They stepped forward together, passing through the thornbreak as if it had never existed.

The real world turned to watercolor and washed away, just as Geoff realized that Matthew had only named *six* kinds of magic.

Slanted American sunlight, softened by smog and the curve of the earth, filtered over Bunyip's shoulder. He turned another page of his newspaper, giving no sign that he was aware of Whiskey crossing the green mown lawn to intercept him, or the earthly knight walking beside him. The paper crinkled under the pads of his fingers, denting where his thick, ridged nails dug into the fibers.

There was a surprising amount of water in paper, trapped.

Bunyip sighed. He missed his billabong—although the women wandering along the lakeside looked like fine eating, and there was enough water and muck close by in the Meadowlands to provide a congenial atmosphere for dining.

Unfortunately, he had business first.

A shadow fell across him, and Bunyip folded his newspaper and settled his hat. He tilted his head back and met Whiskey's china-blue eyes, strange and unsettling in the darkness of his face. Walleyed, they called it in horses. It seemed to make Whiskey squint a little in the sun.

"You're a long way out of the Dreaming, cousin," Whiskey said. Thomas stayed at his left hand, quiet and watchful, as if he understood the danger of the situation.

"And you're a long way out of the Isles," the old man said. He tucked his newspaper under his arm. "Which is why I've come to have a word with you. Will you introduce me to your friend?"

Whiskey stepped aside. "Thomas the Rhymer," he said, making a delicate gesture at odds with the sprawl of his fingers. "Meet Bunyip. Bunyip, True Thomas."

Bunyip rose to his feet, heaving himself up as if he weighed far more than his long, spindly body indicated. The poet thrust out his hand; Bunyip accepted, and for a moment the poet felt him *otherwise,* the long stick and twig hand resolving into a damp clawed flipper. The poet craned his head back as a shadow cooled his face. It wasn't a tall woolly-haired man in a black broad-brimmed hat that looked back at him.

The head that hung over him was jowled like a mastiff and whiskered like a seal, flews clinging to projecting walrus tusks. Black velvet skin, soft as a horse's muzzle, drooped around eyes full of glaring planes of light like black opals. The neck was thick and conical — a sea lion's neck, a bull's — blurring into shoulders like a wall of meat. More black crushed velvet covered the massive muscles, and behind them the ponderous body tapered to a scaled and armored tail, the flukes arched over his back. Bunyip braced itself on one burly leg, which ended in a flippered claw, and extended the other delicately, a cat poking dust motes in a sunbeam.

The poet had shaken the hands of demons and queens and Ben Jonson. He managed not to jump back with a yelp, but it was a very near thing.

"A pleasure," the human said, as Bunyip shifted his weight onto his tail and extricated his hand from the human's grasp without accidentally crushing him to death.

He smelled delicious.

With that momentary brush of fingers, Bunyip brought them into the Dream. The human surprised him again; they usually panicked, trembled, curled into themselves when confronted with the richness of chipped, shifting colors and lights. This human glanced around once, quickly, like a startled bird, and then set his shoulders and crossed his arms over his chest, breathing calmly. He had gone wide-eyed over Bunyip's revealed aspect, but mastered it in a moment, and he didn't seem overly perturbed by the Kelpie's Dreaming shape, the wet-maned stallion pied white and black as a magpie.

He was shaman-stuff, then, and initiated. And perhaps not for eating, no matter how delicious he smelled. Bunyip huffed through bean-shaped nostrils, hiding his annoyance.

The poet stared at the monster in preference to the landscape. It could have been a riverbank in Faerie, mud redolent and primeval underfoot and ferns and mosses rich along the bank. Concentrating on the beast kept the jittering surge of his heart and the shaking of his hands from showing in his voice.

The water itself was cloudy green and as full of light as jade. The whole place had a sense of hyperreality to it, an oil-painting depth and saturation of color, but if the poet looked too closely, it resolved itself into facets and flickers, pointillist dots. Unreal, fractal, unsettling.

Much better to look at the Bunyip, who was preparing to speak again, with peculiarly fair words to ease past those tusks and the flesh-ripping teeth revealed when he opened his mouth.

"Also," Bunyip said, curling his flukes under him, "I am never out of the Dreaming, because the Dreaming is everywhere."

Whiskey snorted and shook out his mane. Salt water spattered the poet's back and Bunyip's face. "Am I here to fence with you, Bunyip?"

Bunyip shifted his weight, slithering, his bulk leaving a broad channel pressed in the malleable bank. When he moved, it was fast as a mongoose, a heave and a twist that sent his meaty shoulder barreling into Whiskey's, his thick neck thrust over Whiskey's back, a resounding body slam that tumbled the stallion over in the mud and sent the man sprawling, diving out of the way. Bunyip thumped across Whiskey's barrel and lay there, his tusks lowered like daggers to press Whiskey's throttle. Pale silken hide dented under ivory scimitars, as the water-horse thrashed and then froze, forehooves pressing, back arched like a rabbit straining at a snare.

"You're here to answer to me," Bunyip said. "Your demesne is unmanaged, your subjects unruled. And I see you without strength, and I hear you have been bound. But there is no chain on you to say why storms and calms intermingle without reason. So answer me: when the seas are wild or merciful, where is the will behind the wave?"

He lifted his tusks and rolled back, like the tide, and left Whiskey mud-covered, struggling to his feet as splay-legged and shaky as a colt.

The stallion put himself between Bunyip and the poet, while the poet, less smutched, also stood.

"I have no heart for it." Whiskey's hooves sucked on mud, each one a plop like frogs jumping. "There is no death in me now, and the horses of the sea are sleeping."

"You are failing," Bunyip said. The poet walked slowly, letting Whiskey's broad barrel fill the space between him and the Bunyip. He did not like the monster's lantern eyes.

"Are you here to eat me for it? Because I'll fight."

Bunyip paused, his heavy head bobbing on the truncated cone of his neck as he lurched and turned. He eyed Whiskey speculatively, and Whiskey watched, ears up and neck arched. Mud and algae clung to the shaggy hair feathering his ankles, splashed up bicolored legs. He didn't seem to notice.

"No," Bunyip said, a rumble like rocks rolling under water. "Not yet. But Rainbow Snake—your Mist, the Dragon—is concerned. The spirits of the sea are restive, and it *is* your fault. Too calm in places, too wild in others. It's not just sirens freed of Promethean bindings running vessels up on rocks, though there is that. But the sea itself goes unhelmed, and the sacrifices taken by the deep are not prepared to the Dragon's liking, and storms rage unchecked, and wrecks are found and looted. Dragons do not like their stolen treasure stolen in return. And when the archmage realizes you're not at your work, Whiskey, she'll turn it to her advantage."

"I have custody of a mortal soul," Whiskey said, an admission that still wrenched. He stomped one hind hoof, ears twisted flat. "Should I damn it for your convenience?"

"That's rubbish." Bunyip's shoulders hunched and his head went down. His black body undulated as he heaved forward. "You should damn it for your duty."

Whiskey's ears flickered. He didn't move, four hooves square on the bank, tail rippling. The poet stroked the stallion's shoulder; warm skin quivered under his touch, but he never would have known otherwise that Whiskey trembled. "And if I don't?"

Bunyip's heavy head swung back, jowls swaying, eyes flashing gold and green. "Then I shall kill you."

A flicker of light and a splash and Bunyip's scaled length vanished down the bank into the river, and they stood in the park—after nightfall, a whole day gone in Faerie—with a cold wind rattling leaves over sidewalks and prickling gooseflesh up the poet's neck, and every black iron lamp burning bright.

Monday afternoon, Felix Luray had fretted a thumb across the iron ring on his right middle finger and tried not to curse as his prey vanished into thin air like the spirits that they were. By Monday evening, he was drowning his sorrows in sake and caterpillar roll not far from Madison Square. He was a slender man, tall, habitually dressed in expensive gray suits with a vaguely Edwardian air that made him look out of place without a bowler pressed over his coarsely waved iron-black hair.

He was just sitting back from the counter, replacing his spoon in an empty bowl, when a sandaled footstep on the *goza* mats and a scent like dragonsblood incense turned his head.

The woman who looked back at him stood out as unusual even in New York. She wore blousy vermilion trousers and an ivory vest stiff with mirrors and silver embroidery, and her arms and face and her chest in the gap of her collar were lined with shiny, knotted scars like strings of black pearls.

The cricket in its bamboo cage by the cash register chirruped and whirred.

"Felix Alexander Luray," she said, her words twining sibilantly through filed teeth. Beads and bangles clashed on her wrists. Her golden earrings twirled, flashing reflections from hammered facets. "I can't imagine why I didn't think to check for your corpse in Faerie, once-Mage."

He pushed a bill under square crackle-glazed pottery and stood, giving her his shoulder. It made her smile almost as much as the iron ring on his right hand. "Did they let you keep that? Or did you have to get another one made? Maybe bought it mail-order, from one of those places that advertise magnetic jewelry on late-night television?"

"Kadiska," he said. He nodded thanks to the chef, who was eyeing his new companion and hefting a cleaver in one callused fist. "Three little, four little, five little Fae in New York in a day. Surely, that can't be a coincidence."

She shrugged one-shouldered, the gesture rolling a sharp-edged collarbone and shoulder blade under her vest, lifting the chains around her
neck. Her shadow coiled and spread a cobra's hood on the floor behind
her. "I only knew about the one," she said. "But once I saw you watching him, I could hardly resist a visit for old time's sake."

"All the cats in Katzenstein," he said. "Do you have somebody holding your tail up too?"

"If I do, I hadn't noticed." Her eyes were a strange, mossy color in
the squint of her smile, paler than skin like polished cocobola wood
warranted. The color shifted, lichen gray-green-brown. A color he
knew; one that marked her an enemy.

As if he hadn't known that already.

Her sandals scratched the *goza* mats against the terra-cotta beneath.
She shuffled, as if unused to walking in shoes, and nodded thanks when
he got the door for her. A brushed aluminum push bar clicked under his
fingertips. The door was painted with hex signs and ward signs from
three cultures, and a garland of zigzag *Shide* strips swung against the
glass, bronze and iron coins wrapped in prayers dangling between the
paper charms. A straw rope twisted with tassels hung over the lintel:
Shimenawa.

Felix looked at the Fae and put a question on his face. Before the
Dragon, *Shimenawa* had been used in shrines, to mark the passage between the sacred and the profane. But they also provided a barrier to
spirits, which is to say, the Fae. It should, he thought, have kept anything
Fae out of the restaurant, even the changelings that made Seekers.

She dropped her ear to one shoulder, and reached out to brush one
of the paper-wrapped iron coins as she walked by. "We never did let you
know everything we could manage, Murchaud, Àine, or me. I'm still a
Seeker, Felix. Though of the Daoine, now." She stuck her fingertip in
her mouth. "Born mortal. It takes more than a little iron over a cradle
to keep me at bay."

"And you're here to steal me away to Faerie?"

"You'd like that too much. Tell me why I shouldn't make sure Jane
finds out you're in her city, once-Mage." Kadiska kicked out of her sandals as soon as she reached the sidewalk, and let them dangle from one
hand.

Felix considered her question. "Do you think she'd react any better to your presence?"

The Fae turned to examine her reflection in a window smeared with neon. "It still hurts, doesn't it? The way your archmage shrugged you off like an outworn coat, took up with a boy whose chief qualification was being one of two brothers with so much magic the Fae would find them seductive?"

"Considering what became of Matthew and Kelly Szczegielniak, and Jane and all her plans for the overthrow of Faerie and the uplift of the Magi?" He paused; she knew his thoughtfulness for mockery. "No, it doesn't sting so much as all that. It could have been me she gave to your Cat Anna, after all. Me, and not that poor idiot kid."

"That idiot kid." More mockery. He smiled through it. They walked through streetlights, their shadows stretching and retracting. Hers had tufted ears that twitched or flattened at any sound. "He had some fire in him. And his brother has some steel. How does it feel, once-Mage, to walk in a city where a broken Magus stands in the place that was rightfully yours?"

"I've gotten used to it," he lied.

"When I was Unseelie," she said, as pedestrians parted to let them pass, and Felix twirled his iron ring around his finger, "I had something to do with Kelly Szczegielniak. And a Prince of Faerie named Murchaud, who had something to do with Prometheus. And something to do with the Unseelie Fae, and Jane Maga. You remember. I do not think you took it so gently then, when Jane turned her back on you."

"Did you take it gently that you had something to do with Kelly, as you say, but you never got your hooks into the brother?" The pebble he kicked off the path skittered into the lawn and vanished.

"Jane never offered us *him*. She kept the strongest for herself, and kept him all mystified as to who her allies were." She laughed, and tucked a braid back under the kerchief wound around her head. "Ah, but you knew that, didn't you? I'm sorry."

Trying too hard: that one scarcely stung. "It hurt then. But if she hadn't used Matthew, I would have died with the rest of the Prometheans. Instead I stand here on their grave, and you can call me mocking names, Kadiska, but I'm whole and Matthew is broken. Oh, don't give me the innocent look"—wide-eyed and incongruous, in a face with filed teeth and so many careful scars—"we were allies once."

"I liked you then, Felix."

"And now you work for Elaine."

"She who was Elaine. Murchaud's daughter, and a better Queen than the Mebd ever was. Aye, or the Cat Anna elsewise."

"Because she's stronger?"

"Because she's kinder."

"What do the Fae know of kindness?"

"Nothing," Kadiska said. "But she is not so Fae as all that. Almost a mortal woman, once, before she sold her name and her soul for a throne. Her mother's as mortal as any Promethean, and Murchaud carried Lancelot's blood. Morgan's a changeling child, Elf-fathered but of iron woman born. And Lancelot was a mortal born, adopted as a pet by Àine after having been orphaned in a war. Elaine's more iron than moonlight. And she freed me from Àine the Cat Anna, who would have sold all Faerie to your Jane. There are no knots in the new Queen's hair."

"You say that as if it matters."

She shrugged, and paused for a walk signal before leading him across Fifth Avenue and past a wrought-iron railing, onto the walkways of Madison Square Park. She tossed her sandals into a drift of hostas. Dry leaves rattlesnaked across the pavement. "Merely making conversation. Why does it matter, Felix?"

He thought about lying to her, but when one's work is tied up in symbols and true names, a small lie laid in the foundation can twist a structure entirely: Jane's mistake, with Kelly and Matthew. Her plan to conquer Faerie all lay on her betrayal of the brothers, and look what it had won her.

"I want what I'm owed." He fiddled his ring again.

"So does Àine. Or what she thinks she's owed." She smiled when she turned to him, the sclera of her eyes flashing white, light filtered through the half-bare trees. She patted his shoulder, offering a glimpse of the curve of her breast and a berry-black areola as her vest swung open. Gold shone on her wrist. He half hoped someone would try to take it from her. It was the sort of night where he might enjoy watching somebody get killed. "You think you can buy your way back into Jane's graces by bringing her Whiskey's head on a stick?"

"Once-Mage is not a title I gladly wear."

"No," she said, thoughtfully. "I would imagine not. Don't try your luck with the water-horse, Felix."

"Because he's bigger than me?" Dryly, a flash of wit. He'd enjoyed her, in the old days, when Hell had brokered an uneasy détente between the Unseelie and the Prometheus Club. Before Jane's change of heart. Before Matthew Szczegielniak, and the end of the war.

"Because I'm here to watch his back."

The city held its breath around them, brisk late-night traveler, wino on a bench with the *Post* spread over his face. *Do not disturb.* This city wouldn't talk to Felix now.

He curled his nails out of his palms. Of course he didn't miss it. What sort of idiot wanted a dragon's attention? What sort of idiot wanted *the* Dragon's attention? Matthew was welcome to it, chapter and verse. Felix didn't need it any longer. New York City with its thousand-chambered heart wasn't his anymore, and hadn't been since Jane Andraste decided Matthew made a prettier sacrifice.

Any other city would be better.

Any other city wouldn't curl and drag in his bones. Promising so much. Delivering a dragon's heart, when it gave anything at all.

Lily slept past three.

She awoke with sticky face and lashes adhered from leftover makeup, her cheek pressed to a dingy pillowcase dabbed with last night's lipstick and eyeliner. Sunlight had crept through the heavy curtains and warmed her ear and the side of her head, and when she reached up, half-aware, to push the irritation away, a cracked fingernail snagged in her hair and tore to the quick.

She yelped and pushed herself up on her elbow, examining the drop of blood on her fingertip. Sticking it into her mouth converted her curse to a mumble. She briefly considered burying her face under the pillow and sleeping until dark, but an insistent pressure in her bladder convinced her otherwise. She slid her legs out of the tangle of unwashed flannel, dislodging Max the piratical cat from her backside, and padded to the bathroom to swill down two Cortef with a palmful of tap water and contemplate waxing the soft dark down on her upper lip. The sound of running water followed, and a sigh.

For his part, after a somewhat ungainly leap to the floor and a better one back up again, Max regained the portion of sunbeam that spilled across Lily's bed. The bed was actually a battered and repurposed—but once darkly gorgeous—fainting couch, which didn't trouble the cat at all. He bulldozed the pillows into a more congenial prospect with his head and settled among them, purring in the sun that bleached his glossy coat from black to darkest auburn.

He was fast asleep by the time the mobile telephone on the unrefurbished Shaker end table that served as a nightstand rang. Lily scurried from the bathroom naked, droplets of water and body jewelry flashing like sequins sprinkled across her skin. She wrapped a green towel around her plum-colored hair one-handed and fumbled the phone up before it quit beeping out its off-key version of "How Soon Is Now."

A flat steel disk with an anodized red caduceus soldered to one side flashed from a heavy bangle as she slapped the phone against her ear. "Hello?"

"Hello, Lily. Did I wake you?"

Despite herself, she smiled at the voice. "Christian. No, Max handled the waking. And I bet you haven't even been to bed."

"I had breakfast with the coven and then went in to work for a few hours. We missed you last night."

"Moira was asking for me, I take it?"

"Afraid you might slip out of the snare. You went Gothing?"

"I'm tempted to open a club myself. Or maybe just shoot every third DJ. *Pour encourager les autres.* You know, to buy some new music or something." She caught sight of herself in the mirror propped against the far wall and paused. Gooseflesh pimpled her skin and her small brown nipples were crinkled with cold around circular barbell piercings of green and black titanium. Her ribs were sharply defined by the shadows between them. *Eat,* she told herself, and frowned. "I should have come to the Sabbat."

"You should have. Gypsy brought the food."

"Oh, *man.* You know how to torture a girl." He coughed, and she smiled. She could almost hear him blushing, and her hip bones were sticking out too. She wondered if he was one of those shy boys who got all toppy when you got them backed up against the wall, or if he was quiet *all* the time. "Hey, Christian, you want to get dinner tonight?"

He paused, a faint clicking revealing that he was consulting his PDA. "I'd love to. What time?"

She checked the time on her phone, which necessitated pulling it away from her ear. Max had cracked open pumpkin-colored eyes, and was staring at her through the slits with uncanny feline intensity. She mouthed words at his reflection. *Three hundred years ago, you'd have gotten me hanged as a witch.*

He smiled at her. Black cats were the devil's watchglasses, or something. Maybe toothbrushes, given the way his tail could bottle up.

"I have a class at six. Afterward? Chinese? And if you want, I'll get you into Ceremony. It's Monday night—I think Object 775 might be playing unless I have my dates mixed up."

This time he did laugh, rich and dark and almost out of character in its chocolatey irony. "You were just bitching about the bad music at Goth clubs, and now you want to take me to a Goth club?"

She let the towel drop uncoiling on the warped wooden floor, where it lay exhaling warm moisture like a serpent on a sun-heated rock. Behind the drapes, the window was fogging, and her hair tumbled over her shoulders in snarls of violet and black and rose, rose-red. " 'A foolish consistency is the hobgoblin of little minds . . .' "

Christian never disappointed. He cleared his throat and finished for her, in a tone that slid from portentous to teasing. " '. . . adored by little statesmen, philosophers, and divines. With consistency a great soul has simply nothing to do.' And are you a great soul, Lily?"

She smiled against the phone. "If not me, then who?"

"Good girl," he said, and that didn't annoy her. "I'll pick you up at seven thirty."

"Harvard Square S'bux?"

"*Please.* Algiers."

"Algiers it is. Cheerio!" She thumbed the phone off with a shaking hand before she went to find her leather pants, which she was sure were somewhere in the pile on the floor.

*   *   *

When they emerged from a dark tunnel that Jewels could never say exactly how she entered, it was like stepping into a watercolor. In, into, and through, to come to the other side—like finding the world behind a rain-washed window of fish-eye glass, suddenly thrown wide. She clutched the Merlin's fingers tight in her left hand, Geoff's in her right, and tried to remember to breathe in between blinking back tears.

They emerged into Faerie at the top of a long sweeping hill not unlike the one they'd left behind in the iron world, but on five times the scale. It was spring here, the grass underfoot the shade of glass stained green with ferric oxide, the sky overhead like cobalt blue. The colors had that same pure transparency, so concentrated they might tint the light that fell against them. Even the air smelled different: sweet, faintly of rain, with an overtone Jewels at first thought might be the Merlin's elusive perfume, but the wind was blowing the wrong direction.

Despite the breeze, mist clung like a gauze gown to the curve of the hills. Geoff let his coat fall closed as Jewels stepped from under its black leather wing. She paused on the crest of the hill, hands by her sides to pin her skirt to her thighs, leaning into the wind that snaked her hair in writhing tendrils. The Merlin's beads clattered as her braids swung, and every charm on Matthew's coat jangled like harness bells. Only Geoff was unruffled by the wind. It picked at the rats in his hair, but snarls and denim and leather defeated it and it spurned him. "Which way?"

The Merlin gestured through the swirling mist, the scent of sandalwood and roses following the sweep of her arm. "Into the valley and down to the sea," she said, and then planted her hands on her hips. "I hope you all brought good walking shoes."

Jewels was still standing, staring, breathing so deeply that the rise and fall of her ribs showed under the loaned-out sweater. Geoff nudged her, and she turned to him and grinned, her eyes bright as sunlit water. " 'Up the airy mountain,' " she whispered, " 'Down the rushy glen, / We daren't go a-hunting, / For fear of little men—' "

She jumped as Matthew's strong arm in its velvet sleeve came around her shoulder, his withered hand scratching her arm. She would have stumbled, but he held her up. She snuggled into the embrace, and let him move her.

"Don't forget the rest of the poem." He shepherded her down the hill.

> "They stole little Bridget
> For seven years long;
> When she came down again
> Her friends were all gone.
> They took her lightly back
> Between the night and morrow;
> They thought she was fast asleep,
> But she was dead with sorrow."

Repressed anger rattled his voice, a contradiction to the warm protectiveness of his grip. Jewels saw him catch the Merlin's gaze, and the Merlin looking down—and she also saw Geoff drop his chin to hide an expression that was torn halfway between worry and jealousy.

Which was fine. She stuffed her hands inside the drooping sleeves of the sweater, the roughness of scars along the insides of her wrists catching her fingers. Jewels didn't mind being wanted. But she didn't *belong* to anybody, and it was best if Geoff didn't forget it.

And best if she didn't let Matthew dismiss her the way he so obviously would like to. She pressed her shoulder into the curve of his arm, and turned to study his profile as they walked. He seemed intent on the mist-shrouded distance; she pitched her voice teasing rather than accusatory. "You *really* didn't want to tell me about witchcraft, did you? The not-Wicca kind. Don't think I didn't notice you ducking that half of the question."

Matthew paused, and made a decision. "You know any fairy tales? Bluebeard? You put the key in the lock, you can't ever get the blood out again. One-way gate. That's a power by initiation. Bought and paid for with a sacrifice. Shamanistic power is similar, although the nature of the sacrifice varies."

She paused, thoughtful, and kept snuggling. "So you can learn power on a dream-quest, or—" She touched the knotwork of scars around her hairline.

"Yes. If you go about it right. Sundance, forty days in the desert. Ritual scarification, sure. The powers tend to be unpredictable, though."

"So what do you sacrifice to become a witch?"

"Your body. Sexually speaking. To the Christian Devil."

"You say that like he's real," Jewels said, and Geoff said, "You mean there're others?"

Matthew's grin was a little cold. Jewels wasn't sure she liked being the target of that much cynical mockery. "You believe in Faeries, and you don't believe in the Devil?"

"I've *seen* Faeries," she said.

"Touché, Matthew," the Merlin said. And then she turned her wicked grin on Jewels. "And I've seen the Devil. So I can assure you, he exists."

Jewels subsided, but pursed her lips when she thought that over. A little later, she pitched her voice low and asked Matthew, "And is that what you did?"

"What *I* did?"

She blushed red-hot. "With the Devil. You know—"

His outright laughter turned the Merlin around, and brought a curious glance from Geoff, who stared with arched eyebrows but stayed back. The Mage doubled over, leaning on her for support, his whole body shaking. He had a nice laugh. Uninhibited.

"Oh, God, no," he said, finally, releasing her briefly to lift his glasses and cuff tears off his cheeks. "Quite the opposite, I assure you." That got him a sharp look from the Merlin, but he didn't bother to explain, and Jewels was still blushing too fiercely to ask the next question.

At least Matthew took her elbow again, if he didn't rest his arm across her shoulders anymore.

They walked through mist that never quite touched them and never quite revealed the horizon. The way was rolling, the path that Carel and Matthew followed faint. Geoff trudged beside them obediently, subdued and trying not to stare. Shapes loomed from the fog on one side or another: embankments, gnarled trees, once a dry stone wall in very good repair despite its air of mossy abandonment. They splashed through a ford and gained the embankment opposite, and all the while Matthew kept his hold on the Otherkin child—not really a child, not precisely, but not any older than his students, either, and thinking of her as a child kept other interests from emerging. Better to indulge his old, harmless crush on Carel; she was safely impossible anyway.

"How far is it to walk?" Jewels said, when some of the tension seemed to have glided off Matthew's body. He didn't answer, but the Merlin did, after a brief thinking pause.

"That depends."

"On where we came out?"

"On whether the Queen wants to see us," the Merlin answered. "We could be walking forever if she doesn't—ah. And apparently we're welcome."

Jewels followed her pointing arm as the mists rolled back, unveiling a sunny prospect: a long line of beeches edging an airy wood, all frothy green and silver with spring, and the viridian sweep of a lawn up to a turreted fantasia of a castle. Towers snapping with banners glowed against an azure sky, golden stone so translucent ripples of twisted light showed in the shadows it cast. A cobbled road curved up the hillside, joined by the path they followed. From the murmur of waves and the tang of salt, not too far beyond the palace was the sea.

Matthew stepped away from the girl, pretending not to notice when she pouted after him. He settled his topcoat and pushed escaped strands behind his ears. "Well," he said, shoving his hands into his pockets, licking his lips as if that could get the taste of acid off his tongue, "here we go again."

Seven years out of Faerie. Seven years crippled, seven years in hiding. Seven years pretending he hadn't lost anything more than he could stand to lose. That it wasn't his choice that had destroyed friends, allies, acquaintances, on behalf of the ancient predators he'd spent his life fighting. Seven years chill and alone, pretending he hadn't walked out of Faerie as broken as anybody else who dared its gates.

Seven years, and here he was back again.

When they were halfway along the road, the flat clack of hooves greeted them. Jewels, who had taken Geoff's hand to mollify him, squinted to distinguish two big shapes clattering abreast over the cobblestones. The riders reined their animals in and turned them, bowing and snorting, to greet the travelers without the sun at their backs, although she did not know if it was implicit threat or courtesy.

She saw tall narrow-faced black horses with riders in outlandish costumes, as elaborate as anything in a Tudor painting. Both men were dark, black-haired where black meant the true color and not poetry, but otherwise as unalike as apple trees. The one on the left was burly, bearded and stern, his hair long in ringlets over the layered patchwork cloak curling from his shoulders in a heavy drape of brocade, velvet, silk, and humble homespun. A cased harp rode at his saddle and a sword upon his hip, and the hands on the reins seemed shaped to manage either one.

The one on the right was of moderate tallness and moderate breadth, paler of complexion. His skin was ivory, redhead-fair, his eyes green enough that the color was bright the width of a road and the height of a horse away. He sat his mount straight as a sword blade on a long-stirruped American saddle, and he wore black velvet, a doublet and breeches slashed with flame-colored silk taffeta, rubies and carnelians sown about the standing collar. A silver circlet crossed his brow, almost vanishing under the gloss of long bangs parted to reveal ears that lifted to a delicate point.

Jewels gasped, and crowded into Geoff's arms.

The Elf-prince's horse curvetted. He gentled it with a hand against its mane, then bowed in the saddle like a herald in an old movie. "Matthew Magus. And my lady Merlin. And master and miss, whose names are not known to me"—Jewels thought his gaze and his cool little smile lingered on her scars and her pointed ears with amusement, and she ground her teeth, feeling grubby and small—"I am Ian MacNeill. My companion is Cairbre the Bard. On behalf of the Queen of the Daoine Sidhe, I bid you welcome in our hall."

"Ian," Carel said, glad of her skirt as she dipped an awkward curtsey. She stepped forward when Matthew didn't, extending her hand. Ian leaned down from the saddle to clasp it, bony fingers strong. "Wolf and heir. It's good to see you. Our companions are Juliet and Geoffrey. Your mother's waiting?"

"Aye, and Morgan too." He shrugged, and when Carel put a hand on his horse's silver bridle, he threw her the reins and swung down with a coursing hound's leggy grace. He tossed his head, flicking hair from his eyes, and dusted his hands on his velvet. He didn't ride with gloves.

❁   ❁   ❁

Ian swept an eye over the travelers. The Mage was clad in some barbaric finery that didn't seem out of place in Faerie, the human boy was
hung every inch about with animal hide and steel—in particular, the
pins lining the outer seam on his left trouser leg, and the closures on his
coat—and the Merlin could dress as she pleased, but the girl looked
cold and unwashed, and Ian wasn't about to feed any mortal girl with
elf-cut ears to his mother clad in yesterday's dirty jumper.

Cairbre smelled angry, but then, Cairbre often did, and the sight of a
Promethean—even this Promethean—was enough to set the bard's
teeth a-clench. But Cairbre would do as Ian asked.

"But," Ian continued, "they're not so eager to see you that they can't
wait on a bath and a change of clothes. And then perhaps join you for a
meal, if you'll accept my safekeeping and a promise that the hospitality
is a gift, and what you accept here will not bind you. My word as the
Queen's son."

The boy's brow creased. The girl looked at Matthew Magus, and
Matthew shrugged, returning Ian's scrutiny.

Ian MacNeill. Matthew knew the name, although he'd never met the
Prince himself. "Carel?"

"His word's as good as Morgan's," Carel said. "How does it feel to be
back in Faerie, Matthew?"

"Strange," he said, and followed the Merlin and the Prince and his attendant up the path, Geoff and Jewels at heel like cygnets behind a
swan. "Stranger than I had thought it would be, coming back again."

❧ Chapter Seven
If I Should Fall from Grace with God

The Fae came to Boston. Not comfortably. Not commonly. But with a tourist's curiosity. They explored doorways and ancient graveyards sandwiched between office towers, and the tree-clotted banks of the wide brown Charles. They were occasionally seen threading through the pack at rock concerts and Red Sox games, and generally behaved themselves with decorum. Their Queen had let it be known that those who ventured into the iron world would follow mortal law or pay a price of her choosing, and few were eager to discover what that choosing might be.

Even among the Fae, there is a certain amount of awe reserved for the one ruthless enough to sit on the White-horn Throne, and the Queen's ruthlessness was not reserved for herself.

Boston was bemused by the attention. There was concern for a few weeks over a string of suspected supernatural killings in Cambridge and Somerville but, like the manticore reportedly sighted in Franklin, they proved of human agency. The Beacon Hill vampire was another matter, however, and so was the colony of redcaps that infested the Common one autumn. The details were never made public, but enough suspicion and innuendo had crept through the city that wreaths of garlic joined the iron and thorn hung on doors throughout the metropolitan area.

It was the age of wonders, and it had everybody who was interested in an uneventful life running more than a bit scared.

Lily loved it. She made Algiers at seven fifteen and staked out a table.

Tea came, and she was surprised to discover they offered a full menu. She'd never been inside before.

She was contemplating the merits of hummus and lamb sausage when Christian's shadow fell across her table. "Maybe we should just stay here for dinner," she said, as he slid into a chair opposite and let his backpack thump onto the floor. Something clinked inside. Lily picked up the pot and warmed her cup.

"What's in the bag?" She smiled at him around the rim of her cup. He looked tired but remarkably alert for somebody who must have been up for almost thirty-six hours.

"Beads, mostly. Samples I didn't have time to look over at the store. You're sure? You want to eat here?" He gestured around the Algiers, the college students and unpopular poets.

"I just suddenly realized that I was dying for lamb kebab," she said. "And hummus. And enough garlic to terrorize every vampire in Massachusetts. So yeah, I think I'd like to eat here, if you don't mind."

"Well, I wouldn't have suggested it if I didn't like it," he said. She noticed that the waiter brought him Moroccan coffee without being asked, and he smiled and said thank you.

She always paid attention to how people she was interested in treated the waitstaff—and how the waitstaff treated them.

She settled back in her chair, the casters scraping lightly, and rested her forearms on the table. An enticing melange of roasted meat, garlic, coriander, and other spices floated on the air, almost disguising an ingrained aroma of tobacco smoke. She imagined if she closed her eyes she could pick out layers and strata in the scent. Instead she smiled at Christian and leaned forward over her folded arms, watching his face to see if he glanced down her top. The black crushed velvet was cut down to *there*, while the brocade bustier she wore over it provided a *there* for it to be cut to.

"You're not exactly dressed for Gothing," she said. Not that the jean-jacket and white T-shirt looked *bad* on him—anything but, with the copper-colored ponytail spilling over dark-blue denim when he ducked his head to look at the menu—but it wasn't club attire.

"Is there a dress code?" He didn't look up, but he might just have blushed a little, as if he'd gotten caught checking out her cleavage.

"Only when the Red Sox are playing," she answered. "I'm not sure where else we'd go, though."

"Well, clubs aren't exactly conducive to conversation. Why don't we start out here, and see where the evening goes? If it comes down to it, either you can dress me up however amuses you, or I've got a bottle of shiraz and a box of crackers at my place; we can watch *Shaun of the Dead*."

"I thought that wasn't on DVD until Christmas."

He grinned. "It's not. Officially."

"Oooo. Racking up the negative karma there, Christian."

A sideways slant of his head, and he put the menu down. He leaned forward, with an inviting air of conspiracy, and murmured, "I don't wait well. I should probably tell you that in advance. So what do you say?"

"I should say, *in advance of what?* But I was never very good at coy." She glanced up. The waiter had noticed Christian's gesture with the menu and was already coming toward them.

Christian smiled at her—if you could quite call it a smile.

"Well, it's a good band," she temporized. And then grinned right back. "So, want to show me your samples?"

"Beg pardon?"

She gestured to his bag. "The beads. Haul 'em out, let's have a look. I can tell you what all the Gothy girls will want."

After dinner, they went for a walk. The night had grown cool. Christian buttoned his jacket against the chill after offering it to Lily. She, however, had a Russian goat's-hair shawl that crushed into a space as small as a pocket handkerchief thrust into a side-flap of her purse, and wrapped the cobweb knit around her shoulders for comfort.

"That doesn't look very warm," he said. "You're so thin; you must get cold easily."

She tugged the shawl tighter and said, "It traps the air next to my skin. Is this going to turn into a lecture about taking care of myself?"

"Not at all. I saw you dive on that baklava. You must burn it off—"

"It's a good joke, that. By rights, I should be as round as I am tall. My endocrinologist thinks I'm a space alien."

They strolled side by side, as if arm in arm would be too much of an admission, stealing giggling sideways glances like children. Lily bought a bag of popcorn and they shared it, salt and slick butter extinguishing the last honeyed traces of the baklava. She liked the way Christian licked his fingers to clean them, eyes half-lidded and the red red tongue peeking between digits long and pale as bones. She liked the way he leaned close to her without saying a word.

Lily saw auras sometimes. Not always, not something she could rely on. But once in a while, when she was thinking of something else, like the way a red-haired boy's freckles clustered up against his hairline as if pushed there by a current, something would flicker at the edge of her vision, and she'd just sort of *know*.

The way she knew now: that the long flickering cloak curling like burgundy-black bat wings from his shoulders would vanish in daylight, that the shadows that wreathed him and crowned his brow would blow out like a snuffed candleflame, along with the glow that shimmered in the back of his eyes, brightening their hazel to amber. "Do you believe in any of it?" she asked, surprising herself.

"Any of what?"

A steady, appraising glance, and she met it with calculated forceful-ness. "Wicca. The threefold law, the left-hand path. Do you think it works?"

She expected him to consider, but he shrugged and rolled his shoulders back, the unreal cloak fanning and tattering on a breeze she couldn't feel. She stared at him directly and it vanished, long curling streamers peel-ing away to flutter down the street. Vanquished by attention, like so many mysteries.

"Yes. I absolutely believe that magic can effect our will. I presume you're not asking me if I believe in magic—"

"Not in this day and age."

"I didn't expect so." He smiled, a streetlamp casting long shadows down his face, making his eyepits skeletal. "So you must be asking if I believe we have any power over the world. And yes, I believe it. As much power as we're willing to take responsibility for."

"Maybe that's my problem, then." She kicked a tin can. "Did you say you wanted to watch a movie?"

"I said I had a bottle of shiraz."

"Lay on, MacDuff," she said, and made a languid arm.

"And damn'd be him that first cries, 'Hold, enough!' " he answered, and took her wrist to lead her on.

They took the T back over the river, and she pointed out that if she stayed too late he would have to drive her home, because the trains stopped running soon. Something spined and too big for a cat scurried monkey-quick into the shadows as they crossed a street against the light. "Don't worry about it," he said, and held her hand to lead her under the horseshoes and thorn branches hung over the apartment's front door.

His apartment was on the third floor of a gaudy, peeling, converted Victorian with a practiced sense of irony. Blue light still flickered under the door of the second-floor apartment as they climbed past it, and she leaned on his arm, straining to make out the television words.

Christian dropped his grip on Lily as they achieved the landing. She stood aside and stared at the door. "No wards?"

The boards were bare. Just brown wood with peeling varnish. He laid a hand flat over the doorknob and pushed; the door swung open. "Anything I have to fear, a little iron wouldn't keep back. Welcome in, Lily. Take off your shoes; I'll get the wine."

He latched the door behind them and walked toward the kitchen, shedding his jacket across the spine of a ladder-back chair. Lily didn't hesitate about the shoes; the lace-up granny boots looked great with the softly shiny superskin of her glove-leather pants, and they had good arch support for walking, but heels were heels and they didn't breathe. She slid them across the old swaybacked floor and dropped onto the futon with a sigh.

He found her there when he came back, balancing glasses and a freshly opened bottle, the viny, vivid scent of the shiraz twining the apartment. She'd unhooked the busk of her bustier, and it hung open like a vest over the velvet peasant blouse. Small breasts pricked naturally under the clinging cloth, lifted by the sprawl of her arms. The leather pants pulled taut against ridged hips, conforming to the soft curve of her belly and pudenda, clinging in the hollow of her thigh. The hide dimpled and stretched oddly, though, and he smiled softly to himself. That explained where the power came from. She was a creature of the chinks and intersections, neither bird nor maiden. There was power in transformations.

"Drifting off on me already?" He set the wine and the glasses on the coffee table, and lifted her feet to slide underneath them. She started to pull out of the way, but he held on to her ankles, and a moment later she relaxed and let him rest her feet across his lap.

"If you're plotting what I think you're plotting, you'll have me at your mercy in a moment," she said sleepily. She slid her arm down from across her eyes and pushed up on elbow. "Pass me my bag, Christian?"

He did, without comment, and she rummaged around loose change, credit cards, condoms—fresh today—a cased syringe, and a mostly empty tin of Flavigny rose pastilles until she came up with her pillbox. It was actually an antique silver snuffbox, and Christian watched as she rattled it and slipped it back into the bag without opening it. "Should I ask?"

"I just wanted to make sure I had my hydrocortisone if I need it."

"Allergies?"

"Not exactly." She jangled her Medic Alert bracelet, the crimson caduceus welded to a hammered steel disk on a stainless steel bangle Michael had made to replace the ugly standard-issue one. "If you ever find me incoherent and vomiting or dead to the world, there's always a syringe in my bag. Just jab it into the nearest available muscle tissue. I'll thank you for it later."

He nodded, and leaned forward over her feet and ankles to pour the wine. "Liquor's okay?"

"Liquor's positively indicated," she answered, accepting the glass before slumping back against the bolsters. The wine tasted of oak and black cherries, round and tannic. He flicked on the television—a smallish set on a cherrywood cabinet that was much nicer than the TV deserved—with a remote control, and Lily lolled and sipped wine while proletariat stiffs identical to the living dead shuffled through their routines.

And then she moaned, "Oh, Christian—" as he balanced his glass on the other arm of the futon and dug his thumbs into the arch of her left foot.

She had big feet for such a little girl. But she was heavy-boned for her height, with bony masculine hands. Not at all surprising, though the curve of her hips and the jut of her breasts was convincing, and so were her graceful arms. She pressed her foot into his hands, head arched back in abandon as he slid strong digits over her bones and flesh. "Just yell if I push too hard."

"Got a jackhammer?" she quipped, then groaned heavily as he worked sore skin and tendons. "Oh, God."

"Only in my off hours," he said, and bent over the task. She shivered and stretched against him, surrendered, the movie forgotten in favor of the pressure of his erection against her calves. He slid one hand up her left leg, over the leather, and didn't stop at her knee. She caught his fingers.

"Christian, before you go any further, there's something you should know. I'm—" She hesitated, searching, and he stepped into the breach.

"Not like other girls?" he asked.

Her hand tightened on his, and the light that soaked her skin guttered and brightened, a blown flame. "How did you know?"

Not accusing, but curious, and he squeezed back before he answered. "The pants are *very* tight, Lily. And you mentioned an endocrinologist. Are you pre-op?"

She half sat up, but awkwardly, with the glass in her hand and her feet in his lap. "Not exactly. I have congenital adrenal hyperplasia. Do you know what that is?"

"Not a clue," he lied. All fairy tales aside, he couldn't really see into human souls. That would have removed all the challenge, and besides, it wasn't *his* job to measure sin against virtue. But he was a very good guesser, and not much else was a mystery to him. Modern medicine included.

"I'm intersexed," she said, bluntly, holding his eyes. He didn't look down, and he saw her smile. "Which is to say, I'm a girl—genetically—but—"

"But," he said, and very gently disentangled his hand from her fingers and laid it across her crotch. She pressed against him, her hips a broad, lean arch. Men didn't *do* that, didn't take her bravado at face value and answer with their own. Didn't watch her face with inquiring eyes while deft fingers molded engorging flesh, outlining, exploring through warm leather.

"Stop?"

"Not if I have anything to say about it."

"You know," he said, as she purred and coiled into his touch, "once, you would have been raised a magician or a shaman, for being born as you were. Maybe you found us for a reason."

"Us?"

"The coven."

"You talk too much." She lifted her arms to him as he turned and slid from beneath her legs. "You are a bad, bad man."

"Not really," he answered, meaning *not a man* and knowing she would hear *not really bad*. He set her wine aside and moved his own to the coffee table, and then he kissed her, tugging an earlobe with his teeth, flicking his tongue across the skin between her piercings. She tasted of salt and earwax and the bitter astringency of her perfume, and her combs and hair clips scratched his fingers when he cupped her head in his hands and nuzzled over stark collarbones to the knob of her sternum.

The old house shivered with her pleasure, the power awakening under her skin, creaked as it settled its stout old beams and bawdy dowager facade. Her fingers disheveled Christian's hair, took his ponytail apart and spread the locks over his shoulders, a translucent curtain of copper and saffron that turned the wavering television glow into streaked light through stained glass. She found the hem of his shirt and tugged it up, her torn fingernail snagging threads, the shirt tousling his hair more as she drew it over his head and down his arms. He sat back and untangled himself, dropping the shirt on the floor.

The flicker on his skin wasn't just the television, though Lily couldn't see it yet, and he had eyes only for her. But the old house saw, and stretched under them, warming itself on the heat of her light, of his darkness. She arched up and pulled him down, skin against skin interrupted by the cold steel of her busk brushing his chest, the rucked-up velvet shirt. Her legs wrapped his and heels hooked knees, pressing her groin against his. "You'll have to teach me how to touch you," he said.

She grinned against his neck, her nails describing lazy spirals on his back. "The penis is just a supersized clitoris anyway. What I have is sort of in between. I have faith in you."

"I'm glad someone does," he answered, and kissed her again when she giggled. Her joy filled the room with heat; the old house offered warm drafts to caress her skin, to fan that trembling brightness. She fumbled in her purse and came up with a condom in a bright foil package. He pulled it from her fingers and set it next to the wine. "I'm sorry. Were you in a hurry?"

"No," she said. He blew a raspberry against her belly. She laughed and pulled his hair. "But it might come in handy later. And I wanted you to know—"

"That I could?"

"With me, anyway. We're all unique snowflakes." She smiled through her irony and bit his jaw. He hissed pleasure; she took the hint, pulling hair, rolling his nipples between her fingers until he gasped wet heat against her ear.

"Harder," he said, and, grinning wickedly, she extricated a butterfly clip from her hair. She held it up before his nose. "How hard do you want it?"

He closed his eyes and shook his head. "Hard," he said, and she pushed him onto his back as tinny shotgun blasts plinked from the television's speakers. Their weight on the futon bowed the old floorboards, and the old house yearned in to them with all its shadows, swaying around their coupling, humming as it sustained them in its embrace. She was so bright, moth-wing bright, flicker of strength like the tremble of her pulse in the hollow of her throat, and the angel who held her was so weary, and so dark in her arms when he left his mark upon her skin.

And the old house loved them for their tragedy as much as for her brilliance, like a corona trailing a falling star.

The protocols, such as they were, for dealing with a Fae crime in the mortal world were simple. One reported it to the Fae consulate, and the consulate reported it to the Queen.

But that was for places that were not New York City, and crimes that didn't involve a suspected wizard as the first responder on the scene. Not to mention the complicating factor of Ernie Peese filling out the paperwork, and the mayor's office getting interested so fast they must have roused the old man out of bed before the body was cold.

That was probably Ernie's doing too. Suck up, kick down. If Ernie ever made captain, Don Smith was moving to Connecticut.

The autopsy was finished by noon on Monday, and Don finally made it home late Monday night. Monette was in the kitchen still, home from her shift at the restaurant, showered free of grease and wearing a towel wrapped like a turban and a long marigold caftan with fringe that tapped her ankles. She cut flowers in the sink, under ice-cold water. Don paused to kiss his sister on the cheek as he went by, en route to the coffeepot. She was a rangy woman, rawboned, smelling of fake freesias from her shampoo. "Isaih," she said without looking up, "you drink that stuff now, you be awake all night."

"I go sleep just fine," he said, relaxing the careful diction of the middle-class accent he put on with his tie in the morning and wore all day, and for the same reasons he used his middle name on the job. "What you cooking up?"

"If you be home for supper, there would be food for you on the table."

"If nobody went got killed for just a month, I'd be here every day."

She huffed and turned her back on him as he poured coffee. She replaced the flowers on the white cloth–covered shrine in the hall, and the glass cylinder of the vase was chilly against her hands. She straightened statuettes and centered the white candle and the water glass. "Bad day?" she asked, finally, bringing the old flowers into the kitchen to dispose of.

"Little girl," he said. "Twenty-one." Unconsciously he pawed at his chest through the shirt, pushing aside the untied necktie. Monette caught his wrist and pulled his hand down, away from a scar too old to have any right to itch. "Mama home?"

"She home," Monette said. "In bed. Don't rub at that."

He dropped his hand as she opened the refrigerator. He could still feel it, a tight inflexibility in the center of his chest, a shape like a Spanish Dancer mollusk or a centipede. Only a single bypass, and he was taking better care of himself now. But the medical leave and the divorce had taken it out of him.

And besides, his mother and Monette could use the help. And there had been room in the apartment for another. Easier than finding his own place, in New York City.

"Got rundown chicken ready here," Monette said.

"Rundown and rice."

"I should warm it up?"

"Cold is fine," he said, and she fixed him a plate while he sat down and drank his coffee, then kissed the top of his head and went off to bed.

A dream of opalescent eyes flashing shattered planes of color awakened him Tuesday morning, fretful and cold, before the alarm. He slept with the window open when he could, but that wasn't the reason for the chill on the back of his neck. Sweat beaded his forehead over gooseflesh, and his hands were shaking as he grabbed the edge of his water bed and swung his legs out from under the burgundy comforter.

"Shit." He hadn't had it this bad since Times Square—which was to say, ever. He pushed himself out of bed, carpet harsh underfoot, and reeled to the bathroom to inspect his clammy skin under green fluorescent light. He groaned. The frosted window by the toilet was cold, and he leaned his shoulder on it while he got yesterday's coffee out of his system. His gut clenched and he gritted his teeth. The taste of toothpaste didn't soothe his nausea, but he brushed twice anyway, hard enough that pink curled through white foam when he spat in the rust-stained sink.

It didn't make him feel clean, and neither did the shower.

Hot water and steam eased his chill. But they didn't clear his memory of those gigantic eyes, observing, weighing.

Don had been at Times Square, when he was still another anonymous figure in midnight blue. Don had seen the Dragon. And more, the Dragon had seen him. Had noticed him, and bowed her great head down to look him in the eye. He'd fallen to his knees under her regard, and he'd been prone to night terrors ever since, and to knowing things he wasn't supposed to know. Like the fact that those two scared kids had had nothing to do with the murder of Althea Benning, and that it wasn't just a coincidence that Matthew Szczegielniak had turned up where he'd turned up, as awkwardly and habitually close to the action as any Peter Parker or Clark Kent.

Any cop knows that there are people in his city who don't seem important and whose appearances are deceptive. They're campaign coordinators, quiet millionaires, the unacknowledged illegitimate children of important men. They're the childhood next-door neighbors of senators. They're investigative reporters without a talent for self-promotion, whose scoops get appropriated by the guy with the television hair. They're the guys the mayor calls at two in the morning when the martinis aren't helping him sleep.

Don Smith knew who Matthew Szczegielniak was, when he wasn't a junior professor and student of English literature. And if Don hadn't known it just from shaking Dr. Szczegielniak's hand the very first time he turned up unexpectedly and dropped a few shy and useful hints about some weird-ass crime, he would have known it when he discovered who paid his rent.

Jane Andraste was one of the people whose importance *wasn't* transparent, even now that she was back in private practice and semiretired. At first Don had assumed Szczegielniak was her much-younger lover, a kept man, a rich woman's toy. But there wasn't any evidence of that; they never spoke, and they certainly never saw each other. And Andraste was widowed and Szczegielniak never married, and it wasn't as if there was much of a scandal in a romance that couldn't even be called May-December, although August-November might come close.

So it wasn't that. And it wasn't political. But whatever it was, Jane Andraste had been at Times Square too.

Don stepped out of the shower while wrapping a towel around his waist. The sky was still dark beyond the window, and in the bedroom his alarm had started pinging. He shut it off, hoping it hadn't woken his mother, and sat on the bed in front of the open closet door considering his options.

Don had his own suspicions about Times Square, and Jane Andraste's part in it . . . and why she was supporting somebody who, as near as Don could figure, couldn't stand her but was willing to take her money if it freed him up to investigate paranormal problems in the city.

Don was a good enough cop to notice that she'd been paying Szczegielniak's bills for years, long before Times Square, and that she'd also been paying medical costs for Szczegielniak's institutionalized brother, who had vanished without a trace around that same time.

It didn't add up to murder, necessarily. But it added up.

And now here was a real murder, a bloody murder, a girl in an alley half-eaten to the bone. And here was Dr. Szczegielniak again, and a Fae connection, and Jane Andraste. Again.

And seven years after the day after Times Square, here was Detective Don Smith waking before sunrise with the memory of a black iron Dragon stirring within.

The coffeemaker perked in the kitchen, which meant his alarm had woken Mama up. Don shook off his lethargy and stood. He found the black pants that went with his black pinstriped suit coat, and a shirt and tie in complementary shades of royal blue, and stuffed his feet into his shoes before he went to check his e-mail.

Mama intercepted him with a mug of coffee as he was coming into the living room. He cupped it in both hands, breathing steam gratefully, and she glowered up at him. Both of Tiyah Smith's children dwarfed her, and both of them still obeyed her with indoctrinated immediacy.

"You had a bad day, Monette saying?" Tiyah put her hand on his chest. "Sit. Let's talk about it."

"Not much to tell," he said, perching on the edge of the couch. "I got a murder. I think the thing is magic, but they won't let me pass it to the FBI."

"Why so?"

"Politics." Don shrugged. "You know how it goes." He sipped his coffee, rolling it over his tongue. "No glory for the city if it's the FBI who crack the case. You know."

She'd never sat down, just hovered—the way she did—and fiddled her fingertips against her waistband. "And you don't want none of that glory?"

"Just don't want to mess up something crucial." He lifted the coffee to his lips, but didn't taste it. The admission made him sick, along with the unsaid word. *Again.*

"You good, my boy," Mama said. "But you must take a chance again someday, Isaih. You can't always look for the door out." She patted him on the head and brushed past him, bound for the kitchen. "What you want for breakfast?"

Donall lowered the coffee cup and thought about it, but his deliberations kept being diverted by the uneasy conviction that he'd just witnessed the opening salvo in another war.

*   *   *

Àine stood on the battlements of a white castle in Faerie and held up her hands to the moon. Its blue light drenched her, glistened off her glossy ebony hair and her ivory face and her lips red as blood scattered in snow on a windowsill. Her gown drooped in sunflower-embroidered pleats from her arms as she raised them, her train puddling behind her feet in a gold and green swirl. A tiara shimmered, diamonds like dew in her hair.

She was the Queen of the Unseelie court. She was Leannan Sidhe, a fairy-muse with old blood on her tongue. The fangs that dimpled her lip were not for show.

She was waiting for something with wings.

It wasn't long in coming, hawk's body making a cross against the moon, though the sharp-edged shadow it cast across her face was the shadow not of a hawk but of a man.

It landed on the battlements beside her, wings cupping air like a gargantuan pelican, the stag's head tossed up as it checked. Cold light turned moss-green wings matte black and cast no reflections on the fluted antlers adorning its long-nosed head: a stag's head, except for the blood on its breath and the teeth that glinted cold silver when it smiled.

"Cat Anna," it said. "I have done as you bid."

Àine reached up over her head and smoothed the lanceolate feathers at its nape. They might be black in moonlight, but the margins were gilt. The peryton clucked and rubbed into her hand, talons flexing on the white, white battlement. "You have done well, Orfeo. What intelligence?"

"I saw no unicorn." It settled feathers with a rustle and turned its head to preen, careful of her flesh and the razor-edged antlers. "There are Fae hunting the city. All that mortal meat, all so unwary."

"Aye. My children will not be forbidden the hunt. Let Jane Maga entreat with her daughter and the Daoine. I'll not bend to Elaine's command."

"I do not think the archmage will have entreaty on her mind." Orfeo permitted Àine to stroke warm velvet skin and rub between its eyes. She did so, as careful of her nails as the peryton was of its horns.

"Dear Orfeo," she said. "Let Hell and Heaven and the iron world claw each other's throats, and bring Elaine down with them when they fall."

"We lack for nothing."

Àine laughed brightly. "We lack a great many things, brave one. We've traded an overlord for a mistress. But that's just a matter for patience, with our new allies. And as you're content so long as you have meat, we're in no hurry at all."

Jewels hadn't expected to be stripped out of her filthy skirt, sweater, tank top, and sandals like a horse being untacked. It was disconcerting—but she was comfortable in her skin, armored in ink and scars and silver.

She would not show them fear. Not here. Not now that she was, finally, *here*.

And she was so entranced by the chamber she found herself in and the creature doing the undressing that she barely raised a hand in protest. She'd never been in a castle before, and she'd had the idea that they would be drafty, tattered places, with rough mortar and bits of stonework protruding at odd angles. But the room they brought her to was cozy, a little chamber under an angle of roof with two dormered windows. Light prismatized through the bevels on dozens of watery diamond-shaped panes, scattering rainbow splinters on the bed, the clothespress, and the wall.

The Fae servant that peeled her clothes off with long twiggy fingers never spoke. It was a creature like a doll twisted of shredded alder bark, with a face that was mostly a suggestion of knots and undulations except for quick alert eyes, soft as brown water under mottled lids. It unbraided her hair gently and combed snarls away with a comb dipped in scented oil.

The Fae was hesitant to touch her at first because of the colors and metal in her skin, the confident scars across her back and shoulder blades that delineated a phoenix arising in glory before a tattered sun whose rays were picked out in brilliant red and orange knotwork. The braid around her hairline extended two of those rays, ink twisting into scar at the base of her skull. Gently, the creature reached out one tapered fingertip and aimed it at the loop of metal through her lower lip.

It didn't feel a pins-and-needles prickle across the little space, and she seemed to understand the gesture. "Silver," she said, touching it. "And there's no iron in my tats. The black is logwood. You can touch . . ."

It did, running a fingertip down the bony edge of her scapula. The scars twisted in slick ridges across the softness of her skin, and it understood. Scars, like Kadiska's scars. Some mortal alchemy. The girl was wrong, though; there was iron under her skin. Not much, but it felt like a current, a trickle, a tickle. Enough to tingle, not enough to burn. The Fae let its hand fall away, and she turned and smiled, showing dots of color and more wire on her teeth.

"Bath?" she said, so the Fae showed her a corner opposite the bed, screened from the room, just where it would get the benefit of the light through the southern window. She couldn't remember seeing these dormers from the outside of the palace—though the smooth translucent golden stone was right—and the gardens below weren't the ones they had passed through. Voices floated up to the window, women's voices, sounding pleased.

There were steps up the side of the claw-footed tub. She ascended, pausing at the top for the different angle into the gardens, and found herself looking into the bead-shiny black eye of a raven with a drooping wing as it settled itself on the window ledge. "Shoo," she said, but she didn't mean it.

Slick hair fell over her shoulder when she leaned down to brace one hand on the edge of the tub, and floating rainbows spiraled from the strands as she slipped into the water. The scent of the oil refreshed; roses and something Jewels didn't know the name of: dragonsblood incense, a deep resinous scent that clung to her skin like smoke. Hot water stung the raw places her sandals had rubbed on her feet. She gasped, and jerked forward before she settled back.

The tub was a revelation, deep and broad, the bottom curved to accommodate her body. She sighed and leaned back, the water rising to the points of her breasts, heat saturating her joints, relaxing her neck until her head lolled against the scrollwork.

The raven watched, expressionless, as the alder-doll Fae loomed alongside the bathtub and offered the child a sponge dripping with scented suds. She took it, rubbery roughness dimpling under her fingers, soap clouding limpid clarity when it dripped into the bathwater. The scent of roses grew stronger, twining the air currents that wound in and out of the open windows. The raven flapped for balance in a freshening breeze. Its old injury twinged: it wasn't the wing, but the breast muscle, a wound long healed but never forgotten.

Jewels rubbed the sponge down her left arm, shoulder to fingertips, and started to cry.

The Fae stayed with the human a little while, concerned by the trembling shoulders, the flushed skin, the mucous slicking her face and dripping into the bathwater. It stroked her hair back with tender fingertips. Maybe the human was injured. It had never heard an Elf make noise like that, but animals did. They howled when they were hurt, squeaked and cried.

Shuffling splayed feet on spidery limbs, it retreated, found the door, and slipped into the corridor, as the raven cawed twice and flapped and the human sobbed into her hands.

The Prince liked changelings, humans, mortals. Iron things.

The Prince might know what to do.

But the Prince was with the Queen, and by the time the Fae came back with the Elf-page Foxglove in tow, the mortal girl was floating in the water with her long hair drifting around her, eyes closed, serene as a flower petal.

Matthew wasn't about to surrender his coat or his clothing, and after a first hard stare when a crackle-faced servant like a garden gnome in a mud mask tried to undress him, none of the Fae asked. There was a washbasin on a stand, and a mirror behind it, and once he'd shown his would-be assistant to the door and propped the handle with a wooden chair, he crossed the carpeted floor to stare into the looking glass.

His ponytail was coming unbound, strands falling loose around his face. It gave him a bad moment: there was symbolism in that binding, just as there was in Carel's braids and in the iron oxides and magnetite in the pigments tattooed under his skin. But after an entire day, it was far more likely simple entropy at work than any malign force picking at his defenses.

A simple, logical reason. Which didn't help the sick terror, sharp as a fist clenching his heart. He'd rather have walked into a killing zone than back into Faerie again.

But he couldn't allow it to matter. He was here for Althea.

Deliberately, with willed-steady hands, he peeled his glove off and reached behind his head and unbound the twisted wire and elastic bands holding his hair back. The strands swung forward, ends beveled even with a prominent jaw, releasing a headache he hadn't even noticed he had. He frowned at his hair. It needed washing, but he wasn't about to strip down and climb into a tub. Still, that didn't stop him from scrubbing hair and hands in the washbasin, using hard yellow soap scented with civet musk, and cold water from a crackled blue pitcher that never seemed to run dry. He wasn't sure he wanted to smell like a harem, but he desperately wanted to be clean, for reasons of comfort as well as thaumaturgy. And it was this or the steaming bathtub in all its vulnerability, a thought that was enough to make him happy he hadn't eaten: his stomach heaved just thinking of it.

He compromised and laid his coat over the back of a chair before struggling out of his T-shirt, which smelled rather like he'd spent the night in a police station, even though he hadn't been wearing it at the time. He washed his face as well, and then his chest and armpits, grimacing when a trickle of cold water wet the waistband of his jeans.

He did smell like a whorehouse. An expensive one. And he needed a clean shirt.

There was a wardrobe beside the narrow canopy bed. If the pitcher never ran out of water—yes, shirts and suits, shoes and underthings. He picked the plainest shirt out of the pile and pulled it over wet hair, unbuckling his belt to tuck in the tails. When he combed his hair back into the ponytail and resecured it—there was a trick to it, with only one working hand and a half—he noticed that the linen was translucent, and the dark edges of his tattoos showed through it as plainly as knife blades pressed to the other side of stretched leather.

He slid his topcoat back on, contemplated his glove before stuffing it in a pocket, and then picked shed hairs off the comb and out of the washbasin. He wadded them up with his discarded T-shirt. A moment's thought, and he pitched the lot onto glowing coals in the fireplace, wondering what he'd missed.

Greeny-yellow flames were licking over the cotton when someone tapped on the door. He remembered he'd barred it before he called "Come in," and went to move the chair.

It was Carel, and she held out her hand with an empress' grace, wrapping ringed fingers around his left biceps to draw him into the corridor. "You smell much better now. If your taste runs to small predators in lust."

"I feel more like Shere Khan at the end of *The Jungle Books*," he admitted. " 'Brother, I go to my lair—to die!' "

"Mmm," she said, and squeezed his elbow before she led him downstairs. "Go get 'em, Tiger."

Mage and Merlin proceeded down the spiral stair hand in hand, and from there she led him to a back hall with an air of spotless desertion, as if people passed through only to clean. Carel's steps were firm, though; she knew this place well.

The palace was not built for defense. The walkway they followed was ranked with bow windows as wide as the span of a man's arms. Some of the window bays held love seats, or dwarf fruit trees—persimmons, lemons, quinces, and more exotic things—in pots. The prospect revealed an expanse of gardens lining white-graveled paths below a broad verandah, if castles had verandahs. Matthew heard plucked strings and voices blown on a gust of wind, and recognized Ian, Cairbre—and Morgan le Fey, her laugh like a dagger point pricking his sternum.

He licked his lips, then glanced guiltily at Carel, who didn't seem to have noticed. The Merlin craned her neck, footsteps eager enough to set her beads swinging, skipping like a schoolgirl.

They came through a fluted Gothic archway, the golden stone around the opening fretworked into a trellis that dripped blue, fuchsia, and violet morning glories. Their pale herbaceous scent colored the air.

On the broad patio below, Ian MacNeill lounged against white stone balustrades beside two women who took their ease on benches, a small table between them. The woman on the right, the Queen, was dark and tall, broad-shouldered, sharp-chinned. Morgan, on the left, was as tall but didn't hang so sparely on her frame, and her hair was a plain ribbon-wrapped braid trailing heavy over her shoulder, a gold-shot red so glossy in the sunlight it should have been leaving stains soaked into her blue man's shirt. Two leggy hounds lolled at her feet, the silver one raising her chin in unison with Morgan's as Morgan took note of Matthew and Carel coming down the steps from the trellised arch. The knife-prick in Matthew's gut turned into a pulse of heat, but he disciplined himself. Unicorn. Magic. Sacrifice. Carry on.

Cairbre sat a few yards away, his layered cloak furled over his shoulders to puddle on the flagstones, a mandolin with a beautifully inlaid face resting on his knee. He ran his thumbnail across the strings, provoking a clean rill of notes.

Carel gave Matthew's arm one last squeeze before floating down the steps, leaving him behind. Her scent, tea tree oil and ylang-ylang, surrounded the Queen when she leaned down and boldly kissed her on the mouth. And the Queen kissed the Merlin back, shameless and smiling.

Carel's mouth was resilient, and bittersweet with fennel and myrrh from toothbrushing. Her lips were softer than other lips the Queen had kissed, and the Queen's cold heart warmed a little at the brush of the Merlin's lashes across the velvet of her cheek.

Only a little, though. Love, like shame, was not something the Fae were made for. This was the memory of love, the memory of shame. A love someone else had known.

Carel kissed her anyway, for the breath of humanity that might warm that Fae chill. Because mercy and hope and faith were not Fae things, either. The Fae did not love, and they did not forgive. They *owned*. But sometimes, the Queen could be coaxed to remember what it had been like, when she had a human heart. Could be coaxed to remember mercy, and love.

Once upon a time.

There were worse things than loving a dragon.

The women leaned together, Carel's hand brushing the Queen's hair, her braids fallings around them like a beaded curtain. Matthew swallowed and averted his eyes . . . and found his gaze transecting Morgan's. The witch smiled at him, a teacup lifted in her sharptendoned hand, watching his reaction, and treacherous memory suddenly superimposed—over the image of Carel and the Queen kissing—the tactile sensation of Morgan's body in his arms, her clinging lips, the molding softness of her breasts against his chest.

He gasped, remembering too well, and then saw the witch's smile, the curve of her lips and the creases beside her eyes, and knew it for a glamourie.

It didn't ease the heat that flickered through him, imaginary tongue-tips over imaginary skin, or the tightness in his throat. It had only been one kiss—

—but it was the only kiss he'd known, in a chosen, monkish existence.

And she was Morgan le Fey, whose love and whose lovers were legend. "Hello, Matthew Magus," she said. "Welcome back to Annwn. We've missed you here."

Ian's tilted head and the ripple of notes from Cairbre's mandolin disagreed, but the Queen's son at least smiled a little before he looked down at his hands.

"So what have you brought us, Promethean?" the Prince asked in a courtier's murmur as Carel leaned away from the Queen.

"Mortal children," Matthew said. "And I come to complain of a murder, Your Highness." The Queen was listening, but he had been addressed by Ian, so it was to Ian he responded. "A mortal girl was killed in my city, and I think the murderer was Fae."

"The others claim kinright?"

"They're what kin she had. There are blood relatives." Matthew dismissed *them* with a turn of his crippled hand, and he saw Ian's eye snag on his rowan-wood ring. Rowan, and not iron. The Prince's eyes flicked up to Matthew's, and Matthew was glad of his spectacles—which *were* steel.

Best to get this part of the conversation completed before Geoff and Jewels arrived. "They don't want payment."

Carel moved behind the Queen's chair and leaned on her shoulders with a friendly familiarity. The Queen was content to watch and sip her tea, the sleeves of her gown swaying under the stiff weight of pearl- and crystal-studded embroidery. She said, "Have you asked them what they want? Or are you just speaking for them?"

Touché. The charms strung across Matthew's chest jangled counterpoint to Cairbre's soft-picked melody when he spread his arms. "Your Majesty," he said. "Tell me you had nothing to do with the death. Tell me you know nothing of it, and Whiskey's presence in New York was coincidence."

The Queen didn't answer at first. She set her cup down on the saucer so softly that it didn't click, and folded her beringed fingers together. And then she brushed Carel's hands from her shoulders and stood, one slippered foot and then the other, the gown's weight making her rise very straight. She looked at the Mage, his earnest eyes, the frown lines that hadn't been at the corners of his mouth when last they had met. When last they had met, in the dappled shadow of a willow on the bank of a man-made pond, and she had won Carel away from him.

Or rather, when Carel had permitted herself to be won.

In the days when the Queen was the Seeker of the Daoine Sidhe, and when she dressed in jeans and boots and wore chained souls braided into her hair. She smiled, and saw the recognition in his eyes, and wondered if he knew what it had cost her to beat him, in the end. Him, and all the rest of them, the Magi with their iron rings.

"Do you remember what you said to me, Matthew?"

"When?"

"The last time we spoke."

"You told me there are three chances, in Faerie." His gaze slid sideways, to Carel, who had stepped back and to the side. She folded her arms, equidistant between them. Morgan stayed in her chair, and the Queen saw her lay fingertips on Ian's wrist when he started forward.

"I did. And this is the third time we meet."

"Third, and last?"

"Third, and decisive." She reached forward, imperious. "Show me your hand."

Silently, he held it out, three fingers curled useless against the palm, stiff and frail as sticks. Like Kelly's feet, after Kelly had danced himself nearly to death in Faerie. She touched him lightly, and teased his fingers open, against their rigor, prickling gooseflesh over his shoulders. Severed tendons had hardened, clenched, bunched. He shivered where she touched him, flesh quivering in isolated places like a horse flicking away a fly. It hurt, what she was doing, and the rowan ring on his thumb was useless to hurt her in turn. Matthew Szczegielniak had laid his hands on a unicorn. They had no power to do harm.

She lifted the hand and pressed it to her cheek, and his heartbeat rose dizzyingly, adrenaline humming through his veins like a plucked harp-string. He hadn't been afraid of her, before. He hadn't been afraid of a lot of things.

Carel fell back without speaking. Ian watched as silently.

"You said to me, 'Come home, Elaine. Don't stay with the monsters now that you don't have to anymore.' Do you remember?"

"I do."

"And now?"

"And now you're Queen of the monsters."

"Yes," she said, with a bloodless smile. "I am. And you're the ham-strung smith, aren't you, Matthew? Crippled, flesh and heart. Lame as Vulcan, or Weyland. You remember Weyland Smith as well, I imagine."

"It's all paid for, the blood and the transmutation." His folded fingers slid down her cheek; he couldn't quite feel the softness of her skin against the backs, but he brushed it with his thumb, and she leaned into the caress like a cat. He returned the hand to his side. He would have stepped back, away from the challenge in her regard, but intransigence made him hold his ground.

She laughed. Behind her, Carel was pouring tea. "Playing with fire, Promethean. No, it was not one of mine murdered your girl. Though it'll make no difference to Jane. Has she Magi around her again?"

Matthew shrugged. "She's barely gotten them through apprentice-ship. Don't your auguries tell you?"

"She's lost none of her wit at keeping secrets." She turned away for a moment and accepted the cup from Carel, then extended it to him. "Do you want another war, Matthew?"

"No," he said. "No. I do not want a war. You know what she can do if she chooses."

He took the cup and the saucer, and hesitated. The steam smelled of fermentation, tannin, roses. He didn't drink.

The Queen nodded. The Promethean juggernaut was a tectonic force: it relied upon the manipulation of history and the weight of collective consciousness for its power. It might take thirty years to accomplish its goals, and Jane Andraste would no doubt be dead before they came to fruition, but if she lived long enough to set the machine rolling again it could mean another four hundred years of cold war, and Faerie would not withstand that. The Prometheans had paid a graver price in the past war than the Fae, but Faerie was worn to the bone by long years of attrition. The Queen ruled a divided and exhausted kingdom, and the Prometheus Club had succeeded in one goal: the iron world remained largely inviolate, its preconceptions strong.

Faerie had to prevent a siege. They could not endure one.

The Queen gestured to Matthew's cup. "It's safe," she said. "You have my permission to come and go as you please, Matthew Magus, anywhere in Faerie."

"Thank you," he said, and touched his lips to the rim of the cup he'd taken from the Elf-queen's own hand. The tea was hot, and faintly sweet, but not as if with honey.

"Was it my grandmother's murder?" Ian, his black-clad body sharp as a sundial shadow cast on the white stone behind him.

"I don't think so," Matthew said. "It doesn't taste like Jane manufacturing support. She's ruthless enough, but she would be flashier." *And might yet be.*

The clink of china as Carel stirred her own tea startled them out of the silence that dragged after. "Maybe somebody is giving Jane an excuse," she said, without raising her eyes from the cup and the spoon. Her opals and silver and amber glittered on her fingers when she set the spoon aside.

"Yes," Matthew said. The Prince was nodding too—as if he knew Jane Andraste at all. "But why those children in particular, I don't know."

"Still." The Queen paced a few steps away, her train shimmering behind her. Crystals caught rainbows out of the sunlight and sprinkled them over her form. "We have an enemy in common, it would seem. And from the look on your face"—without turning—"you'd rather me safely on the other side of the war."

"Where you belong," Matthew said, and let the wryness drip off it. He finished his tea; it was good, and he was dry. They had spent a long time walking.

His comment got a turn, a lift of her head, and her face rearranged in an arrogant grin. "What do you want, Matthew Magus?"

"Want, Your Majesty?"

"Want. That thing that's so much more pleasant than *need*."

He blinked. The cup rattled on the saucer. He set them both aside. He fancied he heard the others holding their breath.

Such a simple question.

He shook his head. "I haven't given it a lot of thought lately, Your Majesty."

"Consider," she said, "asking Mist for direction. If she doesn't eat you, you might learn something. And if war comes again, Matthew Magus, those who won't choose a side will be the enemy of all." An ironic statement? The last time, she and Matthew had both abandoned their 'sides.' The Queen's smile widened, and she turned inside the helix of her gown, the train an elegant swirl.

"Oh, look," she continued, and lifted a hand in a little girl's wave, fingers wiggling inside the pointed sleeve of her kirtle. "The children are coming."

"Excuse me," Carel said, reaching into her pocket. "I need to make a call."

Of course, the Merlin's cell phone would work in Faerie. Matthew rubbed the line between his eyes. He *had* to learn how she managed that.

Tuesday morning, Autumn got up early. November was tree-digging season, but the operative word in summer help was *summer*, and the day off had set her behind. She checked her messages and found no word from Carel: unsurprising, as she'd slept with her phone on the nightstand, and its warble would have woken her. The big rickety bed they shared was cold with one person in it, even with Rumpelstiltskin purring against the small of her back.

She called one of Carel's teaching assistants—the ambitious one, Wade—and told him Dr. Bierce had been summoned home to Texas to handle a family emergency. "I had no idea she was from Texas," he said. "She doesn't talk like it."

Not unless she wants to, Autumn thought, and thanked him for taking Carel's classes.

He wouldn't mind. He was, after all, the ambitious one.

After she hung up, she showered, braided her hair, shoveled down a bowl of Grape-Nuts and listened to the forecast while the teakettle was heating, then wrestled into jeans and a T-shirt, layering a flannel shirt and a sweatshirt over that. It might warm up later, or they might get wind or a little rain. This time of year, there was no telling what *partly cloudy* might mean. She grunted when she bent down to twist the cords on her boots through the speed lacers: winter was definitely coming, because her pants were getting tight.

She made sure she had her ID. She'd stop at the school on the way in to work and vote in the dark, before the sun came up and the lines got bad.

Fortified with sweet tea in a travel mug, Autumn crunched through low-lying mist and across frost-laced maple leaves, and tossed her pack behind the seat of her secondhand crew-cab Chevy. They wouldn't be selling plants this time of year, but she was looking forward to a good physical day digging and moving trees now that the heat of summer was gone. If she had time she'd push some dirt around too, and make new holes to plant more trees in tomorrow. It all had to get done before the ground froze, and there were the hoop houses to set up too.

She had the big green pickup backed halfway down the fissured asphalt drive when her phone made its noise. In traffic, she would have let the call go to voice mail, but in the driveway she hit the brake and left the transmission in reverse. Her arm snaked back and slid the phone from its pocket. She read the name on the display and had it against her ear by the second ring. "Hey, sweetheart. I called Wade for you, and told him your cousin Cate blew up and you had to go to Texas. How's the weather in Hy Bréàsil this morning?"

Carel's laugh rolled as musical as her voice, even over the tinny little speaker. "Still here. I just ducked out on a queen, a prince, a Mage, and a semiretired goddess to call and say I love you. How's that evil cat?"

"Sulking. Do you know when you might be home?"

"How long have I been gone?"

Time ran differently in Faerie. Autumn pinned the phone to her ear with her shoulder and skinned up the left sleeve of her Windbreaker and her sweatshirt. "Twenty-one hours, more or less," she said. She let

the cloth fall back as a late-traveling V of Canada geese honked overhead, gaining altitude.

"It's been about six here. I should be home very soon. I'll ask Elaine
to move things along a little."

"That'd be nice. We have that Hort Society potluck tonight, if you
can make it."

"I'll do my best. What am I supposed to be cooking?"

"You're *not* bringing back Faerie food for a bunch of landscape de-
signers." Autumn put the truck in neutral and set the parking brake.
She slumped in the driver's seat and kicked her knee up against the
steering wheel, leaning unconsciously into the small distant voice over
the phone.

"Aw, *Mom.*" But Carel was laughing, silently. Autumn heard the clink
of her beads as her shoulders shook. Autumn closed her eyes and
breathed deeply, letting the sound warm her. Sometimes you waited a
lifetime for the right one.

Sometimes it only felt that way.

"Hey," Carel said, and now Autumn could hear gravel crunching
under her boots, and a soft passage of notes in the background, under
indistinct voices. "Is that control-freak high priestess of yours still trying to shanghai every passing pagan into her coven?"

"We don't say 'control freak.' We say 'She hasn't processed her inse-
curity issues.' You are *such* a bad lesbian."

"Am I really?" Low and sultry, like the flick of fingers across the nape
of Autumn's neck. This time Autumn laughed.

"The worst. S'why I love you. You have a victim in mind?"

"For lesbianism?"

"For *Moira.*"

"Oh, yes. An old friend of mine rescued this skinny little Otherkin
girl off the street. She's, oh, twentyish. Hippie type. And wants magic
so bad she can taste it when she closes her eyes. I was thinking—"

"She might fit in with Lily and Michael. Right. What's her name?"
Autumn's breath clouded the windshield. She rolled the driver's-side
window down and flipped the defogger on. The morning air was still
crisp, the haze not yet burning off. She shifted the phone to the other
ear, and watched the foundation lights around the old house illuminate

tendrils of mist between the maples and silver birches. It almost looked tangible sometimes, at night and lit from below: shapes like ghosts and wandering animals. And sometimes real deer snuck right up to the house, never mind the fencing, and devoured the irises. An outline there, in fact, had a long horizontal line like an animal's back. If Autumn squinted, she thought she could see the wet shine of eyes. Her right thumb hovered over the horn.

"Jewels." Carel paused when Autumn gasped. "You *don't* know her." Magic was coincidence, but there were limits.

"No," Autumn said. "But you're not going to believe this."

"What?"

Autumn blinked at the fog-pale shape. It could be a stray Angora goat or a young llama. There were people in the neighborhood with livestock, and livestock got out. But as it picked its way around the corner of the shed and paused by the cellar hatch, she saw it clearly: white as egrets, with burrs snarled in its silvery beard. It lowered its head and rooted among the leaves Autumn had heaped over the flower beds and weighted with stones, using its horn to sweep the earth bare.

"Carel, there's a unicorn eating your lily bulbs."

Silence.

"Carel?"

"Well," the Merlin said. "Whatever you do, don't go near it. Those suckers have a temper like you wouldn't believe."

The raven with the draggled wing sailed low over the gardens. Roses glowed in warm whites and colors, side by side with chrysanthemum and hollyhock and the high, wind-silvered walls of burgundy and violet lilac bushes. The scent that scrolled from them under the warmth of the sun was heady and powerful, thick enough to texture the air under his wings. There was jasmine too, redolent and sweet, and iris and crocus and lilies jumbled together, a thousand seasons or none at all.

Bright day in the Summerlands.

His shadow flicked across graveled paths and geometric hedges, across all the bright flowers and the scented fruit trees, and set a rabbit scurrying before it realized he wasn't a hawk. There were people by the golden palace, women and men, dark and fair, and more passing under the arbor to join them. His sister's hair blazed like red amber in the sun.

The raven settled on Morgan's shoulder with a snap of wings. Her hair was sliding from the braid, so the bird preened a strand behind her ear, whispering a few words as he did. The Queen had drunk at the hazel pool, and the secret language of birds was plain to her, so the raven spoke softly and briefly.

The birds don't have the answer, he said, as she rubbed her temple against his head. His feathers rasped stray hairs out of place again, and it tickled when he smoothed them. *But they are asking. Something winged will know. Oh, and the pigeons had an interesting story —*

The stroke of her finger down his beak said, *Tell me later.* She found a bit of cake on the table and held it up for him, and turned to watch the young mortals and the page Foxglove progress down the stair. The Queen, flanked by her son, went to meet them.

"I am but an attendant lord," Morgan said, mostly to the raven, but it was Matthew who gave her the curious glance.

"A little modern for you."

"One tries to keep up." She grinned at him again, and he blushed and turned back to the newcomers, pushing the tails of his patchwork coat aside to shove his hands into his pockets. "Mallory's so dreary, after the first two hundred years."

He laughed, of course, and shot her a shy sideways glance that landed on her mouth more than her eyes.

She almost felt sorry for him.

Jewels' heart hadn't stopped beating staccato since the alder-twig Fae had returned with a slender page — this one unmistakably an Elf of the storybook sort, if a young and furtive one — and they had dressed her in suede trousers and boots that didn't chafe her sore, scraped feet at all. They'd put a blouse with wild full pirate sleeves and a brocade bodice on her, and they had combed her wet hair halfway dry in the sun and braided it in two tails down her back, with copper and verdigris ribbons and tiny dust-blue sprigs of rosemary woven through, so it smelled thick and sweet and resinous.

Geoff, when they brought him to meet her in the hall, was dressed as he had been, except his hair was wet and his shirt was clean. He still had his backpack slung over one shoulder, and the Fae avoided him and all the steel he wore.

Despite the bulky jacket and the every-which-way elflocked hair, he seemed diminished, like a wet cat. His elbows pressed to his sides, denting the leather of his jacket, and the light reflecting from it cast blue shadows under his chin. He breathed out as she came to him, his shoulders lowering. "You're okay?"

"Yeah." She patted his arm. Geoff was a funny creature, big-eyed and skittish as a lemur, so phobic about blood he couldn't watch Jewels tend to her implements, but all lashing tail and claws when he needed to be.

They followed Foxglove through the castle corridors—the alder-twig Fae stayed behind—and down a different flight. The castle seemed deserted. Jewels would have expected a bustle of servants, but other than the pitter-patter of a brownie in ragged coveralls, rose briars pinning the side seams, she didn't hear a footfall.

"It's quiet in the afternoons," she said, and Foxglove gave her a small soft smile.

"It's quiet always," he said, tossing his head so his silvery hair broke in locks across his forehead and around his ear points. "There are not many of us left." A peridot gleamed near the tip of the left ear, a citrine lower in the right. Geoff took Jewels' hand.

They walked through a long sun-dappled gallery and out into the day. The Merlin waited there, the Mage beside her: also, the men who had met them on the road, and two women.

She recognized the beaked nose and blowing dark hair of the Queen of Faeries, though she couldn't have guessed that the stern, wickedly beautiful redhead behind her was Morgan le Fey, two dogs at her feet and that crooked-winged raven on her shoulder. Still, Jewels caught her breath. *This is real.*

Steps gritted under Jewels' boots as she stepped down them, chin up, forcing her hands to hang naturally at her sides. The Queen came forward, her dark boy beside her, her train and sleeves spreading on the marble of the patio to glitter in the sun. It seemed she rose from the same substance, a sculpted plinth with a living woman trapped within. The bard on his chair never looked up, though disapproval stiffened his neck.

Jewels swallowed and glanced at Geoff. He winked—he must have been waiting for her to look—and it made her feel better. And then she saw Foxglove stepping away from them and stooping before the Queen, his hair sliding over his bead-sewn shoulders. Trousers made a curtsey stupid, so Jewels tugged Geoff's hand and went down on one knee too, as they issued from the stair.

She held her breath, suede stretching across her seat and thighs, sun-warmth prickling the nape of her neck, her streaked ashy braids sliding over her shoulders, still damp. "Your Majesty," she breathed, as Geoff ducked his head.

"Juliet," the Queen said, when Jewels was sure she was going to faint from lack of oxygen. "Geoffrey. Rise."

They did, hair haloed in sun, the thready sweetness of the gardens cloying in their throats. Geoff regretted his coat, but he hadn't been sure of leaving anything in the room. He didn't think it was wise to assume, in Faerie, that one could return to get anything one left behind.

The Faerie Queen watched quietly, her dress translucent with the sunlight behind it, her lips twisted in an odd and very human sort of moue. She reached out with a bony graceful hand and touched the silver in Jewels' ear, then tapped the pointed tip. Her own ears were barely slanted at all—no more than anyone's might be, and her features were not Fae. Ian shifted beside and behind her. "Oh, kid," she said, in broad Midwestern English. "You don't want that, you know."

Jewels squeezed Geoff's hand for courage. His palm had gone clammy, his pulse trembling under the skin as hard as her own, but he didn't let the fear reach his eyes.

"Can you see my heart?" Jewels asked, her voice very clear considering how dry her mouth felt.

"No," the Queen said. "I can't see your heart, though I'd bet Morgan could, or Cairbre."

She angled a smile over Geoff's shoulder, and Cairbre responded with a soft trill. It was a fierce smile, and Ian transferred his weight from one foot to another at the bard's answer. This time, in discomfort.

"Mother—" She stopped him with an upraised hand.

"Let her speak for herself."

Jewels cleared her throat. "Then how do you know what I want?

Your Majesty," she added, belatedly, and winced. This was not, she suspected, how one spoke to queens.

"I know," the Queen said. She turned her back, the white gown twisting around her legs, and drew her hair forward over her shoulders with a swanlike lift of her arms. She slipped the buttons down the bodice and let the whole glittering assemblage slide off her shoulders and breasts, taking her chemise with it, baring her to the waist.

Even Jewels gasped.

The Queen's skin was a golden olive, fine-grained and flawless over smooth muscle and bone. Except for the patternless scars that crisscrossed her back in meandering lines, thick and white and stiff as worm-tunnels through the green meat of a leaf, so there was scarcely the span of two fingers between them. They chipped her entire back into facets, and Jewels could see that they extended below her waist and the length of both arms in beaded keloid lines.

The Queen turned to look over her own shoulder, and pushed her hair out of her eyes. She showed the scars on her breasts and belly too: they weren't so dramatic, the pierced puckered stab wounds of an old hart's tines, but they were enough that the Queen saw Matthew turn his head and flinch, his undamaged hand clenching—in empathy, rather than in horror, she thought.

"This is Faerie," she said. "No one who enters comes away unmarked."

She saw the girl swallow, her slender throat convulsing. And then Jewels raised her own hands, unlaced the borrowed bodice she wore, without speaking, and shrugged it down her arms. She pulled her blouse out of the waistband of the trousers and jerked it over her head, then threw both to the stones. And turned, arms folded over a narrow chest, colors glowing on her skin over the rise and hollow of her ribs and spine.

"I was born in the otherworld," Jewels said. "Don't you think it's already marked me enough?"

The Queen sighed and slid her chemise up her torso again, worming her arms into the sleeves. Foxglove came to help her, and Carel did her buttons up, smoothing the gown below her collarbones, the air even more full of Carel's rosewood scent than the scent of flowers.

Jewels had turned back before Carel stepped away, arms still crossed over her breasts defiantly, without modesty.

That would serve her well. The Queen turned for a moment and found Matthew frowning at her. He'd angled his head so the light glinted off his spectacles, hiding his expression, but the curve of tense biceps under his coat and the pin-scratch between his eyebrows gave him away.

"On your head be it," the Queen said, twisting to look the half-nude mortal girl in the eyes. No Faerie mix of shifting colors there: they were clear and brown as brook water. "It may kill you, child. But you can stay."

"Elaine!"

The Queen smiled at Matthew, and made sure he knew how false it was. "What about the boy?" she asked.

"Oh, I'm just here with Jewels—" Geoff sputtered.

The Queen talked right over him, watching Matthew's folded arms tighten across his chest. "Can't you feel the power in him, Matthew Magus? Don't you want him for your very own?"

Matthew coughed, but if he would have answered, it was lost under Jewels' protest. "He's not Otherkin."

"Otherkin is a *joke*," Matthew said, sharply. "Do you want to know what changeling children look like? Elaine is one," he said, jerking the back of his hand at her. "There. Look at Morgan. She's one too. An Elf-knight's bastard. If you were a changeling, Jewels, somebody would have come to kidnap you by now—" He blinked, as if suddenly awakened to his tirade, and settled back on his heels.

Morgan stepped in. "Geoff's a Mage. A Mage-in-waiting, anyway. He could be like Matthew, is what the Queen means."

"Gee, I can hardly wait," Geoff muttered under his breath, and Matthew couldn't blame him.

Chapter Nine
Babylon

Ernie Peese waited for Don after the briefing. Predictable, but not anything Don wanted to deal with when the remnants of the nightmare headache still scratched at his temples, and before his second pot of coffee. Even when Ernie was smiling.

Especially when Ernie was smiling.

"And?" Don said, before Ernie could start the guessing game.

It didn't, unfortunately, deflate him much. But Don would cheerfully use his own height and bulk as a weapon against bullies, and he did so now, closing the space between them and forcing Ernie to tilt his head and look up at him as he said, "Those kids you let go aren't answering their cell phones. Service unavailable. The girl's mailbox was full this morning, but I guess nobody ever calls the boy."

"So maybe they went to the beach. We've got addresses for both of them, right?"

"For what *that's* worth. Do I actually need to tell you there's a lot of people unhappy about this, Don?" Peese sighed and unfolded his arms. He turned to open up the space between them—a tacit invitation for Don to walk on. He took it, and Ernie kept pace.

Peese was a thoroughly odious human being. Unfortunately, he was also a pretty good cop.

Don hated moral ambiguities. "Yeah, I'm getting my ass kicked too."

"From the mayor to the chief and on down the line, everybody adding his little teaspoon of shit to the avalanche. I got a call from a

Christian Bergstrom last night." Peese shook his head, just once, an irritated twitch. "Guess what he is?"

"Dare I?"

"Personal assistant to former lieutenant governor Andraste. You wanna tell me what the hell *she's* doing involved in the case?"

Don stopped. "Dammit. That Szczegielniak guy is one of Andraste's pets too. What did Bergstrom want?"

Peese drew up short half a step after Don, and turned to stare at him, sucking his uneven teeth. "He wanted to know if there was anything Mrs. Andraste could do to help with the investigation. And if there was any chance that it wasn't a Faerie murder."

"So what if it turns out not to be Fae? What else would it be?" Don stuck a stumpy finger in his ear and scratched absently.

"Something that will fuck us up. I dunno—it goes to Washington anyway. If we rule out a mortal agency. And—"

Don's heels clicked on gray-flecked linoleum tile, worn paler under scarred wax near the center of the corridor. The woodwork was old, the floors new—on a system that considered 1950 *new*. "Have we ruled out a mortal agency? Or is that why you wanted to keep a leash on those kids?"

"If it's a Fae crime we're off it. The mayor wants the city to have it. It doesn't do him any good if it goes to DC."

Of course Ernie knows what the mayor wants. Don kicked an imaginary can. "What, you studying law nights? Going to run for DA? That's not a collar you can *make*, Ernie. They have their own rules. The faster we hand this uphill, the better."

Peese sighed and stuffed his hands in his pockets, and stopped. Don slowed down and turned around, walking backward.

"I've just got a feeling about those kids," Peese said.

"Well, I'll tell you what," Don said. "As soon as you want to charge them with something, I'll drive up to Hartford and fetch them myself."

He grinned at Peese and turned his back, pretending an urgent appointment with the men's room. Once inside, though, he only washed his hands and checked his hair and tie.

It was probably a Fae crime. It *was* probably a Fae crime, and he was a fool to keep chasing it.

But maybe it was something else.

And if it was, Don thought he knew who to ask.

You don't just call people up and ask to talk to them. It's ineffective. They respond much better to a face and a firm handshake and a badge. And it's harder to hang up on somebody when he's standing on your lawn.

Cop work was a lot like selling vacuum cleaners.

Don walked down the dished granite steps from the brownstone police station and into a morning much sunnier than the earlier overcast had promised. Long rays warmed his scalp and shoulders, picking out the odd gnarl of silver in his wood-brown hair. The city breathed around him, a thousand pulses and rhythms blending seamlessly into one gigantic beat.

He followed it down into the subways, and ascended into the light again near the gray-white Romanesque revival facade of the Museum of Natural History, where a tropical butterfly vivarium was that particular winter's homesickness-inducing display. It was a nice day for a walk, and Don crossed the street to pace under trees, along cobblestones, as he strolled south on Central Park West, hands in his pockets.

That was where Whiskey picked up his scent and recognized it, even without the overlaid reek of blood and magic from two days before. Thomas' magic trick to locate Jane had worked, and led him and Whiskey to Jane's building. Getting inside was more of a trick, however, and they had spent some time watching people come and go, hoping to catch Jane leaving or somebody they knew to be visiting her going in.

Whiskey nudged Thomas—the bard was half drowsing on a wall at the edge of the park, under a barren tree—and folded his arms. "Our ship of passage has arrived."

"Pardon?" Thomas lurched upright, rubbing his eyes. "I don't take your meaning."

Whiskey's gesture was slight, an uncurling of his fingers. "Remember him?"

He would have been hard to forget: a massive, square-shouldered black man in a well-cut suit, who was putting up a pretty good fight against a middle-aged paunch. He was bigger than Ben Jonson, and just as confident in his rolling stride.

"I do. You think he's going into the tower?" Thomas nodded to an apartment complex across the street.

"If he doesn't, I'll be interested to see where he does go." Whiskey stood, and Thomas stood beside him. The poet hung a glamourie on their shoulders, a whistled phrase of pass-unseen, and they followed, sidestepping midmorning joggers and commuters hurrying for their trains in business suits and tennis shoes. A minor hazard of functional invisibility.

Don found the building he was looking for and paused before the entry to straighten his tie, frowning a bit at the rippled smears of color sliding across the glass behind his reflection. The optical illusion was so strong he actually turned to see if someone was standing there, but the sidewalk was empty.

The doorman became considerably more cooperative when Don showed him a badge. "Shall I call up for you, Detective?"

"Just point me to the penthouse elevator." Don had a pretty good idea that he'd call up anyway, as soon as Don's back was turned, but it wasn't as if he had a warrant, or was even checking out a lead.

Whistling, he followed the doorman's directions across a marble atrium to the brass-doored elevator concealed behind a potted palm. The elevator was smooth and spacious, with brass rails and burled walnut paneling, but Don couldn't shake that ghosty feeling that someone was standing behind him, staring over his shoulder.

It figured a wizard's tower would be haunted.

Jane Andraste waited for him in the elevator lobby when the doors scrolled back. He'd only known her from a distance, back then, but the years out of the public eye had made a difference. She looked frailer. An old woman now, in her pink Chanel suit and low-heeled pumps, her hair gone stone-white instead of iron-gray. But she was perfect and poised, delicate jewelry glinting at her throat and ears.

"Bringing trouble to my door, Detective—"

"Smith," he said, and stepped out of the elevator. He had his folder in his hand; the ones with money always wanted a long, hard look at the badge. But she barely glanced at it and stood aside, gesturing him on, gesturing him in.

Whiskey and Thomas had followed him, cloaked by Thomas' magic, crowding the far wall of the elevator. They moved for the doors as quickly as they could without noise and without stepping on Detective Smith's heels. The doors whisked closed behind them as Thomas swept his cloak out of the way, and they entered a small elevator lobby, white-walled and marble-floored, bright with sun from a skylight. An archway led to a bigger room beyond, and through it could be glimpsed stark modern furniture and the corners of richly framed art.

"Trouble?" Don said.

Jane brought her hands together and fiddled one cold iron ring. She halted when the elevator closed, so abruptly Don almost walked into her.

"You can drop the pass-unseen," she said, without turning. "I know you're there, although what a Mage I've never met is doing in New York, I haven't the faintest. And walking alongside a Wild Fae and a mortal man. What an interesting alliance."

The poet almost choked on his spell. "Archmage," he said. "I'm an idiot." Because of course things had changed in four hundred years, and what had worked a charm on Richard Baines wouldn't necessarily work on Jane Andraste.

He let his pretenses fall.

Don had rounded when Thomas spoke. His eyes widened, and he reached, reflexively, under his coat before he froze. He might have expected all sorts of things of Jane Andraste, but materializing a blue-eyed, six-foot-five black man in an immaculate white suit—and a considerably shorter dirty blond dressed for a Renaissance festival— hadn't been high on the list. "Son of a bitch—"

Jane folded her hands before her hips, demure as a girl. It should have been a collar of pearls glowing at her throat, and not winking mar-casites. "Oh," she said. "I know you after all."

"I have never had the pleasure of a personal introduction," Thomas said. "I presume you are Mistress Andraste."

"You're four hundred years dead, on the books. Am I to understand the Master of Records was misinformed?"

He stepped forward, gallantly, and made a bow. "Perhaps a little. But it is only because we are enemies."

She smiled a little purse-lipped smile. "Quite. And you, Whiskey.

Brave to come after a wizard in her tower. I assume you are not here as Her Majesty's messenger?"

Whiskey scraped a foot across the marble floor and looked everywhere but at Jane Andraste.

"Mmmm," she said. "I thought not. So if you're not here to bargain, then you are here to assassinate. Well, have at me."

Don, who had been watching the conversation with the brow-furrowed attention of a tennis fan at a football match, stepped forward, his hand upraised. "Just *one* minute, please! Now, nobody's laying a hand on you, Mrs. Andraste. And I don't know who these people are—"

"One of them is not precisely a person, Detective," she said, unbuttoning her suit jacket. She shrugged it down her shoulders and let it slide from her wrists unregarded. In an off-white silk shell and the trim rose-colored skirt, slack-fleshed arms folded over her chest to show the peridot bracelet, she looked a peculiar warrior. But Don noticed that the big guy stepped back nonetheless, and not as if shocked by her charge of intended murder. No, as if he were nerving himself to take her on, and wasn't sure he had the muscle to do it.

Which was ridiculous; he was twice her size. But his head went back and forth as if he were a horse trying to shake off a bit, and his nostrils flared.

Jane reached up and pulled a lock of hair loose from her chignon. It curled coarse and colorless between her fingers as she combed them to the end, and pulled it taut. "Do you think I don't have the power to do it? I know you carry her name, and I gave her that name, water-horse. *By my hand and my heart, by the name of your soul . . .*"

"Wrong choice," Whiskey said, and grinned. "I've already danced that dance with your daughter."

He stepped forward, reaching for her wrist. Don grabbed his arm, squeezing hard enough that bone should have ground on bone, and the tall Fae—he had to be a Fae—knocked him off like a kid tossing aside an unwanted doll. Don went down on his ass, sliding on the stone tiles, shocked into a yelp. He burrowed for his piece, fingers closing on warm metal and crosshatched black plastic, and had no idea what happened next except the little blond guy made some sort of negligent sideways gesture and Don froze, locked in place as if by an electrical current. He pushed against it — *dammit, there are not supposed to be Fae in my city* — and surely the semiautomatic was a big enough chunk of steel to break a Faerie enchantment, and his fingers were *on* it, and these two were going to kill Jane Andraste right in front of him before he could ask her what the hell had happened to the girl —

He strained, fingers aching, every nerve and muscle in hand and wrist and elbow stretched against the spell, as the big guy in the white suit started to swell, to bulge in unnatural places like a horror-movie monster, until he blurred and a spotted stallion snorted and pawed in his place, droplets scattering through sunlight from his shaken mane. The creature's eyes grew huge, glaring like the blue fire closest to the wick before it sears itself into invisibility. He stepped forward, water flooding from his hooves, wetting Don's shoes and trouser legs as it puddled on the stone. Beside him, the blond guy had yanked a glittering blade from somewhere under his cloak and was advancing as well.

The horse reared up, an argument against cathedral ceilings, hammered silver gleaming on his forehooves. And Jane still stood calmly, ropy old-woman's arms folded again, that single lock of hair drifting against her cheek as she breathed. The Kelpie towered over her, and she saw his crushing hooves and white-rimmed eyes.

And she brought him crashing to the tile with a gesture of her hand. "Enough," she said. "Enough."

Whiskey fell like a sliding mountain, marble splitting — *splintering* — under his hooves and knees. The whole building pitched, a roll and drop like a seismic shock, and blood dripped dilute pink down his fetlocks when he struggled up.

A hand raised, a flat palm, and she turned the poet's blade without even turning her eyes. She caught his wrist, pressing iron to skin, and smiled when he showed no pain. "Mortal man."

"Once," he answered, as she drew him close, unresisting. The strength she used was greater than her own; she stood in her own tower, and the walls and beams and the deep roots into the earth themselves were her strength, in this place. An alarm rattled, distantly. Overhead sprinklers kicked on, two, four, eight, dragging Jane's hair into her eyes, sluicing off the poet's cloak and soaking his shoulders.

"Children," she said. "Children who don't observe the niceties." He wore no rings at all, neither steel nor silver, and not on any finger, but every finger bore scars at the root, round and round. "Christofer Marley," she said. "Excommunicate of the Order. What is your purpose?"

"Your destruction, archmage," he said calmly, setting his heels. Her touch was a command; he could no more struggle against it than Whiskey could advance past the wall of her other, upheld hand. The Prometheans dealt in symbols and constructs, real and imaginary. There were forms, as she insisted, and she was *enforcing* them.

"Tell me why, Christofer."

"That is not my name anymore, madam. Nor am I numbered among the Prometheans, not for some little while now."

"It's my place to say who is or is not so numbered," she said. She looked him in the eyes, and smiled. "So tell me, Christoferus Magus, why is it that you seek my death?"

He heard Whiskey breathing like a pipe organ, leaning, straining against the archmage's magic, his hooves slipping on the broken stone, rattling and cracking it. But they were in her tower, and as soon as she had noticed them, they had been doomed. Jane Andraste was a Promethean archmage: in her tower, she could draw on the strength of all those who swore fealty to her. She was all but untouchable here.

Still, there were forms. And Jane Andraste was not the only one who could exploit forms. There was one way to force her out of her tower, and to force her to rely only on her own strength to defend herself. All it required was that the poet challenge her as an equal.

The poet released his blade, winced when he heard it clatter on stone. The anger he'd been swallowing for seven long years flared hot, dimmed, and blazed like blown coals. "The Fae do not have souls. When they die, they *die*, madam."

"And?" Quizzical, eyebrows lifting under wet white hair.

"We had a lover in common, you and I. And he is dead by your doing." And Kit—he supposed there was no point in calling himself anything else if everyone he met was going to recognize him in a heartbeat, even if it wasn't his name anymore—Kit let his unrestrained hand dart to his belt. There were gloves there, soaked burgundy leather, and he had them slipped free and in his hand and was striking a sharp, wet, stinging blow across her cheek before the archmage could flinch. It left a welt; he was not a man for striking women, but he did not pull this blow.

Jane Andraste gasped and staggered back, one hand raised to the weal on her cheek, and let go Kit's blade arm.

"I await your seconds," Kit Marley said, and turned his back, and stepped away, a curt, imperious gesture that he would pay for later, beckoning Whiskey to his side. He was almost to the elevator when her voice pursued and collared him.

"Christoferus Magus!"

He stopped and turned. "Madam archmage."

Her hand drew back. She hurled something to him, a glittering something that flashed silver in the glow through the newly cracked skylight. His hand shot up, and he caught it: red power twined through iron and platinum, clear in his *otherwise* eye. "Your ring," she called across the broken stone. "My second will find you in the morning."

He smiled, and slipped the ring onto his smallest finger, where it fit tightly enough to chafe. "I shall look forward to it," he said, and having seen the detective do it earlier, made short work of summoning the elevator and commanding it to open.

When they were gone, Jane glanced around, watching the water run over the cracked stone, and remembered the police officer sprawled on the floor. The spell Marley had used to immobilize him was a good one, but an old one, archaic. It wouldn't have worked anywhere but here, where Promethean power was concentrated—as her own attack on Whiskey would have failed elsewhere. Promethean magic was either very subtle—the ability to see things, to convince persons, to create resonances—or so vast in its effects as to be nearly undetectable. Forest for the trees.

Jane untangled the spell with a few passes, and offered the policeman her hands. He looked ashamed, but he took them, and as he did she happened to glance into his eyes.

Jane peered into the abyss, and Mist gazed back at her, a complacent monster sharpening her claws on stone. And Jane looked down.

Hello, Detective Touched-by-Dragons. "You wanted to ask me some questions?"

"I understand," he said, extricating his hands from hers without trying to hide how they were shaking, "if now isn't a particularly good time."

Matthew had to walk away. There was a garden down there, graveled paths for walking, and he needed to be somewhere else. Somewhere away from Jewels and her butterfly flurry of delight and questions, her carved-up back, and her saturated eyes. *And you have so much latitude to throw stones, Matthew Magus.*

Unconsciously his fingers fretted the cuff of his shirt, scratching at the ink-labyrinthed skin beneath. His marks were different. They had a purpose. They chained power.

And hers chain power too. In a different way.

He frowned and put one foot in front of the other, pretending he didn't hear the boots crunching along the path behind him until Geoff gave up and called out. "Matthew?"

He slowed his step, but didn't halt. "What do you want?"

"Are you all right?"

And that stopped Matthew. He turned, and frowned at the kid. Geoff's pants jingled when he walked, as bad as Matthew's jacket. *Sleigh bells*, Matthew thought, and laughed.

It wasn't a pleasured laugh. "No," he said. "You know what your girl-friend just did is seven kinds of dumb, right?"

"It's what she's always wanted."

"Like a kid's book about a magic kingdom."

Geoff paused, and tilted his head as if he were really thinking it over. Beside them, translucent in the sunlight, banks upon banks of daylilies mounted, rioting in tiger shades. "And at the end of the magic books, the children go back through the wardrobe, or Dorothy goes back to Oz, and they're stronger and wiser for their journeys but no time has passed in the real world, and they're ready to grow up and take charge. But that's not what Jewels needs, you know?"

Matthew kicked at the gravel and started walking again. "Those are bad books. Well, they're very good books, but that's not the point. They're wishful thinking. Besides, if you read on in either series, the children inevitably go back to the magic kingdom. The authors may preach responsible adulthood, but deep down, they don't believe in it. They can't make it stick." He took a deep breath of the dense air of Faerie and shivered at its sweet, heady strength. "Books are lies. All books are lies, but the books that say you can walk out of Faerie unscathed are more so. It's not that you come back and not a moment has passed—it's that you're gone a moment, and fifteen years have gone, and everyone you loved has forgotten you."

Geoff squared his shoulders. "How about *Peter Pan*?"

"I am an English teacher, you know."

"Yeah, I'm finding that out. Answer the question, Matthew."

"*Peter Pan* gets it right," Matthew said. "The book, not the movies. You can't have it all; you have to choose. The iron world, or Faerie. You can't have both, and once you visit one, you can't return untouched. The otherworld is greedy."

Geoff lifted his chin, settling his weight, hipshot with his hands in his pockets, and Matthew let him command the moment, stopped and turned. Geoff said, "Some of us are born in the wrong world. Born the wrong species."

He wasn't talking about himself. Matthew could see that his gaze was past Matthew, over his shoulder and over the garden and on Jewels, if she hadn't moved from where Matthew had left her.

"Some of us are," Matthew said. "Sometimes people are born the wrong sex too, or missing a limb, or with a mathematics learning disability when all they really want out of life is to be a physicist. It's sad, but it happens." His epaulets jangled. "Every one of us is a minor tragedy. Most of us learn to cope."

Geoff's snort of disgust was forceful enough to knock Matthew back a step. The Mage tilted his head quizzically and spread his hands. *Well, keep talking.*

Geoff shrugged and brushed past him, hesitating only for a parting shot. "Well, what's your minor tragedy, then? You seem pretty blessed to me."

His bad luck that Matthew knew the answer. "My minor tragedy? I never wanted a damned thing to do with magic, kid."

"Pity," said a third voice, a rough contralto that prickled on spider feet across the back of Matthew's neck. Morgan's hand followed, warm between his shoulder blades, undeterred by the talismans strung around him like ornaments on a Christmas tree. "You used to be so good at it."

So maybe Geoff hadn't been looking at Jewels after all. Morgan smiled at him first, and then, for a little longer, at Matthew. "Am I interrupting?"

She knew she was. And by the blush on Geoff's face, he didn't care. "What you said earlier. I could be a Mage?"

Matthew swallowed to ease a dry mouth. "A good one."

"Thanks," Geoff said. He pushed his hair out of his eyes, and now he *was* looking at Jewels, past both Matthew and Morgan. Matthew turned to follow his gaze, an excuse for a sidelong glance at the witch. She was smiling right at him when he looked, freckles crinkling across the bridge of her nose. "But no thanks," Geoff finished. "Not my scene."

"At least one of us has some sense."

Morgan laughed. "He knows what *he* wants. And you, Matthew Magus? I overheard what Elaine asked, and have a question of my own. In seven years, have you decided yet whose side you're on?"

He knew what she meant. When last they met, she'd given him a choice, and he'd refused her. Refused her to go home to a city he didn't trust, and a wardenship he didn't want, and a vow that he'd betrayed. "No," he said. "I don't know what I want."

"An honest man. There had to be one in Faerie." Her hand grew warmer. She let it slide down his spine. "Do you *want* to find out?"

"Are you offering to tell me?" More sharply than he might have, if Geoff had not been watching, blinking wide light-colored eyes in confusion.

"No," she said. "I'm not all that interested in what you want, Matthew Magus. But as long as you're here, you could always take the Queen's advice a step further, and go and ask the Dragon how to be rid of that magic you carry, if you truly wish it gone."

He shouldn't tell her. She was far more like an enemy than an ally, no matter how sweetly she smiled. But there she was, and here he was. And even if he couldn't trust her, it wasn't as if he had anything to lose.

"I can't control it," he said. "Not since the war. I can't do a damned thing with it that's more complicated than tying my shoes. When I'm out of Faerie, I'm half drowning in signal all the time."

"I can solve that riddle," she said, lifting her hair over her shoulder, smoothing it behind her ear. "All you must do is stay in Faerie, then."

Felix Luray arrived too late. As he stood on the grass of Central Park, watching the Kelpie and the Mage follow the cop into the archmage's tower, he twisted his ring in frustration. He'd wanted to speak to Jane before she found out from other sources that he was in New York, but if the water-horse was here, then Kadiska was likely just behind him. She might choose to keep her own counsel, or not.

He interlaced his hands behind his back and slowed his breathing. This wasn't a disaster—or even proved a setback, yet. And the information he had now would at least buy an audience, if nothing more.

Meditation would pass the time. And perhaps he could find his own way back to the heart of New York, without Jane Andraste. He tilted his head back and fixed his gaze on the penthouse where she lived now, the one that had been a Promethean meeting hall and ritual space in brighter days. Things changed, but the city pounded along, underfoot, overhead, protean and powerful.

Like the city, the beast has many hearts. As many hearts as there are empires, so one might swell as another shrivels. As many as there are mountains, as many as there are treasons, as many as there are pearls. Even the beast cannot know the truth of her soul. All books are lies, and all stories are true.

Felix pressed bright-polished oxblood loafers into the grass and felt the blood and bedrock underneath, found the old mad power running there and invited it in, invited it through. The beast was a rough lover, and the Promethean discipline had been to keep it chained, caged, channeled, tamed—a tiger in a magic show. But those chains were broken now, and what had once been demands upon its power had become supplications.

Felix was not comfortable with surrender. But he let it happen, laid himself open and gritted his teeth, and thought about the wild young city thrusting under his soles. *"Fallen, fallen, is Babylon the great, that hath made all nations drink the wrath of the impure wine of her passions."*

Not yet, though. There was blood in this dragon yet. And that was part of the secret too. There were many Babylons, one for every fractal heart. Felix found New York in his memory, as he had first seen her on a sun-drenched morning in 1973. He'd known no one in America—not a soul. He'd gone to Central Park because that was what one did, and been a little dizzied by the sun and the bell-bottoms twined with amateurish satin-stitch embroidery and the pretty, long-haired, soft-bellied girls with nearly nothing on.

The prettiest girl had a transistor radio on the blanket beside her, tuned to WNEW. Through synchronicity or destiny, it was playing Paul Simon's "American Tune" when Felix wandered past. He'd stopped, thunderstruck—and the city, or the beast, had reached inside him and made him a Mage.

Not long after, Jane Andraste—heartsick and furious and building an army to win her stolen daughter back from Faerie—found him and trained him. And then she'd taken New York away from him, but she hadn't been able to take his power, even if it wasn't the equal of hers—or her darling Matthew's.

Felix heard the city singing, millions of threaded melodies, a massive, surging fugue . . . and it would not sing to him. He laid himself open, nails driven into his palms, eyes clenched tight as his fists, and the power rolled over and through him and took no notice of him at all.

He opened his eyes and took one deep, raw breath that he wouldn't call a sob, only seconds before he felt the wards around Jane's tower ring like a steel drum hammered hard.

Felix knew the way up. As a crackle of discharged energies still rattled the apartment complex, he adopted valor as the better part of discretion, crossed Central Park West against the light, leaning on his luck hard and bending it in the process but not quite breaking it, and made the doorman think he was flashing a badge as he galloped past. The elevator awaited.

The funny part was, he thought—impatiently counting flashing numbers—that he wasn't sure to whose defense he was charging. Or what he thought he would do when he got there. He held on tight to his luck all the way up, white-knuckled with the grip.

It was over by the time the elevator doors opened. Jane, her cream-colored blouse plastered to her skin and revealing details of her lingerie, was helping the equally soaked cop to his feet, and neither the Kelpie nor his associate was visible. She turned at the *ding* of the elevator, frowning in expectation of building security, and stopped dead as Felix put his hand on the door to prevent it from closing in his face. He killed the sprinkler system with a sigil sketched left-handed on air, and picked his way across shattered tiles, wet marble dust gritting under his shoes.

"I see my assistance wasn't required after all."

"Felix," she said, the detective forgotten as she squatted to pick up her soggy jacket. "What on earth are you doing here?"

"Well," he said, as dryly as possible, "I came to slay a monster for you, but I hope you'll settle for the key to a murder mystery." He gestured to the cracked stone and dripping sprinkler heads. "Thaumaturgical error, or equipment failure?"

"Pitched battle." She hadn't moved, heels set and jacket clenched in ringed fingers. "*Do* tell me what you want."

He stopped, not quite willing to push past her to enter her space, and aware—if Jane wasn't—of the weight of the detective's attention. "I want what I want," he said. "My place at your right hand, as the cliché goes."

"Power."

"That's wrong?" The arched eyebrow and the wrinkled nose belied a coldly sardonic smile. Same old Felix.

"No," she admitted. "One second. Let me call the alarm company and tell them it was a malfunction before I wind up paying for a ladder truck."

She turned away and fussed with her cell phone briefly—damp, but functional—and then turned back. "And you think you can buy that? Your old job back?"

"I think I can earn it," he said. "Should we be talking so frankly in front of your friend?" His gaze flicked to Smith, and away, back to Jane's face. Earnest and friendly and nothing more than a calculated surface, a mirror reflecting expectations.

"Don won't talk," she said, and made it so with a gesture. Whatever had touched him—and she meant to get to the bottom of that at her earliest convenience—he had no mastery of it. Which made him valuable.

It tickled her bones, a tingle of excitement in her fingertips. For the first time in seven years, she felt hope, like a brush of feathers on her hair. *Fuck* the vultures, her poor, scavenged, half-talented apprentices of whom only Christian had any potential at all.

Prometheus was not dead.

Jane said, "We've found common ground for an alliance, haven't we?" And Smith nodded, confirming her assessment.

Felix wet his lips. Double or nothing. "The murder," he said. "The Otherkin girl."

Jane hadn't expected him to know. It showed in the faint relaxation across her cheeks, the slight flattening of her smile. "What do you know?"

"Something for nothing, Jane?"

Her hand flicked dismissively, beads rattling on the turn of her wrist. "You want New York. I can't give you New York. It doesn't *like* you anymore, Felix. It doesn't even like me."

"It wouldn't have a choice, would it? If Matthew were gone?"

"Whoa," Don interrupted. "What you're going to say, don't say that. Felix, that's your name? Felix, don't say that."

"I don't mean *murder*," Felix said, tiredly. "More like a sacking. Or a relocation. Jane, I need *something* after the manner of a guarantee."

She thought about it. "Prometheus."

"Yes."

"You still have the ring."

He smiled, and held up his hand.

"Right," she said. "Detective, you should probably go now, unless you plan to arrest somebody, or you have a warrant you haven't happened to show me."

"Oh, no," Smith said. "That dead girl's my problem, Mrs. Andraste. I'm staying right here."

She turned, and frowned. "It's a Fae matter, Detective."

"It's a murder," he said, and crossed his arms.

Felix held his tongue, though the drip of water grew louder in his ears each moment. Finally, Jane snorted, flicked strings of hair from her eyes, and clapped her hands together like Pilate calling for a bowl of water.

"On your head be it," she said, and even Felix almost didn't see the manipulation. "We'll just have to extend your jurisdiction. Donall Smith."

"Yes, ma'am?" Brows beetling over watchful eyes.

"Do you solemnly swear, avow, aver, and affirm that you will uphold justice in the service of humankind, that the Promethean flame of art and science may be evermore preserved in the furtherance of that service, and the sacrifice of the fire-bringer remembered?"

Smith thought it through before he answered, and Felix, for a moment, wasn't sure which way he'd choose. But then his lips thinned and he nodded, slowly, thoughtfully. "To serve and protect? I can promise that. Is that all there is to it?"

"That's all there is to it," Jane said. "Felix, give that ring of yours to Don. I'll get you a new one in a minute. Don, welcome to the Prometheus Club. And now Felix will explain who killed your murder victim. Won't you, Felix?"

So easy. As easy as that. Felix pulled his ring off and slipped it on Don's finger like a wedding band. It fit, just barely, as they always did—despite the size disparity in their hands. "Peryton," he said, over his shoulder to Jane. "A bound one. Fae. I don't have the name of its master yet, but I will."

"How'd you find that out?"

"Because New York doesn't like me anymore doesn't mean I can't hear when I choose to listen. I called up the memory of its shadow in the alley, and its claw marks on a roof nearby. There aren't too many monsters with an eagle's talons and a man's reflection."

"Nothing Matthew couldn't have done."

Felix smiled. "If you hadn't intentionally limited his education. Admit it, Jane. You missed me."

"We need better weapons. We need allies. I have half-trained apprentices, not warriors."

"I beg your pardon," Don said, "but what's a peryton?"

"The soul of a murderer reincarnated as a winged, carnivorous stag," Jane said. "Not a pleasant thing to meet in an alley at night."

"Not pleasant at all," Don said, remembering shredded flesh. "That's what we're up against?"

"No. We're up against its boss. By the way, Felix?"

"Yes?"

"Now that there is a Prometheus Club again, I need a second. For a duel. Or else you may find yourself rather abruptly with a different archmage than you bargained for."

Damn, Felix thought, with dull finality, as the strings snapped taut. Don Smith wasn't the only one who didn't see Jane digging the trap until he tumbled into it.

"How do you feel about a trip to Faerie in the morning?"

Tension flowed from his neck as he finally let go of his luck. "It seems to me that I'm the only man for the job."

Chapter Ten
Devil in Blue Jeans

Michael looked cold. She was standing on a rooftop when Fionnghuala—a white swan skimming through cold rain, over the ice-tipped branches of the trees—found her, her arms crossed and the longer ends of her hair whipped forward in cords around her jaw and throat as wind and wet turned the A-line bob into a plastered cap. Michael stared through netted tree branches that made a stark damp silhouette in the streetlights. Her head was dipped as she watched something at ground level, the line of her neck sloping gracefully, and she didn't seem cognizant of the rain that rolled down her spine and plastered her T-shirt to her bony shoulders. Only her crossed arms gave any hint of discomfort as the rain slid down her face, scattering from her eyelashes each time she blinked.

She stood still as a gargoyle, grim and prescient, poised above her prey. She neither turned nor flinched when the swan's wings folded behind her, and Fionnghuala rose from a crouch, her mantle of white feathers clutched tight at her chest in white fingers. The rain soaked her feathers and draggled her hair in ragged spirals down her cheeks, streaming in rivulets over the pale, naked skin underneath. Unlike Michael's, *her* flesh prickled up in goose pimples, and a shiver rattled her teeth.

"Cold after Hell," the angel said, with the manner of one offering an observation to an empty room. She didn't turn, and her folded arms dropped to her sides, palms against her thighs, smoothing the jut of her shoulder blades under her soaked shirt.

"Cold *as* Hell, I'd rather say," Fionnghuala answered, and came to stand beside the angel. She might look like a skinny girl in a white tank top with the words IT'S ALL MUSCLE printed on the front, but Nuala knew who wore that form, and no one would notice them here. No one would look up and see, as long as Michael stood beside her. Angels passed unnoticed through the world. "Still unsmiling, I see. Is this your storm, then?"

"It is not serving," Michael said. She extended her right hand, a flick of her fingers, the rain tumbling off them. In the street below, two figures entwined, kissing in the shadows at the edge of a streetlight, oblivious to the rain.

"Wouldn't you like to jump down there and put your sword through his heart?"

Michael sighed. "You know the answer to that."

"You don't have to obey."

She turned to glance at Fionnghuala then, her mouth wrenched sideways by an expression that could have been despair, if despair was not a sin. "No one *has* to obey. Lucifer also was an angel once."

Fionnghuala shrugged. "And is His love and regard worth so much?"

"You've been to Hell. You tell me what it's like to live without it." Michael's fingers flicked, significantly, to the street below. "The ones who don't believe are such easy prey."

Fionnghuala peered down. She recognized the man, but not the woman, and she knew from Michael's words what must be transpiring. "Does it matter when they can't be damned?"

Michael turned and gave Fionnghuala an eyebrow, frowning. "You were. And how is it you are out of Hell now? Or come you on Hell's errand?"

"Can't you see my heart, angel?"

"The Lord thy God gave thee free will, creature."

"The Lord my God," Fionnghuala said, "came along a bit after I did. The fact that my story was consumed in His doesn't change what I was before that. And don't play the innocent with me; it was always you who walked among humans. You know us well enough to know that too, Prince of the Presence. Isn't it beneath an angel of the Lord to bait an old woman?"

"Any other old woman, perhaps." Michael never smiled, they said. She hadn't since Lucifer fell. And so Fionnghuala could only call the change in her expression a softening. She turned back to the clinching couple. "You didn't answer my question."

"She'll catch a chill and die in this," Fionnghuala said, the rain freezing on the ends of her hair.

"She won't get cold with *that* one holding her."

Fionnghuala frowned, and tucked her chin into her feathers. "The answer is no, Michael. No, I'm not damned. Damned is different than *sold*, and God does not condemn for acts of pity."

Michael did not answer. Silently, they watched the lovers kiss and break apart, but not too far. The man pulled the woman inside his embrace, and kissed her again. She laughed out loud and clung to him. Michael raised her eyes to Heaven; a stinging curtain of rain froze on Fionnghuala's feathers and melted on her skin, and pelted the lovers below.

Fionnghuala shivered, teeth chattering, huddled under her cloak, and waited. There was more than patience to dealing with angels, but patience was a very good place to start. Ice crackled under her toes as they passed beyond pain and into numbness. Roof gravel bit the soles of her feet.

"What does Lucifer want?" Michael asked, finally, after five hard minutes of rain. Warmth cupped Fionnghuala's shoulders, living feathers over the frozen feathers of her swanmay's cloak. She leaned into it gratefully, protected by a curve of broad jade-colored plumage, Michael's wing like a heron's.

"Forgiveness," she said.

Michael snorted and drew her under the one arched wing. She was cold and clammy beneath her cloak. It wasn't Lily who needed to worry about catching her death. "It's his for the asking."

"He doesn't think he's the only one at fault." She shrugged, and found herself dry and warm. "He has his pride."

"And pride goeth before a fall." Michael peeked at the swanmay sideways, and accidentally met her eyes.

She didn't flinch. She smiled.

The angel's eyes flared warm and green through the tangled briars of her hair. "Pride is the one thing He won't contend with," Michael said. "His word is law. He doesn't compromise."

"I know," Fionnghuala answered. Under the shelter of Michael's wing, she lifted her hair from the collar of her cloak and spread it out to dry in netted tangles. The couple were still kissing in the street, as if they enjoyed the storm and the cold. "And the Morningstar has never mastered the art of humility. You know, though—He'd get on better with people if He negotiated once in a while."

"That's what the stories are for," Michael said. "You may tell the Prince of Lies that his message has been received, and will be considered." Reaching out, she darkened the streetlight over the lovers' heads with a *pop* and a shatter of glass.

Matthew had never seen the Dragon face-to-face. On television, on the news in the days leading up to the Promethean assault on Faerie, he had seen the images over and over until, like an Escher print, they lost their value as representation and only the pattern remained. But by the time the Dragon descended on Times Square, he had been in Faerie.

If he had stayed in New York, it would have been different. If he had stayed in New York, with Jane, he would have been in Times Square. He would have seen the Dragon.

If he had stayed in New York, Faerie would have fallen, and Weyland Smith's hammer could have done nothing to prevent it.

He watched Morgan walk away—toward the woods rather than toward the Queen—her dogs trotting at her heels, and her raven winging ahead, and he sighed. Geoff waited until the sound of gravel crunching faded, and rubbed his nose with the back of his knuckle. "You two've got history, I take it?"

"No," Matthew said, without looking away from the witch's retreating back. "Not as such. Do you hear that?"

Whatever it was, Geoff didn't. But he followed Matthew anyway, as the Mage set off in pursuit of Morgan le Fey like a hound on the trail of a rabbit. "What are we listening to?" he asked, hustling to keep up. Matthew wasn't particularly tall, but he could move when he put a mind to it.

They hastened along the pale gravel path side by side with their coats belled out by their speed. What Matthew had heard—hoofbeats crunching gravel—was soon clear enough to everyone in the garden, as a man's head and a horse's ears appeared over the hedges and flower beds. They came into the clear a little beyond Morgan, who paused in the path with arms spread wide as if to make wings of the sleeves of the gown she was not wearing.

Old gestures betray us. Matthew caught up to the witch and her dogs before he stopped, Geoff just a step and a half to his left. He knew the horse, but not the man in a bard's bright, waterlogged cloak—although the ring on his left pinky finger was familiar, and something about the cast of his features was more than accustomed, like the face of someone known as a child grown to manhood.

Morgan let her hands fall just as Matthew added another thought: *She makes it seem that we heel like the hounds.*

"Kind Kit," she said, reminding Matthew of an emissary of Hell named Murchaud and a conversation on a sidewalk in New York. He knew who this had to be—thinner, ten years older than in the famous portrait, his beard redder than his hair.

"Morgan," Christopher Marlowe answered, and bowed stiffly from Kelpie's back. "And thy companions, my queen?"

Morgan glanced over her shoulder, an artless turn of her head shifting hair that had come unbraided. "Sir Christofer," she said. "May I present Matthew Szczegielniak, a Magus of the Prometheus Club. And Geoffrey Bertelli, a mortal man. Matthew and Geoffrey—"

"Sir Christopher Marlowe," Matthew said, swinging wide around Morgan's red hound. "The knighthood came in Faerie, I presume? And you wearing one of the archmage's rings."

"Are you her second, then?" Kit said. He pushed damp hair from his eyes before swinging a leg over Whiskey's rump and sliding down his side. He dusted his hands on his soggy cloak and extended the right one to Matthew, cautiously. Whiskey stood silent and stern as a blue-eyed statue behind him, his knees oozing blood from a hatch-work of shallow cuts. Kit continued, his hand hovering in midair, "You arrived in better time than I had anticipated. My apologies, sir Mage, to have kept you waiting. I made what haste I could."

"Second? No," Matthew said. He held up his right hand by way of apology and saw Marlowe's eyes widen. It was a measure of his day that he found himself standing in a garden in Faerie, making small talk with Kit Marlowe, and his chief thought was embarrassment that he could not shake the man's hand. "I've had nothing to do with her in years. . . . Sir Christopher?"

"Aye, Matthew Magus?" The poet took his hand back, tilting his chin up to examine Matthew with a wicked humor in his squint. He turned briefly to Geoff, but whatever he saw didn't hold him, and his gaze settled on Matthew again.

"You're implying you've challenged Jane Maga? To a duel?"

Marlowe smiled, sharp and sweet and utterly disingenuous, and Morgan le Fey began to laugh. "And neglected to arrange for seconds, I take it? Where are you going to find one on such short notice, Kit?"

Marlowe looked down at his hands, and then gave her a wider, slyer grin. "I'd thought to ask a certain sorceress of my acquaintance."

She was going to refuse. Matthew knew it as clearly as if it were spelled out in city signs and portents. With a sick sense of inevitability, he stuffed his hands into his pockets and said, "I'll do it, Sir Christopher."

Kit jerked as if shocked. "You know me not."

"Only by reputation," Matthew said. "But I know Jane."

They regarded one another. The gaze stuck, and held, and Marlowe nodded once. "So be it."

"Well," Morgan said briskly, "that would solve the Promethean problem. Welcome back from Hell, Kit." Stepping forward, she leaned down and kissed him quickly on the mouth. Then she settled back on her heels, crossed her arms, and glared up at the piebald stallion. "And you, water-horse? What *have* you done to your knees?"

The animal nickered, ears settling forward. "You should see the other guy," he said, a strange deep mellifluous voice to come from an animal's throat. Matthew bit his lip hard against comparisons to Mr. Ed, and when he looked down, he saw Geoff doing the same.

Until Marlowe slapped his hands on his thighs and said, "Aye, she walked away without a scratch," and gave them both an excuse to laugh.

He was a man who knew his audience too. He waited for the chuckles to die and turned back to the witch, and crossed his arms over his chest. "Well, Morgan," he said, "aren't you going to introduce me to our Queen?"

For the second day in a row, Lily woke up smug, clean, and not the least bit sorry. Christian's white cotton sheets smelled of copal and frankincense. She rolled over and slid an arm around his waist, pressing her face into his disarrayed hair, inhaling his aroma: salt, sweat, and warm human animal.

He murmured something unintelligible and leaned into her arms, turning his head to face her. "Good morning, sunshine," she answered, and kissed him, trying to spare him her morning breath until he wrapped his arm around her neck and pulled her down for something a little more lingering and thorough.

"How did I get so lucky?" she asked, when he let her go.

"I don't think it's luck," he said, arranging himself to make a pillow of her shoulder. "I think it's power finding its time. I think we were looking for each other."

"Okay, Faerie magic is one thing. But do you really believe in all that giggly new-age stuff?"

"I own a magic shop," he answered. "I'm not a *complete* hypocrite. Yes, I really believe. And I can show you some of it too. You have the potential to be very powerful."

Another time, and she would have laughed. But there was a certainty in his voice that was different than Moira's cloying need to *be* somebody special, or Jason's pedantry. So she stroked his hair off his forehead and said, "Then show me."

The sun drifting through Christian's batik curtains seemed to dim a little as he sat up, the sheets sliding down his belly. Light trickled through his hair, haloing the edges gold. He turned, cross-legged, and the house encircled and drew close around them, as if leaning in. *Interested*. It had seen other lovers in its weary mortal years, but these two, with their secrets and the runnels of life so vivid under their skins — they were intriguing.

Christian laced his fingers together, palms out, backs toward his chest, and exhaled a painstaking breath. And on that breath, the sheets slithered off her body and Lily floated into the air. "Christian!" she yelped, and thrashed and clutched at his hands. He caught her, steadied her—sitting tailor-fashion in midair now, nude as an angel—and held her hands lightly, firmly, in his own. "Breathe. Think about breathing."

She obeyed, focusing her attention away from the tickle of vertigo in her belly and the cool air currents caressing her buttocks and thighs. "I'm flying." Her voice was self-consciously level, but her hands grew sweaty in his grip.

"You're levitating," he answered. "Flying requires wings. Do you believe me now?"

"Will you drop me if I say no?"

She *did* mean it as a joke, a transitory smile breaking through her lip-bitten concentration. "Now do it on your own," he said, and loosened his grip but didn't pull back his hands.

"Whoa!" she yelled, and grabbed again when she started to rock in midair. "Don't *do* that." More giggles followed hard on the demand, bubbling out of her depths, only slightly hysterical. He already felt the strength in her answering, the core of energy learning by his example, ready to follow, ready to *learn*.

He smiled.

He hadn't had one like this in a long time.

"How?" she asked. The air was cold. Her hair was cold on her neck, still a little damp where she'd slept on it, and gooseflesh bristled the hairs on her arms and legs so she felt the breeze more now, the air stirring over her skin.

"Relax," he said. "If you fall, you fall on the bed, and I won't let you hurt yourself. Okay?"

"Okay." She shivered, but held herself steady. She closed her eyes and took three deep breaths, and without opening them again said, "I'm as relaxed as I'm going to get, Christian."

"All right," he said. "What you need to do is feel that power in you. That euphoria. Do you have it?"

"I think so."

"Do you *know*?"

Lily listened. The sunlight glowed flesh-red through her eyelids, her body rocking on air currents and the force of Christian's will. She remembered his kiss, the rain pouring over them that should have chilled her to the bone and had felt like a baptism instead, washing her skin, washing her soul. There was something like that down there, something potent as the sunlight and cleansing as that rain, a restless energy. "I know," she said, because she did.

"Then know this," Christian said. He almost didn't sound like Christian; his voice was deeper, more mellifluous. She leaned toward it, sightless in the radiance. "That power is your birthright, Lily. Thou art God, and it doesn't take a sevenfold kiss to make you so—only your own decision as to which rules you will and won't choose to abide by. And the law of gravity is one of those rules."

She cracked an eye, squinting through her lashes, her face laced with shadows from the wild snarls of her hair. "Roadrunner physics, Christian? Magic's one thing. *God* is another."

"Why do you think the Church forbids it?" he said, his voice mocking and reasonable, all at once. "If you knew what you were, you wouldn't need them to talk to God for you. You'd know where to find him whenever you wanted. But there's a price. And so you choose to accept their judgment that you are poor little children. Not gods, not angels. Sheep in need of a shepherd, and about as smart and moral as sheep, as well: can't even be trusted to do what's right because it's right. No, it's God and the Church holding the devil over your heads like a housewife on Valium squeaking, 'Wait 'til your father gets home!' "

"Christian!" She swayed, shaking. A draft rustled through the gabled bedroom, and she rocked in midair, her breath quickening to a moan. Her hands flexed, big hands that creaked his knuckles as he held on tight. "Don't *yell* at me."

"I wasn't yelling," he said, but softened his voice. "I was explaining. But if you want this power, you have to take responsibility for it. You need to put that *childishness* down right now. You have free will. You have freedom of choice. 'Do as thou wilt shall be the whole of the law.' Can you be trusted to make your own bed and take out your own trash, or do you need God shaking his stick at you?"

"I don't know," she said, her eyes wide open. She swallowed, but settled back into place and eased her bone-aching grip. "If everybody just did what they wanted—"

"Grown-ups," he said, "also do what they *should* do. Without being told. What they *should* do, even when it's not what they're *supposed* to do. Even when they get punished for it. Grown-ups don't need to be threatened to get their chores done."

"You don't think it's . . . condescending . . . to say that anybody who acknowledges a higher power is an undisciplined brat? That's more judgmental than I expected of you. . . ."

He smiled. "Not at all," he said. "But I think we can do better for a God than one that's paternalistic and suffocating, don't you? Leave that one for the angels. They're into being told what to do. Now let go of my hands, Lily, and hold yourself up."

She set her jaw and jerked her hands back all at once—and flopped onto the bed like a landed fish, laughing until she choked, giddy unto hysteria. He pulled her tight and kissed her neck and stroked her back, his body warm and smooth in her arms.

"Well, I fucked that up," she said, when she stopped coughing. She lay under him, panting, her hands clenching and unclenching on the sheets.

"Nonsense," he said, and kissed her mouth this time. "You're doing great. Come on. Let's try it again."

"Sure," she said. "Just let me go pee and take my pills."

A smiling man dressed for a dinner party wandered through the bright November afternoon, twirling a silver seal-headed cane and tipping his hat to the ladies, unaware that a shadow tracked him. Padding on lynx feet, tasting the air with a serpent's tongue, flittering across walls and tree trunks on a spider's eight bristled legs, it moved unremarked, without hesitation, through the park. Its eyes watched Bunyip from the shade of every withered leaf and blade of grass, a bee-vision kaleidoscope that would have dizzied most.

Custom can inure one to stranger things.

When the crowds thinned and the evening cooled, Bunyip tucked his cane under his arm and drifted west as if headed home along with everyone else. He passed under a sere wooden wisteria arbor on the Lake's southwest edge and paused to catch a glimpse of shoebox towers like God's own dominos lined up beyond the treetops, hazy in the failing light. Those haunting shadows coalesced, and when he turned back, a running woman caught his attention and he turned to watch her go.

Too much temptation. And she was already running. What predator could resist?

He never seemed to move much faster than a stroll, but her strides opened no distance between them as he followed her over grass and through rustling leaf litter, down a slope to the western bridle path. Her black braids bounced and her footfalls thudded dully on the packed clay trail, echoing from fern-hung boulders as she came up on the rustic Rift-stone Arch, in the shadow of the Dakota but concealed from its view by high embankments. She trotted under the bridge, vanishing in blue twilight, her running shoes squelching in mud.

The perfect place, and *now* Bunyip hurried. He wanted to catch her under the gray mica schist, press her back on rough stones and taste her fear for a moment or two, feel the rumble of her heart in her chest. He wondered if she was brave enough to feel her death or if her pulse would stop when he touched her, like a fist-clenched bird's.

He undulated forward, mud cold and slick under his belly, his clawed flippers churning broad tracks alongside the smooth curve pressed by his abdomen. A sharp thrust, a crashing lunge after her fleeting shadow in the dimness. He called out, a weird bitternlike wail that crashed and reverberated in the confined tunnel to startle and confuse her. She turned, crouched, hands raised before her face.

She did not look afraid.

A cabled shape writhed underfoot and snapped around him in brusque convulsive flexion. The coils wrapped hard, a king cobra's man-thick body wrought of shadow and glamourie twisting, thrashing him to the ground. Scales rasped scales, belly to belly, scraped, scarred, slid. He thumped and rolled, flippers scrabbling mud and shadow-stuff, slashing as they'd slash flesh. And then he was on his back, stunned with the force of the fall, a woman's small face hovering and her filed teeth smiling while the coils of the shadow-serpent tightened around his neck. Her left hand was uplifted, poised. A glimpse of knapped black-glass blade flecked with pale crystals showed between curled fingers, and something *big* flared shadow-ears like tent flaps behind her and trumpeted mockery.

"D'you think I could steal a Bunyip's shadow?" she asked, in an off-hand manner belied by her own panting breaths. "If I cut it off with my little knife? You're big and strong. But I'm smarter, and sister *ndovo* is stronger, isn't she? So maybe I should just give you the cobra, and the spider bite, and not have to worry about you anymore. Little fishie."

He writhed and snarled. Her coils ground tighter, bending back his scales, tugging his pelt. She'd pinned one flipper in her coils and bound the other with her right hand grown magically powerful, but even the elephant's strength couldn't hold *him* long. She'd been wise to trick him, to catch him off guard and surprised.

He let her think she'd cowed him, and surrendered in her grip. "What do you want, Kadiska?"

"Stop following the water-horse."

"What is *that* to you?"

She reached past him, past his tusks and staring opalescent eyes, and laid the blade of her obsidian knife against the path. It tugged as it pricked his shadow, and he winced. "He belongs to my mistress," she said. Hiss of her breath, warmth of it on his cheek. "And if she ever decides she's done with him, he's mine."

"Oh." She might be strong—just as strong as her sister-shadow, power shrugged around her shoulders—but she was *little*, despite the cobra coils. "That's no path I can walk, Seeker."

"What mean you?"

"I mean he is failing his charge, and if he cannot keep it, then one who *can* will. I carry the word of the Rainbow Snake."

"Assassinate him." A nose-wrinkled snarl.

"Is there another way for power to pass from hoof to hand, in Faerie?" He said it wryly, quietly, and when he saw her lips twitch in answer, he slammed both flippers upward, hurling her back and sideways, toward the hand with the knife. She clutched after him, coils tightening with all her stolen strength, but he had already pulled on his man-guise and slipped free, shoving the coils down and lifting his legs clear, heaving himself to his feet. A twist of thighs and hips and he stood upright, and then shifted again, reared over her, balanced on his flukes like a breaching cetacean, flippers spread wide to embrace and crush her before she could throw her shadow-coils round him again.

He came down like a tsunami, expecting to meet her strength for strength, elephant shadow to elephant seal. But she was gone, rolling away, cat-shadow quick as she somersaulted aside, mud smeared in her braids and down her back, caked clots on her cheek and her thigh. Claw-quick flash of her black knife and a *rip* like caught and shredding skin.

He rolled, reared back and howled, thrashing in the tunnel like a gaffed fish as she skittered away. The shriek rose over the city, rang, resonated, churned, turned heads and shattered windows. Trees swayed, their last shopworn leaves sailing free. Dogs howled on Staten Island. In Jersey City, babies woke crying, and wouldn't be soothed.

Kadiska stood up with Bunyip's black shadow twisting and squirming in her right hand, and watched him contort on the muddy New World clay. He lay still, finally, moaning his pain as Kadiska folded the shadow small and tucked it into the bottom of her pocket, weighing it down with the knife. She folded her arms over her chest, smearing the red elastic of her sports bra with still more mud, and waited until Bunyip was silent.

"Go back to Australia," she said. "There's nothing in New York for you. And another thing. You tell Mist that if she wants Kelpie, she can come and get him herself. And if you want your shadow back"—she smiled, with all her teeth—"you can go and get it from Elaine."

Ian's irritation all but colored the air around him. The Prince paced, ignoring the Kelpie and the Mage and their gathering coterie at the bottom of the garden, stealing sidelong glances at the Merlin and his mother and the girl who stood beside them, so earnest and strangely uncowed.

Ian's place in the court was complex. His father, Keith MacNeill, was the Dragon Prince—the champion touched by the Dragon and doomed to sacrifice and horror, his own life forfeit for the lives of whatever nation he fought for—and his mother, who had been Elaine Andraste MacNeill, was the Queen of the Daoine Sidhe. But the Mebd—Ian's great-grandaunt (and the wife of Elaine's father) who had been Queen before—had named Ian her heir, not Elaine. Elaine's intervention had left Ian more human and Elaine more Fae, and it had spared Ian the embrace of the White-horn Throne.

And cost him his lover, and his daughter. For which he had forgiven her.

Perhaps.

So it wasn't unusual that Ian was irritated and restive in his cold mother's presence. Nor was it unusual to find him pacing, a dark world flung in orbit about her pale, stationary star. But the anxiousness was something new.

"The girl's not that pretty," Cairbre whispered under his breath as Ian swung near. Too soft for the Queen or the Merlin to overhear, and far, far too soft for the girl. But Ian's wolf ears made it plain, and he paused with one foot in the air and set it down slowly. His hands unfolded and fell to his sides, palms turned against his thighs as if to conceal glistening sweat.

The Elf-prince shot the bard a green-eyed stare. "It's not about pretty," Ian murmured. "But why does *she* get to stay and play Barbie-dolls in Faerie, when she hasn't a glimmer of strength?"

"Because she wants to?" Soft, so soft, Cairbre's lips barely moving and the sound no more than a brush of breeze across Ian's neck.

Ian gritted his teeth, the first sharp edge of canines cutting his gums. "That tune's not so pretty in my mother's ears when it's her son that plays it."

Cairbre's hand brushed his elbow, strong as oak sticks. "She is less consistent than another might be, in her place."

"She doesn't love anything. She's the Queen." But either the hand on Ian's arm or spitting out his own venom calmed him, and he managed to settle back against the wall and fold his hands over his arms.

"And you so much want to be King and sit in that chair?" Cairbre's mildness was deceptive. Ian checked, but didn't see mockery on his face, or find it in his scent. To all appearances, he wasn't even looking at Ian. His regard rested on the Queen.

Not quite. But Ian didn't say that. Because he'd managed, suddenly, to put a name to his rage.

"If she's staying, then," he said, "well, let her stay." He stepped forward, passing by Cairbre, and paused before the Queen. He made a bow, and addressed her when she looked down. "Mother."

His curls broke at the nape of his neck, showing pale skin unadorned by a collar, and she reveled in that nakedness before gesturing him to rise. "Are we so formal, then?"

"She's to be of your court?" Ian asked, not so quietly that the mortal girl couldn't overhear.

"What else shall I do with her?" Light, and mocking.

Ian met her gray-green eyes, dark and soft as moss in shadows, and waited for the colors to shift to chocolate and autumn while he bit his tongue. "Give her to me," he said, and refolded his hands.

If she had been the Mebd, her fan would have been open between her fingers, flick-flick-flicking a little wind. But she was Elaine, or she had been Elaine, and her hands stayed curled loosely by her sides. Her high court diction would have told him she mocked, if the frankness of her scent did not. "Do you think that . . . seemly, Ian, my son?"

"What cares the court for seemly?" He rolled one shoulder. "Give her to me. Unless you think I'll misuse her. Unless you think I'm not owed something for what I've lost. Unless you'd rather make her a lady-in-waiting. Waiting for what?"

The Queen angled herself away from Ian, staring over his shoulder. "Did you hear that, Juliet?"

White-lipped, the girl nodded. "What do you want of me?"

Ian turned to look at her. "What are you good for?"

Her smile startled him, white and bright as a wolf's. Ian stepped back at her voice. "I can cut you. Or pierce just about anything you want, if you're not afraid of a little pain."

"She's not pretty," the Queen said, such a sharp echo of Cairbre that Ian laughed.

"I brought her in," he said. It wasn't exactly a lie, and he stared the Merlin down when he said it, as if she would challenge him, but she just tilted her head and smiled, and let her beads swing. The smile on her lips could have meant anything, and that was Carel all over.

Jewels' voice clipped the silence short. "Is *pretty* all you care about?"

"My mother is making an assumption," Ian answered. "Do you want to stay in Faerie, Juliet?"

To her credit, she paused. Her gaze tended sideways, seeking out the boy with the badly dyed hair. "He won't want to," she said. "He doesn't like blood."

"I wasn't asking about him." *And a Fae wouldn't think of him. Iron girl, this land will kill you.* "What do you *want*?"

"To stay." Sharp and flat, and she hadn't paused to think about it, just slapped it down in challenge.

"Not to stay and go? To come back and forth? To go up and down in the world, and see what is good in it and what is not?" Ian felt Cairbre's eyes on him, Carel's, his mother's. It didn't matter. All that mattered was the girl.

"*Can I?*" Just that. *Can I stay and go? Can I travel back and forth?*

"You cannot live here," Ian said, and raised his hand when she would have protested and told him that the Queen had said she could stay. "You can't. Not yet. My mother the Queen has said you can stay, and her word is law. But even her word cannot keep you alive and safe here without power to call your own, Juliet. And when I look at you, I can see that you were born without power. Faerie will destroy you."

She shook her head, raising her voice over his. Her hair flowed in wood-pale waves across her shoulders, breaking into stray curls and locks in the wind. "I'm not—"

"*Without power.* And the lies you tell yourself will see you eaten all the faster, here."

"Your mother said I could stay, Y-...Your Grace."

Highness, but he didn't correct her.

"It was what you wanted," the Queen said, with a tip of her head as Jewels turned toward her in supplication. "But Ian is probably right. I promised permission to stay, Juliet. Not protection. If you cannot protect yourself, you will not live."

There is always more than one test. Jewels swallowed, and settled the bubble of fear in her gut. "But if you give me to ... to Prince Ian?"

"I'll protect you," he said. "And you'll serve me."

"And you'll teach me?" Fine and defiant.

He smiled. "I won't forbid you to learn."

Her pause was long. She peeked at Carel. Carel spread her hands. "I know somebody who could teach you a little of the old religion. It would be a start."

Of course she could. She might speak quietly, but a wolf's ears could hear even what the Merlin whispered into her phone.

Another silence, this one soft and pregnant. Jewels sucked her lower lip into her mouth and rolled it between her teeth. An unattractive habit. Cairbre laid his mandolin aside and smiled. "Well, Juliet Gorman? It's a rare thing you're offered, permission to walk into the mortal realm and then back out again. It's not something he'll extend to you twice. I'll promise you that."

She turned the other way, a flash of light in her eyes, and found Geoff, walking toward her, a rose stem in his hand. His face transformed when she smiled at him, and she looked quickly down. "My Prince," she said, "I accept your terms."

She lifted her slight chin and smiled shyly. Ian breathed deep on the rush of relief sliding through him. He'd won. A brief match, and one that the Queen hadn't cared to fight him on. Or Carel, or Morgan, for that matter. He'd won the girl.

She was just a girl. Alive or dead, it shouldn't matter. But it did. He pitied her, in his foolish human heart.

And the *power* of standing up to his mother and having her agree to his choices mattered more.

Yes, Ian thought, as he glanced over his shoulder and winked at Cairbre. *Yes. I want to be King.*

Chapter Eleven
The Gypsy Laddie

As the sun set and a moon like a Spanish doubloon usurped its place in the sky, the scent off the gardens shifted and sweetened, jasmine and honeysuckle replacing the almost-rancid richness of rose. Eternal day gave way to endless sunset, soft blue twilight laid over everything, and then—sudden as a set change—there was moonlight and an indigo velvet sky rich with stars, like no sky Jewels or Geoff had ever seen.

Dinner revealed another manner in which the Queen was unlike her predecessor. Kit in particular had expected they would make their way inside to grace the long tables in the Great Hall. He had been rather wickedly looking forward to finding where he sat in the Queen's estimation: above the salt, or below it. But the new Queen was as American as she was Fae, and she summoned the page Wolvesbane and had platters and plates and more chairs and small tables brought out to the patio, where they could dine alfresco, cooled by the evening breeze.

It was a pleasant change, much like Faerie after Hell. Not that the games here were any cleaner, but flowers and soft music were an improvement over any devil's taste in decor. Not that Faerie wasn't *also* Hell, after its own peculiar fashion, but the Queen's chosen exile from God was more humane than Satan's, or even Lucifer's.

Morgan had a subtle hand in the table arrangements. If Kit had been willing to dance as led, he would have found himself sitting with Cairbre and Geoffrey—whose name reminded him of another Geoffrey entirely, so that he wondered what had become of his old acquaintance—but instead he managed to arrange a conversation between the boy and the elegant-necked woman who they said was Merlin the Magician, and excuse himself to the place at Morgan's table that Morgan had intended for Carel.

He seated himself there, Whiskey on his left hand and Matthew on the right, and Morgan directly across, while the Queen sat with Jewels and her son. An unsubtle manipulation: Morgan would know very well what he was up to. But then, they'd played this game of old, and after answering the Queen's ill-concealed hunger for whatever news of Keith MacNeill that Kit could give her, Kit found he didn't have the heart to sit and look at her. Not when he could see her father in the shape of her mouth, in her arrogant nose, in the powerful bones of her hands.

So he rearranged things to suit himself, to play spoiler both to the interest he suspected Morgan had in the boy Geoffrey and to her cat-and-mouse pursuit of the unexpectedly generous yellow-haired Mage.

Petty spite aside, they needed the time to conspire. Kit wanted to know Matthew Magus before he trusted him to guard his back. Besides, he felt a certain kinship to anyone whom Morgan le Fey was working *that* hard to bed.

Matthew ate awkwardly, the fork in his left hand and the knife pinned under his right thumb. Kit resisted the urge to cut his meat for him, and instead turned to Whiskey. "You are not overmuch interested in your supper, water-horse."

"It does not satisfy," Whiskey said, pushing the peas around his gold-rimmed china plate.

" 'Tis no fault of the chef's." Kit smiled. "Not that I can detect, at any rate. I wish you a better appetite in the future." He sipped his wine. "Matthew Magus, I am curious."

Matthew looked up. It *was* an effort not to stare, and finding himself addressed, he indulged. "Curious as a cat?"

"And as likely to die of it," Kit answered complacently. "I mean not to intrude—"

"Intrude." Matthew snapped his knife across his plate.

"How does a Promethean come to Faerie?"

"I might ask the same of you," Matthew said. His hand ached. He hated eating in public. Every bite was an epic of concentration. He reached for his wine, hoping the alcohol would ease the pain, a little. "But you left us, didn't you?"

"I was expelled," Marlowe said, with a sidewise smile at Morgan, who was applying herself to her plate with apparent unconcern. "At the prick of a knife."

"Mine came on the tip of a unicorn's horn," Matthew answered. "You want to know why I said I'd second you."

"Not to put too fine a point on it," Kit said. Matthew smiled at the pun, only a flicker, but it eased the tightness across Kit's chest. "Yes, of course."

The bread was more manageable. Matthew could hold it well enough right-handed, and butter it with his left. Whiskey was doing something similar, breaking off bits of bread and soaking them in the juices of his meat. "If Jane Andraste weren't archmage, I might have a reason to come back."

"Or lack reason to stay apart?"

"If you prefer." Their gazes crossed, and locked until Morgan cleared her throat.

"Shouldn't your opposite number in this little pavane have sent her dog by now?"

Kit looked up at the moon. "I should think. Unless we're faster than the mortal world today?"

The witch poured wine. "Perhaps he's lost on the borders."

"Perhaps." Kit swirled his wine in crystal, and buried his nose in it: plums and oak, radiant as sunlight on loam.

Morgan toyed with her fork, turning the warm, heavy silver over and over in her hand. "Perhaps you should go look for him, Sir Christopher, if you're so eager."

"Perhaps I will," Kit said. "After dinner."

He enjoyed Whiskey's chuckle. But Matthew pushed his plate away and made as if to rise, his left hand tightening on the arm of his chair. "I'll go. If someone will tell me where I'm likely to meet him and draw me a map. I am your second, after all. And know the forms," he continued, ending Marlowe's interruption before it properly got free of the poet's lips. "Probably better than you do. I've only been to New York recently, not Hell."

But Marlowe's hand, which he had raised, continued out. The poet stared at Matthew's shirt, or maybe at his chest behind it, and half stood to catch the laces at Matthew's collar. Marlowe steadied himself on the table edge while Matthew stood still, allowing the poet latitude to continue his action.

Which appeared to be tugging Matthew's shirt open and staring at his ink. He touched a black line with a fingertip, his skin warm on Matthew's flesh, and drew it back. "There's iron in this."

"That was the purpose," Matthew answered. "It's armor."

"It's more than armor. Morgan?"

She didn't look up from cutting her meat. "Oh, aye, I've seen it. Nice work, no?"

"I know these patterns."

"They're Promethean symbols," Matthew said, stepping out of range of Kit's hand. "You would."

Kit let soft-washed linen slip through his fingers. He shook his head and sank back in his chair. "No, you don't understand. I've worn the like. Painted by the hand of Prometheus himself. Where did you come by those?"

"My brother and I both had them," Matthew answered, hoping Marlowe wouldn't see him shiver. "What mean you . . . I mean, what do you mean, 'the hand of Prometheus himself'?" It was far too easy to get tangled up in Marlowe's archaic diction, especially with everyone else around code-switching.

The voice at Matthew's shoulder that interrupted wasn't exactly a *voice*. It was more like the immediate and vivid memory of someone having spoken, moments before.

:Indeed, Kitten. Whatever do you mean?:

Matthew, trapped between his chair and the table, turned so abruptly that he spilled his wine. Whiskey intercepted the tottering crystal with inhuman speed, crimson splashing his hand and arm. He set the glass back down, and lifted his hand to his mouth to sponge the remaining droplets away with his tongue.

Whiskey knew better than to look up and meet the Morningstar's star-blue gaze.

Matthew was not so well-versed. And in fairness, didn't know who he was dealing with at first. He looked, and caught his breath at the shadow-crowned beauty of the being who confronted him. Someone stood at heel on the stranger's left; Matthew barely noticed him.

:Sir Christofer, Queen Morgan, Kelpie,: the entity continued. :I am content to see you all well. And Matthew Szczegielniak. I am pleased to make your closer acquaintance.:

Matthew just managed to shut his gaping jaw. He made a little bow between the table and the chair and stepped free. "You have me at a disadvantage, I'm afraid."

"So he does everyone," Whiskey murmured into his wineglass.

The beautiful stranger twisted the toe of a glossy black boot on pale marble and folded his hands behind him. :If I am not mistaken, my dear Kit was about to offer introductions.:

Matthew's heart quickened when the stranger smiled at him. *Another Elf-knight?* he wondered. And then Kit disentangled himself from the table and stood, and Matthew realized everyone else was standing too—even the Queen—standing silently, as if at attention, having made no sound at all other than the scrape of chairs and the rustle of cloth. And Matthew also now realized he knew the man who hovered at the stranger's left hand like a coursing dog about to slip the leash.

"Felix," Matthew said, rolling his shoulders under his jacket to make the talismans jingle. He wore his city on his back like a snail. Felix he could handle. One-handed or two. "Sir Christopher, I would hazard a guess that your enemy's second has arrived. Did you retrieve him at the border, sir . . . ?"

The angel smiled. :Morningstar will do. Unless there's another name you prefer, Matthew Magus. I have so many. Kit?:

"Of course, introductions," Kit said, stepping close enough to feel the warmth of the devil's radiance. "Lucifer Morningstar, Matthew Magus. I hope you don't expect me to believe that timing was coincidence, old Snake."

:I love your pet names, Kitten.: Caressing, as if he meant it. A lover's tones.

Felix smiled and turned his ring with his thumb, and said nothing that his folded hands couldn't say for him.

Kit forced a laugh. "Matthew, forgive me when I say that I hope very dearly that you two do *not* get along."

:Nonsense,: Lucifer said. :We're going to be tremendous friends. Matthew, my hopes are simpler than Kit's. *I* hope you'll permit me to examine your hand?:

"My hand?" Matthew could hear the thick stunned stupidity in his own voice.

:The ruined one,: Lucifer said, as Felix hung behind him, a pilot fish off the stern of a shark. :Perhaps we can make it beautiful again.:

Matthew caught Kit's warning glance, sharp enough that it cut the seductive sapphire haze of Lucifer's regard. "Thank you," Matthew said. He pushed his glasses up his nose with his thumb. "I'd just as soon not owe you that."

Lucifer sighed and winked over Matthew's shoulder at Kit, lifting his shoulders and letting them fall again under black velvet. It was the most beautiful, negligent gesture Matthew had ever imagined. :What's one thing, more or less?:

"Still," Matthew answered, with a shrug of his own, a far less lovely, more awkward one.

:Yes, still.:

That breathtaking smile. Literally. Matthew had to stare down at his shoes to get air in past the pain that filled his lungs when he tried to look the Devil in the eye. Something warm pressed his shoulder: Marlowe, unexpectedly, standing beside him like a brother warrior.

Lucifer's smile caressed Marlowe as well, and Matthew felt him shudder. It didn't feel like a shudder of pain.

:As you wish, Matthew Magus. For now, then, I've brought you Felix Magus, who was lost along the way. So if you will forgive my haste, I must be about the errand I delayed to fetch him. Good day.:

The Devil excused himself with a faint, gracious bow, clean of any hint of mockery, and turned toward the waiting Queen. And Felix Luray stepped forward, extending his right hand exactly as if he'd forgotten that Matthew couldn't accept it, and said, "Do I have the honor of addressing the second of Christoferus Magus, late of London?"

Matthew squared his shoulders and nodded, and didn't bother to show Felix his hand. "Yes, Felix. You know that you do."

❀   ❀   ❀

A traditional ratatouille takes time, and there are just enough burners
on the average stove to manage it. When the dish is constructed *classi-
cally*, the eggplant, zucchini, and green pepper are cooked individually,
and added to a rustic tomato, garlic, and onion sauce only at the end of
preparation, to allow the flavors to meld without muddling. The dish is
seasoned with *herbes du Provence*: basil, fennel, lavender, marjoram, rosemary, savory, tarragon, and thyme.

Gypsy looked upon cooking as a ritual.

Which is to say, his interest was more practical than ceremonial, and
he was willing to sacrifice liturgy to pragmatism. He started with one
pan, heavy-bottomed and well-oiled, not cast iron—because of the acid
in the tomatoes—but copper-clad steel. As the oil heated, filling his
kitchen with the memory of seven thousand Cretan summers, he sliced
onions, no motion wasted.

The oil shimmered in the pan, and when he glanced into the bottom,
he scryed those summers: sunlit lads in fierce competition, their bodies
gleaming with Homer's "liquid gold"; Solomon and David; sun, stone,
drought, silence, and solitude; the olive-crowned heads of athletes and
warriors; Athena's stern, helmed countenance.

With both hands, Gypsy shoveled sliced white onions in and stirred
them with a long-handled oaken spoon. The visions vanished in a hiss
of piquant steam and a few drops of oil spattered the white and green
tile backsplash. Onion for autumn, onion for healing. He lowered the
heat: a sauté, not a sizzle. Garlic next, when it wouldn't burn, its pun-
gent raw scent mellowing to sweetness as it melted into the gilding
onions. Exorcism and relief from nightmares. A spell to keep witches at
bay. He smiled, appreciating the irony, as he brushed papery skins into
the compost bucket and wiped his blade.

His knife was good steel, with a black wooden handle, sharpened
until the blade slid through the crisp flesh of bell peppers without a
whisper of resistance. He only had one knife.

He only needed one.

Peppers in, cooking gently so there would be no bitterness. And then
the tomatoes, out of the sink in the colander where he'd left them drain-
ing. The coring and scalding and peeling could be done in advance.

Summer was over, so he opened a can of tomato paste and added two spoonfuls for the flavor. Wolf-apples, deadly nightshade's sweeter brother, gift from the Americas to the world. Olive oil floated in rose-tinted lenticular dots on the lightly simmering surface as the tomatoes melted. Salt and pepper. He brought herb bottles down from a cabinet well-removed from the stove, where he kept them in darkness to compensate for the ridiculous clear glass.

Before the herbs, a taste. Too much acid, so he added a pinch of sugar—brown sugar, to sweeten the tongue. And then he opened the jars one at a time, and measured into his palm.

Basil, to summon scorpions—although probably not in Massachusetts, whatever Pliny said—and to ensure prosperity. Fennel—he crushed it in his ceramic mortar before sprinkling it into the pot—for sweetness and cleansing. Fennel, too, to drive off witches. Gypsy chose to interpret that as malign magic, a symbol of witchcraft rather than witches per se.

Besides, he was fond of fennel.

Lavender, rolled between his fingers before he laid it in three gentle sweeps across the surface of the sauce. Lavender, sharp and sweet, the blossoms releasing their acrid, musty scent when he crushed them. Lavender for peace, for purification. Lavender for dreamless sleep, and thyme for purification too, purification and courage and protection and the powers of the mind: each one another pass of Gypsy's knotty left hand.

He sang as he cooked, sock-footed in his kitchen, standing in the angle between the chipped enamel face of the gas stove he'd salvaged from a condemned house in Woonsocket and the pine-green painted cabinets with the slightly crooked doors he'd cut and hung himself. It would do for an incantation.

After thyme he added the savory—mental powers again—and the marjoram, for protection and health. And then rosemary, rolled between both palms to break the needles, silver-gray, redolent of summer and hope and pine. Rosemary for remembrance, rosemary for youthfulness, rosemary for all things honest and true. Rosemary to bind and rosemary to ward. Rosemary over the crib to fend the Fae away.

He scattered the crumbled leaves across the sauce, and stirred gently. Nothing left now but the tarragon, which he bought fresh because it lost its flavor in the jar. It would go in at the end, after the rest of the vegetables, but he stripped it from the stems and chopped it now, his knife glittering in the overhead light.

There was no magic in tarragon. Oh, some hardy souls would say it was cleansing or soothing, for polishing chalices or banishing unwanted obstacles, for averting the bites of venomous things. It had none of these powers. Gypsy suspected that to say otherwise was pity for the nervous, woody little plant with no virtue but sweetness.

There was no magic in tarragon. But it tasted good, and he inhaled its licorice aroma as he swept it from his cutting board into a bowl, for now, humming another verse. No history, no images shimmered over the blue and white rice-grained ceramic as he turned his attention to the zucchini and the aubergines.

There was no magic in tarragon. Its French name was *esdragon*, the little dragon, from the Latin *dracunculus*. Gypsy pushed the floating pieces of eggplant and green squash down in the sauce with the back of his spoon, sampled the sauce one more time, and covered the pot to wait while it cooked on down.

The spell was a ward, a come-hither, a simple thing meant to protect and bring trust, ease communication. It worked like the charm that it was. The heavy old harvest-gold phone rang before he had finished cooking. He answered on the second ring. "Hello, Autumn."

"Dammit." She laughed. "I know you don't have caller ID on that old rotary dial—"

"Magic," he said, and then laughed and spoke before she could realize she had had no reason to call him. "Hey, as long as you're on the line, are you and Carel doing anything for dinner tonight?"

"Tonight?" He heard a rustle as she sat up straighter in her chair. She might have been dozing over the paper. "No, um, I mean, Carel's not home yet. And I was just contemplating making supper out of an orange and a bag of Doritos, actually."

"Well, don't do that," he said. "I made stew and bread, and I have nobody to help me eat it. My date stood me up. So what do you say? I'll be over in about an hour."

"You don't have to ask me twice," she said, and laughed at him when he made quick excuses to get off the phone.

He'd noticed something, when she'd dropped by Moira's house the night before to talk to Moira about the friend of Carel's who might be interested in the coven. Something new. He'd always liked Autumn. She was a tough girl, in a crunchy-granola sort of way. But one thing she'd never had was any real power.

Gypsy'd been able to see power, intermittently after a sun dance on one hot North Dakota day in 1975, and consistently since the Dragon. And Autumn had never owned any of her own, though she'd carried a faint nimbus like glitter-dust on her skin, brushed off from Carel.

But now . . . It still wasn't power. Not *her* power, anyway. But now looking at her made his scars warm, and he had to *know*: what she'd seen, where she'd found it.

Whether it had changed her.

He bundled the stew into the car, still in its big enamel pot. Autumn didn't have a woodstove like Moira's, but she had a warm and cozy kitchen, with a big oven for heating the bread and the ratatouille in its blue-flecked enameled pot. It shouldn't take long; the stew retained a lot of heat, despite transport.

Autumn made honey-butter with a hand whisk while Gypsy set the table with mismatched stoneware bowls she'd bought in Provincetown. He ought to have felt guilty. But he could still see the aura, something else's power like a scatter of snow on her shoulders, and her air of distraction had thickened.

There was nothing wrong with buying a little insurance.

When she turned around and brought the honey-butter to the table, Gypsy took advantage of the opening to rescue the bread from the oven, using a pair of tea towels to protect his hands. He set it on the cutting board and fetched out the ratatouille while Autumn went to find a bottle of wine in the rack down in the cellar, then spooned the stew carefully into the bowls.

The one he'd picked for himself was rough and unfinished on the bottom, the artist's name pin-scratching the palm of his hand. The glaze was a rich variegated blue that had feathered cloudy white. The flaws added to the beauty; it was a shame to cover it with food.

He sat down to wait as Autumn came back up the creaking stairs into the kitchen, a waft of cool, moister air following her. She set the wine bottle in the sink and wiped the dust off. Gypsy got up and handed her the corkscrew from the rack beside the fridge before she reached for it. "What did you pick?"

"A Pinot Noir. I should have opened it sooner, but I suppose it can air out in the glass as well as anywhere."

"Heathen," he said, cheerfully, and pulled two wineglasses out of the hutch.

"If I wasn't, we'd all be in trouble." She worried the cork from the bottle and laid it aside, joining him at the table a moment later. She lifted the glasses out of his hand one at a time to pour. "So this must be a new girlfriend?"

"Pardon?" Gypsy paused, the bread knife in his hand.

"Nobody who'd *eaten* your cooking would stand you up," she said. She took her seat as he sliced the bread, and held out her hand for the heel. The aroma of rosemary, garlic, and olive oil steamed from the cut surface, filling the kitchen, and she sighed and breathed deeply, closing her eyes. "Not that I'm complaining of the errors of others by which I benefit."

Gypsy dipped a knife in the honey-butter and smoothed it over the rough crumb of the bread. Not enough milk, a little too much oil. He chewed slowly, an excuse not to talk. Autumn's silence as she dug in to the ratatouille was gratifying.

"You should open a restaurant," she said, when she paused in her methodical eating long enough for a sip of wine. "I bet you hear that all the time."

"I thought about it," he said, cutting himself another slice of bread. Autumn had the good honey. "But who wants to work that hard?"

"I own a nursery," she said, with a dry halfway laugh. "I'm the wrong one to ask."

"So what should I be asking?" He stretched his feet under the table, sock heels slipping on worn linoleum. The warm draft from under the refrigerator blew across his toes. "Carel's not really in Texas, is she?"

She stopped with a slice of bread halfway to her mouth. "Setup," she said.

"You wound me."

She didn't laugh. Her hand trembled as she balanced the piece of bread on the rim of her bowl. "Gyp—"

"I can *see* something's wrong, Autumn. Ever since you and she got together, there have been things you haven't been telling anyone. I worry." He gave detailed attention to the movements of his fork as he teased out a cube of eggplant and speared it through. "I'm just looking to be a friend."

She grinned stiffly and gulped wine. And sat back in her chair, loose joints in the wood complaining, and folded her arms. "What's in the ratatouille?"

"Eggplant, zucchini, tomatoes, and *herbes du Provence*." He answered with his mouth full, and took another bite. "And a small blessing. Pocket-sized."

"Uh-huh." But she picked up her fork again. The seduction of good food, and warm company. "You wouldn't believe the truth if I told it to you."

"I do believe in Faeries. What else do you need?"

"Hah!"

"Autumn." He let his fork clink on the edge of the bowl as he rested it. "Look. You're shedding fairy dust every time you move and you're obviously worried sick about Carel. And whatever else you've got going on. Would it kill you to tell me?"

"Well, Carel might." But she didn't close the door any tighter than that. Instead, she kept eating, and got up for seconds when she reached the bottom of the bowl. He was right. She could push it aside all she wanted, dig trees until the cows came home, work her hands blistered—and she would still be left standing helplessly on the sidelines, the princess in the tower, while Carel rode off to a war she couldn't even describe.

Autumn did not fancy herself a Penelope.

Standing before the stove, her back toward Gypsy, she closed both hands on the pull bar of the oven and sighed. "Funny you should mention Faeries," she said.

She turned, hands crossed behind her back, and leaned on the oven door. Gypsy watched her, letting his arms fall to the table. "Don't set yourself on fire."

"The burners are off." She took a deep breath, tasting it, and let it out again. "Hell, Gyp. Have you ever seen a unicorn?"

It is not many times in one's life that one can count upon the Devil to make obeisance. But there he was, kneeling before the Queen, shadows a circlet on his golden hair. She touched his shoulder, where a wing should have been, and bid him rise.

"You don't actually come in supplication," she said as he rose to his feet, so close she could feel the breeze his body made uncoiling.

He bent over her hand, brushed it with his lips, and stood, lips quirk-ing. :The forms must be observed.:

"Must they?"

:If not us, who? Your mother sends greetings, Your Majesty.:

"She would." The Queen began walking, bringing him along with a gesture. She glanced over her shoulder and caught Carel's eye. The Merlin moved forward, falling into step at the Queen's left hand as Lu-cifer did on her right. "And you are nothing but her messenger? I find that unchancy."

His smile was unbearable. She would have glanced away from its brightness, but she was Queen. Instead, she lifted her chin and smiled in return. She had felt worse pain, now and again.

:Angels have always been messengers, Your Majesty. Don't I seem a common sort of errand boy to you?:

The Queen could almost stop her hands from shaking. "An uncom-mon one, maybe —"

"Then let's have the message." Carel, more plainly than the Queen would have dared, for after all she owed Lucifer no fealty now. Keith had settled that debt forever.

:The Prometheans think they own me, Mistress Merlin. They also think they own *Him*.: Polite as the very devil, not to say the name of the Divine in Faerie.

"And are they right?" Carel's earrings spun as she flipped her braids over her shoulders. She had long, strong fingers, lightly fleshed over the bones.

:After a fashion.: Something flashed behind him, a sweep of white feathers, glazed blue in the moonlight. :Insofar as they work to control all stories. Jane Maga wished you to know that she does not welcome Fae intrusions into her domain.:

"Hardly a revelation."

The Queen heard it this time, and there could be no doubt from Lucifer's half smile that he did, as well. Carel was defending her; that note in her voice was a flat territorial growl. "And?" the Queen asked.

:If you deliver her the miscreant, along with Master Marlowe and her other runaway Mage, all is forgiven.:

Under the jasmine arbor, the Queen paused. "Did she happen to pass along a reason why I should turn her prodigals over? Or does she expect my filial devotion to carry the day?"

:She said to appeal to your better instincts.:

"There's a lost cause. If I had better instincts, they'd tell me to protect Matthew and Kit, not hand them over for . . . what, reeducation?" The Fae formality slipped into unadorned Midwestern English.

The Queen's steps picked up speed. She lifted her hem to allow herself a swinging stride, out of place in the silver-gilt stiffness of the gown as her face and posture became animated. Carel was not as tall, though more practically dressed. She hurried to keep up.

Lucifer paced them easily. When the Queen turned to him, a stare that layered ice over heat like the core of the sun, he balanced himself to a stop with his wings, unveiling them broad and worthy in the moonlight.

:She offers peace,: the angel said. :She offers an end to the war.:

The Queen stopped so short her gown overbalanced her. Carel's quick hand on her elbow saved her an upset, though it cost her some dignity. She turned, gravel knobby through the soles of her slippers. "A true end. Not a cease-fire."

:Gestures toward an eventual alliance. Promethean and Fae.:

"We've won *out* of your service, Morningstar. Would I blithely walk in again?"

Rose-pink lips caressed the smile thoughtfully before he let it out into the air. :She will rebuild the Prometheus Club, Your Majesty. She's begun doing it already. And though you rule a thousand years in Faerie, you will not reign forever. Think of war. Think of your son.:

"When do I think of anything else?" the Queen asked. Carel's hand tightened on her elbow. She turned, away from Lucifer and his temptations, and glanced back up the path and the sloped flight to the assembled Magi, mortals, and Fae, all of them pretending they were not sneaking glances at the Devil, the Merlin, and the Queen. Marlowe stood apart from the others, arms crossed, one foot kicked up as he leaned on the rail. He was watching Matthew and the English Mage with the graying black hair, their heads bent close, as they argued the terms of the duel. *Can he beat her?*

That was what it came down to. A deal with Jane, or a deal with Marlowe after he defeated her. If he could defeat her.

If the Queen was willing to help him destroy her mother.

Lucifer folded his wings.

"I'll think on it," the Queen said, quietly, turning. She waved both Lucifer and Carel away when they moved to follow her. "Leave me alone," she said. "And send me Whiskey. I'm going for a walk."

Chapter Twelve
I Guess the Lord Must Be in New York City

"You know, Felix," Matthew said, "I haven't thought of you in years." It was a calculated cruelty, the more so for its truth, and Matthew felt a little guilty for not disliking himself more when he could apply it with such precision. "You haven't changed a bit."

Felix rubbed his nose with one finger and offered a pinch-mouthed smile. "If we're indulging in pleasantries, Matthew, the only response I can make is that you have changed rather a lot." The finger flicked left and right, indicating Fae and devils and misplaced mortals. "I'm surprised to find you in such mixed company. What happened to the boy who wanted to see them all dead like the parasites they are?"

"He reassessed his opinion that the iron world was any better," Matthew answered. He pushed his hands into his pockets to hide the way his fingers wanted to tighten, and pretended a relaxed slouch. "And you? I imagine you've been busy? Going up and down in the world, as it were?"

"As it were," Felix answered. He seemed genuinely at ease, amused, while it was all Matthew could manage to keep his own voice from shaking. He didn't *want* to face Jane, even indirectly, and he was already regretting having told Marlowe he'd stand as his second.

On the other hand, it wasn't as if he could have lived with himself if he'd left the poet to face her alone. Sometimes a man had to get involved.

Felix cleared his throat. "Are you with me, Matthew?"

Matthew nodded, forcing his attention back to the conversation at hand. He would rather have been anywhere else. Tilting at windmills. You name it. "Jane's the challenged party," he said. "Choose your damned venue. We'll be there."

"The Arthur Kill," Felix said. "The marine scrapyard."

"Damn," Matthew said. A heck of a choice, and not good for Kit, whose familiarity with modern naval technology might not be strong. He couldn't come up with an immediate reason to dismiss it from consideration, though, and the crumbling ships had been used as a Mage's dueling ground before. "All right. This week." The less time Jane had to prepare, the better.

"Next week," Felix answered. "Think of it as a concession. It will give you time to familiarize your man with the . . . turf. And maybe shake the dust of Faerie off your own boots. *As it were.*"

Matthew glanced at Kit, who stood under the arbor, arms folded, studiously ignoring them. "What's wrong with you, Felix, is that you're too goddamned small and too goddamned smug. You never cared for anything but the power, and it wasn't enough, and now you're like a—a spurned lover, and I'm the other man. And it's twenty years ago now. Let it *go.*"

"You really think I'm motivated by envy? How about justice? Fairness? You only ever wanted *revenge.*"

Matthew took the hit well, he thought, though it stung enough to silence him for a moment. He grabbed a quick breath, and shot back, "You should have been born a Faerie. You'd have fit right in."

"Funny you should say that," Felix answered, cheerfully examining his fingernails. "Considering where I find you."

"Sunday," Matthew said. *I should not let him bait me.*

"Sunday," Felix agreed.

Marlowe hadn't moved in minutes. He stood a little apart from the others, near an immense burgundy-blossomed lilac that embraced the balustrade, shading and scenting one entire corner of the patio. The leathery hearts of its leaves brushed his shoulders, their shadows sharp as blades in moonlight that laid the patio brighter than a candlelit room. The blossoms nodded over his hair, heavy stems echoing his bowed neck. Out of earshot and nearer the wisteria trellis, Matthew and Felix stood closer than they wanted to, the devious breeze that teased a few strands out of Matthew's ponytail powerless against Felix's slicked dark waves.

The table the Queen had occupied was empty. Jewels and Geoffrey sat side by side now, his hand resting on her forearm as if she needed the reassurance more than he did: a blatant lie. Jewels leaned against him, upper arms brushing, but her attention was firmly fixed on Ian, whose black-clad form made a knife-cut silhouette against the golden stone of the palace wall. Cairbre crouched beside the bench on which he'd played, packing his mandolin carefully away—thick velvet wrappings inside the hard wooden case—and Morgan and Whiskey still sat at their table, toying with trifle and port as Merlin and the Devil returned. "She wants you," Carel said to Whiskey.

Whiskey nodded and set his napkin aside. Three steps from the table he shifted midmotion, showing Lucifer all the regard he might a fence post, clearing the steps with indifferent power. Lucifer stared after the waterhorse as he cantered in pursuit of his mistress, all collected grace and dignity. Then the Devil looked up and caught Kit watching, tucked a stray curl behind one ear—a picture of innocence—and beckoned. And Kit, squaring his shoulders under his particolored cloak, went before he paused to think if he willed it or not. He felt the eyes upon him as he moved: Felix Luray, Matthew turning in his chiming coat, Carel reaching out to brush his sleeve and letting her hand fall before it clove the silence Kit wore like a cat's bared teeth and prickled fur.

He stopped short, and Lucifer took the last few steps to close the distance between them. :He does not care for my presence in Faerie.:

Kit chuckled and lowered his voice, hoping to keep his words for the angel alone. He felt the strength around his shoulders when Lucifer encompassed him with a wing, for all he didn't see its arch. "Few enough do, I warrant. Art leaving?"

:Art following, when I do?:

"Thou hadst thy use of me," Kit answered. He turned in the lee of the angel's pinions and folded his arms atop the balustrade, looking over the night garden. The crunch of Kelpie's hoofbeats faded into the distance. "Enough and more than enough."

Lucifer laughed almost silently, his hair escaping around his face in coiled tendrils, his face creasing beside the nose and eyes. :Thou'rt prideful as I, Kitten.:

"Aye, and for almost as long. Mayhap I'll be archmage, an I win the combat. Would it please thee?"

:And so comest thou on a spiral, from mastered by Prometheans to mastering them?:

"There's a certain poetry in it." Kit turned to the Devil. "And, as thou didst but now proclaim, I am prideful as thee."

:Aye,: Lucifer answered. :Thou dost *thee* the Devil. There is a detailed pride in that.:

"Methinks I've earned familiarity."

:But thou aspirest to virtue now?:

Kit shrugged. "Virtue untested is no virtue at all. Thou knowest I loved thee. The Devil can see in human hearts."

:Ah. Would that that were so.:

Lucifer sighed, eyes downcast, and Kit cleared his throat. "So tell me—"

Polite attention, a stirring of invisible wings and a lift of a golden brow.

"—*is* it better to reign in Hell?"

:No,: the Devil answered, with rare, plain honesty. :But then, I am thy Lucifer, thou-who-wert-Christofer Marley, and not John Milton's Satan. Thou wouldst achieve a different answer in another story, sir.:

"You came back for me. Back through history."

:What's time to the Devil?:

"I'm sorry."

:Think not on't.: And Lucifer stepped away, leaving Kit's shoulders cold with the brush of a swan's hard feathers. :There are worse images to be made in. Ah, and thy second appears to have made thine arrangements. Wilt speak with him?:

The Devil furled his wings with a flick Kit heard, though he saw nothing but a shift of shadows in the moonlight. Matthew peered worriedly through his glasses. The Mage had paused just outside of Lucifer's reach, and he stood there, fingers rippling against his jeans. "Yes, Matthew?"

"Sunday the seventh," Matthew said.

" 'Twill serve. Where?"

"Not Manhattan," Matthew answered. "Nor Faerie either. Rossville, Staten Island. I'll take you there later."

"Good," Kit said. He rubbed the back of his hand across his mouth, and looked away. "I'm going to find a drink."

It was odd, Matthew thought, that it didn't seem *more* odd to find himself standing on a verandah in Faerie, kitty-corner to Lucifer Morningstar, watching a long-dead poet stalk away. *What am I doing here?*

He didn't quite know. He'd lost everything, in Faerie. And gone back to Manhattan because it was what he knew, what he'd been raised to. He just kept doing what he'd been doing because he didn't know what else to do, and passion and devotion—to a *cause* he had believed in—had become habit as tired as any moribund marriage.

"A measure of a misspent life," he murmured. Well, he was due a midlife crisis, wasn't he?

:Master Marley?:

"No," Matthew answered. "I meant mine. You know, he's not what I would have expected, if you had told me I was going to meet Kit Marlowe."

:They called him Kind Kit, you know.:

Matthew laughed and brushed his topcoat open with his thumbs so he could shove his hands in his pockets. "I had heard it was meant as mockery."

Lucifer's wings rustled, and now Matthew could see them, manifest in the darkness. The Devil smiled. :He was never less than kind to me.:

The next day was Thursday, and Don knew he was going to have to tell Ernie something. Don planned to take the subway in, the way he always did, but the sidewalks chilled his feet through leather soles and he needed coffee first. He'd have to trade in his loafers soon enough, but for now, he was reluctant to let go of summer. Even if it meant cold feet in the morning.

Monette and Mama were both still in bed when he got up. Breakfast was Starbucks from the shop near the precinct and a self-delivered lecture to take better care of himself. He paused outside to sip his latte and contemplate the pigeons and the pedestrians, the wind icing his neck. A

black-haired girl with Snow White skin turned and smiled at him without breaking stride, a girl in a yellow skirt, sunflower barrettes framing
her face.

It struck him odd. Middle-aged black man in a suit doesn't get smiled
at so often by a white girl his daughter's age, even if he is drinking a
four-dollar coffee. Not unless she's on the job, and she didn't look like
she was on the job.

NYPD was the only metropolitan police department in the US with
an international counterintelligence presence. In enforcement strength,
the department numbered more than thirty thousand officers, the pop-
ulation of a good-sized suburb unto itself. Most days, Donall found that
a comforting thought, as if the sheer mass of the armies of the law must
have a relativistic effect on the fabric of society, bending it toward what
was right and honest. The brotherhood. The thin blue line. *We hold these
truths to be self-evident . . .*

But in the shiver of recognition that spidered up his spine, he found
himself entirely alone.

It was a hunch, a stark absolute certainty with nothing under it but
instinct. Don slurped the last gulp of latte, tossed a cup light as a shed
insect husk into a keep-your-city-clean barrel, and waited for the street
traffic to fill up the space between them before he followed her on
down.

What the hell. He could call if it looked like he was going to be late.

The residual heat of the coffee cup still warmed his palm, but the ring
Felix Luray had pressed on him retained nothing of it. It was cold, cold
and tight, a serpent wrapped around his finger, constricting. He
clenched his fingers against it, squeeze and release. The cold soaked to
the bone, demanding and reassuring. Another compact. Another oath.
New allies.

He needed a different brotherhood now.

People hunched in their jackets, steam drifting from their lips, the
manhole covers, the subway grates. And maybe that was what it was
about the girl, besides the warning chill in his ring. Bare legs, a skirt
like a garland of dandelion fluff, her hair all down her back in a dark
cascade, restrained by those plastic barrettes. She wore marigold
Converse All Stars laced up her skinny ankles, the holes frayed

where the grommets had been picked out, black socks bunched around the tops.

She doesn't look Fae. But, then, what did Fae look like? Anything they wanted, Don supposed.

He followed her around the corner, watching her avoid the subway grates as she *trip-trop, trip-trap, trip-tropped* along the sidewalk. The ring was an ache up his arm to the elbow joint, cold or pain conducted by the bone. She turned onto Sixth Avenue, and he was definitely going to be late. He checked the time on his phone and winced. The desk was on speed dial, and he used the phone to hide his face while varying his distance and keeping the bulk of the crowd between him and his quarry. The skirt made her easy to keep track of, as they whispered like a breeze through the city.

And what am I supposed to do if I catch her?

Something snagged, something caught—as if a silk thread brushed on a stucco wall, tugging. One thread, and a whole stocking laddered. The city wore them like a garment, brief decorations on a persisting being. But just now, the snag and ravel brought a focus of attention into the street, the eyes on cornices and drain spouts observing sleepily, a gleam behind the lashes of an immense, drowsing beast.

They wound through the dance of the streets like children playing tag through a pavane. The rawest of apprentice Magi, somber in navy wool, followed a girl bright as a spatter of paint through labyrinthine ways that could not be solved by the expedient of keeping one's left hand on the wall. In this maze, that solution would only walk one in circles endlessly. A different sort of maze, New York: one with a thousand ways in or out, and a hundred hearts, and more than one minotaur.

The girl in yellow needed no scroll of yarn behind her. She was seeking a man, as girls in mazes have for centuries, and her own magic was more than enough for finding him, even if she hadn't known that he'd await her at the tangled intersection of Bleecker, Carmine, and Sixth Avenue.

The tree-edged West Fourth Street basketball court hosted a desultory cold-weather handball game and Don paused to watch it for a moment—and beyond it, the girl, through two layers of chain link. She extended one hand and trailed fingertips along the wire, jerking them back and knotting the fist in her skirt as if she'd been scorched. The cold locking Don's hand into a fist intensified, and he had quickened his pace, intent on catching her up, putting a hand on her shoulder, and turning her around to ask her a question or two, when a completely unexpected silhouette detached from the onlookers by the fence and fell into step alongside her: Ernie Peese, hands in pockets and a knit cap pulled over his ears, the tip of his nose ruddy. He rubbed at it with the back of his hand as Don hesitated, fading against the trunks of slender, leafless maples.

Ernie and the girl moved fast. She had a good stride; she kept up with Ernie and from what Don could see of the conversation, the exertion didn't distress her at all.

He wouldn't get close enough to overhear, unfortunately. Tailing the Faerie girl was risky enough. Ernie would make him in a second.

It explained some things, though. Like how eager Ernie was to prove that Althea Benning's murder hadn't been a Fae crime. Of course, Ernie talking to a Fae didn't mean anything, except that a Fae was impolite enough to come to New York, and thought she had some reason to talk to a cop. Maybe a Faerie would be as worried about retaliation as a homicide detective. Maybe a Faerie would snitch, if she knew something a cop should also know. He thought about what Jane had told him, about a monster with a murderer's soul, and the murderer who had sent it to do his killing for him, and left a girl's guts spread out on the waking stone of New York City.

Maybe a Faerie wouldn't want another war either.

Don didn't know.

Which was why he was still watching Ernie and the girl, keeping the basketball court between them and ignoring the cold pull in his ring, when another joined them: a tall man, a broad-shouldered man with a trim black beard and a sleek black ponytail, wearing boots and black trousers and a retro patchwork jacket closed with leathern toggles at the front. He wore a guitar case slung over his shoulder, and he forgot himself enough to bow a little, or perhaps the reflex was too ingrained, though his hair stripped back over his ears hid the most obvious evidence of his heritage.

Don knew him at a glance. Another Fae, and one better known: Cairbre, the bard of the Daoine Sidhe, who rode at the right hand of the Queen. Don had seen him in *Time* magazine.

Curiouser and curiouser, Donall thought, and withdrew behind a tree to call Jane Andraste. Call him crazy. He was sure she'd want to know.

He was scrolling speed-dial numbers with his thumb when the phone buzzed in his hand like a hyped rattlesnake. He almost dropped it. *Duty beckons.*

The archmage would have to wait. Another girl had been murdered.

Sensible folk do not gallop a horse bareback through trees in the dark of the night. They don't discard their court gowns over a lilac bush and cling like a burr in the cresting mane, shifts rucked about their thighs, brown legs clasping prickling hide. They don't close their eyes and duck their heads and let the horse run, a milk-white shade bending between the smooth boles of silver beeches, a pale, thundering outline in the leaf-shadowed dark.

But Whiskey was not an animal who stumbled, and no rider fell from his back until he chose to throw her—and the Queen, not even then.

And Whiskey could see in the dark.

He stretched out, running hard, ears up, hooves a staccato on cracking leaves and litter. He was broad-barreled, his gait as smooth as brown river water when he chose to make it so, and the Queen didn't need stirrups to keep her balance. She had the strength of her thighs.

They crested a hill, twigs fouling the Kelpie's feathers, the bright streaks in his mane and tail flashing as he and his rider broke into moonlight along the ridgeline. The scent of running water rose from the gully on the left. It would be a crashing descent through gorse and briar down the bluff, and the Kelpie hesitated, silver horseshoes striking thick, blue sparks from exposed flint. He danced sideways at a trot, legs scissoring, then curvetted as he straightened, hoofbeats caroling like bells, the echoes ringing from each side. The Queen rode the short skips lightly, then settled back, slid down his withers, relaxed her grip on his mane. He slowed to an amble, almost a shuffle, click and clatter of metal on stone dulling as he crossed to chalk and stony, mossy earth in the shadow of a wind-stunted tree.

His thick neck arched, ripple of hot muscle under the Queen's hand as he turned and nosed her knee, tickle of whiskers and a moist pink nose spattered with dark freckles. He huffed warm air across her skin, welcome as the night breeze cut her shift and chilled sweaty skin.

"Ride on?" he asked, rejoicing in the clasp of her legs, the caress of her hands.

"Here," she answered, and slid down his shoulder before he'd quite halted, hopping a step or two alongside with her hands still in his mane. "A word in your ear, Uisgebaugh."

He shuddered when she said his name, a flinch that trembled the tender skin of his neck and shoulders. "Do not forbid me Jane Andraste. It's gone too far for rescinding."

"Do you think I care for her?" The Queen leaned her shoulder on Whiskey's shoulder, and found herself, a moment later, snuggled under the heavy curve of his arm, his solid naked flesh slick with clean sweat.

He bent and lipped her hair, tangled with beech leaves and sticks. She smelled of husks and sorrow, a wintry smell for the Winter Queen. He wondered what would happen to her soul, if he should die. Surely it wouldn't revert to her, not unless he could find a way to make her accept its return. It would be his then, for more than safekeeping.

Immortality beyond the body. Eternal life. Once, he would have said honestly that it had never tempted him. "But you're unhappy, my Queen."

"Kadiska brought me something," she said. She reached into the pocket of her shift and drew out a flat, black, tightly folded tatter. "After Carel went to fetch you. Uisgebaugh—"

He knew what she held. He snorted. "Vixen. Say it."

"Who's hunting you, Uisgebaugh?"

"No one I can't handle," he said. He turned her in his arms and kissed her forehead, her nose, her mouth. "Or, apparently, that your Seeker can't handle for me."

"My Seeker," she said, and kissed him back, a lingering glide of tongue between clinging lips. His mouth was soft and warm, his teeth wide plates of ivory. She flicked her tongue-tip across them. She leaned into his hands. "Your paramour."

"Call her an ally," he said. "Put that thing away."

It vanished into her pocket again. Her skin slid under his palms as he lifted the shift to her shoulders, silken and moist between the waxy lines of her scars. Her hair came with it, tumbled over her face. She shook it back as he went to his knees and tugged her palms away from her body, slipping the sleeves over her hands. "You're angry." He nuzzled the humid joint of her belly and thigh, the shift dropped to one side.

"Not with you." His hair between her fingers was like lamb's wool, springy and fine.

"Jane?" A guess, hazarded between kisses.

"Lucifer," she answered. She touched his cheek, his neck, his shoulders, her head bowed over him, her body pale in the moonlight. He balanced her with dark human hands, silver rings curved around the second joint of each thumb. "And then I tell myself there's no point in being angry at the Morningstar."

"But in opposing him?"

"Always a point to that." She shivered. The feather-light brush of horn-callused fingertips across the backs of her knees, half tickle and half delight. "Uisgebaugh—"

"Can't you see I'm kissing you?"

"Then wait. First that word."

He settled on his heels, hands folded in his lap, all demure stallion falsity. Tilting his head back, he regarded her, pale eyes weird in a dark face. "I await my lady's pleasure."

"I can't protect you from Mist," she said, her fists at her sides. The wind prickled gooseflesh across her and snarled her streaming hair. Moss dented softly underfoot. "I can try. But I can't guarantee."

"I never asked your protection, my Queen."

A lie, but she let it slide by. "You have duties."

"Take back your soul, and I will complete them."

"And if I order you?"

"Order me?"

"To kill," she said. Her left hand unfolded. She reached out and pointed. If Whiskey had stood, he would have seen the ocean glinting like hammered metal beyond the beechwood and the palace far below. He didn't need to stand to *feel* it. "To fulfill your nature. To serve the sea." The gesture closed, her arms folded over her heart. "You're thin, Uisgebaugh. Thin and worn."

"Take back your soul," he answered. "Take back your name."

"You'd eat me if I did."

He wouldn't. At least, he didn't think so. But she didn't need to know that, and besides, one never could tell how things might change. It was not in his nature to be always blue and calm. "Set me free."

"Give Ian the throne?"

"He wants it."

"He thinks he wants it," she said. She sighed and dropped to her knees, a sharp rock gouging her kneecap. The pain barely registered. "He thinks he wants all sorts of things."

"Then let him choose his own mistakes," Whiskey said. It was an old argument, the sort married couples have, where they can mouth both sides of the debate while knowing nothing will ever be resolved.

She sighed and reached up, and touched his face. "Do you love me so much?"

"Don't be foolish, mistress. Nothing Fae can love." And that was half a lie as well. But then, he wasn't Fae. Not quite, not anymore. "What does Lucifer want from you?"

"Dominion," she said.

"Besides that."

"The Mage and the poet, bound up in satin ribbons and delivered to my mother."

"That's Jane's price, not the Devil's. What does he get in return?"

"A treaty," she said. She shrugged. He laid his hands on her shoulders and felt the rise and fall, and pulled her against him. She moved closer, swaying forward as he went back. The twigs and stones on their mossy bed bothered him more than they did her. He brushed them away with a hand before lying back. "Peace under the dominion of Hell."

"I think not," he said. Her buttocks filled his palms, a soft weight, more scars. The night was cool, and she was warm. "Back the poet. You'll get the same, without the Devil. We have that in common; Master Marlowe's won free of Lucifer too."

"Marley was dead to begin with," she quipped. "Morgan says he's a Merlin, or was once, in his own time. Could he be still?"

"No," Whiskey said. "And no doubt glad to be free of the Dragon's hand. He's outlasted her attention."

The next question weighed on the Queen more. "Can he win?"

"I don't know," Whiskey answered. "Can you afford to let him lose?" He drew her down astride him. She tasted of flesh and the sea. Her breasts rippled as she moved over him, the ocean in a woman's body, wave upon wave in the endless deep. She moaned and held tight, her fingers clenched on his hands.

No struggle, this time. No surrender. Once she would have fought herself, a piquant edge of rage on the seduction before she acquiesced. He missed it, missed the challenge and the hunt.

But the Queen knew what he was, and what he had been, and how far he had fallen. He was her animal now.

⮞ Chapter Thirteen
Chasing the Dragon

I an and Cairbre had gone to bed at midnight, when neither the
Queen nor her steed had returned, leaving the mortal and angelic
guests in Morgan's care. Lucifer took his leave with a tilted head
and a wing cupped in farewell, to see Felix home just as Matthew was
considering how best to disentangle himself from the Devil.

And as for Matthew, he went from Lucifer to the Merlin and leaned
down to speak in her ear. "If I *did* want to find a Dragon, where would
I look for one?"

Carel grinned at him through her fingers and took him by the elbow
under the morning glories—replaced at sunset by moonflowers, now
fading as the sky grayed—and said, "You're not about to do something
dumb."

"Because anything Morgan and Elaine suggest must be dumb?"

"Because I've done my share of dancing with dragons." She
scratched the tip of her nose. "There's nothing a dragon can do for you
that you can't do for yourself, Matthew. There's nothing she can tell you
that you don't already know. And Morgan only agrees with people
when she has an ulterior motive."

Matthew leaned a shoulder on the wall and folded his arms. Leaves
tickled his neck. His face itched with the need to shave, and he blamed
his light-headedness on adrenaline and exhaustion. "So what's her motive this time?"

Carel smiled over his shoulder. He didn't have to turn to know she
was smiling at Morgan le Fey. "Fifteen hundred years," the Merlin said.

"And no one's ever been able to answer that question. I think she rather enjoys playing the cipher."

Matthew followed the Merlin's gaze. With moonset, pages had lit lanterns and set them along the balustrade. Morgan stood beside one such, straight-backed as a pillar and flanked by lazy hounds, a glass of wine in her hand. Marlowe lounged opposite, sprawled in a chair, one knee drawn up and the other leg extended, his head back and his chin lifted. It put Matthew uncomfortably in mind of a dog showing its throat, and Morgan's smile was idly predatory.

"She wants him," Matthew said. "And he knows it too."

Carel laughed, richly throaty. Matthew followed her as she strolled to a table that still held a half bottle of wine and an unused glass. "What's so funny?"

"Foolish mortal. Mind if we share?"

"Not at all," he answered. The wine breathed a deep scent onto the air, cutting jasmine sweetness. He could taste it in advance. "You're dodging the question."

"She wants *you*. He's a toy. She's gotten her use from him." Carel poured and passed Matthew the wine. "*And he knows it too*," she mocked. "See what he has in his hand?"

Her eyes were better. Or she'd already known. "Something dark. A flower?"

"A pansy. From Elaine's garden, which was the Mebd's garden before. 'Unwilling love.' I'll wager there's a history there."

Matthew sipped the wine. It was sweet and dark. "She's Morgan le Fey," he said, and handed Carel back the glass. "There's *always* a history there."

She laughed. "And what's the history that has you standing as his second, Matthew? That was an abrupt decision."

He let the breath go slowly, once the tightness in his chest reminded him that he was holding it. "You remember Kelly."

"With tremendous clarity."

"Jane killed him." Matthew turned and stared down at Carel until she dragged her gaze off Marlowe and turned it on him. "That's how she built her *fucking* bridge."

"And you never did anything about it."

Matthew smiled, cool bitterness. "Lady Merlin," he said, and held out his hands, the strong one and the broken, "I touched a unicorn."

She looked at his face, at his hands, back at his face again, his eyes half invisible in the shadows behind his spectacles. She licked her lips. "East," she said. "Follow the stream. Mind the troll. Through the beechwood, past Morgan's cottage, into the hills. East until you reach a gorge. There's a cave under the ivy. Mist lives there."

"That will take all day," he said, when he was sure she'd finished speaking.

"You're a Mage in Faerie," she said, negligent. "Tell me you can't manage a pair of seven-league boots."

"Thank you."

"Don't thank me," the Merlin said. "She'll probably just eat you. And take a friend. Somebody to drag the body home."

"Do I have any friends in Faerie?"

"You have Sir Christopher," she said, with a brushing gesture. "And he looks like he could use a rescue."

Across the patio, Kit knew that he was watched. He didn't turn, however. His eyes were on Morgan, side-lit by the lantern. More than half a century since he'd braced Morgan le Fey, and the edge hadn't gone off it. He doubted that it ever would.

Especially when Morgan smiled at him, as she was smiling now. "I would have been thy second," she said, her hands folded in front of her belt.

"Aye." Kit twirled the love-in-idleness between his fingers like the stem of a wineglass. "I imagine you would have welcomed the chance of a little vengeance. 'Tis dear work, replacing a tool so worn to the hand as Murchaud."

"Christopher." Disappointed, with a cold tilt of her chin. His cruelty cut a little, though he'd never believe he could hurt her. It wasn't in Kit to understand that love and control could be warp and weft of the same cloth. But then, he'd never understood, had he, that she had loved Arthur too, and Accolon, and Mordred—and Christofer Marley himself—even when she drew her power from their obedience.

Morgan let her hands fall apart and crouched between her hounds, resting her elbows on her knees. "He was also my son. Dost think thou didst love him more than his mother, Sir Kit?"

" 'Contrariwise,' " Kit quoted, letting his head arch against the back of the chair, eyes staring upward into the graying morn, " 'if it was so, it might be; and if it were so, it would be; but as it isn't, it ain't. That's logic.' "

"They *will* keep letting you read." Morgan reached out with a splay-fingered hand and let it rest on Kit's ankle, over the cloth of his trousers and the leather of his boot.

He lifted his head and let his other foot drop to the flags, iron nails thudding on marble, but didn't pluck his limb away from the witch. "Hell and Faerie have extensive libraries."

"And you've a Bard's memory."

"Latin grammar school," he said, and almost smiled. "God bless Henry the Eighth, and keep Great Harry's rotten corpse 'til Judgment Day. Can I remember Ovid for four hundred years, I've no fear to not recall Lewis Carroll after fifty."

"And yet you still affect that ridiculous accent." She smiled. One of her dogs twitched in his sleep, whining, claws scrabbling stone.

Kit laughed. "It comes and goes."

"And what wilt thou do, now that thou art without service, Master Marley?"

"I will not serve. 'Twill make a pleasant change." Her hand slid up his leg and his eyebrow rose with it. Footsteps: Matthew was coming up behind him. Morgan, who must have seen the Mage approaching, gave no sign. Kit flicked the flower at her. It tumbled end over end until she picked it from the air. "There *can't* be any use thou hastn't put me to already."

"No love for remembrance?"

"I'll send thee a wreath of rue," he said, and shook his leg out from under her hand as he stood. She stayed in her crouch, grinning up at him with a child's smile crinkling her eyes and plumping her cheeks, a long lock of hair fallen over her eyes. He bit his lip and stepped aside, forbidding himself the heat her touch engendered, if he lingered on it. *Aye. I'll give thee remembrance.*

"Matthew," he said. The blond Mage drew up ten or twelve feet away as Kit turned to face him. "Tell me you've come to take me to . . . Staten Island."

"No," Matthew said, his gaze flicking from Kit to Morgan and back without comment. Morgan stood, straight-backed as ever, and withdrew against the balustrade, removing herself from the conversation. Matthew greeted her anyway, before turning to Kit. "Good morning, Morgan. Sir Christopher, I've a favor to ask."

Kit stepped forward, opening his hand, sweeping it away from his body in a broad, stagy gesture that spread wide his cloak and tossed it over his shoulder. Matthew turned to walk alongside, enough taller that Kit craned to see more of him than his shoulder and the line of his cheek and jaw. "Ask it."

"I'm going to consult an oracle. The Merlin suggested I might bring company."

"What oracle would you consult?"

"The Dragon," Matthew answered.

"Oh," Kit said, and turned to retrieve his pack from where he'd left it beside the wall. "Yes, I know the way."

The path was as Carel described, and Kit and Matthew walked it with strangely light hearts. Gray mist curled between pewter trunks, smoky and strange in the slanted light of the rising sun, and the litter underfoot was scrambled as if by the passage of something large and hurried. Matthew dropped one knee beside the path where the bank was soft and traced a shod hoofprint as broad as his outspread palm. He glanced up at Marlowe and shrugged.

Marlowe shrugged right back. "Even a queen wants to run away once in a while."

"Especially a queen." They began walking again.

"There's a troll," Kit said, when they'd come within sight of the river, and Matthew answered, "The Merlin told me," and they grinned at each other like truant schoolboys.

"She said something about seven-league boots as well."

"Could speed our travel," Kit admitted. He unslung his rucksack and rummaged under the flap, retrieving a long black feather, each strand lustrous. A little more digging produced a chamois pouch that clicked softly when Kit handled it. He tucked the feather between two fingers and poured a handful of semiprecious stones into his hand. Before returning the rest to the pouch, he picked out a nearly flat, square-faceted piece of tourmalinized rock crystal the size of a dollar coin. The quartz was transparent as a palmful of water, the tourmaline crystals rayed through it from one corner unusually limpid and a deep coniferous green. Kit returned the pouch to the pack and the pack to his shoulder, then blew on the gem and held it to the light.

"I've but one feather," he said. "But quartz is symbolic of reception — even put to Promethean uses, in radio — "

Matthew's brow beetled. "How do *you* know about crystal radio sets?"

"Murchaud went to the teind in the year of your Lord nineteen hundred and forty-eight," Kit said. "And we did get television in Hell."

The worst of it, Matthew decided, was that the mad poet was as serious as broken glass. "And the tourmaline? We don't use *that* much."

"No one did," Kit said. "It's ideal. A stone with no weight of symbolism, one which, to the ancient magicians, might as well not have existed. And one that can acquire a static electrical charge. So, you see, I can take this stone" —and he demonstrated—"and this feather, and transfer a virtue from the feather to the jewel, and from the jewel to a subject."

"Subject?"

"Victim," Kit amended with a wink, and cupped the feather and the stone together in his hands. When he drew them apart, the feather had vanished. Matthew, who had been looking for a sleight of hand, had seen nothing.

"That's not Promethean magic."

"No," Marlowe said, crouching to tug up his trouser cuff and slip the stone inside his boot. "It's not witchcraft, either, or storyteller's magic. But it owes something of process to all three. Come on, take my hand."

Bemused, Matthew did so—his left hand, Marlowe's right—and found himself striding along beside the poet at a comfortable and considerable rate of speed. Marlowe's hand was dry and smooth, callused across the grip, a swordsman's or a sportsman's hand. "Witchcraft?" Matthew asked him, as the trees whirled by.

"Shocked?"

"A little," Matthew admitted. The low-hanging branches never seemed to strike his face, though he flinched at the first three or four. "So is *Faustus* a story from life?"

Marlowe glanced at him, breaking concentration a moment, the corner of his mouth curled up behind the beard that was so much redder than his hair. "Never kidnapped a pope," he said. "Though I killed an Inquisitor once. And would again. No, rather, call it an example of life imitating art. I chose witchcraft, Matthew Magus, because the Promethean arts would not avail me, and because my soul was already damned for being too fond of my sins of heresy and sodomy to repent them, and because I had already sold Lucifer my name and my fame for other considerations. So you see, I had nothing left to barter the Devil, and God does not bargain."

Kit's voice came out raw and soft, stripped of passion in its honesty until it rang with a parody of innocence.

"I'm sorry," Matthew said, because it was all he could think to say.

Kit flickered a smile. "Don't be. It was pleasanter than you might expect, and it all came right in the end. More or less. And unlike God, the Devil comes when he is prayed to. But it doesn't matter; I don't do that sort of thing anymore."

" 'Nor will we come, unless he use such means / Whereby he is in danger to be damn'd. / Therefore the shortest cut for conjuring / Is stoutly to abjure the Trinity / And pray devoutly to the Prince of Hell,' " Matthew quoted, ducking needlessly under another low-sweeping branch as they broke out on the breast of a hill.

They staggered to a halt as Marlowe stumbled. "You know it?"

"I teach it," Matthew replied, regaining his balance. He shook loose of Kit's suddenly moist hand. "Well, if I haven't been listed as a missing person by now. I was not expecting to spend a week in Faerie."

"An English teacher."

"You'd prefer a sturdy vagrant or a masterless man?"

Kit stared for some seconds, then laughed and pushed his hair back with his left hand. "Oh, are a relief to talk with. Matthew Magus, whatever of mine idiot scribblings do you teach, there's another three hundred years of it in Faerie. And a few stray bits by some other men, that may not have survived in the iron world. The Puritans and the Protheans were not in all ways our friends."

And you have a talent for understatement, Master Marlowe, Matthew thought, but he didn't say it. "Other men?"

Kit dropped his chin. "Ben Jonson and Edmund Spenser and Will Shakespeare, and all the poor doomed Toms, Nashe and Kyd and Watson. I saved what I could—"

Matthew's mouth went dry. He spoke slowly, so there could be no mistake. "Those are names to conjure with, Sir Christopher. And what do you want in return?"

Kit knew it was madness to trust this creature so easily. It was Matthew's sharp good looks and the lonely smile, and the air of calm that surrounded him and never seemed to touch the Mage himself, and Kit did not fool himself otherwise. But he had always been a gambling man. "It's yours," he said, with enough gravity to indicate that he understood the generosity of his offer, and did not take it lightly. "No bargains. It's not the sort of thing that ought be bargained for, and I've hoarded it long enough. And *that* should see you safely landed, if your patronage is spent in Faerie, seconding a secondhand Mage. Morgan knows where to find it, if I do not survive Jane."

"If you don't survive Jane, I'll have bigger problems than a few missed classes," Matthew said, seeing his opportunity. "Tell me about Morgan."

Marlowe grabbed his hand again, and they charged down the hill. It was almost like hang gliding, except Matthew's feet brushed earth between each enormous bound, water sparkling as they cleared the stream in a prodigious leap, though they never quite seemed to take flight. "What would you know?" Marlowe asked.

"*Is* she a witch?"

"Is she Lucifer's, you mean?"

"Yes."

"No," Marlowe answered, with a hang on the end of it that told Matthew there was more to come. "No, not precisely. She's what we used to call a cunning woman. Not really a witch, not really a bard. Not a priestess or a Promethean, either. Her magic is in stories, and in the intersections between stories, in what she can make a man do without his understanding why, because of who she is. She knows her own legends, and she . . . rides them, like a gladiator astride a team of horses."

He glanced at Matthew, as if to be sure Matthew understood, and Matthew nodded, encouraging.

Kit's voice came to Matthew strange and attenuated over the rush of the wind. "She has many hounds, Matthew Magus. You do not wish to be one."

"She has nothing to offer me," Matthew said. He noticed Kit's bitter, answering smile.

"She'll find something, if she thinks you have aught to offer her. *I* am just a toy, at this juncture. She teases me because it amuses her, but like a cat, she'd be after fresh prey were it presented."

Matthew remembered her mouth, her kiss, and wished he dared blink. At least Kit would likely think the sting moistening the corners of his eyes was from the wind. "What does she want?"

"With you, or me?"

"Overall."

"Power," Kit said, and slowed at the edge of the beechwood. He pointed through the trees with his free left hand. "See? There's her cottage now."

It was a rustic affair, thatched stone tumbled over with roses. Matthew took it in at a glance: a warm meadow, a path, buzzing bees and an empty paddock with the grass grown high and tasseled gold along the rails. "Why show me this?"

"So you can find it again when you want it."

"And if I don't want it?"

Marlowe laughed at him, a cruel joy that made him beautiful. "You will."

They traded a look, light hearts gone to quiet in the heat of morning and the insect hum. Matthew cleared his throat, unwilling to loft words into a silence so heavy. "How is it you of all people walked out of Faerie unmarked, Sir Christopher?"

Matthew had thought the previous spate of laughter a transformation. If it had been, this one was a seizure, and Marlowe was choking, doubled over, one hand on his knee and the other on his mouth by the time he was done.

"Oh, Matthew," he said, sinking down between his heels, red-faced and breathing hard. "Oh, if only."

Nimble fingers opened the lacings at Marlowe's collar, baring a pale chest, collarbones and the shadow of ribs visible beneath. And under them, over his heart, Matthew saw a white, sharp cicatrix, a pale crisp outline of a Hebrew letter, *mem*. A brand: the skin was taut and hairless. Most striking, a thin horizontal line bisected it, distorted the edge.

Matthew recognized that scar, angled so as to slip between the ribs. His fingers shook as he opened his own collar, left-handed, baring flesh and black ink charged with iron, and his own thin, perfect white scar.

"One on the back too?" Kit asked, bright-eyed.

Matthew nodded. "Not a unicorn?"

"No," Kit said. "But nearly. Angel." He stood, and shrugged. "You get your Christ symbolism where you can."

It broke whatever tether held Matthew's trembling hand at his collar. He let it fall to his side and sighed in relief, and then chuckled, shaking his head.

They started forward again. Some little time later, they came out of the trees alongside the stream, on a grassy moor that bordered a high, stark hill—the first in a serried rank of hills just like it. Downs, lonely and empty, their silhouettes more ragged than the smooth curve of Horsebarn Hill, and a gloomy mist tangled around their shoulders, though what Kit and Matthew had just left behind at the edge of the wood had become broad midday. Kit slowed their pace, and let go of Matthew's hand. "Not too much farther."

He crouched to slip the stone from his boot, while Matthew set his hands on his hips and looked around. The cold landscape did not invite visitors, but he could see the path, wending beside the stream into a gorge between the downs, as promised. He breathed damp air scented with moss and chlorophyll. "So Morgan wants power."

"Morgan wants control of herself." Kit scratched behind his ear. "Control of her story. She always has—"

He stopped short, and Matthew turned to see what had distracted him—and froze as if his blood had crystallized. The hillside was pale brown and yellow-green, high-summer colors contradicting spring-sour air. And there on the brow of the elevation, surrounded by soft gray mist and watery light, gleamed the small white shape that had arrested Marlowe midsentence. "Oh."

"You summoned him," Marlowe murmured. "He heard you speak."

"She," Matthew said. "She's a jenny."

"You've seen her close enough to know a stallion from a mare?" The poet didn't take his eyes off the animal. Five hundred yards if she was an inch away, and she stood out as crisply as a mother-of-pearl figurine in a stained-glass window. What light there was caught her, glittered off her shoulder and horn as if someone on the ridge flashed a mirror into the vale. Matthew could *feel* her looking back at them, could feel her vast bottomless eyes and her shivering feral presence, could feel her warm, solid flesh against his hand.

"Close enough," he said. "She put her horn through my heart, Sir Christopher."

"I cry thee mercy," Marlowe said. It had the sound of something mouthed by rote, an apology out of habit. He was not hearing his own voice. And then cracked disappointment. "Oh, she's gone."

And so she was. Matthew breathed deep, and looked down, blinking as if she'd left an afterimage in her brightness. He stood for a moment, silently, as Marlowe scuffed his palms on his trousers. The silence was breathtaking.

"You're sure that was *your* unicorn?" Marlowe said, finally, when it seemed like sound might carry again.

"Hard to tell at a distance," Matthew said. It fell flat. It felt cheap. But there were no words for the ache in his breast, like a wild thing pulling its chains.

"That explains what Morgan wants with you, then. She desireth a leash on everything, up to and including Lucifer. And since I didn't suffice, you could be that, very well."

"*Lucifer?* Me?"

"A Promethean Mage bound to a unicorn?" Kit asked.

"Yes, but—"

Kit placed a warm hand on his elbow. " 'What would be now the state of us / But for his Unicorn?' You listened not to what I said regarding Christ, Matthew Magus."

"Sir Christopher—"

"Kit."

"Kit," Matthew echoed. "I'm not a Christian."

"Neither is Morgan, but she's not the sort to let worship interfere with damned practicality."

"And you?"

Kit turned and smiled at him, sunlight through the mist that rolled along their path. "Oh, aye, I am that. Both Christian, and damned." He pushed his hair back again. The damp air annealed it in strings clinging to his brows and his cheeks. "Come along, Matthew Magus. Your Dragon awaits."

They picked their way downstream along the dirt path, which wound between cracked flint and granite boulders, worn testimony that the water ran high in flood season. Kit went first, sure-footed and possessed of two good hands, and Matthew followed less nimbly. The cliff Carel had described loomed before them, a louring face roped with thick vines, green and glossy in the mist rising from the stream. Kit drew up before it, and Matthew paused at his side. If he hadn't seen the outline of the mouth behind the vines, he would have felt it. A warm draft, dry and scented like heated stone, turned the leaves on their stems and brushed a few stray strands of Matthew's hair against his face.

"Coming?" he asked Kit, who was in the process of leaning against a boulder and folding his arms.

"I'll pass, if it's all the same," Kit answered, as if bored to tears by the prospect of bearding a Dragon in her lair. The prickle of humor in his voice gave him away. "I shall stay right here."

Stay in the old sense. *I will wait for you.* Matthew smiled as he turned away and squared his shoulders, that blank fear lessening for the first time since he'd stepped through into Faerie. What an unlikely place to have found a friend.

He pushed the vines aside and entered the cave, while Kit pretended not to watch him go.

His first thought was that he'd been foolish not to bring a flashlight. The tunnel was broad, the floor not precisely flat underfoot because it was worked in a pattern of briars and tended to a downward slope. The light through the heavy foliage obscuring the mouth was filtered and dim and Matthew could tell the cave went a long way back.

He rested the knuckles of his right hand against the wall and began to walk, sliding each foot forward and testing his weight against it before trusting the floor. He could call light; he felt the potential like an itch in his fingertips, but he didn't trust his own strength, and he didn't wish to disturb what dwelt here any more than necessary.

He'd see how far he got in the dark.

And it grew very dark. The blackness of caverns has a quality all its own. A texture. Time is suspended in that darkness. The space between heartbeats grows enormous. Matthew felt it, the slumbering awareness that surrounded him, the warm dry air stirring his clothing.

There is a curious phenomenon known to meteorology as the foehn effect. Dry air cooled by a glacier becomes a katabatic wind, which is to say that the heavier, colder atmosphere drains away from the peaks. Sinking from the mountain slopes, this frigid exhalation is transmuted through the alchemy of adiabatic compression into a hot, ionized dragon's-breath reputed to provoke madness, wickedness, and sickness where it blows. These winds have names: *Chinook, Sirocco, Koembang, Simoom, Samiel*. And those names are stories.

Matthew, descending like Inanna in the darkness, breathed the mother of them all.

It was good that he trailed his hand along the wall, for the passage curved on the broad pleasing arc of a grand staircase, spiraling down. His sweat was not all from the warm air. His neck felt clammy, and his heart jostled painfully against his ribs. It seemed a very long time before he saw a faint red glow ahead, painting the wall, picking out the details of relief carving that his numb knuckles and shod feet were too insensitive to discern. The dark-adapted eye picked out new brightness easily, and a scent arrived alongside: a bitter sun-baked smell, a mineral reek with overtones of heated metal, of petroleum and juniper and incense. Rosewood, sandalwood, dragonsblood, myrrh.

He'd been smelling it for some time, he realized, as some atavistic awareness halted his foot in midair. Fear coiled and slid in his belly, rising behind his pounding heart to close his throat. Static as a hare in a lamper's light, reduced to a bunny's defense: stare, crouch, gather. Be ready to run.

He heard the predator breathing.

Just around the curve.

Matthew inhaled shallowly through his mouth, through the panic in his bowels, and dropped his hand away from the wall. One step at a time, he closed the distance between here and there, moving into the light. Into the presence of the Dragon.

It would have been arrogance to consider himself prepared, and he knew that. But standing there, framed in the high, arched gateway to the abode of the mother of dragons, her carnelian glare painting his face with blinding brightness, he understood that it was arrogance even to come here. Arrogance merely to force her acknowledgement of his existence. Arrogance to so much as allow himself to come to her attention. The sort of arrogance that would be paid for sooner rather than later, he feared.

He took a breath, and came the last five steps to the cliff edge.

The tunnel didn't open out at ground level, and for that he was grateful. Instead, he had a view of a chamber big as a football dome. It seemed at first firelit, although there was no fire in evidence. The coals across which the glow crawled were the scales of the Dragon herself.

She hung from the cavern's domed cathedral ceiling like an enormous bat, furled in massive wings, drowsing over the banks of her treasure. Matthew steadied himself on the lip of the tunnel left-handed and craned his head back to observe her slumber. She seemed to shift before his eyes, her cabled hide scaled and ropy as ironwood boles, the skin shimmering under char-dark scales with an ember heat. Her head was pulled up between her shoulders, her eyes closed. The fog sliding around her glowed rosy with her furnace light.

He swallowed the fear in his throat, and tried to find his voice. "Mist?"

The name cracked coming between his teeth and fell broken at his feet. He swallowed painfully and said it once again, failing his attempt to draw a breath. "Mist!"

One eye slit. The wings fanned wide, stirring the hot wind, two long fingers on the leading edge grasping at air. The pops as her joints responded to the stretch resounded like the cannonball thunder of river ice breaking.

Matthew flinched. The bat wing morphed, smoothed back into her shoulder, one spiny five-taloned foot on a twisted pillar of a leg reaching to the floor. Claws flexed sleepily through heaps of misshapen coin and cracked, discolored jewels, marred by the heat of her flesh. She arched her back, long and lithe, wingless and then winged again—this time with a third set of limbs at her shoulders. Her sturdy neck elongated into a snaky curve as she slithered to the cavern floor. Her back feet released their grip only after her front half was securely on the ground, weasel-lithe, unholy grace in a beast the size of a jetliner.

The thump of her hind feet striking knocked Matthew into the cavern wall. He braced himself, scrambling back from the lip. *She could bring the whole cave system down with a breath.*

She settled on her haunches like a gargoyle, wings flicked tight, and brought her muzzle down beside the opening. "Matthew Szczegielniak," she said. Her voice was a mountain's voice, a bass choir or an arrangement for viola and cello, a dozen voices in one, deep and slow and dull as iron even as it sparked rich brutal harmonies. "Mage," she said, turning her head to inspect him with each eye in turn. "It was your folk who bound me here, before I was freed. Have you come to make amends?"

He hadn't thought of it, but an apology cost him nothing. He bowed low and spread his hands, feeling like a mountebank in his gaudy finery. "On behalf of what remains of the Prometheus Club, I do, O Dragon."

"Plain talk suffices," she said. The dizzying stench of charred meat washed over him. "You do not speak for Prometheus. Or for the Prometheans."

"I am one-quarter of them," he answered, swallowing against his rising gorge. "My saying so is as good as anyone's. And I am sorry we bound you. I did what I could to end that binding. Not without cost."

"Magus, you disturb my rest." Her nostrils flared. Her breath curled his eyelashes and scorched his eyebrows until he could smell the burning hair. He might have stammered. He might have apologized again.

Instead, he opened his mouth to speak, and said nothing, because he realized that he did not know what he intended to ask for. He almost squeaked on a sharp, hysterical giggle, because it also occurred to him that if there were anything more dangerous than lying to dragons, it was probably waking them up without a very good excuse.

He managed a painful inhalation. The breath that should have settled him reeked of Mist. A flawed plan, obviously.

"Speak," she instructed, and coiled back just a little, as if to give him space. Or perhaps to strike, like a snake. There was that anticipatory tautness in the curve of her neck. A low hiss followed the flicker of a tongue. "Matthew Magus. Ask."

Matthew braced himself, tugging his topcoat closed. He couldn't hear the jingle of talismans over the rasp of the Dragon's scales on gold, but it would have to do. He might be a bad Mage, a broken and disloyal one, but he was Promethean and he had his pride. There were so many questions. *How do I heal my magic? How do I free myself? How do I stop Jane Andraste? How do I protect the iron world from Faerie, even now?*

He opened his mouth and unfolded his arms, and the question that emerged was not the one he had intended. "How can I stop being a Mage?"

Mist laughed like waves breaking on rocks. Her tail writhed, rattling, over gold. "Die. Matthew Magus, ask again."

His scars twinged and Matthew stopped. Just stopped. He pressed the balls of his feet to the floor and admonished himself to courage. Cold fear-sweat was lost in the dripping heat. *Stupid*, he thought, and *Answer me, these questions three.*

One down.

Two more left.

He pushed his hands into the pockets of his topcoat and thought, while the Dragon smiled at him through sulfur-stained teeth as long as his arm.

Morgan le Fey had told him what to ask. And the Queen of Faerie had too. Leaving him one question of his own. A wasted question, now.

Think like a Mage, damn you, he told himself, and closed his eyes. The Dragon was too much, too present, too real. He couldn't think and look at her, both. She filled him up, slammed him against his own edges like water in the vessel into which is dropped a stone. He held his breath to clear the scent of her from his senses; the hot iron was gone and now all he could smell was summer, roses and jasmine and fresh-clipped grass. Morgan and the Queen had told him what to ask.

And what if he didn't want to ask their questions?

Well.

That had been his problem all along, hadn't it? Being too biddable.

So he knew the answer to the Queen's question, and to Morgan's. What he *wanted* was his freedom, his life untouched by Prometheus. Kelly back, hale and sound, as they had been when they were boys and Matthew had worshipped him. Things that, short of a deal with the Devil, he could not have.

What he *needed* was to want something else. Something attainable.

Except—and here was the true irony—having identified his problem as one of being too obedient to the whims of others, Matthew now couldn't think of anything else to ask.

Amazing, the clarity one could obtain while standing on the doorstep of a dragon.

He opened his eyes.

She waited still, fire pooling in her maw as she yawned elaborately, wreathing her nostrils like a dancer's transparent veils when she closed her mouth again. Her vast eyes gleamed with planes of color, blue and green and a lucent, vitreous vermilion like fire opals. She smiled at him, and didn't speak, and her heat stung his skin like too much sun.

And then he grinned. *What the hell*, he thought, pulling his hands out of his pockets. He hooked the topcoat tails back with his thumbs. He knew when he was beaten. If he was just going to stand here and vacillate, he might as well play to type.

"What do you think I should ask?"

A pause, as if the Dragon considered. She bowed her neck, her whiskered chin resting on the stone by Matthew's feet, her pupil level with his face as she turned her head. The heat was a pressure, pushing him back, and whatever numinous strength rolled off her was the only thing that allowed him to stand his ground. His breath rattled in and out; he heard himself whimper.

"What should I ask, were I Matthew?" she asked, mildly as a woman, modulating her choir of a voice. "Is that your question?"

"Nearly," he said. "Answer the question you wish I would ask. I commend myself to your mercy."

"A dragon's mercy is a fickle thing," she said, the echoes rolling around him.

He shrugged, falsely insouciant. "So is a unicorn's."

"Yes, that." She didn't draw back, but she did appear to hesitate. He waited, sweating until his shirt clung to his chest and back, showing no impatience as he cycled a mantra through his head. Perhaps no one could outwait a dragon, but he suspected that a show of impatience would provide no advantage.

He was a Mage. He could stand up to a Beast. No matter how it terrified him.

He was still waiting when she drew back—not far—and opened her mouth. He prepared himself for the reeking heat of her breath, but what followed was a summer breeze, as redolent of flowers as the Queen's garden, ruffling his hair and soothing seared skin. "You were close the first time," she said. "Close, but too limited in your vision. It is a failure that will much afflict you."

"It's a failure that already does," he said. "Your Merlin said you would probably eat me."

She chuckled. He *did* step back from that, echoes shaking dust into his eyes. Dust, but no pebbles: the tunnel was solid enough for a Dragon, at least. He blinked furiously, sliding his fingers under his spectacles to wipe his streaming eyes, leaving dabs of skin-oil smudging the lenses.

"I probably will. I eat most things, eventually." Translucent fire curled up her muzzle. "Do not ask how you can be free of your magic, Matthew Magus, for you cannot be free. Ask rather how you can encompass it, how you can learn to use your gift so it no more cripples you."

Matthew nodded, and hunkered down on his heels. He reached up, left-handed, and tugged his hair loose of the ponytail. It fell about his face in sweaty tangles, cloudy droplets spattering from the soaked ends. No wonder the cavern seemed to swirl around him. He put his hand on the wall for support. "Tell me, then," he said. "How can I encompass it?"

The Dragon's tongue flicked, forked tips fluttering inches from his face, as if she could taste his sweat. "I have never said this to a Mage before," she said. "But you are too much surrendered, Matthew Szczegielniak. You have given yourself over to the magic, to the voices of your city. You have kept yourself soft, receptive, as you were taught, accepting even where it wounds you. And it has availed you; the strength of your city fills you. But if you do not rule it, it *will* rule you."

Her voice was plain, matter-of-fact, suddenly unornamented. It shocked him. He had expected a lecture on meditation, on openness, on feeling the flow of the power and letting it direct him. "I can do no harm," he said.

"Control is not harm. Matthew, you are a man and a Mage. Your destiny lies not in surrender, but in struggle. Kick, claw. Stand *up*."

He stood, bootheels gritting on stone. "Mist," he said, carefully. "Are you telling me to go out and get laid?"

A dragon's shrug was an epic undertaking. "It couldn't hurt," she said, and folded her wings. "Now leave, as you have your answers, and may you have pleasure of it, Matthew Magus."

He bowed and backed away. It didn't seem right to turn his shoulder to her until he was around the corner and out of sight.

The path up was easier. He was climbing toward light.

When he pushed aside the hanging vines, Marlowe was still waiting for him, and from his glance at the sky—where the sun was still hidden by clouds—Matthew's descent had taken less time than Marlowe had anticipated.

The poet folded his arms. "She didn't eat you?"

"Apparently not."

"What did she tell you?"

Matthew wiped the sweat from his face with the back of his glove, and stuck his hair behind his ears. It remained plastered there. "She told me I'm insufficiently phallocentric," he said, filling his lungs with a deep breath of cold, misty air. "Come on, let's get some lunch. And then I'll take you to Rossville."

Chapter Fourteen
An Englishman in New York

Whiskey slipped the shadow from the Queen's pocket and into his own while she wasn't watching. He brought her shift to her, folded over his arm, and once she'd struggled into it he combed his fingers through her hair to pick the worst of the twigs out. "You're going back to New York?" she asked, without looking at him. The sunrise gleamed cold on her near-black hair.

"I will." He planted his forelegs, hands hardening to hooves, and leaned his head on her shoulder so she might feel the weight of muscle and bone. His mane spilled over her, coarse hair streaked white and black, as long as her arm. "Since my Queen will not hear me, I will defend her as best I may."

"If your Queen heard you, she would not be your Queen for long, little treachery."

"Ideally." He backed a step and snorted, shaking his head as if a fly buzzed around his ears. "I'm not hunting Jane Andraste now."

"You'll be there when Marlowe takes the fight to her." She might have been talking to her shadow, for all the attention she paid him. There had been a time when she wouldn't have turned her back on him, in fear for her life.

"Oh, aye," he said. "That I will. But I'll confess myself curious that something Fae stalks mortals in New York City. I'd have a look and see if I can trace the hand behind the killing."

"Who do you suspect?"

He didn't answer for a moment. The sun inched higher, warming their shoulders, two white-clad figures in stark relief against gray stone and scrubby trees. "I suspect everyone," he said. "Thou art a popular Queen with some, and thus the more hated by others. A conqueror sleeps not easy."

"No. I've noticed that." She turned, quicksilver, and smiled at him. "Whoever acted got their will, wouldn't you say? Faerie and Magi in open confrontation?"

"No," he said. "I don't think they got what they wanted. Your throne is in no danger yet."

"Only from you."

He shook his mane and pawed. A spring trickled from cracked stone where his hoof hammered, a thin line of water pure as rain. She closed the space between them and reached up to drape an arm over his withers. He turned and lipped her hair. His whiskers tickled, and she pushed his head away.

"You think my throne is the target."

"I think you are, so long as you sit that throne."

"Proclaim me no false mysteries, then, Whiskey. You think it's Àine stalking me."

"I think it's logic and sense to abdicate, lady, and accept my vow that I will neither harm you nor see harm come to you, once you have reclaimed that which you forced on me."

"And feed Ian to that thing."

"He wouldn't mind," Whiskey said. "He's a wolf. He'd survive it."

The Queen sighed. When she closed her eyes, the sunlight lit her whole world red, silhouetting the capillary patterns in her eyelids. "And if Sir Christopher and Matthew manage to overthrow Jane Maga, and they grant me an alliance anyway? We'll ferret out our enemy then—"

"They'd grant one to Ian too."

"Probably," she said. "But would he know how to manage it?"

For that, Whiskey had no answer. He stood, tail stinging his flanks, and regarded her with high-pricked ears. And she shrugged and dismissed it. "Majesty," he said. "What if Ian is the enemy?"

"All the more reason to keep him off the throne." Said with a tight, bitter smile. And then she shrugged, and passed her hands over her body—shift and tangled hair and bare feet—and stood before him in riding breeches and a white button shirt, her hair braided back over her ears. "Go on," she said, with a dismissive gesture. "I'll make my own way back."

He didn't argue. He whirled and plunged down the steep side of the hill almost on his haunches, brush abrading his chest and belly, a bramble scraping a thin raw line across his foreleg. He splashed into the rocky stream and the cold water stung the cut.

Spray dashed around him, flashed and shattered in the light. Whiskey reared, warm sun and chill water on his hide, and let himself collapse into the cold immaculate stream, his blood and bones melting. He crashed down, an unexpected waterfall, wetting the banks, and then slipped away, free, running downhill to the sea, his father and his flesh, and from there to the wide ocean and all its tributaries.

When he stood up again, it was in New York. And Kadiska was waiting for him, at a shady bench on the sere, autumnal banks of the Central Park boating pond.

"You've been watching for me." He settled on the bench beside her, his white raw silk suit dry as if he hadn't walked out of the lake, wearing the shoes he hated even in winter.

"I asked the shadows," she said. She wore a quilted coat today, red and gold and crusted with embroidery, and she was throwing crumbs of popcorn to the fish in the lake. Their mouths made popping circles on the surface, ripples spreading faster than the iridescent discs of grease that diffused from each bit of waterlogged grain. "Just got here."

She looked like she'd been there for hours. She leaned against him, bursting her paper bag with her palm. "Did Elaine tell you about the Bunyip?"

"I already knew about the Bunyip," he said. He put an arm around her shoulders. She turned and sank filed teeth into his wrist, above the bone, blood blotting the cuff of his suit jacket. A quick nip, piercing the skin, leaving her mark like a ring of red pearls on dark flesh. He tugged sharply, left hand in her braids shaking until she opened her mouth and drew back.

She turned, smiling, her mouth lipsticked with blood. He gave her one last rattle and let her go. She snuggled back against his side. "You are too thin."

He didn't answer. He stroked her braids, listening to the jangle of coins.

"You fail us, Whiskey."

"I'm failing no one but myself."

"On the contrary." She lifted his wrist to her mouth and licked away the blood congealing in streams across the heel and the thumb. Her wet, rough tongue ferreted stringy red from the lines braceleting his wrist; his blood was musk and salt, seaweedy. "You give the Prometheans more advantage than they have already. It's neglect, and you know it." She smiled, and let his hand fall. He didn't argue, just watched as she turned toward him, her eyes narrowing. *You are not doing your job.*

"My *job*?" A braying snort. "Fae is not a profession."

"No. It is an obligation." Her tongue curled across her lip, eradicating a last trace of red. "The sea is blood. Blood is the sea. You must be what you are, Whiskey, though what you are be terrible."

He untangled his arm from her shoulders. One of the pockets that hadn't existed when he wore his horse-shape, his water-shape, produced a linen handkerchief: an antique thing, a froth of yellowing lace and ivory cloth. He could not remember the face of the girl he had taken it from. A redhead, he thought. Maybe a blonde. "Is that a Seeker speaking?"

"Or a huntress." She tipped her head in dismissal as he bound his wound. "Bunyip is right. You've gone soft. Humans manage their evils burdened by souls, and none can say that their beasts are less beastly than you . . ."

"Aye," he said. He stood, and tucked the edges of the handkerchief in, forming a tidy package. "Their mortal, human beasts are beastly enough, when they do not have Fae to blame for the teeth in the night. But when I was what I was, Kadiska, it was not . . . evil. Terrible, perhaps"—he hesitated, as if savoring the word—"but the sea, as you say, is blood. And evil is an iron concept or an angelic one, of no concern to the Fae. But now I have a soul, and I would as soon not sin."

"Mm." She paused, considering. Her shadow lashed a tail and flared a hood behind her when she stood and paced, the short fluid steps of a caged panther, stalk and wheel and stalk again. She did not look at him, her head bent, considering. *She* would not bow to convention, insofar as shoes. "Coward. Out of a little fear of Hell, you give away strength."

"Like water," he answered. She didn't laugh. Whiskey drew one foot onto the bench and clasped his hands around the knee. "Get Elaine to take the damned thing back, pussycat, and I will be all the monster Mist could wish of me."

Donall Smith was straightening his tie in the window beside the revolving door when Felix walked up Central Park West, northbound under a sky like a slate casket lid. The creases laddering the back of the detective's blue suit coat informed anyone who cared to know of hours slouched at a desk.

Felix paused behind him. Don's eyes slid sideways in the reflection and he straightened up before Felix cleared his throat. "Long night?"

"The longest." Don tugged the hem of his jacket ineffectually, and stifled a yawn against his palm, his Kevlar vest chafing his armpits as he moved. "What brings you here, Kemo Sabe?"

"Returning from errantry in far lands," Felix said. He ushered Don through the door. The doorman did no more than glance at them. Jane must have left instructions. "I'll share the rest upstairs."

"No point in telling the same story twice," Don answered.

They shared the elevator ride in silence, Felix straight-backed, hands folded, and Don sleepily studying his thumbnails. "She knows you're coming?" Don asked, as the penthouse alert dinged.

"To the minute." Felix softened his tone with a smile. "Figured that out, did you?"

"She do this sort of thing a lot?"

"She's a great believer in efficiency." The doors slid open, and Felix stepped out.

This time, Jane wasn't waiting for them. Workmen were in evidence amid a mayhem of plastic sheeting, ladders, and marble dust. One of them caught Felix's eye and gestured a path around the edge of the room; he nodded and obeyed, Don still following.

The inner door swung open as he came up on it, and Jane's paperyskinned hand drew a sheet of translucent four-mil plastic aside. She beckoned them into her home.

Even having seen it once before, Donall found his awe unabated, though he concealed it behind professional cynicism. Felix's reaction was at once more open, and more pained.

Jane had taken the great, empty, echoing chamber that had once been the meeting hall and mystic center of the Prometheus Club, and turned it into a domicile. As if she could not bear to leave the place where her Magi had gathered before they had fallen—or even, in particular, bear to change it much—the vast sunlit space Felix remembered was still undivided. Soft music threaded from concealed speakers, supplied by a sleek laptop propped open on a coffee table. Here and there, clusters of blond wood and ivory raw silk furniture huddled under potted palms and ficus, circling Caucasian and Afghan carpets hand-knotted from burgundy and gold and white and indigo wool. The floor underneath was pale hardwood, broad expanses visible between the conversational groupings, its stark pallor ameliorated by the glittering-eyed shapes of coiled and tendriled five-toed dragons, crafted from inlaid cherry, purpleheart, olive, cocobola, and other colored woods. Orchids and cacti clustered near the windows, arranged in pale-glazed pots with restrained simplicity.

A few strategically placed paper-and-lattice screens broke sight lines. One of them concealed a door that led to service facilities, including what had once been the Prometheus Club's coed locker room, and a restaurant-sized kitchen. Another screen provided a private nook for Jane's bed.

It was a calm, soothing room. All that open space, all that airy brightness. Room for hundreds to gather, if they didn't care to sit.

All that comforting pallor made the black, twisted hulk in the geometric center of the floor seem so much more uncanny. It could have been the carcass of a steam locomotive, warped and bent from some unimaginable explosion.

Dislocated, out of context, dominating the single enormous room Jane lived in, it was the wreck of a wrought-iron stair.

"Tea?" Jane asked. She shut the door firmly behind them, and engaged the alarm as her sound system offered up tinkling Tchaikovsky.

"Please," Felix said.

Donall pulled his gaze away from the ruined stair. "Coffee, if you have it?"

"I can get it," she answered. Felix could not resist reaching out as they walked past the fused lump of iron and stroking one hand over what remained of the railing. He remembered it as it had been, a lovely thing, a spiral as tight as a nautilus shell, as a unicorn's horn, a masterpiece of the Promethean Art—beauty, function, science, and magic wrought into one devastating artifact.

It filled him with a great, bewildering homesickness to stand in this room again, so changed and so changeless, and it wounded him hot and deep to see what Matthew had done.

His fingers brushed metal. He expected roughness, the ambient warmth of iron. Cold spiked and writhed under his fingers, a shock that made him snatch his hand back as if something small and venomous had sunk teeth into it.

"It's still alive," he said, stupidly, looking at his hand.

"Matthew severed it," Jane said. "He didn't *unwreak* it. Nothing short of his death would manage that. His blood is bound up in it, his and Kelly's. The bond between them makes a road to Faerie. Though"—a thoughtful hesitation as she turned to examine her favorite student's handiwork—"the way is tangled now, and dark."

She smiled over her shoulder, and Felix swallowed a chill as he and Don followed her behind a screen. "That's why you've been protecting him."

"Don't be ridiculous," Jane said. "I love all my Magi. Even the wayward ones. Christian, are you there?"

"I am indeed," a gentle voice answered. Felix stepped wide of Don and Jane to see who spoke; it was a red-haired, hazel-eyed man in a plain white shirt and a pair of jeans, who rose from Jane's cream-colored sofa to extend his hand.

"Christian Magus," Jane said, "Felix and Donall Magi. Christian is my apprentice of longest standing."

"Not yet Proved?" Felix asked.

"Next year I ascend to full status," Christian said. "I've heard a great deal about you, Felix."

Felix smiled, showing teeth. "I wish you luck in your trial." Somehow, he managed to modulate the wrath out of his voice when he turned to Jane and continued, "Matthew is standing second to Marlowe."

"Hah!" Jane threw her head back hard enough on the laugh that strands of her careful bun slid down around her ears. She tucked one back up, and let the other fall. "I should have known. All the better. The arrangements are settled, then?"

"As they're likely to be. Sunday in Rossville."

"I'll look forward to it," Jane said, as she led them through the door. The enormous kitchen was far beyond her needs; a few small appliances clustered in one corner of the stainless steel and black-and-white granite countertops. Only one burner on the stove showed signs of regular use, and beside it rested a stainless steel Russell Hobbs electric kettle, a toaster oven, and a Braun coffeemaker with the usual accessories. "Christian, be a love and get the beans out of the freezer, please?"

He did as she instructed, and measured them into the grinder too. The whine of the blades defeated conversation for a moment. Then he said, "There was another murder yesterday. A young woman named Nancy Rivera."

She took the cylinder from his hand after he unplugged it, and tapped it into a paper filter, clearing the blades with a forefinger while Felix ran water into both pots. A warm, earthy aroma rose from the grounds until she swung the basket closed. "Related?"

"Fae," he said. "Not the same animal, I don't think. Something big. Wet. With claws. The girl looked like she'd lost two separate fights, the first one with a rhino and the second with a tiger."

"Bunyip," Felix said. Jane looked at him sharply.

"Not our usual mythos."

"I saw it talking to the Kelpie in Central Park earlier this week."

"And you didn't mention anything?"

"There hasn't been a lot of time." Felix rubbed a thumb across the band of his ring. Donall felt echoing cold in his own fingers, while the other apprentice, Christian, fetched cream and rattled cups.

"Well then." Jane took the pot from Felix's hand and poured water carefully into the coffeemaker, a sparkling, trembling stream. "That certainly helps us make our case against Elaine."

She sounded disappointed, and Donall felt a flush of affection for the old woman because of it. No matter what, she wanted to think the best of her child. He picked up the beans from the counter and turned to put them back in the freezer, and stopped with his hand on the door. "Oh."

"If that was meant to be reassuring, it failed utterly," Felix said, when Don let the resulting silence drag on a little too long, broken only by the hiss of steam from the coffeemaker.

"This Matthew?"

"Matthew Szczegielniak," Jane said. "My former apprentice."

"He was the first person at the scene of the first murder," Don said, with real unwillingness. It wasn't his job to *like* people. It was his job to arrest them. "We questioned him as a witness, and he took those two Gothy Otherkin kids home. And I'll tell you something else. Before I got called to the scene yesterday, I had my thumb on the button to call you."

Jane didn't turn away from her contemplation of the thin brown aromatic stream drizzling into the bottom of the glass carafe. *This* was magic, and she loved it. She rested the backs of aching fingers against the warm glass. "Out with it, Donall."

"I followed my ring," he said. "And I saw a cop I know on a street corner, talking to a couple of Fae. One I didn't recognize." It left him cold inside. He squeezed his fingers around his ring, and asked himself sternly whether it was worth protecting a cop who might not be such a good cop after all, if the price was a little girl's life. *Dammit, Ernie. Tell me there's an innocent explanation for that.*

She didn't speak. Christian filled up the silence for her. "And the other one?"

"Elaine's bard," Donall answered, and tried not to feel like a traitor for saying it.

Her first time into shadow, Fionnghuala had ridden a white mare decked with bells, the Morningstar riding beside her. This time, only the click of her shoes accompanied her, like the tapping of dainty hooves. Dainty slippers for a dainty foot.

She descended the long stair straight-backed and unmolested, her cloak shimmering faintly in the darkness. It was all the light she needed. Fionnghuala knew the way into Hell, and the oppressive stillness in her would have told her she was on the right road, even so. The loneliness was an ache in her breast, a hollowness like a scooped-out heart, a gasping stillness that echoed when she listened into it. No lightness filled her, no faith. She had no hope, and she had no song.

God despised this place, and she could feel His disdain as a shunned child feels a parent's scorn: like a thorn in her palm, like a stone in her bosom. Hell is not merely the absence of God. It is the knowledge of His disregard.

For a moment, as she always did when she came to this place, she pitied the stiff-necked Lord of Hell.

She emerged on basalt paving stones long as a coffin and wide as a grave, the black rock as sharp-edged as if they had just been laid, mortarless, without space to slip a knife blade between. A road curved before her, down to a span of bridge over a calm green river. Beyond it rose a spired and twisted castle like some barbaric wrought-iron crown, Hell's banner snapping from every tower. *Gules, simple*: the red of flame and the red of blood, the red of roses and the red of a fox's brush. Windows glinted like rough-cut diamonds in each minaret, reflecting light though no sun shone in the coiled sky overhead.

Fionnghuala's footsteps scouted in advance, the echoes resounding in layers, some crisp and some curved as she crossed the bridge. *Tip tap, tip tap.* No point in trying to sneak. Lucifer knew she was returning. And here came a horseman now, clopping along on a red bay caparisoned black and leading a silk-gray mare. Fionnghuala paused beyond the bridge, amused by the heavy cloak flowing from his shoulders—dense, soft wool lined with silk so dark a red it gleamed purple where the shadows fell—and by the archaic breastplate, and the gauntlets on the big hands gentling the reins. At least he wasn't wearing a helm. His hair curled over his shoulders in fussy ringlets. The horse dipped his head as the rider reined him to a halt, and stood, whuffing softly, calm as if he gazed over green fields and not the hollow pasturage of Hell.

"You have to stop letting the Devil dress you, Keith," Fionnghuala said, folding her arms under her cloak. Feathers tickled her neck as she shook her head. "You look like a Dürer self-portrait."

"Except not going bald," he answered, and leaned down to offer her the reins on the mare's bridle. "What brings you back to Hell?"

"A message for His Majesty," she answered. Her shoes were unsuited to riding, but she swung up. The mare barely noticed the weight across the saddle. Fionnghuala had bones like a bird's. The horse turned willingly, though, at the caress of the reins on her neck, and Keith wheeled his broad-chested steed the opposite way and brought him parallel.

"I wish you wouldn't do this," Keith said. "I knew what I was walking into. You shouldn't risk yourself for me."

The gray mare shook her head. Fionnghuala eased her grip on the reins. "There's no risk. I'm merely playing messenger, as befits a wingèd thing. He told you?"

"Why would he fail to? Any lever he can lay his hand on. You know how he is."

"Yes," Fionnghuala answered. The green scent of the river followed them uproad, and she could hear the lost souls singing from its shallows. It was one thing to go to the teind, willing or unwilling—another entirely to do the Devil's bidding once he had you. The old snake had a knack for getting what he wanted, though. "I was surprised he took you. Dragon Prince."

"Don't remind me," he said. The sideways glance he shot her revealed pale eyes under shaggy ginger brows. He'd kept his beard clipped close, though he'd let his hair grow, and it did give him a Renaissance air. "Not all the perfumes of Araby—"

She knew him too well for the mask of dignity to fool her. "It's hardly a *little* hand," she said, tartly. "What use has he for a soul already damned?"

Keith chuckled, keeping his restive horse to a stately walk. The gate loomed faster than he wanted, anyway: a great alligator-jawed portcullis, tall enough for a cargo train to pass through. Of course, there were railroads in Hell.

"It's a moral victory if you go willing?" Keith said. "Better ask what use he has for a Dragon Prince, Nuala."

"What's a Dragon Prince for? Lucifer considers conquest."

"We're not for conquest," Keith answered. "We're for sacrifice. Last stands and being the stone the hammer shatters itself upon. Alas for the stone, it does not survive the experience." Strong shoulders rolled, straining the straps on the breastplate. "I'm still waiting for the sacrifice. History isn't done with me yet."

The mare swerved at the pressure of Fionnghuala's knee, and brought her rider close enough to Keith that she could lay a hand on his gauntlet. Her fingers looked ridiculous there, laid on scaled iron, and when she squeezed she could not dent the armor.

"The last defender of Hell," she said, and let her hand fall to her saddle.

"Beats Camelot," he answered.

They shared a grin, and rode side by side under the high, fanged gate. The horses were whisked away almost before Keith could offer Fionnghuala his cupped hands to dismount, invisible servants leading them to airy stables deep with straw. The Devil is a horseman.

They crossed the courtyard side by side, as they had ridden in. The great doors stood open before them. Striking against the dark stone of the palace, they were broad slabs of pale wood, pied with irregular patches of satiny charcoal and silver: spalted oak, lovely in its rottenness.

"Is the master at home?"

"Of course," Keith said. She had always seemed a rock to him, an iron woman with her iron hair. Even here in Hell, she stood as straight as an angel. He stripped off his gauntlets and laid them on a table in the hall; another invisible servant whisked them away. Convenient toy. "He's waiting for you. And the table is laid. He said to ask if your old room would serve, and to say he kept it for you."

"There are a thousand rooms in my father's house," Fionnghuala said, not hiding the irony. "Am I meant to stay long enough to need a bed?"

"Traveler's rest," Keith answered. He offered her an elbow, and she accepted, light on her toes, long-necked and lithe.

The hall was broad, the flagstones dark and silver slate strewn with rushes, the walls tapestry-hung. "He kept my room?"

"Aye," Keith said. "Did you ever serve him?"

"No," she answered. "Not as he wished. I never did."

"Murchaud did."

"Murchaud had his reasons." Her shrug rippled the spread of her cloak like wings. "Hell's not so bad, I understand, after Faerie. And Murchaud never had a relationship with God to forfeit. So no, I didn't serve him. But we were, I suppose, after a fashion, friends. As much as he in his loneliness can call anyone friend."

Her footstep hesitated. At the same moment, Keith paused and stepped away from her, clearing a space to swing the sword he wore at his hip, should the need arise. He wasn't surprised by who strolled out of the shadows to greet them, and neither was Fionnghuala. But he didn't pull his hand from his hilt, although he bowed stiffly to the slender, red-haired man who came forward, one hand extended.

"Speak of the devil," Keith said.

"I didn't know the Morningstar had guests," Christian answered, tugging his gloves off one finger at a time. He laid them on an end table, where they vanished as smoothly as Keith's gauntlets had, and shrugged out of his denim coat as well. "I would have dressed for company."

"I'm resident," Keith answered, settling on his heels, easing his shoulders and neck. "What brings you to our half of Hell? Shouldn't you be out going up and down in the world?"

Christian smiled. "I was invited. For the masque. All Hell is coming, and perhaps even Faerie. Marley is leaving us, going back to the Snow Queen. You didn't know?"

"Always the last to," Keith temporized. "And Lucifer's throwing him a ball."

"I imagine he's sending invitations as we speak. Perhaps that's why he's summoned you, Nuala." Christian acknowledged her with a bow. "Or has it to do with your assignation with Michael, the other night?"

Of all the stories, he was the devil she liked the least. Dante's Devil was easily avoided, an idiot god ceaselessly gnawing, crouched on his idiot throne. Milton's had a certain urbane bravado, for all his groaning wings and reek of brimstone. Lucifer was what he was, broken and beautiful. . . .

Christian was the youngest, cat-cruel and cat-clever, the master of bad deals and worse bargains, a cinema trickster. At least the Morningstar loved what he destroyed. Christian went at it for the sheer joy of malice.

"I am but a messenger," she said. In another shape, she would have fanned her wings and hissed; it came through in her voice. "And I have a message to deliver. If you will excuse us?"

"Of course." He nodded and turned to watch them pass.

She hurried, and Keith kept up with her, their cloaks fluttering behind them, dark wings and pale. Neither one liked wearing the weight of Christian's gaze.

"Michael offered a bargain?" Keith asked, when they were out of earshot.

Fionnghuala hitched her feathers tighter about her shoulders. "Michael offered nothing new. If Lucifer would bend his neck, his Lord would love him again."

"In four thousand years," Keith said, rubbing the line between his eyes, "you would think that one of them would have grown up a little."

Fionnghuala's laugh was anything but ladylike. "As below, so above," she said. She took his arm back, and squeezed his elbow hard. "I've missed you."

"And I you," he answered. "I'm a dog on a chain here, and you know how this place weighs your soul." He covered her hand with his own for a moment, as they paused before another great set of spalted oaken doors. These were carved in elaborate filigree, and glimpses of the room beyond could be seen through the openwork. It was a long room, richly appointed. Someone indistinct, all in black with golden curls, stood at the far end, head bowed before the fire. Keith lowered his voice. "Have you seen Elaine? Or Ian?"

"Not of late. I can bring them a message, if you like."

"With their invitation to the ball?"

She snorted. He stepped forward, leading her, and the doors eased open on silent hinges. On the right was a cozy nook of three or four chairs and a settee arranged around a low oval table. On their left stood a long table laden with scented platters. Three places had been set, one at the head and one on either side, and the vast empty length stretching below it sent Fionnghuala's loneliness aching across the bridge of her nose.

Lucifer did not raise his head as they came forth. He stood before the fire, shoulders hunched under his tight-folded pinions, one hand cupped loosely around the bell of a glass, and Fionnghuala could see that his eyes were closed, the corners pinched as if he addressed some inward pain.

He's a snake. But it didn't stop her from pitying him.

"Morningstar," she said, stepping away from Keith MacNeill as the

Dragon Prince released her arm. "I bring a message from Michael." He didn't move, didn't flicker a feather or raise one fine-boned hand to stop her words. She thought of Christian, smug in the empty, echoing castle, and Michael with foresty wings bowering the girl in the rain. It was information, and information was currency.

And if she didn't trust Lucifer, she called him a friend. And she didn't like Christian at all. "And there's news, as well, old Swan."

And perhaps I know a way around Michael's obduracy.

He straightened, wings fanning for balance as he turned, and held his glass out to her with the single faint lip-print smudging the rim. He smiled like a shark as she took it, the grief vanished as if it had never been. "Please," he said. "Nuala. Drink. You have traveled far."

Rumpelstiltskin finally resolved that Gypsy wasn't an immediate threat to the health and well-being of all concerned around suppertime on Thursday, after the assemblage had broken for sleep and daylight duties and reconvened to continue discussion of unicorns and Faeries and points between. The cat celebrated by slipping from his usual vantage in the hallway behind the wrought-iron plant stand to twine the big man's ankles and beg for crumbs of cheese, which Gypsy fed him whenever Autumn wasn't looking. Rumpelstiltskin pushed them around on the carpet with soft white-rimmed toes until he was satisfied they weren't going to bite him back, then consumed them with a great show of satisfaction and a flipping tail-tip.

Gypsy sat in Autumn's usual armchair with a pile of reference books beside him and Carel's ThinkPad open on his knee, the sound dialed down to counteract the tinny MIDI files infesting half the Web pages he surfed. Autumn, her hair held out of her face with the back of her left hand, sprawled on the floor, where she drew charts and family trees on a big sheet of craft paper with repurposed dry-erase markers. All three lifted their heads when the front door swung open, cooling the house with a draft.

"Carel?"

"I've brought company," Carel called back. "Is that Gypsy's car in the drive? . . . Oh, hi, Gyp."

"Hey your own self," he said, and set the laptop computer aside before heaving himself to his feet. And stopped halfway, blinking, while

Autumn knelt up, and Carel and her company appeared in the hall doorway. "You weren't kidding."

Three children clustered behind her, two boys and a girl. Well, Gypsy allowed, *children* might be an uncharitable description. Young men and a young woman, twentysomething. A black-haired boy, slender and well-made. The second boy a Gothy type with his dye job showing red at the roots, and the girl ash-haired and contrasting hippie chic with the scars and piercings decorating her flesh. *She* made Gypsy's old scars itch, in particular, which was odd because there was nothing to her, metaphysically speaking, and he could see the power dusting the boys as if they'd been rubbing their hands over soft, silvery schist and the flakes of compressed mica had coated their fingers and palms.

Carel, as she always did, glared with power like the coals in a black iron furnace. She hesitated in the doorway, met his eyes, smiled a little, and then turned her attention to Autumn. "Sorry there wasn't more warning," she said. "I didn't think to call. Autumn, Gypsy, I'd like you to meet Ian MacNeill, a Prince of the Daoine Sidhe; Jewels—the young woman I spoke to you about on the phone, Tums"—Autumn winced at the nickname, but couldn't hide her smile—"and Geoff."

"And who's Geoff?" Gypsy said, collecting himself enough to finish rising from among the books, step over Autumn's legs, and extend his hand.

"Nobody in particular," Geoff answered, but he was the first one to put out his hand. His grip was firm, a little cool, as if he had been not wearing gloves outside. The safety pins lining the outside seam of his pants jangled as he stepped back, giving way to the girl.

She smiled as Gypsy took her hand, careful of her bones, and shook it lightly. No shock of power, no initiation, for all her scars, but he saw the sallow yellows and violets that swirled around her and knew her inner bruising and her pain. He set her back on the shelf like a china cup; there was a deep crack there that would take more skill than his to mend.

Autumn had risen to her feet and come up behind him, making soothing noises to the girl while Gypsy introduced himself to the Prince. The young man seemed amused, and Gypsy supposed he'd broken some protocol shaking hands with the others first, but he'd never had much to do with royalty. Gypsy did notice the way the girl kept one corner of her attention on the Prince no matter where she was, even when Autumn led her to the sofa and insisted she and Geoff sit.

Gypsy released his grip and leaned back on his heels, huffing into his beard as he planted his hands on his hips. "A house full of the Fair Folk," he said, and turned to his hostesses. "When you told me Carel was Merlin, Autumn, I didn't think you meant it literally."

Carel looked up sharply. "What's she been telling you?"

"It's my fault," Gypsy answered, as Autumn lifted her hand, paused, and said, "I'll just make more tea" over her shoulder as she brushed past Ian and fled the living room.

Carel smiled at him. "I knew you were trouble from the minute I met you." It could have been worse. It could have been Moira, or Jason, God forbid. She actually didn't mind Gypsy *knowing*. But she hoped he hadn't been *telling*. "What'd I miss?"

"You've been in Faerie," he said.

Carel shrugged, as good as an admission with an Elf in the room. "I get around."

Gyp laughed. Rumpelstiltskin, normally shy in the presence of strangers, came and rubbed himself in loops around Carel's ankles, sniffing and purring. She squatted to pick him up, and his long limbs gangled over her shoulder and out of the cradle of her embrace, an armful of cat and more.

Gypsy said, "Mostly, we've been trying to figure out whether it's a portent of some sort that Autumn saw the unicorn. And no, we haven't told Moira. A thing."

"Well, that's a relief then," Carel said. She dropped her chin for the cat's convenience, and smiled as he hid his pointed face against her neck.

The tension that had held Ian static by the doorway snapped and he came into the room and selected a chair, confident and in command.

Jewels had dropped her head, and with her face and hands concealed in the fall of her hair, was listening to her cell phone messages with an expression of concentration. Four and a half days' worth: she hadn't checked since Sunday night.

"Actually," Carel said, "it's just as well you're here, Gyp. You see,

Jewels has been accepted in service by His Highness"—she nodded to Ian, as the cat bumped her chin hard with the crown of his head—"and she needs training."

"How do you teach somebody to survive in Faerie?"

Ian settled himself on one corner of the sofa, not far from Jewels. "I can teach the lady that," he said, crossing his legs and folding his hands. "But I cannot 'prentice her in mortal magics, for I do not know them."

"And I do."

"Better than Moira, anyway," Carel said. "And Autumn hasn't a lot of interest in anything beyond meditation—"

"I heard that!" floated from the kitchen.

Carel smiled. The cat squirmed in her arms, and she let him down. When Gypsy looked at Jewels, though, she was frowning at her phone, and Geoff had his hand on her shoulder and was leaning forward.

She must have felt his gaze. "I have to call that cop," she said. "He's left three messages."

"Peese?" Geoff said, with a wince.

"War," she answered. They grinned at each other, leaving Gypsy completely lost. "I'll call him in a minute. I'm sorry, Gy-Gypsy?"

"Gyp," said Gypsy.

"Gyp," she echoed, with another ghosty smile. "You're a magician?"

"I'm a Pagan," he said. "Shamanistic tradition. I can teach you something, sure. If you can tell *me* something."

She leaned forward, swallowing, her hands folded over the warm plastic of her phone. "I'll try."

He pointed to her forehead, blunt finger and a bitten nail indicating the line of scars braided like a tiara across her brow. "How'd you manage to get scarred up like that and *not* earn any power of your own yet?"

Her chin went up, her hair shaken back from her face, slipping behind the points of her much-pierced ears. "I don't know," she said, blunt confession that pleased him.

"We'll find out," Gypsy said, as the phone rang. The landline, not anybody's cell.

Autumn dodged in from the kitchen with a tea tray in both hands, and slid it onto the table beside the telephone as Carel starting forward. "It's Lily," Gypsy and Carel said, in unison.

Autumn's hand paused over the handset. She glared through the veil of her hair. "I *hate* it when you do that."

Lily had something she wanted to talk about—whatever it was, enough to make her voice flat with emotion—and didn't seem deterred when Autumn told her the house was full of strangers. "I'll be over as soon as I pick up my car," she said. "Want me to get a couple of pizzas on the way? It'd do me good to be around people."

Autumn cast a jaundiced eye around the room, as Jewels leaned toward Geoff and mouthed *You don't suppose she means Lily Wakeman, do you?* "Pizza sounds like a great plan. Make sure you get one veggie; I'm not sure everybody's a carnivore."

Lily laughed, as if Autumn's voice had eased whatever it was weighing her down, and hung up. Autumn looked up to see the slender boy with the eerie green eyes hovering at her elbow. Ian. "I beg your pardon," he said, "I couldn't help but overhear. You saw a unicorn?"

She nodded, setting the phone back on the cradle. "I did."

Ian touched her elbow, lightly, leaning in as if to catch the scent of some perfume she wasn't wearing. "I know a Mage you should talk to. He knows a few things about unicorns."

Detective Smith said he needed to talk to her as soon as possible, and that he'd cheerfully drive out of the city to do it. Jewels, the back of her hand pressed to her mouth and the phone pressed to her ear, its transparent lime-green plastic cover clinging like a kiss to her cheek, hesitated longer than she should have. It was Thursday evening. He'd think she'd been ignoring his calls for most of the week. She'd have to find an excuse—or just plain tell him where she'd been.

She couldn't bring him to Carel's house. And she needed an advantage, the advantage of home turf. It didn't matter how *nice* Smith was, how much of a relief it was to hear his musical voice on the phone and not Detective Peese's nasal tenor. But—she checked the display on her phone just as Detective Smith cleared his throat—but it was Thursday. And there was probably a bus to Springfield. If she couldn't convince somebody to drive there.

"Have you ever heard of a place called the Rathskeller?" she asked, ignoring Geoff's stare. "In Springfield?"

Don, thumb-punching on his PDA with reckless speed, had not. But the girl knew the street address, and it was easy enough to find the Web site and Google a map. "I'll be there at ten," he said. "I hope you'll recognize me."

The laugh that answered, though made tenuous by the crackling mouthpiece of her phone, was more relaxed—more mature—than he had expected. "You're hard to miss, Detective."

Ten o'clock—which left him with barely enough time to shower, change into something that didn't look either slept in or too conservative, collect his car, fight the last half of rush hour over the Triborough Bridge, and start driving north, if he wanted to be there in time to have a look around before committing to the arrangement.

He told the shift lieutenant where he was going and why, filed his paperwork, arranged a midnight check-in, and hurried back to his apartment, stopping at a coffee shop along the way.

The drive was no worse than it had to be, the weather cooperating and the steady stream of headlights south and taillights north dispersing slowly as he left Fairfield County. The highway was featureless by night, broad lanes of well-maintained blacktop picked out in reflective paint, and it took him less time than it seemed it should to reach Hartford. Springfield was less than an hour up 91 after that.

It was a postage-stamp city, a skyline you could take in at a glance, without detail or complexity. A cluster of a few boxy curtain wall buildings and one old-fashioned stone office spire dwarfed by its modern cousins lounged on a low bank of the broad, brown Connecticut River, and once in its cluttered streets, Donall had no difficulty finding the address, although it did take a few circles through the one-way corridors to locate parking. He turned the collar of his leather trench coat up— he hadn't worn it in a year and a half—and slid from behind the wheel into a chill night, the tang of early winter frosting the sour scent of garbage.

The boots got worn more often. And were more comfortable because of it; the coat strained across his shoulders. He knew from the people passing out front that he was twenty years too old for this place, but he was hoping he'd get made for a creepy guy trolling for inappropriate women rather than an officer of the law. He checked the tuck of his black turtleneck in the side window, squared his shoulders, and went to meet his doom.

It was as loud as expected. He felt the bass line through the sidewalk cement half a block away. The faded red and yellow sign on the cinderblock front of the old warehouse advertised LAZER FLASH. The ghosts of festive colors haunted its facade.

When Don followed Jewels' instructions and walked around back, he found a loading dock with two-pipe steel railing up either side of the stairs and along the length of the cement. Young people huddled there, some skinny and some voluptuous, their hair spiked or ratted or allowed to tumble in sheer ebony and carnelian waves. Embers glowed by their fingertips: the smoking lounge. The breeze snaked through the reek of clove and Don sneezed, climbing the stairs to enlist in the line.

The kids queuing were kids: he figured if he started checking ID, he could probably collar half the freshman class of Springfield College. The bouncer *was* checking—most of it fake or borrowed. Don had his ready—NY driver's license, in the wallet without the shield—when he got up there.

"Eight dollars," the bouncer said, bored. Don had six inches' height on him, and the girl just before was waved through without paying. But Don wasn't wearing a corset. He paid.

The main entrance seemed to be a sally port just left of the big, rusted loading bay doors. A sign hung to his right, hand-painted purple on black. A gleaming violet neon script capital R illuminated it. RATHSKELLER.

"This must be the place," he said to himself, and so he passed within.

In the darkness he stepped right, as if the percussive wave of the music had brushed him out of the way. Alongside the door, against the sealed loading bay shutter, where he could scope the place for a minute or two before he walked out in it. His hand dipped into the pocket of his jeans and found a cracked hard plastic case, from which he withdrew custom-made earplugs.

They were for the shooting range. He praised a couple of random deities in passing that the plugs had still happened to be stuck in his jeans, and seated each one in turn. It lowered the deafening rattle of the music to an uncomfortable roar, and gave him time to inspect the venue.

His ducked head and hands cupped before his face presented the convincing illusion that he was indulging in a couple of fingernails of blow.

The Rathskeller had been a laser tag labyrinth before it became a dance club, and the reminders of its former employment were evident. Salvaged fire escape stairs rose to a grillwork balcony that circumnavigated the vast chamber, chained to the ceiling and braced by frequent pillars. The far side of the space was one long bar, worked by three bartenders.

Also on the left, a drop led to a dance pit, reached by two broad steps carpeted in leopard print. The far left wall was a stage, complete with maniacal DJ and towering speaker stacks. The dance floor was an incandescent darkness writhing with bodies, a Bosch painting wrought animate, cluttered with forms made mutant by strobing crimson light and elaborate clothes. Black-painted pillars in front hosted two men and a woman chained in various states of dishabille. One of them was offering himself to be flogged, ten knotted ropes braided into a handle clenched in his teeth and hopeful tears staining his cheeks. The dancers were far too busy just now.

The walls were cinderblock, matte-black, and the surreal, intentionally disorienting fluorescent designs left from the club's previous incarnation smeared them in great, random whorls. On Don's right, the leopard-print carpet extended under a seating area composed of repurposed cast-iron lawn furniture. Beyond even that, a portion of the labyrinth remained: a plywood maze three stories tall, confounding with mirrors and disconcerting with switchbacks. The booths, such as they were, were situated in its recesses, and other things went on in shadowed and curtained corners. Everywhere was the groan of leather, the hush of velvet, the glint of plastic.

Right now, the best-lit part of the club was a patch of newspaper-clad concrete near the labyrinth, which was set off by still more two-pipe railing, this painted dull crimson and crowded with onlookers. Don couldn't have missed Jewels if he'd meant to. Wearing a smock and a surgical mask, she commanded the middle of that bright spot at the back of the room. She bent over the back of a half-nude young man who hunched in turn over the back of a reversed chair, a blue plastic-handled scalpel in her right hand, making his red blood run. The boy she said wasn't her boyfriend was nowhere in evidence, but another young man had been permitted inside the rail and leaned against it, arms folded, watching. He made Don's Promethean ring cold, but not sharply so, and whoever the young man was, he had no apparent difficulties with the iron.

Don stuffed his hands in his pockets and slipped between tables, toward Jewels and her acolytes, pressing against the current of tension that hung on the air. The shirtless boy was Caucasian, hair ratted around his face, his eyes closed and his teeth clenched as he pushed out tightly controlled sobs. Jewels worked with absolute concentration. The teeming crowd, the breath-held observers lined up along the gallery rail, the thumping music and the shouts of the drinkers and the bartenders might have been the murmur of wind through long grasses. She never glanced up, even when Don eased his bulk between two curvaceous velvet-clad women and claimed the railing directly in front of her and her subject, where he couldn't see too clearly what she was doing.

He could smell it, though. Over the perfume of the ladies he'd nudged aside—one darkly redolent of grave-sweet lilies and sharp with ylang-ylang, the other musky rose and myrrh—an abattoir savor threaded the air. Attenuated chrysanthemum streaks curved around the boy's pale, corrugated torso, drying on his chest. Don imagined his back must look like a fireworks display in reverse, dark on bright. It wasn't *much* blood, though.

He wondered what Jewels was carving on his skin.

She set the scalpel aside on a TV tray covered with paper and picked up something else. Her hands deft in red-daubed vinyl, she moistened a cotton ball in some viscous substance and stroked it into the pattern of wounds, her lips moving as she murmured to her client, or maybe herself. Don couldn't imagine that either one could hear what she was saying over the music.

She patted him on the shoulder at last, and stood back, stripping her gloves inside out. The boy remained where he had been, eyes easing open a little at a time, his face flushed strawberry bright in patches on skin like bone.

Someone nudged forward a bucket. Jewels pulled off mask and smock, and they went in on top of the gloves. The recapped scalpel followed, wadded in the paper from the tray. She crouched, murmured something in the ear of the boy, who was still aswim in his endorphin cocktail. And Don, nerving himself, slung a leg over the railing and moved forward.

He expected to be grabbed, intercepted. But no one reached out for him, and instead he found himself the center of attention, bathed in a flood of incandescent light, towering over a skinny child with a Faerie's ears pricking through her brown-blonde braids. "You wanted to see me," he said as a young man came up to them.

"Come on," Jewels answered, stepping away from the blood and the bleeding boy. "We've got a booth. This is Ian. Ian, Detective Smith."

She'd meant to rattle him. Make him run a gauntlet, force him onto her turf. He followed her, coat swinging around him; they resembled a mantling raven pursuing some twig-and-bent-grass creature. Ian brought up the rear.

The Bertelli boy was holding down a table inside the maze, past two clinching couples and an argument, and a shortish girl with violet hair was sprawled on one of the wooden benches, her back in the angle of the corner, a drink cupped in her hands. She rocked her head in time to the music, eyes closed, and Don thought Jewels looked sour-faced over Geoff's attention to her.

It was quieter here; the walls baffled sound. The booth had two sides flanked by benches built into the wall and the other two buttressed by chairs. Once Jewels placed herself in a chair, she managed introductions without shouting while the men sorted themselves into seats.

"Are you sure you want to talk in front of all these people?" Don asked, when he'd waited for her to regain her drink and click nearly melted ice against her teeth.

"Unless you have a warrant," she said. "These are friends."

But Don thought the guilty sideways glance that she shot Lily said something else. Not a threat: she was on edge, but not scared of them. Don didn't know what to call it yet. He waited, folding his hands, resisting the urge to fiddle his ring. She was at ease here, at home. Not at all the trapped fey thing she'd been in the interview room.

Jewels set her drink aside. "You wanted to talk to me, Detective Smith," she said.

He smiled and awarded her the point. "Interesting place you've got here," he said, with a vague gesture of his left hand. Somebody tromped overhead, dancing or running through one of the twisting corridors on the second level. "What you were doing out there—"

"This is where I work," she said, tracing a finger through the luke-warm condensation that had left rings puddled on the tabletop. "One of the places. This is my job."

"Cutting people?"

"Decorating them." She shrugged. "I wouldn't expect you to under-stand. I'm trained—"

"You seemed very confident."

"She's good," Geoff said, leaning forward on his elbows to intersect their conversation. "Well-known. Respected. You don't get the kind of buzz Jewels gets unless you do good work."

Don held up his hand. "I wasn't questioning that. Is it an apprentice-ship sort of deal?"

"Mostly," she said. "And most people are too squeamish to do a good job. So yeah, I found a guy who did body modification, and said I wanted to learn." She looked down and counted on her fingers. "Six years now."

"She studied with Sergei," Geoff said—if that was the name, exactly, under the music. Don could tell he was supposed to recognize it. More, the purple-haired girl—Lily—did. Her head tilted with reluctant respect.

Jewels dismissed it with a blush and downcast glance, but she was pleased. "Ask me what you wanted to ask me."

"It makes me a little nervous," Don said, leaning back with folded arms that got his itchy fingers a little closer to the butt of his gun, "to come all this way to talk to you about your friend's murder and whether the agency behind it was Fae or mortal, and find you hanging out with a changeling."

Ian smiled pleasantly. "I've just met the lady," he said. The first words out of his mouth, and Donall was surprised by the light sweetness of his voice and the gentle Scottish burr. "She came to my mother's court for assistance in solving the murder. And I am that. Assistance, I mean."

"Your mother's—" Don had never experienced the sensation of being dumbstruck before. His mouth opened and closed, until he swallowed and tried again. "You're *that* Ian. Ian MacNeill."

A lingering constriction in Don's chest released pain he hadn't even realized he carried. There *was* an explanation for Ernie's clandestine conversation with the bard. "*That's* what your mother's courtier was doing in New York."

Ian looked uncomfortable. "I beg your pardon?"

"Queen Elaine's bard," Don said, aware that he was volunteering too much and gambling anyway. "I saw him in New York City. Meeting with a homicide cop who's working the murder of Althea Benning . . . and another Fae, a woman."

"What did she look like, the woman?" Ian's hands had gone still on the table, and his voice was very calm.

"Black hair, very pale skin. Maybe five-ten, not over one thirty-five. She was wearing yellow, and barrettes with sunflowers."

Ian's lips thinned. "I don't suppose you can draw?"

"Not good enough for that." Don licked his lips, and cast a sideways glance down at his ring. What assurances *did* he have that Jane was on the right side? In retrospect, his agreement to help her seemed hurried, unconsidered . . . unwise. He was not usually so quick to choose sides. "Can *you* draw?"

"As a matter of fact," Ian said. "Pass me a pen."

Lily provided one, a violet rollerball, and a folded sheet of paper with a shopping list written on one side. Ian hunched forward over the table with his long-nailed fingers twisted through his hair, supporting his head as his other hand scratched with the pen.

Don tried not to stare, but it didn't take more than a few lines to convince him. "Different hair," he said. "Different clothes. But that was her."

Ian capped the rollerball and handed it back to Lily. Jewels leaned over his shoulder, one hand resting on his arm, oblivious to his raised eyebrow and sideways glance. "I've seen her too."

"Juliet?"

She leaned away from Ian. "In New York. On Halloween."

"Thank you," Ian said, and crumpled the paper into his pocket.

Don, in the process of reaching for it, frowned. "I take it from your reaction that your mother didn't send anyone?"

"Not Cairbre," Ian answered. "Curious . . ." He paused, looked up, and jumped to his feet sharply enough to rattle the table. Jewels squeaked and grabbed her drink. "Aunt Nuala!"

Don hadn't seen her arrive. He glanced up, and there she stood, a pale woman in—perhaps—her vigorous sixties, her gray hair tangled in wiry waves around her shoulders, wearing a white button-down shirt and indigo jeans, as out of place as a dove in a rookery. "Your father sends his greetings, Prince Ian," she said, with a nod.

Ian's hand went to his mouth, covering his expression. "Only his greetings?"

"And his love," she said more gently. "And he inquires if you still wish to claim your throne, when you have had time to think on it. Also, his master wishes me to extend an invitation to you and your family, to attend a masque in Hell tomorrow, as a farewell to Master Marlowe." She seemed to notice Don's startle when she said *Hell*, and smiled at him with the corner of her lip as she extended a sealed, folded paper to Ian, who accepted without comment.

The woman glanced around the table, fixing each one in turn on her gaze. "And you, Mary Wakeman, who calls herself Lily . . ." she said, when she paused.

Lily pressed into the corner, pulling her drink against her chest. "Who told you my name?"

The gray-haired woman smiled. "That isn't the matter now. You and I need to talk, my dear, about your choice of paramours. Please, come with me."

Whatever it was—Lily's whole name, so blithely delivered, or the old woman's grace and poise, or the way her voice (harsh, not melodious, but resonant and deep) cut the noise in the club as if it were murmured direct in Lily's ear—Lily got out past Geoff, who slid from the booth to facilitate her passage, and looked from Jewels to Ian and back again.

Jewels was the one who nodded. "We'll be here."

"Thanks." She scooped her wrap out of the booth, just in case, and fixed a hair clip as she stood, feeling the music shiver through the floor. Laibach, and the DJ was stressing the system with it.

She'd gone by Autumn's house with the intention of talking to her about the possibility of disentangling herself from Moira without losing contact with others in the coven—*You, and Michael,* she'd planned to say—but then Gypsy was there and between the two of them they'd broken it to Lily about Jewels wanting to come in and learn something of the arts, and Jewels had turned out to be somebody she knew from the club scene and kind of vaguely disliked, and Geoff somebody she knew rather better, if a yearlong flirtation culminating in a blow job in a dark corner of the now-defunct Blackthorne, when he'd been tending bar there, counted for anything.

Goth clubs did not have a long median life span.

But he'd been sweet, and from his sideways glances, he remembered it too.

The evening's conversation had somehow, after explanations and digressions, evolved into the three of them and a couple of Fae of Jewels' acquaintance going out clubbing on Fetish Night. At first, Lily's self-discipline had been strained not sneaking her own sideways glances at the Fae, but soon enough she'd forgotten to find him magical, and had just enjoyed sharing with Jewels in the unstinting and ever-so-slightly competitive attention of two attractive men.

And she'd been flying that morning.

Sometimes, it seemed as if everything in life went magical all at once. Synchronicity, or perhaps the hand of Fate.

"You should know," Lily told the stranger after they had stepped aside, "that I'm *not* interested in personal advice from strangers. Or judgments. Especially judgments."

The older woman leaned close. She slipped a hand into her pocket, and brought out something that looked like a popper, amyl nitrate, a little twist of paper that bulged in the middle, except it was silver and Chinese red instead of white. "I'm not here to offer advice, my dear," she said. "I'm Fionnghuala, by the way. T'were rude of me not to offer a name."

She tried to press the popper into Lily's hand, and Lily pulled away. "I don't want that."

"You need it," Fionnghuala said. The girl's hands were cold, but the swanmay caught them—so much larger than her own—and folded the fingers around the scrap. "It will take you to Hell. You, and a companion, if you choose."

"A . . . companion?"

Fionnghuala smiled. "It's traditional to bring a date to a party. You pop the paper open, and breathe it in—"

"I know how they work," Lily said. She tucked it into her pocket, intending to flush it when the opportunity presented itself. "Why would I want to go to Hell?"

"Because that is where your lover will be, tomorrow night." Fionnghuala held out an envelope of fine linen-pressed paper, sealed with dark red wax. It was amazing what a girl could accomplish with the joint cooperation of an archangel and the Prince of Lies. "Here's your invitation, my dear."

Chapter Sixteen
Everything Goes to Hell

The invitation was on thick, soft, high rag-content ivory paper with an embossed crest. Geoff ran his thumb over it before flipping it open with his thumbnail. It felt more like stiff cloth than paper, rich and knife-creased. "I can't believe I'm agreeing to this. You want to take me to Hell."

Lily grinned, lounging on the settee in her cramped apartment, a clove cigarette glowing in her hand. He needed to get over that thing about Jewels. And Geoff *hadn't* agreed to join the exodus to Hell until he'd found out that Jewels was going, as Ian's companion. "Who else could I ask? Without having to explain the whole kidnapped-by-Faeries thing?"

"To somebody who hadn't explained it to you first?" Between him and Jewels and Ian, she'd managed to more or less build a narrative of where he'd been and what he'd done. He handed her back the paper. She struggled for a moment in the three-inch heels of her granny boots, the red metallic fabric of her skirt whisking around her ankles. Automatically, Geoff reached out to steady her, and she accepted, letting him pull her to her feet. She wore a corset over the skirt; once she was up, it pressed her spine into alignment and made her feel as light and sustained as when Christian took her hands and coaxed her into midair. "It's funny meeting you again this way."

"Kismet," he said, with a shrug. He was kitted out himself in Gothic finery, a vintage tuxedo with frayed cuffs that made him look like a refugee from the Addams Family, his hair freshly re-dyed that morning so his ruddy eyebrows looked even stranger on his pallor, eyeliner and lipstick as dark as a bruise. A mask hung around his neck: Polichinelle. "Are we going?"

She glanced out her window at the sunset. "Yes," she said, and tucked the invitation into her corset. She retrieved the twist of paper Fionnghuala had given her, and weighed it in her palm. It felt warm, the paper crisp and crinkly when she pinched the ends. "Ready?"

"This is silly," Geoff said.

"You're telling me," Lily answered, and broke the capsule under their noses as he leaned in close.

Geoff had closed his eyes reflexively. He braced for bitter unpleasantness, but what diffused through the air was pleasant, the deep musty scent of old leaves in autumn, the richness of pollen, the warmth of moist earth tilled over in the sun. His eyes widened, his head went back—

He found himself staring over Lily's shoulder, at Hell.

It wasn't anything that he'd expected. No lava pits, no lakes of flame, no writhing souls nor demons with pitchforks. That dead-leaf scent swept around them, ruffling their clothes and lifting the hair on their necks. They stood in a formal entryway, a tall tapestried room brightened by soothing gaslights, cut flowers—roses and lilies—banked like snowdrifts along the walls. That scent grew enervating as the other faded.

They were alone in the room, but Geoff thought he knew which way to go. More roses strewed the path. He took Lily's hand; they shared a glance, and she laughed. It sounded strained. "I have a bad feeling about this," Geoff muttered.

Lily nibbled her lips, staining her teeth with lipstick. "If I want to learn magic, I need to do this."

Geoff felt the need she spoke of, and something worse and colder underneath: sucking pressure like a vacuum, an emptiness that turned the flowers into funereal wreaths, the faintly heard music into a dirge. The sensation wasn't . . . *crushing* so much as haunting, as coming home to an empty house that shouldn't be. He squeezed her hand and stepped forward, Lily's skirt rustling alongside, but she sensed his hesitation. As they came to a cross-corridor where the foot-bruised carpet of roses tended left, she stepped forward and took the lead in turn.

They rounded another corner and now came upon a great Gothic doorway which soared three times Geoff's height. The doors stood open, guarded on either side by winged figures as still as statues, that shed radiance all about. Beyond the doors were people—a paltry gathering for such a grand ball. Gently, Lily tugged her hand free of Geoffrey's sweaty clasp, and presented the invitation to the angel on the left.

Or, not precisely an angel. As she handed him the paper, she saw the ridged claws, sharply curved over the tips of each finger, and the way his wings dripped feathers when he moved, revealing gray membrane underneath. *A masque*, she thought, as Geoff pulled his own hook-nosed disguise up and settled it over his eyes.

"You may pass, Mary Wakeman," the disguised demon said, returning the invitation. His voice was mellifluous, soft and almost cloying. Feathers shed like snow. Goose feathers, and some swan: the Prince of Hell was not above humiliating his own. "And your guest as well."

"Thank you," she said. She stepped forward, but he barred her path with one horny hand.

"Your mask, Mistress Wakeman."

"Oh!" she said, and unhooked it from the waistband of her skirt. As Geoff was Polichinelle, so she was Harlequin. She tucked the elastic under her hair, took Geoff's elbow when he presented it, and sailed forward.

"Mary?" he murmured in her ear.

She made a face, her skin moving against the inside of her mask. "Mary Theresa. But I've been Lily for years."

"Ah," he answered, still sotto voce. *"Un nom de Goth."*

She didn't quite snort.

The expected crowd wasn't—not so much of one, anyway. Some two dozen figures, a few Geoff recognized from Faerie: the Queen, the bard, the Prince of Hell himself. They clustered in groups, waited upon by more faux angels. "Hell's half empty," Lily said, unable to remember at the moment if it was a quote.

"I don't think the damned were invited," Geoff said, as a servitor angel paused with his tray. Geoff handed Lily a red wine, and paused with another in his hand. "Have you seen what you've come to see?"

"No," she said, turning slowly, heel and toe. "I haven't . . ." She paused, and quickly sipped her wine, rolling it across her tongue until she felt able to speak. "Is that *him*?"

Geoff followed where she stared. "Yes," he said. "It is."

Lucifer Morningstar held court alongside a curved, small stage without a single musician on it, from which sweet melodies nevertheless flowed. He was clothed in white from head to toe, a suit of archaic cut that displayed his calf in hose and a high-heeled, buckled shoe, a coat of brocade silk and matching breeches cut close to the leg, argent as his mantling wings. Silver buttons up each thigh that held tarnish in their creases, dark as the shadow of his crown. Even the leather of his rapier carrier was white, the buckles silver. But the swept hilt of the sword suspended from it was elegant, practical steel, the arch of the guard reminiscent of ostrich plumes, and though he wore a white velvet mask, the hand that rested nonchalantly on his pommel was innocent of any glove.

The conversation was idle, painfully so. Lucifer stood with the Queen and Cairbre—the Queen costumed as Eostre, with flowers twined through her long dark hair in place of the souls that the Mebd had worn there, and Cairbre in a conquistador's helm and breastplate, wrought from silver rather than steel. Matthew the fallen Mage stood nearby, not actually costumed, but still resplendent in his gaudy coat and clothes borrowed in Faerie. He did not speak, and seemed to turn all his attention to the drink in his hand whenever Lucifer glanced at him.

Such a pretty thing, and so flawed at his heart: it made the Devil's fingers itch to mend him.

The Queen's patent unwillingness to show distraction, on the other hand, amused him. She tensed each time someone entered the ballroom, but she would not turn, and she would not ask after her husband. Such pride, and yet the pride of folk who were not angels, be they iron folk or moonlight, was barely pride at all.

She didn't notice when Christian's witch appeared, the mortal boy on her arm, and she didn't notice when they turned this way and that, ac-

cepted wine from a tray, and retired to a corner to observe. The Devil
noticed, though. Everyone was waiting for something: an arrival, a de-
parture. It made a pleasing sort of allegory.

As for himself, Lucifer was waiting for the poet. The Devil didn't
turn a calf for just anyone.

Nor did he *wait* for just anyone, either—however fashionable their
lateness might be. Still, a ripple swept the sparse crowd of guests and
the attendant demons, and Lucifer turned on his jeweled shoe to find
the source, already smiling.

His poet would *never* disappoint him.

The invisible musicians seemed to take a breath, to pause for a moment,
and then a high, skirling lift of violin and flute picked Kit up and swept
him into the room. He'd spent what seemed half a lifetime on his costume—time held no meaning in Hell, even less so than in Faerie—and
he knew every eye in the room was upon him.

He'd left his bard's cloak in his room this once, and wore rose-red, a
doublet and breeches in an old, old style. His mask was red as well, sequined so it scattered light as he advanced, alone, among the revelers.
They drew back as he came forward, and there was nothing to conceal
what he wore harnessed on his shoulders: the sooty half-furled wings,
like a vulture's, the feathers charcoal and inky and black. And much
better made than those sported by the befeathered demons: Kit's wings
did not shed a trail like bread crumbs behind him when he walked, for
trampling underfoot.

Every guest watched as Lucifer came forward, abandoning his conversation with no more than a heedless turn of his head. He came to
Kit on a moment of indrawn breath, as every eye watched, every
mouth stilled. And Kit stood smiling, arms crossed, and let the Devil
come to him.

"You wanted a masque," he said, when Lucifer was close enough that
an unraised voice would carry. "Is this costume enough, Prince of
Lies?"

Lucifer paused, his wings fanning out to each side, the draft bending
his feathers. :You look the very devil,: he said, to be heard, and then
lowered his voice a little. :If you wanted wings, I would have seen to it.:

"Only if I asked."

:Well, yes.: That was the dance. The Devil smiled, and came up another step, side-slipping, encircling them both in the bower of his wings—white living things that made Kit's black feathers a sad mockery. :Repent of thy sins and be free of me, thou-who-wert Christofer Marley.:

Kit didn't uncross his arms. He leaned back a little, looking up at Lucifer. "Of my sins, I repent freely. It is where God and I differ on the meaning of the word, alas, that cannot be mended. Have you come to wish me luck, on Sunday?"

:Wilt use my magic, warlock?: He smiled through the locks of hair that slid forward under his hat.

Kit reached out, brushed the inside of a wing with the back of his fingers, felt the living shiver of skin under feathers. "How many times must I refuse thee, Morningstar?"

:We are alike.: Feather-tips caressed his face, and Kit shivered in turn.

"We have our differences." Kit stepped back. "I thank you the farewell, Morningstar."

Lucifer folded his wings with a clap. :Joy you in it,: he said, and made a bow that swept him away.

Kit watched him go, and finally unfolded his arms, breathing shallowly. "All stories are true," he murmured to himself, about to turn and find a servitor angel of his own.

A voice at his shoulder startled him. "That's the bitch of it, wouldn't you say?"

Matthew. Kit exhaled in relief. He'd jumped, and almost tripped himself on the overbalancing shoulder frames. And then there *was* a glass in his hand, and the Mage was grinning at him. Kit saluted him with liquor. "Unfortunately, I think we're all but crushed under the weight of them."

"You love him." Matthew jerked his chin after Lucifer. He swallowed and covered his mouth with the back of his hand, as if in disbelief of what he'd said. The ladderwork of healed piercings that climbed his ear was sharply revealed when he turned in profile.

Kit pinched the bridge of his nose as if his eyes stung, but didn't drop his gaze. "Of course I love him. I made him. And *he* came back through history to remake me. You don't get to fall out of love with the Devil."

"But Lucifer? Not Mephistopheles?"

"Goethe."

"Ah." Matthew fell silent, contemplating the vagaries of metatextual polycreationism. There might be a paper in it. He cleared his throat. "He's dressed the fallen as angels. Unholy Barbie dolls."

"I beg your pardon?" Kit sipped his wine.

Matthew echoed the gesture and looked back at him, directly into his eyes. "Never mind, Kit. You're going to tell me this is a prelude to Armageddon, aren't you?"

"Armageddon?"

"You know. The end of days, the seventh seal, the Revelation to John—"

"Oh, that old thing. Different John, did you know?"

"Really?"

Marlowe shrugged. "Bit of a break in style, for one thing. And were they written under Domitian; although it is but a slight century after the death of our Lord Jesus Christ, *that* John would have been a patriarch worthy of the Hebrews at the time. Of course, I wrote the plays of William Shakespeare, according to some, and he was so much a kinder soul than I—well, it profits us not. Anyway. Fall of Rome. Over and done with, and on to the next apocalypse."

Matthew rubbed his left thumb against the fingers of his left hand, as if checking for the rings he no longer wore. It still startled him, every time, to find his fingers naked. "What if a lot of people believe it's true?"

"Then it's true." Kit's eyes seemed unaccountably drawn to the motion of Matthew's fingers. He dropped his gaze and restrained himself from touching the scars on his own hands, the ring Jane had returned to him. "The Prometheus Club has been trying to remake God for some four hundred years now. With greater success, or lesser. 'The Lord thy God is a jealous God.' You just get one started, and He tends to get consumed in another. The Pagan stories are easier to work with, these days."

"So it *could* be an apocalypse. In the modern sense."

"We'll know when the Rapture happens," Kit answered. He

stretched his arms out, fingers interlaced, and cracked his knuckles. "Until then, I wouldn't trouble myself with it. We have more immediate worries."

"The duel?"

"The duel."

The grand ballroom in Hell's palace was no simple, airy space, but rather an arched cavern flanked by tapestries and arras and secret tunnels, side chambers with fainting couches and retiring rooms, all the better for intrigue and assignations. Few guests stared into the vault of the ceiling for long; the black stone, sculpted in buttresses and arches and all the soaring shapes of a cathedral, nevertheless presented a tremendous sense of weight as if it were all balanced like a boulder on a knife-tip and could tumble at a careless glance.

In one arras-draped alcove stood Keith MacNeill, dressed in an Elf-knight's green silks and velvet, with Morgan le Fey at his left hand. When she leaned forward, a trickle of gaslight from the ballroom traced the silver at her temples, limned her hawklike profile and caught on softness under her chin. "Go to her," Morgan said against Keith's ear, her hand on his shoulder as she rose on tiptoe. Her voice would not have carried farther.

Keith shifted. "Is it fair to approach her publicly?"

"Is there anything fair in what we do, Dragon Prince?"

He turned, and looked at her. "Better might you ask if it is all so foul," he said, and pushed the arras aside before she could return fire.

All the room was silent when he entered. Alone, for Morgan stayed behind.

Nuala could joke, but the fact of the matter was he *did* let the Devil pick his clothes—and was more or less grateful to him, because the crimson silk lining of the green velvet cloak rippled heavily when he moved, swirling around the heavy blade slung between his shoulders, and he knew he cut a figure he never would have managed on his own.

The sword wasn't Caledfwlch; Caledfwlch was lost in the Dragon's lair. But it was a comfort all the same.

All around him heads turned, attention focused by the sketch played out between Kit and Lucifer transferred. Morgan's craft, borrowed for the occasion like Lucifer's wardrobe. If Keith practiced a thousand years, he would never match either of them for gamesmanship. But a Prince uses the talents of those at hand as if they were his own, and so seems more accomplished than a man has any right.

If he's wise.

Keith was at least trying to prove he could learn. And so every face swung with him, in unison, sunflowers coursing the sun. Every face but one: the Queen of the Daoine Sidhe, stiff-necked, did not turn.

Ian was crossing toward the Queen and Cairbre—Jewels following very quietly alongside, her eyes wide behind a feathered mask—when Keith's gaze caught Ian's across the room, a wolf's awareness passing between. Ian's mask hung around his neck, his shoulders bright with jester's motley, each stride swinging with bells. *Yes*, Ian said, an answer to the question Keith had sent with Fionnghuala, the words as plain as if he'd pricked his ears up and waved the banner of his tail, laughing like a wolf invited to run.

Keith nodded. *Make it so.*

Ian picked up his pace as Keith slacked a little, wolf and his get, the perfect instinctual coordination that served the hunt. Ian's hand rested on Cairbre's elbow. Jewels breathed deep, once, and folded her arms, forcing herself to watch Ian. Waiting her cue, if he had one for her.

She didn't return the smile Geoff sent her across the room. He wasn't, frankly, certain she'd seen it, and he told himself sternly that she didn't want him, didn't need him, and wouldn't thank him for the help if he went to her.

He managed to keep his boots nailed to the floor.

The Queen also did not move, did not turn. She did not acknowledge her son with a nod or a word, even when he cut her bard away and left her standing alone by the dais upon which no musicians played.

Keith paused three steps behind her and one to the left.

"My lady," he said. Sword cleared sheath in the same gesture that left him on one knee, head bowed, the blade laid flat on the stones beside her feet. Rose petals swirled away in the draft and fluttered down once more. "Will you look upon your servant now?"

She was silent for a long while. He thought, any moment, that he would hear the scuff of her shoes as she stepped away. And then, without turning, she sighed and dropped her chin and said, "A servant who can't obey? What good is that to me?"

"Try me and find out. Or step on the blade and break it, and I'll answer you as a husband to his wife."

No chill in his voice. He kept it level and fluid, and every word was like a quill under her skin. She clenched her hands on the tails of her red silk coat, crumpling the white and yellow flowers embroidered along the hem and up the placket. Turning, she placed each booted foot like a horse afraid of snakes. She laid one atop his sword, heel on the flat, but did not press down.

"You look well," she said.

He could have let the sword hilt fall to the flags, reached out, caught her foot in both hands. Drawn it up, and kissed her ankle just below the bone. He answered without lifting his head. "The Prince of Darkness is a clotheshorse."

She snorted. Her hair fell over her shoulders when she dropped her head, releasing the aroma of the lilies braided into it as their petals bruised against her coat. "I mean it. You look . . . quite beautiful."

He sucked air between his teeth. She stank of musk, a stallion's rut. "Must it always be briars between us?"

"Always," she said. She lifted her boot from the blade, and set it back on stone. "Beginnings have ends, and knives cut."

She traced an infinity symbol with her toe on the stones, lifting her foot before the sign was complete. The scattered roses crushed and slid, moist patterns left behind. Keith sheathed his sword without looking and stood. He held out his hand; she extended hers in turn, upturned. Open, expectant.

The antithesis of her expression.

He uncurled his fingers, and let the bruised petals of some shredded white roses shower her palm. "Not just knives," he said. And he stepped forward, and kissed her on the mouth.

She didn't fight him. No, but she was stiff at first, resistant, all the flowers garlanded around her mangled by his touch. He didn't care; it didn't matter. He turned, and leaned her back, and kissed her until her hands came up and clutched his velvet-clad shoulder and his hair, and she kissed him in return. Her lips were chapped. His beard pricked her cheek. He stepped back, finally, still holding her by the shoulders, and the applause almost drowned out her voice. Every pair of eyes in the room, still upon them.

And Keith had finally learned how to play a scene.

"As you defended Faerie, so will you Hell," she said.

He let the frustration twist his mouth. "And die of it," he said. "As you've reminded me—"

"It's what Dragon Princes do. I understand better now. I am more ruthless myself—"

"Yes," he said, and slid his hands down her arms before pulling away entirely. "And will Faerie go to war for Hell? When the time comes?"

"Did Hell go to war for Faerie?" She let her breath hiss from her nostrils, cold again. He almost saw the frost dew her lip. "I think not." She lowered her voice and stepped closer. Heads bent together, speaking softly, without histrionics, they made a far less interesting center of attention. She turned, and paced away. He followed. "He really thinks *this* is the time to reopen that argument?"

"He has," Keith said, with a self-dismissing wave of his hand, "secured the services of a Dragon Prince. Hopeless causes a speciality."

She sighed, and looked at him, and he looked right back. "Infuriating man."

Somewhere, he found a smile that was positively sunny, and gave it to her. "Hey. There's hope for your heart yet."

Her frowning regard, arms crossed, was punctuated by drifting heat and the unexpected stink of brimstone. She turned to investigate, but Keith had already located the source. He'd been smelling it for almost a minute. It was only the hot iron miasma that accompanied a slightly younger devil than Lucifer Morningstar, the bright air groaning under the shadow of his wings as he descended, flames licking around his flesh.

His was a fumarole air, the devil of Milton. He settled amidst the crowd, unattended by familiar demons, and cast around himself. "And where *is* my brother?" he asked, quite pleasantly. An invitation fluttered in manicured claws.

"Who is that?" Across the floor, Ian paused with his hand on Cairbre's sleeve, in the act of drawing the bard into one of the privy alcoves. They had left Jewels behind, with instructions to stay out of trouble.

Cairbre didn't turn. "Another story of the Devil," he said. "Nothing to concern ourselves with." He pushed an arras aside and entered the dark cubby. A pointed arch paned in diamonds looked over a vast and empty sea, or perhaps an abyss only. With no moon to cast reflections, it was impossible to tell.

"Many devils?" Ian asked.

"One for everyone, some would say." The bard held the tapestry for as long as it took Ian to step within. "I hold it is a lesser number, or Hell would not seem such a lonely place. And I know what you're about to suggest . . ."

Ian folded his arms and leaned back against the wall. He could have claimed the velvet-upholstered seat by the window, but it held no allure. "And why not? What's wrong with it?"

"Do you think *he* would let himself be played that way?" The brush of the back of Cairbre's hand encompassed the palace they stood within, the realm that sprawled around them, and the lord of all of it. "Do you think he wouldn't notice, if you tried? Like a sparrow playing off hawks against each other."

"When one hawk's on your tail . . ." Ian answered, and let it hang there. He joined Cairbre at the window, and they gazed down over the end of things. " 'And all was without form and void, and darkness was upon the waters,' " Ian muttered, and grinned behind his hand when Cairbre flinched at the scripture, cupping scarred fingers over his ear. "What did you in New York with Àine?"

"Your Highness?" Cairbre raised an eyebrow in profound innocence, turning away from the window.

"The Cat Anna. The Queen of the Unseelie Court. You met her in New York. Would you demean yourself with a lie?"

"I was looking after your interests," Cairbre said, after thinking it over.

"By consorting with my mother's enemies? I should turn you into a tree."

"Your mother usurped your place—"

"Which I will deal with on my own, at the proper time."

"—and she killed Hope," Cairbre finished.

That brought the Prince up short, as Cairbre had planned. Ian's lover, Cairbre's daughter. Dead in Times Square.

Ian's arms stayed folded and his chin dropped, a stubborn gleam in his green eyes. "As soon say she killed Murchaud. Her father and her granddaughter. No, though I could have hated her then. Those deaths are the Dragon's—"

"I cannot," Cairbre said, meditatively, "seek vengeance on a dragon."

"And must you have vengeance?"

"I need it. If you were the Elf-knight you play at being, you would not hesitate. And you deserve the throne, my liege."

Ian grasped Cairbre's shoulder. "It's treason to say that. And treason to call me that."

"Then let it be treason—"

"No." Ian squeezed, hard, his fingers narrow on Cairbre's meaty shoulder, and drew a grunt. "I'll handle that in my own time. Stay away from Àine—"

"Is that an order . . . Your Highness?"

Not *my liege*. Not this time. The relief went down bitter. "Yes. Can you be trusted to obey it?"

The bard stared at him. "Whelp," he said. "What a King you would have made."

Ian reached out and slid the curtain back, releasing their close atmosphere into the cooler drafts of the enormous ballroom. "I'm my mother's heir."

Ian and Cairbre were not the only ones to note the figure out of *Paradise Lost* gyring from the rafters. A couple who had paused by the entry in particular paused to watch, the woman bird-thin in a dress the color of smoke, hung from one bony shoulder in an almost Grecian style. The silk was no softer than the weathered skin it exposed; Fionnghuala looked very different with her hair upswept and dark pearls gleaming in her earlobes, but the feathered cloak she wore like the richest stole foiled any chance she might have had of remaining incognito. It draped her shoulders more softly than ermine, the blood-dark silk-and-velvet lining clinging to her form.

Michael, muttering darkly to herself, had changed her appearance somewhat. She was at her ease in a man's pearl-gray cutaway coat over a jade waistcoat that matched her pinions. Her hair was greased severely back, a green velvet ribbon trailing over her shoulders and a black silk bag adding the illusion of fullness to a tiny, almost hypothetical ponytail. She wore her wings manifest, a great bowering archway of feathers that rose over her and framed her slight body, and a rapier gleamed at her hip. The carrier hung mostly concealed under her waistcoat, the cutaway falling clear of the scabbard. It could have looked ridiculous, a heedless jigsaw of eras and styles, but her carriage made it sublime.

Fionnghuala was drinking champagne. Michael was not drinking. "I should not be here."

"You promised you would speak with him," Fionnghuala answered. She stepped closer to Michael and lowered her voice, but her eyes never left Lucifer, who was turning in a slow, deliberate circle to greet the black-winged monster closing on him. "It is to all our benefit if they *speak*, Michael. If He pushes Lucifer far enough—"

"The significance of the Dragon Prince is not lost on me." Michael ran her nails along the rapier's hilt. "And the question of benefit is still open. Some of us don't mind fighting."

The devils bowed to one another, one cruel-eyed and smoking, rose petals sizzling under his footsteps, the other white and fair and wearing a crown of dancing shadows on his brow. Around the room, guests stepped into the shadows, crowded against the walls. Finally, the theater they'd come to witness.

"Do you think they'll brawl?"

"It's the Morningstar's party," Michael said. "Satan will purr and provoke, but he would only be humiliated if he started something here. Which is not to say that he won't arrogate any attention he can muster."

"You don't suppose he was invited, do you?"

"Why not?" a third voice interjected. Nuala turned her head, already knowing who she'd see. Christian had come up behind them silently, dressed as a pop-culture superhero, boots and gloves and a scarlet body stocking revealing his physique, a mask that did nothing to conceal his identity shadowing his eyes.

He continued, "*I* was. Perhaps he considers it's better to know where the Devil is than leave him lying about unattended."

"Perhaps he means me to think he is gathering support to renew his war with Heaven," Michael said, without any sign that Christian had startled or discomfited her. She might have been expecting the Devil to speak. "Would you fight?"

"I'm a lover," Christian answered, fiddling his mask. "And you two are blocking this doorway far more effectively than you are my love life. Perhaps we could step to one side?"

Michael glowered; Fionnghuala placed the angel's hand on her own elbow and led her aside. "Do we give way before devils?" Michael asked under her breath. Christian's wink said he heard it, but he passed with a hint of a bow.

"We do when we're causing a fire hazard." Fionnghuala's cloak rustled and hissed where it brushed Michael's wings.

The archangel didn't laugh. But she did send a single, searing glance over her shoulder in the direction of the *other* devils. "Pray let us greet our host and the guest of honor, that I may receive my measure of scorn from each and we may be away."

Fionnghuala nudged Michael, a disrespect bred of familiarity, and when she glared said sweetly, "It's not just Lucifer who is prone to moments of arrogance."

"Maybe not," Michael answered. "But *I* know how to hold my tongue to my betters. When I can find them."

They turned to follow Christian. The other guests were still gathered by the walls, attempting unobtrusiveness or having simply forgotten to reclaim the center of the ballroom. In particular, Fionnghuala noticed that Marlowe and the blond Mage, Matthew, were engaged in a head-bent conversation with Lily Wakeman and the boy she had brought along, the mortal from the dance club. None of them seemed to have noticed Christian's entrance. After Satan's arrival, perhaps the guests were exhausted, and Michael had been mistaken for another servant in angel drag. Now, though, heads turned, voices stilled.

Lily did not look. If anything, she bent closer in her four-cornered conversation, as if she meant to physically step between Matthew and Geoff. The former was lecturing—practically haranguing—the latter.

Matthew's low tones were more than compensated by the violence of his gestures; even Kit found it politic to lay one hand on Matthew's shoulder, as if to soothe a nervous horse. Matthew was not pleased to find Geoff in Hell.

Geoff, surprisingly, was holding his own. Whatever responsibility Matthew considered himself to have assumed for Geoffrey and Jewels, they were not, in the final analysis, Matthew's problem. And Geoff was unwilling to place himself in the position of becoming Matthew's problem, thank you very much.

Fionnghuala turned her attention that way, allowing Michael to sweep her along, and stared at the back of Lily's neck.

It took thirty seconds of concentration, but Lily's chin came up. Her head turned, her expression silencing Matthew midsentence. He shut his mouth and shoved his hands in his pockets.

Fionnghuala squeezed Michael's arm. The angel tugged her glare free of the Morningstar and glowered until Nuala jerked her chin at Lily and the men. The angel's wings fanned, half embracing Nuala like an upended bathtub trapping a madonna.

"Watch," Fionnghuala said, squeezing her arm. "This will work much better than breaking lightbulbs with your brain."

Lily's nostrils flared as Christian covered the distance remaining and paused beside his brothers, taking Satan's hand. The justifications thronging her belly failed as swiftly as she could invent them. *But I'm here*, she tried, a fine stab at denial denied when logic answered, *You're not embracing a batwinged devil as a friend.*

I will think about this later. Abruptly, she didn't want Christian to see her, to know she was here. It felt like an enormous betrayal to have come. Crushed rose petals cloyed, as if the air writhed with invisible maggots, dizzying.

Lily glanced around, reflexively, to see who might have noticed her staring, to get her eyes off Christian before he felt her dismay. And found the gray-haired woman of the previous evening staring back at her, beside a green-winged angel who wore an eerily familiar profile, an aquiline nose and a contemplative frown.

"Michael," Lily said, and felt her knees go weak as they hadn't when she saw Christian on promenade in Hell. "Fuck me. Is everybody I know a devil?"

"What?" Matthew started to turn, Kit beside him. Geoff stepped forward, but whatever he was about to say died on his lips as Lily squeezed his hand, and reached out and grabbed Matthew's with her other one.

"Take me home," she said, turning her back on Fionnghuala, and Michael, and the whole glorious mess. "Get me the fuck out of here. Take me home *now*."

Chapter Seventeen
East Village Buffalo Poppy

To his credit, although Geoff cast a longing look across the ballroom toward Jewels and her new lord, he never once looked as if he was about to abandon Lily. He gritted his teeth and nodded gamely, and turned toward Matthew with a frown. "Can you get us home?"

The implied trust surprised Matthew. Kit's surprise ran parallel, though he hid his smile behind his hand. He hadn't expected chivalry from this ragged-haired, lovesick boy.

And then he checked himself. A boy who wasn't so much younger than he, Kit Marlowe, had been in Rheims, where he had first become a pawn of the Prometheans. Scholar, cobbler, poet, spy—it was easy to forget, in four hundred years of living, in and out of Faerie, in and out of Hell, that twenty-five years was not so very little. "I'll take you home," he said, releasing his grip on Matthew's arm. "Let us find a mirror, shall we?"

"A mirror? What do you need a mirror for?"

Marlowe patted Matthew on the shoulder, and Matthew found himself grinning in naked relief; notorious rakehell, sodomite, and playboy he might be remembered as, but lately Christopher Marlowe was the only person who seemed willing to touch Matthew without some implication lying predatory behind it.

"I'll teach you a trick," Marlowe said. His gesture swept up Lily and Geoff as he turned. "Follow me."

Kit knew his way around Hell. They left the ballroom behind quickly,

eluding the scent of flowers and the strains of music with a few sharp
turns down dustless corridors. There were no roses and lilies here, just
long hallways broad enough for a procession, empty of everything but
perfectly placed statuary, well-framed paintings, and the occasional chair
crafted of rare hardwoods and upholstered in silk and brocades.

He led them to an empty room, one where the furniture was covered
in dustcloths and the art on the walls draped against light. He lit the gas
lamps with a wave of his hand and gestured to Matthew to shut the
door. "We won't be disturbed here."

Geoff had a hand on Lily's arm, not so much directing her as warming that small patch of her skin against the inner chill that huddled her
shoulders and bent her head. She straightened as the door clicked shut,
small breasts swelling over the top of her corset as she breathed deep.
She shoved her mask up savagely, disarraying her hair, revealing violently kohled eyes.

"He said I had power." She glared at pinned Kit. "Show me how to
use it. Christian wanted me, and Fionnghuala brought me to Hell,
and"—she shook her head—"it's tangled up somehow. It's got to be. I
didn't pick it, but I'm *in* this."

Kit smiled. "I suspect I've walked in on the third act of your drama,"
he said. "But as one who's lain down for a devil myself, I can say that
there are worse things."

The words struck her like a pan of ice water in the face. She blinked,
swallowed, and it took a moment for her to get her tongue reorganized
around whatever she had been about to say.

"I beg your pardon?" When all else failed, her grandmother Mary
would have said, good manners never deserted one.

"Christian," he said. "That's what you were brought here to see,
weren't you?"

Lily nodded, dry-mouthed, wishing suddenly she hadn't been so
quick to dispense with her mask. Beside her, Geoff stripped his off, letting it dangle from the strings. It had pinched the bridge of his nose red.
"He's been teaching me magic."

"Witchcraft," Kit said, kindly. "I've used it myself."

"*Christian?*" Matthew said the name too fast, stumbling over it, and
Lily stared at him. "What does your Christian look like?"

"Red hair," Lily said. "A few freckles. Good-looking. He was in my coven—"

"Jane's apprentice," Matthew said.

And Kit covered his face with his hands and laughed. "Bloody hell," he said, and looked at them both. "He's a devil, Matthew. The youngest. Lily was right, and it is all interlinked."

Matthew found no words. Geoff, however, convinced that whatever he was saying was as stupid as everything else he'd said since Sunday night, managed to add, "Someone named Fionnghuala sent her here. She came with a message for Prince Ian, as well, and invitations for both of them."

"Which still doesn't explain why *you* walked into Hell," Matthew interjected, a muscle along the side of his jaw jumping in unconscious counterpoint. "Just after being fortunate enough to get clear of Faerie—"

His anger was a shield for fear, though, and Geoff took a little pity on him when he realized Matthew's hands weren't shaking with wrath. Geoff folded his arms. "Lily needed me. And *you* seem to come and go as you please."

Matthew kept his tone even, but didn't lessen the mockery. "Lily *needed* you? And what would you do to defend her, given you want nothing to do with magic? Or did you tag along when you learned Jewels would attend?"

Lily bit her lip. She took a breath, and said, instead, "And what's *your* interest in how Geoff spends his time?"

It brought Matthew up short. Shorter than she had intended, because he paused and winced, cocking his head. There was a silence, as if he considered her question and thought it through, before answering carefully.

"Geoffrey has power," he said in a calm, professorial voice. "So do you; so do I." He glanced at the poet, who had leaned against the wall and folded his arms, waiting with every evidence of patience. Marlowe straightened and tipped an imaginary hat as Matthew named him. "So does Master Marlowe. The price of Geoff's power is that he will be used for it, controlled and directed, manipulated and seduced, *raped* if that's what it takes. And if he doesn't want it, his choice is to get the hell out, and tend his own garden. Is that clear enough for you?"

"And if he chooses not to?"

Kit stepped forward, reinserting himself into the conversation. He took Lily's hand in his own and turned it over so the backs of his fingers were exposed. An iron ring on one; on the others, only scars. She yanked her hand back.

"Before long," Marlowe said, "like you, like me, like Matthew here — he won't be offered a choice."

As if on his words, she felt the silence, the loneliness come crashing back. The emptiness of Hell. *Hell is not other people. It's no one else at all.*

It stilled her.

And while she was still, Marlowe reached out left-handed, and whipped the pall from a standing mirror with a player's gesture, swirling heavy dust through the gaslight. He let the shroud fall to the floor, and beckoned. "Your hands, please?"

Lily stepped forward obediently. This time, Geoffrey hesitated. "Where are you sending us?"

"Boston?" Kit ventured.

"Will that get me closer to whoever killed Althea?"

"Althea?" Lily said. "Althea *Benning*? Dead?"

Matthew sighed, and Geoffrey nodded and ducked his head. Lily stood, mouth open, until Matthew forestalled her with an upraised hand and said, "I could warn you again — "

"Matthew," Geoffrey said, "she was my friend."

A simple declaration, calm and serious. Matthew felt the boy's sincerity like pain, a thumb pressed into the hollow of his throat. He drew breath to respond, and Geoff cut him off, his tone gone dry with self-mockery.

"I understand that I'm risking my body, my sanity, and my immortal soul. And I don't care. You're the only person I know who has a chance of finding out who — " Geoff stopped, gagged by a visceral memory of the smell of blood and spilled bowels, his voice skying as fragile composure cracked.

He waved off Matthew's concerned gesture with a brusque right hand and pinched the bridge of his nose. "I'm—I'm staying," he said, when he got a breath. "And what about you? You're so damned scared of this all you can do is yell—"

"It was my job to keep her safe," Matthew said, and shrugged. "Scared doesn't enter into it."

Matthew rubbed his eyes, profoundly tired. "I can't promise to protect you. If you get involved in this, it will probably get you killed. And we might very well get killed in our own private little war on Sunday, so now's not the best time for signing up apprentices."

He looked at Marlowe, and Marlowe pursed his lips. "Well," he said. "On the other hand, if we don't get killed on Sunday, we're going to need apprentices."

"Whatever," Lily said. "Look, I already fucked the Devil. Do you think I'm scared of a little war?"

The shifting cold in Donall's ring was unsettling. The detective could have spent all his sleeping and working hours in pursuit of those shadows. And he *did* spend too many of them that way, until his eyes burned and the ache in his feet and legs rose above background noise to become the primary concern of his conscious mind. His back hurt. His neck hurt. He didn't know who to trust, and when he did sleep, he dreamed of dragons.

And today there had been another body. Just like the last one, mutilated and chewed. A twenty-two-year-old girl with a baby and a husband and an office job.

It wasn't as simple as talking to Jane made it seem. His trip to Boston had left him confused, but it felt like the sort of confusion that led to eventual enlightenment. There were factions in Faerie. The tendency was to think of the Elves as monolithic, implacable. But that was the sort of mistake, when dealing with enemy powers, that got one into messy little wars.

He figured now that he'd stumbled across a sort of turf war that had spilled over into the iron world. Jewels and Geoff—and Peese had been right to suspect them, damn him—might be allied with one faction. The ones he'd seen them with at the Goth club.

The question was, was Matthew part of that cabal, or another? And what about Peese?

Uncomfortable to admit that Don himself had become embroiled in yet a fourth conspiracy. He could half convince himself that it wasn't arrogance, that it was what the dreams demanded, what duty demanded. And he half didn't care if it was arrogance, anyway. Somebody was going to have to run interference between cops and Magi. Somebody was going to have to . . . liaise. The world had already changed.

Magic was a one-way gate.

Don caught himself half asleep at his desk, rubbing his temples in one hand, and forced himself to his feet. He'd be no good to anyone if he didn't get some rest.

He took a train toward home, but never found his bed. He was ascending from the subway when a bright spike of cold drove through his hand, an icicle plunged between the bones. He clutched it against his chest, gasping. More pain, enough pain to demote the other aches and pains to irritations. The night was jewel-bright, the city gleaming tawdry and brilliant. Something was happening.

Pain brought adrenaline, and adrenaline brought energy. He charged up the stairs, startling a few late-traveling commuters, one hand on the steel banister, seeking like a compass needle. He'd started taking better care of himself since the surgery, and this was the payoff, now; he was barely panting when he hit the street. If he lived, maybe he'd run the Marathon one of these years. Crazier things happened.

The cold was as fierce as that which had charged his ring on the night of the second murder. He'd gone two more steps before his cell phone rang. He growled, stepping into the corner of the subway entrance, out of the pedestrian flow. "Smith."

"Don. It's Jane." She paused to take a breath, to cement her thoughts, and he cut her off.

"I'm after something Fae," he said. "Something big, moving in the city. Gotta go, call you ba—"

"It'll wait." Her voice froze his thumb halfway to the red button. "Come and see me. Now, tonight. Take a cab."

He opened his mouth to argue, and closed it with a snap. "See you in fifteen minutes," Jane said.

"You ever seen a black man try to hail a cab in this town?" He closed the phone one-handed before she could snap something dire in

return and turned around to trudge back down the stairs to the subway, his ring jabbing pins and needles from his hand all the way up to
his shoulder before subsiding to dull discomfort. The train *would* be
faster than hailing a cab, whatever Jane thought. And a hell of a lot
less frustrating.

As Don jogged through crowds on a subway platform, four of the
sources of his pain and that maddening chill stepped through the reflection of a dark shopwindow, and stood dusting themselves and glancing
this way and that on the empty street.

"In Halloween costumes, no less," Matthew said, rolling his eyes. At
least Marlowe had ditched his wings in Hell—and followed Matthew's
advice about where they should come out. Matthew wanted to be close
to his home base, but not *in* it, in case anyone had left him any surprises.
"My apartment's up the block. We'll find something to change into
there."

Lily looked doubtfully at Matthew and at herself. "I'm fine like this,"
she said, as Marlowe folded his arms and Geoff said nothing at all.

"Is it wise to return to your lodgings?" Marlowe asked.

"We're ready for them if they try anything," Matthew said. "And I
don't intend to discuss plans there. *That* can wait for a safer space. I
wouldn't put it past Jane to bug my apartment."

Kit glanced sideways at him, and Matthew gestured the poet to walk
alongside. He did, with Lily and Geoff completing the square. Lily was
looking up, head craned back, until Geoff touched her arm. "You'll look
like a tourist," he said.

"I am a tourist," she answered, but after that she kept her eyes to the
front as she walked. There were still a few people on the street though
the wind was blowing cold. A dark-haired young woman in bright sunflower barrettes brushed by Matthew, undressing him with a look that
he profoundly ignored, though he wouldn't have if he'd felt the fey ici-
ness that a very particular, very exhausting sort of spell cloaked from
both him and Kit. Kit, panhandled, dropped a shilling in a cup.

Lily hugged herself as gooseflesh crawled across her skin. Her corset
left her shoulders bare, and offered no protection from the wind—and
kept her from hunching into herself for warmth. Geoff slipped his jacket

off and swung it over her shoulders without asking. Matthew and Kit, in the lead, had not noticed.

Fortunately, Matthew's directions had ensured it was not far to walk. Matthew unlocked the security door, ushered everyone into the entryway, and led them single file up the stairs. Meanwhile, underground, Don was on a train rocking westward; Matthew checked his wards, found them secure, and unbolted his front door and let himself into his apartment for the first time in almost a week.

The answering machine flashed with messages. He was sure his cell phone would as well, if he bothered to look, and spared a moment wondering if he'd been reported as a missing person yet. Time enough to deal with that later, although he did place a call to his teaching assistant, who was mercifully not answering her phone, to say that he'd been called away on an emergency and hadn't had access to a phone or Internet connection, and would she please cover his classes until next Wednesday at the latest.

Melissa was a smart kid, a PhD candidate who'd be defending her dissertation any semester, and Matthew had known her since she was an undergrad. She'd figure something out. If he was *very* lucky, she'd been covering for him without being asked. Assuming he was still alive a week hence, he might want to keep his job, and he owed his students consideration no matter what else was going on. Although the bribe Kit had offered would go a long way toward smoothing things over with any English department in the world, assuming the documents had *some* sort of provenance.

He was getting *far* ahead of himself.

He peeled off his talismanic coat, grateful that he had not needed its protection on his journey into Faerie and Hell. That kind of luck didn't bear too much inspection, so instead he crucified the coat on a hanger to air out and changed into far less ostentatious clothing: blue jeans, a T-shirt, a blue flannel shirt, a pair of sneakers. He found a too-tight pair of jeans that might fit Kit if he punched another hole in Matthew's belt. Geoff's clothing was a little dressy, maybe, but not completely outré.

Lily, theatrically unself-conscious, talked Geoff into loosening the laces of her corset so she could unhook the busk and wriggle out of it. Matthew was just coming out of his bedroom with an offering of

T-shirts and a red woolen sweater with a pattern of oak leaves across the chest when she stretched like a cat, her spine cracking as it aligned. The black lace tube top she was wearing as a singlet revealed a band of skin above the skirt slung around her hips, pale flesh pressure-lined and dusted above the cleft of her buttocks with sleek, sparse dark hair. "Lily," he said, forcing his eyes to the back of her head. When she turned, the flash of green metal caught his eye. He experienced about the degree of success ignoring the shadowy detail of areolae and piercings behind the lace stretched over her wide-set breasts that might be expected. "Something a little warmer," he said, and pushed the sweater into her hands.

"Where are we going?" Geoff asked, while Lily was hauling the sweater over her head and Kit was looking for someplace inconspicuous to leave his rapier, and Matthew was staring at his half-renovated kitchen and wondering why he'd never finished ripping out the harvest gold and avocado green. It was as if his life had entered a kind of suspension when Kelly died, a finger on the cosmic PAUSE button.

He needed to move out of this place.

"I don't know yet," he said. "Someplace we can talk." He pressed his finger to his lips, a reminder. *This apartment isn't safe.* Jane paid for it. Jane, he realized now, with an old familiar chill, had never lost her grip on his leash.

On Central Park West, Jane Andraste's grip was concerned with the control of an entirely different set of leashes. Felix Luray sat on the edge of an ivory-upholstered armchair, his jacket sleeves tugged up to reveal French cuffs, his elbows on his knees. Beside him sat Christian, who had not spoken overmuch, but watched, amused. And across from Felix, sipping tippy Ceylon from a gold-rimmed teacup, dressed in close-tailored perfection, sat a monster with a lemony smile.

Jane didn't think the Bunyip intended them immediate physical harm. He had reasons of his own for being there, reasons he laid out carefully and formally to Felix while Jane waited unobtrusively in the background, fondling her marcasite bracelet, and listened.

Felix poured more tea, and looked through his lashes at the Bunyip.

"So what you're saying, so circuitously—or circumspectly, if you prefer— is that Mist will *help* us against the Faeries?"

Bunyip reached out one splay-fingered hand and pinched up his teacup, delicately, the gold-painted china handle warm between his finger and thumb. "You misapprehend."

"Enlighten me." Felix wielded the sugar tongs like an extension of his hand. Each cube drifted through steaming golden fluid, raining granules of sugar into the bottom of the cup. They rippled like sand in a Zen garden before dissolving under the influence of the spoon. A few flecks of tea leaf sailed round and round, caught in the vortex while it lasted.

"Mist wishes Kelpie returned to his proper role as a wild element. Tamed, he serves to support the Promethean influence."

"It's not one of ours who tamed him," Felix said. The tea was tannic even through the sweetness of the sugar, a tang that contracted his taste buds and prickled his tongue.

"That's irrelevant," the Bunyip answered, as a chime alerted them that the elevator was ascending.

"Donall," Jane said, and stood up to see to it, stepping around a rice paper and ebony screen.

Bunyip continued, "The symbolism reflects the Promethean plan: nature chained."

"Keep going," Felix said, as Jane bent her concentration on the new arrival. There was a limit to how much leaning on Donall she could afford. She couldn't risk driving him away, as she had Matthew—and he didn't need her as much as Matthew had. Her only hold over him— besides her own considerable force of will and emotional power—was the NYPD's lack of a methodology for dealing with magical crimes. Seven years is a long time in human terms, but for a bureaucracy, it's an eyeblink. And it's hard to figure out how to screen and hire magicians when you've just become aware that they exist.

As she opened the door, she met the gaze of the Dragon behind Donall's eyes. "Come in," she said, and stood aside.

He came, puffy-faced, red-eyed. "There's something—"

Jane touched her ring, icy cold under the patina of gold. "I know," she said. "Would you like some tea? No, you drink coffee, don't you?"

"Tea's fine if it's made," he said, making no move to shuck off his coat as she locked the door behind him. "I can't stay. What did you want me for, Jane?"

"Come in and meet somebody."

Felix and Bunyip had fallen as silent as Christian when the door opened. When Jane and Don rounded the screen, they were sitting expectant as nestlings, their chins lifted and their eyes bright. She made the introduction and poured Don a cup, which became dwarfed in his enormous hands. "Bunyip's brought us information from the other side," Jane said.

A mug might have eased the arthritic ache of the ring on Don's hand. The teacup was small and eggshell fragile, not designed for cupping one's hands around to absorb the warmth. He put it to his mouth and sipped, wishing he'd thought to ask for sugar and lemon. "What sort of information?"

"We were just sorting that bit out." Felix edged over on the couch toward Christian, offering Don a corner. Don didn't move, except to set his cup back on the saucer balanced on his other palm. Felix glanced at the Bunyip, who sat stiffly upright beside the cushion occupied by his fedora, and frowned. "Please go on."

Bunyip nodded. His hands empty now, he gestured. "I want to offer you an alliance. I need to remove the water-horse, and you wish to avoid a direct confrontation with the forces of Faerie and the potential loss of your position as archmage, Jane Maga. Is that correct?"

"We'd prefer to see Faerie driven entirely from the iron world," Jane said, abandoning her pretense of being an observer when Bunyip stared at her. "And I want Matthew back. Unharmed. He's too useful to be left wandering around uncontrolled."

"It'll be a neat trick to get him to come crawling back," Felix said. He picked up and finished his tea.

"He's not self-directing. If presented with no other choice than working for me, he'll fall back into line."

"Jane," Don said. "Somewhere out there, somebody else is going to be killed and eaten tonight."

She nodded, and raised a delaying hand. "A moment. Bunyip?"

"I need access to the water-horse without his protectors. I can defeat *him*, but the Daoine Seeker and the Mage he travels with are trouble."

"Jane." Don set the cup and saucer down on a plinth, not caring that they rattled, and folded his arms.

"Donall, I said *wait*. Bunyip, assuming I can arrange this thing—and I think I can—what do I get in return? You don't want to see a Promethean renaissance."

"On the contrary," he said, "an alliance would suit me very well. And in return, I can give you access to Matthew and Christoferus Magi, at a time and place of your choosing, before the formal duel. Or even at the duel itself. I would be happy to deal with them for you there."

"What would you do?" Felix asked. "Turn them into black swans?"

Bunyip showed his teeth. "It wouldn't be the first time," he said. "But you'll have heard that story."

"I haven't," Don interjected, which earned him a silencing glance from Felix.

"The form of the duel is set," Jane answered. "It would be very bad symbolism indeed to break that bargain."

"What if I ensured Matthew would not be there?" Bunyip covered his mouth with his hand.

Jane paused. She looked at Christian, who blinked, and Felix, who nodded, and then turned her head to meet Don's gaze.

Don didn't know, frankly, what to tell her. He was rocking from foot to foot with impatience. Somewhere out in the darkness, someone was dying horribly, or was about to—and the ring on his hand would tell him where, if the damned Archmage would just let him go *do* something about it. *She's talking about sending this guy to kill Matthew*. Or take him captive, maybe.

That was the thing. Don *knew* Matthew. Not well, kind of casually—but Matthew had never set off that cold feeling of black dread that crowded Don's gut when he looked at the guy in the pin-striped suit on Jane's white nubby silk sofa. "Let me speak with Matthew," he said, shoving his hands into his pockets. "Maybe I can talk some reason into him."

"Then what can Bunyip give us?" Jane asked.

Don lifted one shoulder and let it fall. "Ask him who killed our murder victims. Ask him to deal with them."

Bunyip smiled. His teeth were yellow, tea-stained, and very sharp. "Murder victims?"

"Althea Benning," Don said. "And now, Nancy Rivera. Murdered and eaten. By something Fae, I think, but the damned governor's office isn't having any."

"Ah." Bunyip folded his hands. "There's an easy answer to that question. But I'd rather not say because I suspect you will act in haste, Detective Smith. You see, there's a good deal of magical energy bound up in a death, in a sacrifice. In a life. And there are those who have neither love for the Fae nor compassion for those the Fae have touched, and who might go to great lengths to pursue a vendetta."

A good police officer is half psychologist and half wicked stepmother. The Bunyip might be Fae. But by the way he settled back against the sofa cushions, by the sharp edge of his smile, Donall knew. Knew that he was being manipulated, of course, and knew that there were things the Bunyip wasn't telling him.

And by the quick compression of Jane's lips as she reached for her teacup, a little too quickly, he understood that Jane knew it too. And that she'd been hiding things from Don that his own fondness for a guy who should have been the first suspect on his list had made him overlook.

But Matthew had been there, first man on the scene. Called it in. Taken the surviving kids under his wing, and handed them off to a pack of Faeries.

And it was Matthew Szczegielniak Jane Andraste was protecting by keeping him here while his ring burned cold agony on his hand. As she had protected Matthew all along: paying his bills, keeping him safe. She shook her head at Bunyip. "Don't be ridiculous."

"Aw, hell," Don said, and turned to walk out of the penthouse.

Christian was there in front of him. "Donall Magus," he said, "give your archmage a chance to speak. She has not lied."

Don checked and met the young man's hazel eyes. The lids narrowed with false earnestness, and Don shook his head. "Learn to lie better, kid," he said, and shouldered past.

He was aware and surprised that Jane restrained Felix with a gentling hand when Felix would have stood. He was even more surprised that he made it down to the street unscathed.

He walked past the doorman and paused on the sidewalk, glancing down at his ring. It hurt. It made his arm ache all the way up to his brain.

He pulled out his cell phone and dialed by rote. "Carmen," he said, as he jogged toward the pain in his ring. "Yeah. How fast can you get me a warrant for the arrest of a Dr. Matthew Szczegielniak? Suspicion of murder. Yeah, wake up anybody you want. And let me spell that for you, hang on . . ."

When he ended the call, he stuffed the cell phone back into his pocket and *ran*.

Vast wings glided overhead, flitting between dark buildings, and the scent of iron and magic turned the flyer's antlered head. A rich scent, enticing—but Orfeo the peryton had been charged to seek particular prey this evening. And *that* scent drew him on, past the unprotected apprentice Mage, past the bound sea god, skimming over the rooftops of New York with the city's light caressing his wings.

A chain reaction. Orfeo came hunting the trace his mistress had left on the enemy, and when Orfeo flew, *he* left a trace that alerted another hunter.

Ernie Peese moved in a world of mages and Faeries, angels and killers and jeweled midnight beasts, hard-luck stories and unhappy endings. He wore cold iron in his shoulder holster, and he believed in the law and he believed in his faith. But he had no magic of his own.

He was brusque, honest, plainspoken. Not stupid, and not for sale, and he took it as an affront to decency and his own dedication to the best, most important job in the world that magic was afoot on the earth.

But sometimes angels spoke to him, for Ernie was a virtuous man. And there is nothing to do when angels speak, except listen, and do what you are told, and do the best you can.

Ernie woke in darkness, to the rustle of mighty wings. He was alone in his bed, in his bedroom, except for the faintly snoring shape of his wife. Lucy slept hard. She never woke when Ernie got out of bed, late at night, and paced out to the living room to watch television with the sound turned off.

She didn't wake now when he stood up in his boxers and pulled that day's trousers off the back of the bedside chair, though leftover change rattled in his pockets. He slid them on, found socks, kicked his shoes out from under the bed as silently as he could manage. He found a polo shirt and a sweater in the laundry basket, folded and clean, groping among textures. The light from the alarm clock turned everything green.

He walked into the hallway still shrugging his coat over his holster, and slipped out the front door and triple-locked it without waking the dog. The note he left pasted to the television screen read *Gone walking. Home for breakfast*.

The elevator took too long to reach the sixth floor. The voice in his ear urged him faster, so Ernie plunged down the stairs, bouncing lightly on tiptoe, trying to keep the old building from ringing with his footsteps.

He hit the street at a trot, accelerating.

Not far away, with a passing thought for irony, Don followed the cold in his hand. And Whiskey, still stalking the city, followed Don. He was curious what went on in the archmage's tower—what brought Mage and Bunyip there in consultation—but he was more interested in what mission sent the hastily summoned officer running into the night like a page on an errand.

The shadows would not hide him in his white shirt and trousers, so he had conjured clothes in plain tailored black when he shifted to human form. Dark skin and dark hair would have sufficed even if he had not been out of sight as he followed, letting the officer's scent lead on.

For his part, Donall ran. Adrenaline shocked his tired cells, tangled his nerves; concrete jarred his knees and hips with every stride. He had no breath to damn Jane Andraste, and so he did it silently, damned Jane and Matthew and Felix and every other Mage who'd ever lived, a relentless liturgy of rage.

It was with himself that he was furious. It was his fault Rivera was dead. He'd had Szczegielniak in his hands, and he'd let the damned Mage convince him—convince him the same way Jane had, with that mysterious plausibility.

He would have liked to blame it on magic, to say he'd had no choice. Another symptom of weakness. Another way he was an idiot. And he couldn't outrace that guilt, a young woman's blood and her horrible death. He couldn't expiate it.

But maybe he could run fast enough to stop it happening a third time.

Orfeo dipped emerald pinions and bent on a curve, gliding now, circling a mortal Mage. The mistress' touch was upon the man, a peppery sunflower scent guiding Orfeo down, sliding, putting a helix and plans of murder under his wings.

The street was tight, and the Mage accompanied. Orfeo must hit his angle right the first time. He must strike from behind, over the heads of the mortal youngsters, like an owl taking a cat: the unheard wings, the stunning blow, the talons piercing skull and brain and the carcass lifted before the victim understood its death, the body's own weight snapping the twisted neck. He did not believe he would get a second chance.

He saw well in the dark, did Orfeo, but the shadows from the streetlights were confusing. Still, the Mage's blond hair stood out. There could be no mistaking his victim.

His feathers were not hushed like an owl's; when he stooped, he could not beat his wings. The flutter would give him away. And the wind was wrong, ruffling his plumage. Fortunately, he realized before committing and caught and nursed a thermal, lifting into the night for another pass.

The city noticed. A vast slumbery beast, drowsing through hungers, not quick to waken to the firefly existences flickering through its heavy-lidded streets unless they forced themselves on its attention—but needing them, half aware even in dreams of their presence, the mitochondrial lives that populated it, that gave it being. Eight million hearts in the city, and every heart a city unto itself.

And the city's dreams were already worn thin by the *trip-trap* of Faerie hooves and boots over asphalt and paving stones, its slumber troubled by the peal of magic and the clamor of sacrifice, its intellect aroused by the tolling of the Dragon's wingbeats on the gasping air. Enough blood can wake even stones.

And these stones knew whom they had chosen, even if the choice had been in dreams, even though their limerence went unrequited. And the object of the choice wore the Summer Queen's touch like a brand on his arm. That touch placed him in danger, and with him, the city.

New York was awakening.

And Matthew would not be permitted to ignore it any longer.

Matthew paused under a streetlight on an empty block, and the bulb popped. Nothing: he barely noticed. An everyday occurrence since the bridge and the unicorn. Kit looked up, though, and quickly down, raising an arm to shield his face, half expecting a rain of soot or glass. "What's that?"

"Signs and portents," Matthew answered, with a glance over his shoulder to make sure Geoff and Lily were following. Lily huddled in the red sweater, head ducked and forearms pressed together in front of her chest. She fumbled with a little box and extracted something from it on a licked fingertip. "Lily?"

"Meds," she said, and tucked the tablet into her mouth, a gesture practiced into efficiency. "I have . . . primary adrenal insufficiency. It's aggravated by stress. Which . . ." She tilted her head in a half shrug, and tucked the snuffbox back into her bag while dry-swallowing the pill. "Just being careful."

Geoff reached out left-handed and squeezed her hand. The length of the block, CLOSED signs flickered and pulsed: red, stop, warning. Matthew stuffed his hands in the pockets of his jeans and balled up his left fist, eyes downcast.

"What's going on?" Geoff's gesture took in the flickering neon, the abrupt wail of a car alarm and flash of headlights.

Matthew turned in the strobing, frozen in a series of stop-motion flashes. "Back against the wall." He put a hand on Lily's shoulder to guide her there. She resisted until Kit, who had caught Matthew's expression, grabbed her wrist and dragged her against brick. It could have been a warning, the city talking to him. Or it could have been someone like Felix trying to distract or attack him.

It didn't feel like Felix, though.

"What's happening?" Geoff again, revolving slowly, scanning the street, as if he could see what made the magic occur.

"It's a warning. But I don't know —" Matthew settled on his heels, a chill creeping under the collar of the flannel shirt. Someone ran toward them: someone big, moving fast. Matthew shouted: "Don!"

The detective slowed as Matthew raised a hand. His eyes moved from Geoff to Kit to Lily, measuring each one in a manner that made Kit feel for the hilt of the rapier he wasn't wearing.

Don drew up about fifteen feet away and stopped, foursquare, his hands by his sides. Sweat slicked his forehead and dripped from the tip of his nose to splash on the front of his shirt, but he forced his breathing and his voice level.

"Matthew Szczegielniak, you are under arrest for the murder of Althea Benning," Don said, wishing he relished the words a little more, feeling the weight of his gun against his heaving ribs. He didn't think Matthew would go for a weapon. But Don had seen Althea's body, and Don knew how deceptive a mild-mannered suspect could be. He stayed well back. "Please face the wall."

"Aw, this is *not* a good time for this," Matthew said, and did as he was told, while Geoff gaped and Lily shivered, and Kit—after Matthew's sharp nod—herded them away.

Don searched him. He didn't resist, as efficient hands pressed his clothes against his skin and Don confiscated his cell phone. Another car alarm deployed, a wailing siren. A shopwindow half a block on and across the street crumbled into a shower of crashing glass as Don jerked Matthew's arms behind his back and snapped the cuffs on. Stainless steel embraced Matthew's wrists, warding, protecting, and the store's alarm climbed the night.

"Stop with that," Don said, and gave Matthew a shake.

"It's not *me*."

"Matthew?" Geoff, sounding plaintive and worn.

"I didn't," Matthew said, craning his neck over his shoulder in a vain attempt to catch Geoff's gaze. Geoff was looking over him, past him, eyes as round and open as his mouth. Looking at Don, no doubt. "I think—"

"Matthew!" A gasping shout in a young man's voice. Too late, too late. Orfeo was stooping, dropping like a tiercel, having found his wind and

folded his wings. The Mage stood tall, head up and shoulders pulled back, and the others around him could do nothing to stop Orfeo's fall.

His legs were extended behind him, antlers laid against his spine to streamline his body, wings furled against his sides. The water towers rushed past, the rooftops, the gargoyles, the walls, the wind, and the night.

The Mage turned, blond head tilted back, following his student's shout. He was helpless, hands bound, magic bound, all his agency wrapped in steel. He started to step aside just as Orfeo cupped his wings, snapped them wide with a thunderclap, creating a bar moored in the air around which to swing his weight. A gymnast's reversal, and his legs came forward and down, talons splayed, striking for the brain, for the eyes. Shattered, scintillating light left a flickering train of images suspended in the night.

At the last moment, the leading edge of Orfeo's wing struck the police officer, knocking him sprawling, and Orfeo's own pinions obscured his prey.

The strike was a second thump, hard on the crack of snapped wings. Orfeo felt the stretched resilience of skin before talons popped through, the crunch and squish and slickness, as if a crow drove through the shell of a garden snail. A loud, sick pop meant the neck had snapped. The dangling weight shivered as Orfeo labored upward, its feet kicking erratically before it went limp. Blood ran over his toes, hot, slippery. It did not affect his grip.

The prey never made a sound. But someone else was screaming, high enough to carry over the warble of electronic alarms. Keening, shrill and thin, like a gutshot animal.

Orfeo sang as he climbed.

Lily didn't have the presence of mind to drop to her knees, or muffle with her hands the sounds she was making. Kit thrust her back against the wall without a word, stooped, and scrambled over the sidewalk, scraping his hands, sick at the warm blood wet under his palms. He didn't look up, not at the climbing wings, not at the dark dangling shape.

He crouched between his knees and grabbed Matthew's shoulder, heaved him onto his back. Blood streaked his face, some of it Geoff's, most of it his own. He'd fallen hard, with his hands chained behind his back. He hadn't been able to keep his face from striking stone.

"Christ wept," Kit said, ducking his head warily as he fumbled for a pulse. But Matthew twitched as he did it, eyes flicking open, sockets already staining on either side of a broken nose.

"Ow," Matthew said, thick and muffled as if he spoke through cotton wool.

Lily's breathless screaming stopped, hiccuped, dropped a register as she muttered, "oh, God, oh, God."

It didn't help. The cars still beeped and flashed; the shattered storefront wailed. Matthew blinked. "It missed?"

Kit flinched. He got his feet under him, still hunched, and started dragging Matthew into the shadow of the wall. Matthew bore it gamely, obviously trying not to wrinkle his face around his nose. "Not exactly. Geoff knocked you down."

"He— Oh. Oh, shit." The Mage tried to struggle up.

On the sidewalk, Don was shoving to hands and knees. Kit snarled at him, while pushing on Matthew's shoulders with both hands. *"Stay down!"*

Don dropped to his elbows and rolled across oil stains and petrified chewing gum until he fetched up against the wall. He burrowed under his coat and came out with a semiautomatic pistol that vanished in the meat of his hand. "Where's the kid?"

"It got him," Lily said, into her hands. Her voice was suddenly calm and level, frictionless as ice. She shoved her shoulders at the wall as if she meant to melt through it, and it wasn't cooperating. "The thing got him."

"And it's going to come back, as soon as it understands it didn't get what it was aiming for," Kit said, his hands stroking Matthew's hair and shoulders, checking for other injuries. "We must retire the street. Matthew, can you stand?"

"I can't do anything with these damned cuffs on." He glared at Don, who patted his pockets one-handed, without looking away from the sky or loosening his grip on his gun.

"I dropped the key when I fell. Can your friend—"

"Kit."

"—Kit help you up?"

In answer, Kit glanced over his shoulder, checked the sky, and stepped away from the wall long enough to grab Matthew under the armpits and haul.

"The shopwindow that broke"—Matthew blew blood off his lips—"we can get inside there."

"Across the *street*?"

"Do you have a better idea?" Matthew clinked the handcuffs at Don petulantly. His nose had swollen shut and gore was still running down his face, into his mouth, staining his shirt. He turned his head and spat blood, hair escaping from his ponytail and adhering to his bloodstained cheek. He wasn't going to think about Geoff. He wasn't going to think about Lily's face, so white under the night-dark violet of her hair.

He took a breath and stared straight ahead. "Can you run?"

"You bet your ass I can," Lily snapped back, icy fear and a shocked emptiness too fresh to really count as grief both shattered by a bolt of annoyance. It never occurred to her that Matthew might be speaking to anyone else. Of course not: it would be aimed at her, because she was a girl. And then she saw the corner of Matthew's mouth twitch as he cocked his head back and studied the sky, and she almost slapped him.

"Shopwindow," he said. "You first."

"Then you," Don said. "It wanted you. You need cover."

Matthew thought about arguing, and nodded instead, half deaf with the cacophony ruling the narrow street. He reached out with a thought and silenced the machines. He melted electronics and left fused plastic behind where he meant only to break a connection. Lousy. No finesse. Too much power. "Whatever."

"Can't you nail it with a lightning bolt or something?"

"Not in the iron world." Not in New York City, even more so. Not even in a Mage's tower, not even if Matthew had Jane Andraste's power. Four or five hundred years of Promethean wreaking had gone into binding magic away, a labyrinth of iron roads girdling the land and the sea, and this was the heart of the spell. The power was concentrated here. It ran violent and deep, like a river chained by canyon walls. And it was not the sort of thing that was amenable to flashy pyrotechnics;

those were—with the exception of the Merlin's tricks—reserved for Faerie, even since the Dragon's return.

Matthew looked at Kit. "You?"

"I could hex it from the sky"—he spread his hands, a helpless gesture—"and so could Lily, if she knew the trick of it. But you know whose power it would take."

Matthew nodded. "Not unless there's no other way."

"Well," Don said, and chambered a round. "I guess that means me. Lily, *go*!"

She was right. Even in heels, she could run.

Bent over, smart enough to hustle on a zigzag, head down, she darted across the street like a chipmunk fleeing a hawk. Her breath echoed from the stones, her footsteps thumping. Don held *his* breath, watched the skies, and Matthew leaned after her like a yearning lover, pulling at the steel that bound his hands.

Not that he had any power to fight for her if the monster returned. For a moment, he allowed himself to hate his unicorn.

And then Lily was halfway safe, or at least shadowed by the buildings opposite, and it was Matthew's turn.

There's a knack to running with your hands tied behind your back. Matthew didn't have it. He stumbled, caught himself, twisted his ankle, went down hard on one leg. His jeans shredded on asphalt, and his skin went with them. Raw heat, a childhood pain: skinned knee. Shocking how much it hurt, enough that the sharp strike of his wristbones against the cuffs was but a grace note.

He grunted, ducked his head, and heaved himself up. The air he gasped burned his lungs. It all tasted of iron, and pain seared the inside of his leg with a white phosphorous fire. He'd sprained his ankle, maybe broken something. By force of will he made it bear his weight. He staggered one step. Another.

If racehorses could run on broken legs, so could he.

The first he knew of Orfeo's descent was the measured hammering of Donall's gun.

Lily saw it all.

The shopwindow had shivered into nonexistence, and she

crouched behind the low wall that was left, shatterproof glass crunching under her boots. She saw Matthew stumble, saw the mighty wings catch the streetlight and become limned, frozen in it like the wings of a fly in amber, trapped for endless moments before they folded and fell. She stuffed her fists against her mouth and pressed her back into the corner, and could not drop her gaze as Matthew strove to his feet.

She bit her fingers and she prayed. And for a moment, the pounding of the detective's gun seemed like an answer. Flame licked from the barrel, lashing out like a serpent's angry tongue, and the monster folded its wings even tighter and twisted, somersaulting in midair, tumbling end over end, jerking from the impacts. And Lily dared to hope.

A breath too soon.

The slugs were steel-jacketed. It helped; lead would have glided through Orfeo, and done no harm at all. *These* bullets tore into his breast and wings and he cried out, the skin-creeping scream of an executed man. His shadow spread human arms and legs upon the pavement as his wings snapped wide, antlered head thrown back, the arch of his long neck sustaining the shriek. His own antlers brushed his back, and he flapped madly, trying to slow his descent until he realized that the target was still directly beneath.

Donall exhausted his clip, stroked the release, fumbled a spare magazine from the carrier before the empty hit the ground. He wasn't fast enough. He couldn't be.

Orfeo didn't have the force of his stoop behind him. Instead he reached out, relying on the forthright strength of talons, and clutched at the Mage's head. But Matthew had turned. Unable to throw his hand up, he ducked his head behind a hunched shoulder, and flinched back and to the side as Orfeo's claws scored his shoulder and neck.

It wouldn't have helped, if a second spatter of bullets had not caught Orfeo across the breast just then, tumbling him from the air. He hit the asphalt on his back, spread-eagled. *Sable, a peryton vert, displayed.*

Don pinched his palm smashing the magazine home. He didn't turn to see who had his back; he'd counted nine shots, and the other guy was likely reloading. The enemy of my enemy—

Don worked the slide and fired. Measured shots, two and wait, aim for the head. Six more where those came from. One more clip in his belt.

The thing had already soaked up an awful lot of lead.

It flopped, twisted, lay still. He couldn't tell if the breast was rising and falling, under the feathers. Don heard footsteps, a clip sliding home, a round being chambered. Whoever it was kept a good spread on him, eight or nine feet, centered on the green-winged creature. Matthew was down, curled on his side between Don and the monster, ear pressed to his shoulder. Donall couldn't see how bad he was bleeding, or if he was conscious. Probably, and definitely breathing; he wasn't limp.

"Don?"

"Fuck, Ernie," Don said, light-headed with adrenaline. "Are you one of the bad ones?"

"Are you? What the fuck is that thing?" Ernie edged one more step forward, and Don could see him now, his semiautomatic in a two-fisted grip, low ready before his heaving chest, trigger finger registered along the frame. Ernie wasn't about to shoot anybody who didn't have it coming.

"Fae." Kit stepped away from the wall, regretting his rapier bitterly. He kept his eyes on Matthew, palms itching with helplessness. "Unseelie. Shoot you it again."

Ernie never turned his eyes from the thing on the ground. "Did you call backup?"

"Did you?"

"Now that you mention it—" Ernie shrugged, and slid his finger inside the trigger guard.

"One second." Don edged forward, trying to get a better angle on the antlered bird. He couldn't see if it was breathing, but he couldn't see it bleeding, either. "It might be dead."

It wasn't.

Orfeo waited. Five mortals now, two of them armed. The bullets *hurt*, but couldn't hurt him, not really. Not for long. He was already dead, dead three thousand years, and so he waited while the bullets worked out of his flesh and lay, hard lumps pressed between his plumage and the road.

He'd have to kill the men with the guns. Not that he minded the blood, but it was extra work. Extra complications. Only the Mage had needed to die.

Humans.

They *would* thrash, and make everything harder.

Beside the wounded Mage, the pale-skinned warrior went down on one knee. He mumbled something, and the dark first one grunted agreement, without taking his eyes off Orfeo. There was a click, the metal restraints being removed. The first warrior rolled the Mage onto his back and, with the assistance of the small bearded Mage, began doing something to his wounds. That crunch had to be the woman's boots on the broken glass. In the near distance, Orfeo heard sirens.

The second warrior adjusted some mechanism on his pistol, and slipped it into its carrier. He spread his hands wide, angled down, and murmured a prayer.

A vast, calm, martial presence suffused the narrow road, a holy peace, the susurrus of settling wings. "Ernie, what are you doing?" Donall asked.

"Whatever I can," Peese answered, and laid his hands on the wounded Mage, praying for a miracle.

In a movement as fluid as thought, Orfeo lofted into the air, balanced on a murderous curve.

And was met.

Not by the bullets he had expected, the sharp-toothed rejoinder of the first warrior's pistol—but by a white-shouldered tsunami.

The sound of gunfire had drawn Whiskey to close the distance between Donall and himself. The water-horse had arrived just as Peese changed magazines, and paused to assess the conflict. If there was no need to show himself, he could linger in the shadows, soft-shoed and inconspicuous.

Conversely, if there *was* a need—

He was waiting for it. And when Orfeo snapped himself off the ground with a sinewy flex of wings and a flick of antlers, Whiskey leaped. It was a spring no mortal man could have matched, and few mortal horses—clearing the parked automobiles that Matthew had ruined with his ill-contained magic, clearing the heads of the crouched and cringing men, hurling himself into the air like the spray of a white wave smashing exultant against a cliff: head up, mane bannering, ears pricked, bugling challenge, and changing as he flew.

He struck the peryton chest-to-chest, and smashed him from the air.

Great wings buffeted Whiskey's head, blinding, deafening. Gnarled talons scored his shoulders and his broad black breast. His hooves rang on the road a mere foot from Matthew's supine form, cracking asphalt, water glittering about him when he whirled. Orfeo struck again, sharp yellow teeth slashing Whiskey's cheek, missing his white-rimmed eye. The stallion screamed and reared, hooves connecting, forelegs scraped by Orfeo's claws.

Orfeo's cries, harsh as a raptor's, carried a far more human tone. The peryton screamed like a peacock, a tattered, bloodcurdling sound. He lashed out with teeth and talons, fighting for distance, needing to win free of Whiskey's weight and momentum so he could bring his antlers to bear. Whiskey drove him with the force of a rising tide, the speed of falling water.

Blood scattered the peryton's plumage as Whiskey tried for a wing and spat out only a mouthful of feathers. The teeth of a son of Manannan could manage what bullets could not. Orfeo's talons connected with Whiskey's muzzle, slicing nostrils. He kicked off, wings pumping furiously, and sailed over Whiskey's head as Whiskey lunged into the air, his hind hooves leaving earth, his thick neck twisted as he stretched after the enemy. He missed, and landed heavily, collecting his hooves under him and taking the impact in his shoulders and haunches rather than risking a careless hoof on the fragile humans just behind.

The peryton flailed higher, air scalding the raw flesh of his wounded wing, bruised muscle in his breast complaining. Whiskey's teeth had torn the soft hide of Orfeo's throat, and blood trickled hot through hair and plumage and tickled as it dripped and dried down his inner thigh.

But in the air, he had the advantage. And the stallion was hurt as well, blood filming one china-blue eye, pinking the sea-slick shoulders and darkening the puddles under his hooves.

Whiskey sidled, snorting, silver shoes pealing on the road like dropped coins, clear and sweet over the clang and stink of gunfire as

Don and Ernie tracked the rising arc of the peryton and pumped shot after shot into him. The young woman stood against the wall, pressed flat beside the empty window frame. And Marlowe crouched over Matthew, who was conscious enough to have drawn up one knee and fisted one unchained hand in the shirt Marlowe had ripped off and stuffed against his neck and shoulder, but not much more.

"Christopher," Whiskey said, "take him to Morgan."

Kit looked up, cold at the words, his bare chest daubed with Matthew's blood. He was pale, wiry with muscle on a slender frame, much scarred. He licked his lips, and glanced at the darkness beyond the lights. The sirens were closing in. It had been perhaps fifteen seconds since Whiskey met the peryton's fall, and though Peese's miracle had sealed the wounds on Matthew's throat, the Mage had left a battle's ration of blood upon the road. "Can you hold him?"

Whiskey tossed his head, swinging his haunches left, turning around the forehand as he followed the peryton's flight. If he was charged with killing Matthew, he would give up—for the time being—as soon as Matthew was out of reach. "I *will*."

"Magus"—Kit waved Donall over—"help me get him up."

Don waggled his head without dropping his attention, or his gun. "It might come back."

"I will be here," Whiskey answered. The street was filled with the raw scent of his blood, of Matthew's blood, of Geoffrey's. "Get them to safety."

Peese was standing again, cloaked in grace, his weapon trained on the sky and pale glory whipping about him as if lashed by a brutal wind. "Go," Peese said, to Don. "I'll stay. Anyway, somebody will have to explain."

"You going to admit it's Fae this time?" Don snarled, but he crouched and slid his gun into the holster.

Peese half smiled, and let his shoulders rise and fall.

"Geoff—" Lily stepped forward, out of the shadows a little. Her hands twisted in front of her hips, but she stood steady, boots planted, and her voice was firm.

"We can help him not," Kit said, more gently than he had thought he would manage. "There remains only the question of meting out justice."

"Justice?" Her incredulity bordered on mockery.

Kit smiled through another man's blood. "Come with us, and live to claim revenge."

She looked up. She looked at Don, who crouched beside Matthew and lifted his shoulders while Kit helped him to his feet. They heaved him out of blood sequined with broken glass, the wreckage of his spectacles. Matthew reeled, eyes closed, still holding the wadded shirt against his throat, his face a blood-streaked mask. Don steadied him, got under his arm. "Lily," Kit said, "open the mirror."

She turned to see where he was looking. An unshattered shopwindow loomed behind her, glossy with reflections. "I remember how," she said, and felt the strength prickle her fingertips. "I don't know how to get where you said—"

"You just open. I'll guide."

She met his gaze, and then sucked her lower lip into her mouth and nodded. "All right, then. Come on."

Orfeo's wounded wing burned as he banked, turned on a feather-tip, and came back around, searching through darkness for the light. The mortals crouched in the street, Whiskey towering over them like a battle memorial: ears up, tail lofted, proud neck arched in mordant challenge.

Waiting.

Orfeo didn't care to accept.

The sirens were coming, and the mortals were moving the Mage. He had one more chance. A falcon stoop, no hesitation. One blow to kill.

He waited until Whiskey had turned his head to scan another quarter of the sky, and dove. The bullets that ripped through his wings and breast made no difference, not even with an archangel's power wreathing the hands of the man wielding the gun. Nothing could stop him—

One of the men dragging the quarry turned, letting the other support all the Mage's weight. The little one, shirtless, who reeked both of Fae magic and Magery. Those things meant nothing in the iron world. Whiskey was moving, leaping, but Orfeo was faster, when the waterhorse had not taken him by surprise, and Whiskey would not be in time. The peryton anticipated the impact already, the grab, the pivot and snatch, sailing upward, out of the water-horse's reach, untroubled by the guns. He was going to enjoy his supper tonight.

Orfeo prepared to spread his wings.

Damme, Kit thought, quite reflexively, as the wind howled in the predator's wings. And, bitterly amused at the irony of his choice of oath, he had just time to raise his hands.

It was an old, sick power, rich and nauseous and irresistible as any unhallowed love he'd ever known. It ran shivery caresses up the inside of his skin, weighed a stone like desire in his gut and his groin.

He hadn't touched it in almost four hundred years.

He reached out with Lucifer's borrowed strength, and ripped Orfeo from the air.

The peryton wailed, tumbled, and struck hard on the asphalt. Whiskey was there when he fell, and Orfeo did not rise again. Kit watched, expressionless, the gauzy vermilion that sheathed his hands guttering back against his skin as Whiskey ripped feathers from flesh, hide from bone, and strewed blood and entrails over the street. Crunching echoed; boluses of meat distended his throat like a snake's as he tore and gorged, and Lily—ever so softly—choked.

Red and blue lights painted buildings at both ends of the street, and the wail of sirens bounced and howled between the canyon walls. *"Go!"* Peese shouted at Don, waving over his shoulder, as Whiskey snorted over his mutilated prey. "Get out of here. I'll handle this."

Don touched Kit's shoulder, and Kit stepped back, shouldering his share of Matthew's weight again. They must have made quite a ridiculous prospect. Don was twice his size.

"Whiskey," Kit called. "Whiskey, *now*."

He thought the stallion wouldn't listen. Doors were opening on the police cars and men crouching behind them as the water-horse finally lifted his head and curvetted back from the crushed body of the peryton, tracking dinner-plate hoofprints that shone glossy black in the dim light. "Christopher?" He turned and lifted his muzzle, no longer a white horse, but red.

"Go to your mistress," Kit said, sharply, as Peese stepped into the sudden flood of spotlights and raised and opened his perfectly ordinary hands. Whiskey shook out his mane, blood showering, and vanished where he stood—a crash, as a tower of water in the shape of a horse folded and splashed over stone, running this way and that. Into the gutters, down to the sea.

Peese was shouting something about being an officer, holding very still, calling to the wall of white-and-black cars and armed men that everything was under control.

Kit didn't wait to hear the details of the negotiations. Lily stepped through the mirror, and Kit and Donall were right behind her, dragging Matthew between them.

Kit hadn't overstayed his welcome for a change. In fact, this once, Lucifer could rather wish he'd lingered a little. Angels were so *boring*. Even in Hell.

Mortals were livelier, and Kit more than most—although there was a transitory amusement to be found in the way the wine smoked and bubbled in Satan's glass. Some stories carried a metaphor a little too far.

Lucifer reached up one-handed and laid a finger against the other devil's clawed, black thumb, while Christian and Michael and Fionnghuala looked on. They stood in the center of the tiled ballroom floor, under a wrought-iron chandelier that would not have looked out of place in the Paris Opera House. :It tastes better unboiled.:

Satan arched a tufted eyebrow, membranous wings folded tight against his back, looking down at the Morningstar. Satan dominated the room, an eight-foot monolith the color of rusted iron, muscled like a Renaissance statue. "If only thou gavest the concern to religion that thou dost to beverages." His voice pealed in the echoing space, and mortals and Fae winced at the crash like a miskeyed pipe organ.

"On the contrary," Christian said, selecting a glass of his own from the tray of a ragged-winged angel, "he thinks of nothing but. Except possibly politics." He turned back, and lifted the glass in Fionnghuala's direction, an understated toast—whether to a lady, or a Christian, or the one who wasn't an angel, she didn't know. The wine in his glass was the color of straw, and it made his lips glossy when he sipped.

Satan reached out and brushed Lucifer's cheek, leaving behind the scent of urine and brimstone. Lucifer stepped away from the touch.

"Politics *are* religion," Satan said. And then bluntly, archly, ignoring Michael as if Michael were not even in the room: "Will you submit to Him?"

Lucifer laughed, as even the angel stared at him. :*None left but by submission*,: he quoted, lifting celestial eyes to meet the lash of Satan's fiery ones. :*And that word / Disdain forbids me, and my dread of shame / Among the Spirits beneath*—:

Satan dropped his glass, so it starred the tile with shards and burgundy. "Do *not*," he said. "You will answer the question."

As if in answer, Lucifer made shattered glass and spilled wine vanish with a pass of his hand. :Pride,: he said coldly, :we have in common. You object to my goals?:

"You have a Dragon Prince. Overthrow Him." Satan's wings stayed folded tight as the great, nude figure gestured to Keith MacNeill, who stood against the far wall, hands over his ears, the mortal girl cringing beside him. "Unite the Hells. Relinquish cowardice."

Michael startled. She folded her arms over the dove-gray breast of her coat and cocked her head at Satan. Fionnghuala laid a hand on the taut muscle of her forearm. "Bring me a war," Michael said, lips thinning. "If you dare."

Satan grinned, showing ragged fangs, and Christian laughed into his wine. "Ask, and you shall receive."

Lucifer rolled strong-bodied drink over a forked tongue. :Would He take me back?:

"If you plead your case. Most likely." The archangel wore beneficence, but never quite a smile. "God is perfect love."

Lucifer snorted. :One Corinthians thirteen,: he said. :Verses four through ten. The New American Standard text.:

Around the circle, Fionnghuala saw two suppressed smiles, one sharp frown. Angels and devils *knew* scripture. And *she* knew it too: both the modern words and the ancient ones.

Love is patient, love is kind and is not jealous; love does
not brag and is not arrogant, does not act unbecomingly; it

does not seek its own, is not provoked, does not take into ac-
count a wrong suffered, does not rejoice in unrighteousness,
but rejoices with the truth; bears all things, believes all
things, hopes all things, endures all things.

Love never fails; but if there are gifts of prophecy, they
will be done away; if there are tongues, they will cease; if
there is knowledge, it will be done away.

For we know in part and we prophesy in part; but when
the perfect comes, the partial will be done away.

:Is the Bible His word?: Lucifer asked. :Would He submit to me?
Why then must my love be proved more perfect than His?:

"Because He owes you nothing," Michael answered.

Fionnghuala stepped away.

:No more,: Lucifer answered, :than the lover owes the beloved, or the
parent owes the child.:

Michael hovered on the verge of rejoinder. She found it and framed
it, and let it pass, as something more urgent came to her attention. "An
attempt has been made to bring the mortals and the Faerie back into
conflict."

"Have they ever left it?" Fionnghuala had meant to remain silent, but
some temptations were too much.

:Where?:

"New York," Michael said. "There has been another death, though
not the death intended. I have an agent there."

And while Christian and Satan turned and stared, Lucifer pealed
bright laughter, head thrown back, fanning his wings. :Michael. You
cheated.:

"Angels do not cheat." Michael glanced at the floor.

"Who died?" Fionnghuala said. "Fae or mortal?"

"The mortal boy, Geoffrey Bertelli." Michael's wings had fanned
wide too, and between her plumage and Lucifer's, the circle cast all but
encompassed the gathered five. She raised an eyebrow and looked from
devil to devil. "And I suppose none here had to do with the provoking
of that?"

:Someone must inform Juliet,: Lucifer said, ignoring the question,

turning to look at the girl. She still stood beside the Elf-prince, her arms folded over her breast, her mask pushed up, revealing eyes bruised at the corners with tiredness.

"I will." Michael's frown pulled the corners of her mouth sternly down. " 'Tis what angels are for." The angel stepped back, turned, and squared her shoulders under the trailing cape of wings. And did not see Lucifer smile behind his hand, as—somewhere above—he felt a war-lock once named Marley reach out and take up the power he had so long laid aside.

:Nuala,: Lucifer said, making his wineglass vanish before he took her arm. :Wilt dance with me, my swan?:

Jewels was not following the conversation. Fortunately, the Prince did not seem to require her comprehension, merely her attendance. And she was *motivated* to learn. She wanted this, wanted the life she could see ed-dying around her, as if she were a rock tossed into a moving stream. She could almost feel its ripples and rills, the lift of a little curl of white water where it stroked her edge, the pressure that wanted her to roll down-stream. She wanted to treat with these winged and elf-eared and magi-cal beings the way Matthew did, or Kit, with his ash-colored hair and his too-dark eyes.

And it started here, in this echoing and two-thirds empty hall, with trying to follow a quick, slurred conversation in a language she didn't understand, between Ian—her *lord*—and the red-haired, sword-bearing giant who was his father. She folded her arms together, her own pulse racing under her fingertips.

She had too much to learn. But it was happening. Finally. All around her. Happening now. She took one deep delighted breath to fix the scent of this place in her heart, and smiled. It might be Hell, but it smelled of roses.

"The odor of sanctity," a young woman's voice said in her ear, and Jewels startled and found herself eye to eye with an angel. An angel her own small height, stern in a pearl-gray coat, with slicked dark hair. "*He* likes to pervert what he can."

"Him?" Jewels asked. She let her gaze slip toward the devils gath-ered at the center of the hall.

"Who else?" Jade-colored wings settled, revealing translucent lavender and gray under the foresty greens. The angel brushed past Jewels
to wait at Ian's elbow until he gave her his attention, a matter of a moment or two. "Your Highness."

He nodded, balancing at the crux of her attention and his father's
without appearing to slight either one. A delicate trick. Jewels caught
herself admiring it, and frowned. The Prince might be pretty, but she
suspected he would not be safe to fall for. Not when she lived as his servant. She'd gathered that nearly everyone in Faerie belonged to someone else—and the rest lived by the sword.

"Michael," Ian said, and waited. No honorific, just the name. It
seemed dignity enough, said that way, though neither the angel nor the
Elf-prince bowed. And people *did* bow here, like they meant it.

Michael waited too, and then brushed Jewels' arm with the leading
edge of one wing. It felt nothing like she had expected, warm and flexible. She almost cried out. "I have a message for your servant," the angel
said, when she seemed to think some responsibility had been satisfied.
"With your indulgence?"

Ian never glanced at Jewels. He nodded, casual tolerance, leaving
Jewels unprepared for the irritation that clenched her jaw. She had
never been good at accepting parental authority.

But she'd chosen this, and she would learn.

"By your leave?" the angel said, and extended her arm. Belatedly,
Jewels understood that she was intended to take it, like a lady escorted
to the ball, and after a moment she accepted, stepping inside the bivalve
camber of Michael's wings.

The angel's air was grave. Jewels let herself be led, thinking of the
warmth and hardness of the slender arm under gray wool, like the marble under her shoes. "A message."

Michael turned an eye on her. The corners of her lips dragged as if
her mouth were a bow, drawn to deliver an unwelcome arrow. "Your
friend is dead." Her steps hesitated as if she expected Jewels to
crumble.

I know, Jewels almost said. *I saw her body.* But she hesitated. "My
friend?"

"Geoffrey," Michael said. "I am sorry."

The words formed in Jewels' mouth without her knowing where they had come from, heavy and round as stones. "You're wrong."

Michael shook her head. Jewels stepped back, pushing Michael's arm away.

"He can't be dead. He's here. I just saw him."

Jewels turned, and Michael turned with her, following her sun. The tall arch of her wings simulated privacy, and also blocked Jewels' line of sight. She jerked back, three steps, intending to step out of the living bower and find Geoff for herself, point him out and prove Michael wrong. But the green wings crossed behind her, fenced her in, and drew her close.

"He left," Michael said. "He went back to New York. And he has been killed there. By that which murdered your friend Althea, and no one could protect him."

When the girl staggered, the angel caught her, balanced her, and kept her on her feet. She swayed, fists to mouth, and Michael's grip on her forearms was all that kept her from crashing to the floor.

"Why would he go back?" It wasn't what she had meant to ask. Not exactly. Her eyes were burning, and she didn't want to blink. When she closed her eyes, she saw him. Poor gentle Geoff, who'd made Virgin Marys with wasabi instead of horseradish. He would have been mutilated like Althea, tangled up in his own blood, and blood made him dizzy and he'd loved her anyway, even when she didn't really want him to—

"Why New York?" That was closer to it. She forced herself to lower her hands and breathe, watching the angel's eyes.

"I cannot answer that," Michael said. "But there are others who may know."

She half turned her head when she spoke, not quite looking Jewels in the eye. *Do angels lie?*

But Michael cleared her throat and continued, "Vengeance takes its own time," and peeked quickly back at Jewels' face.

And so maybe Michael wasn't avoiding her gaze. Maybe she was looking over Jewels' shoulder, craning her head past the sweep of her wing. Toward Ian, and his father, the so-called Dragon Prince. Jewels licked her lips.

She must have stopped shaking, because the angel let her stand on her own. "Thank you, Michael."

The angel folded her wings, left hand dropping to her rapier's hilt. "I am but the messenger."

Keith listened with folded arms while Ian laid out his plan, and then said, "Elaine won't forgive it."

"She won't have a choice," Ian said, lowering his voice again as he checked the position of those who would have the most interest in this conversation. Cairbre stood with the Queen, and the girl, Jewels, was still distracted by the angel. Scents threaded the air in the ballroom, each aroma knotting through the others until the whole made a sort of net, smells woven into a palimpsest of who was there, and who had gone. "She did what it seemed she must, and now it's done."

Another man might have made a gesture, a flick of his fingers as if brushing something away. Ian stood very quiet, with folded hands, and waited for his father to answer.

"She would have done more," Keith said.

"Do you *want* to see her suffer?" Ian amended his question before Keith could object. "No, I don't mean it. You went to Hell in her place. I just—"

"You were raised to be King," Keith answered. He leaned forward, his cloak falling over his shoulder, draping in sculptural folds. "And you want it. Ambition's no sin—"

Ian flashed a look over his shoulder, in the direction of Lucifer Morningstar, who danced with Nuala in a sway of alabaster feathers.

"All right," Keith allowed, with a laugh. "There's ambition and there's ambition. You know I want Elaine off that damned throne, and I want her to be herself again. And you—"

"I am a wolf," Ian said, with quiet pride. "I do not need to sell away my heart or soul to endure the White-horn Throne. No matter what mother thinks of me. I can do what she cannot. And if there are four that love her, three of us I *know* would see her released, and I do not think Carel would be opposed."

Keith bit his lip at the mention of his rivals, but had the sense to nod. "She says the Fae can't love—"

"They can," Ian replied. "I have loved as one, and loved as a wolf as well, and as a man. It's not the same love. But it is love nonetheless. And she acts in love now—she *does*"—in the face of his father's arched brow—"but it's a Fae thing, cold and implacable as ice peaks in the sun. We need a ruler who chooses to rule, rather than enduring it. Too many of her subjects would see her replaced—and mother will not kill Àine, and Àine will never leave her alone. The Mebd was the Summer Queen, the elder sister, and now it is Àine's role, and mother is the Snow Queen—"

"And you want it," Keith repeated.

"And I want it," Ian said.

Ian felt his father decide. In wolf-shape, Keith would have settled his haunches, flipped his tail over his feet, and waited, alert, to see where Ian pointed.

The man just nodded once. "Then how to make her abdicate?"

Ian let his hands fall apart and pressed damp palms to his thighs. "She won't do it for herself. So we make it the only way to save our lives."

Keith schooled himself, breathed deeply, and frowned. "What do you mean?"

"Michael," Ian whispered. "Do you think you can take her?"

Keith's gaze went over his son's shoulder, to the frail dark-haired girl with the dappled jade wings. And then he frowned. "We'll talk later. Your friend returns."

Ian turned to meet Jewels and waited. She wobbled somewhat; the news had not been good. He might have felt pity, if he had permitted the emotion. Instead he pressed his tongue to the roof of his mouth and thought of what his mother would have done.

Jewels' throat worked. "I need your help," she said. "Geoff is dead. And I want—I want revenge."

"And you appeal to me as your lord to obtain it?" Conscious and careful, Ian arched an eyebrow and accepted a small smile, and didn't think of the boy in his black leather and his ridiculous badly dyed hair. He felt Keith fading away behind him: a diminishment of presence, a diminishment of scent.

"I—" She hadn't thought. No, not really.

"Let go of the iron world," Ian said. "It's not yours anymore. You chose."

Her fingers blanched as she balled her hands. "*You're* sending me back there to learn."

A temporary thing, to secure her future in Faerie, and she knew it. It was a false trail, and he wouldn't pursue.

"It will break your heart." Calm and stern. The way, he fancied, Cairbre would say it. "You shall live a long while. Will you seek vengeance every time something mortal you cared for dies? It will keep you very busy."

She closed her eyes. "You're laughing at me."

"No."

"Do you . . ." She swallowed. "Do you forbid me?"

He let it hang for a moment, so she would remember that he could. "No," he said. "Not this time."

"Then what?"

"I won't forbid you to seek your revenge," he said. "But I will not weep when I bury you, when you fail."

"I don't like prophecies. Who killed my friend?"

"Àine," he answered. "The Queen of the Unseelie Fae. The girl with the sunflowers in her hair."

She swallowed that too. Calmly, with a little smile. And then she dropped her head and murmured, "I can wait."

Lily had bitten off most of her lipstick and what remained was a bruise-colored stain around the margins of her mouth. She stood in the warm rain, outside Morgan le Fey's cottage, where the roses wouldn't drip down her neck, and worried at her cuticle with her nail.

She could have stayed inside, but the cottage wasn't big, and she was in the way as Kit and Don and a red-haired woman scrambled over Matthew. And she couldn't bear standing in the hearth corner, fiddling her Medic Alert bracelet, helplessness breaking over her. The rain was better.

She stepped onto a graveled path and strolled between banks of white and gold lilies, growing madly out of season. Except this rain held no hint of November. It was warm and mild, summery, as sweet as the flowers.

The stone cottage looked medieval and the damask roses overgrowing it were antique, but the lilies were every variety Lily had ever seen and more: modern cultivars, white, speckled, orange, yellow, red as the heart's red blood. She bent over them, burying her face in the petals, and breathed their fragrance down. The petals clung to her cheeks and water dripped under her collar. She closed her eyes.

She licked up the sweetness of the flowers in the rain that wet her lips, and turned to face Christian before he came up on her. The flowers brushed her fingers as she folded her hands behind her back.

"You're angry."

"Angry?" Matthew's sweater clung to her shoulders, dripping cotton swinging at the hem. The charm on her bracelet jangled as she twisted her hands. "Because I found out you've lied to me, and so has Michael, and there's some sort of . . . cosmic game of chess going on?"

"I care for you." He shook his head. "I would have told you."

"But you didn't."

"No. Not yet. I wanted you comfortable with me and with your power. I wanted—"

"You wanted to seduce me. You wanted me *invested.*"

"Yes," he said. The rain straggled his hair down his face in lank red coils. It looked too much like blood. She turned her back, and stared down at the lilies instead. "You need me more now than before, Lily. You're in Faerie now, and you've fallen headfirst into the argument I wanted to keep you out of."

"Until you could use me."

"It was inevitable, one way or the other." He reached out and turned her around. "Michael would have done no less in her time. Your potential is irresistible. My lady, you are a song."

She breathed out across her lower lip and let her hands fall to her sides. She wondered if she would ever get the drying itch off her palms. "You're a devil."

"I'm a little more than that." He touched her cheek, and stroked his fingers across her mouth. "And you need me more than ever. You drank the water."

"Yes. So?"

His hand fell. He dried it on his trousers. "Faerie owns you now. I have a lot to teach and little time to teach it in."

She could still taste the pollen and rainwater when she swallowed. "What do you mean, *owns*?"

"I mean it will kill you to go home."

He took no joy in it when she blanched, and was ready when she sat down hard on the garden border, cushioning her fall as best he could, though his grip burned her wrists and pressed her bracelet into her flesh. At least she believed.

"*Kill* me?"

"If you are absent from Faerie for too long. Yes. Ask your new friend Marlowe what it means."

"But he was in the iron world—"

"You will notice he did not stay long."

Her hands were shaking when he let her go, and the chill was back. The cold and trembling worried her. It wasn't just the rain. "I can't," she said. "I'll need my medicine. What about my classes? Who'll take care of my *cat*?"

"You see?" He squatted beside her in the wet that was soaking through her skirt now, and pulled her out of the grass and crushed lilies, and lifted her to her feet. "I can aid you."

She twitched reflexively toward the cottage, gray stone streaked with fading whitewash, all rose-draped in the rain, with its vivid crimson door. *If she's really Morgan le Fey, surely she can help.*

Christian touched Lily's arm. "You know those hounds of hers? And the raven?"

"Yes?" She didn't want to look at him. When she looked at him, if she actually let herself hear the timbre of his voice, the hurt came swelling back up her throat and her eyes burned, her sinuses swelling until she had to open her mouth to breathe.

"They were men once." When she blinked at him, he stepped back far enough that she could feel the distance between them. "Let me help you, Lily."

She pressed her elbows to her sides, rain dripping from her lashes. Thoughtfully, she reached out, and took his hand.

Chapter Nineteen
Dirty Old Town

"That was foolish," Jane said, as the door closed behind her apprentice. She reached with steady hands to pour herself a cup of tea. The last few drops trickled from the spout flecked with bits of leaf. "And not congenial to a sense of community."

"You won't win him back," the Bunyip answered. "Though you do not wish to let go."

"Donall?"

"Matthew Magus," Bunyip said. He folded his hands around the cup, held it fragile and strong as an eggshell. "He's lost to you. You think you can use him, to straddle the boundary between iron and moonlight—"

It was what the Prometheans had made him for. "You think not?"

"I think you're a fool to try it," he answered, and sipped. "My way is better."

"Your way." Felix, who stood, precise and cautious in his bespoke suit, and crossed to examine the flowers tumbling from a tall verdigris vase on the floor before the black-and-white shoji screens. "I believe we're still unclear on what that might be, old man."

"Ally yourself with me. Ally yourself with Heaven—"

"That has always been our goal. But Heaven has not been open to allegiances."

Bunyip covered a bubbling chuckle with the back of his left hand, and Jane understood what she was meant to: that he knew something she didn't, and intended to raise her curiosity. She glanced at Christian. Christian shrugged.

"Times change," the Bunyip said.

Jane settled back on the couch—not lolling, but erect and graceful, her saucer balanced on her hand. "Do finish your tea," she said. "I'll fetch more."

"Thank you," he said, and set the empty cup down, scraps of tea leaf clinging to the sides. "I've had enough."

"You wish us to choose sides," Felix said. He ran a fingertip along the orange-yellow spike of a bird-of-paradise, and down the stiff dark stem. "It would be a compromise to our principles to negotiate with Fae."

"Your principles? Of conquest? You don't want another war."

"We lost the last one," Jane said. "It would mean starting over from scratch. And Faerie is forewarned this time." She let herself smile, though her face felt tight, and did not permit the cup to rattle on the saucer. "Three hundred years, give or take, it took us to chain the Dragon. One hundred years of peace it bought us, and Faerie undid it in a week, once they learned the symbols. You cannot make me believe that once freed, she'd permit us a wreaking like that again—and you cannot convince me that it would be worth the cost, if she did." She glanced aside, at Christian, his expression dreamy over his folded arms.

Christian shook his head. "The wards on the iron world are still strong. We wouldn't be starting from scratch."

"Of course not," Bunyip said. "Which is one reason Kelpie's laxity concerns the Dragon. His weakness weakens Mist, as well. But you know her strength isn't drawn only from Faerie. It comes from the Promethean power also. She's as much in New York as she is the rock beneath it, if you know how to look. The *Dragon* doesn't care who wins. She doesn't care to see a winner at all."

"Dynamic equilibrium," Felix said. "You're suggesting we readjust our goals."

"I'm suggesting you examine the source of your goals, and determine if the course you were set, half a millennium since, was really to human-ity's benefit, or . . ."

"Or become yours?" Jane was allowing Felix to take the lead. He tried not to revel in it.

"Or reinvent yourselves. You have accomplished so much. Your path may have been flawed, but let's speak the truth; it is Promethean power that's healed the sick, raised your iron miracles into the sky, built a world where mortal men and women never even had to *believe* in the Fae, never mind fearing them."

"Lost now," Jane said.

Bunyip dismissed it with a pass of his hand. "As Christian says. The wards are strong. If you have the strength to win your duel and bring your prodigals in line, those shan't be lost. And should you fail—"

"Marlowe has no loyalty to our goals," Jane said. "Nor any love of our works. He'll leave the iron world unguarded."

Bunyip's eyes crinkled at the corners. "And you can be assured that Faerie will not hesitate to ally itself with your other enemies as it must. You need your own friends."

"You're that enemy," Jane said. "Why wish us victory?"

"It's not that simple. There are factions in Faerie that would see you and Elaine destroy each other, resulting in their own elevation to power. If they cannot set you at each other's throats, they'll find other ways to strike. There's factions in Hell, and Prometheus has been allied with only one of those, and the others will not be kind to you. There are factions in the iron world. Your choice is to choose whom you will be used by, who you will use. The only monolith is Heaven, and they do not give up information to outsiders. And for the first time in a very long time indeed, the Divine has extended its hand."

"What do you mean?"

He dusted his lap off as he stood, and straightened the crease of his trousers before lifting his hat off the sofa cushion. His smile sent prickles of unease through her, though she forced herself to reply in kind.

"Michael has returned," he said. "And you *can't* claim you missed the unicorn."

She sat dumb for seconds before re-collecting herself, setting down her cup, standing to escort him to the door. "What do you get out of this?" she asked, as he shrugged on his coat.

"Simply put, your help in reclaiming what the Queen of the Daoine Sidhe and her minions have, that I need."

"Which is?" A clink from behind the screen told her that Felix and Christian were collecting saucers and cups.

"My shadow," Bunyip answered. "And the sea. I'll be in touch. Only

see what you can do about the Daoine Seeker, and I'll handle the rest."
He bowed and left Jane standing by the door, the handle chilly in her
palm. She closed it and made sure of the latches, and went to help Felix
and Christian.

She found Felix staring into the bottom of Bunyip's teacup, a frown
souring his mouth. "What is it?"

He tilted the cup so she could see the pattern of leaves adhering to
bone-white china, below the golden rim: wings, a crown, a cross, a
blade, a rose. For a moment, they stood with their heads bent together,
a study in perplexity.

"Damn," Jane said, when it became obvious that Felix wasn't about
to. "He was telling the truth."

"He was," Felix agreed. "What the hell do we do now?"

"Win the duel," Christian offered. "Re-create the order. Save the
world."

Ian brought Jewels home—not to her own home, but into the capable
hands of the Merlin and the Merlin's mistress, on a chill Saturday morning not quite a week after the murder of Althea Benning had started it all.

Perhaps *started* is the wrong word. Because it was not, truly, so much
that the killing *began* anything as that it brought it dripping into the
light, a flash of color in the pan.

When it broke, then, rather than when it began.

And so Ian delivered a grimly determined Jewels onto Autumn's
front porch before breakfast, when the sky behind bare trees was transparent golden and cold birds sang in their limbs. He didn't enter the
house this time, though there was no rowan over the doorway, and the
only iron was a horseshoe nailed to the lintel in the attitude of a waxing
moon. Instead he put one hand each on Jewels' thin arms, and presented her before the door as if he were bringing home a recalcitrant
stray.

She obeyed, and that was all he required. She lifted her hand and
knocked—it was important to knock rather than to ring—and waited
gentle on his glove until the door popped free of a sticking frame. Autumn beckoned from the other side of a coir fiber mat the same color as
her unraveled braid. "Your new apprentice," Ian said.

"Not mine." But she took Jewels' chill hand and drew her over the threshold. "Gypsy said he'd be here by lunchtime. In the meantime, Jewels, you look as if you ought to have a cup of cocoa and a nap. Thank you, Ian."

"You're very welcome," he said, and retreated down the porch stairs.

Inside, Jewels drank the cocoa fast to keep from dozing off into it. It was Swiss Miss, with the petrified marshmallows, but Autumn had twisted a small carton over it and plopped a dollop of half-and-half into the hot water and powdered chocolate, so it was good. Just not good enough to keep Jewels awake.

Like an overtired child, she couldn't recall how she made her way to the bed she woke up in. It was a daybed, a white metal frame and a lumped mattress covered in a green store-bought quilt. The covers were warm, and tucked up around her shoulders, and she'd been sleeping soundly despite the brightness that pushed through yellowed eyelet curtains and filled the clean, worn room under the eaves. A few moments later, she realized she'd heard the rattle and thump of a weather-swollen door.

She swung her feet onto cold wide pine and stood: misplaced, disenchanted. Wendy waking up in her own bed, alone, with no shadow, no Tink, and no Pan. The quality of the light, the smell of the air, were all wrong.

She couldn't find her shoes, but her face was clean, the makeup scrubbed away, and she was wearing a woman's enormously oversized sweatpants and her own undershirt as pajamas. Anxiety writhed in her chest as she descended the stair, and it couldn't just be from—what— *missing* half an hour or more. She'd probably gone through the motions with closed eyes and numbed fingers, head nodding into microsleeps. She could still taste stale sugar, cloying in her mouth. She'd forgotten to brush her teeth, or even run a finger full of toothpaste around the inside of her mouth and rinse.

Voices below climbed past her up the stair. She paused with one hand on the silken old banister and listened. Autumn and Carel, and the tingly rumble of the old guy, Gypsy, with the barrel chest and the beard. Her teacher, or whatever.

He sounded okay. He'd smelled okay too. And he'd known what he was talking about, when he asked her about her scars.

She turned, still steadying herself, breaking the octagonal shaft of sun that tumbled through the skylight at the landing, gilding the dust and cat hair hanging on the draft. "Geoff . . ."

Her voice fell dead, without an echo. She let go the banister and put her fingers against her mouth, as if she could stuff his name back in. But the word was long flown.

When Carel walked from the kitchen down the hall to wake Matthew's stray, she found the girl sitting on the steps, her head bowed over her hands. Jewels didn't hear Carel coming, and Carel paused there a few moments and watched as the sunlight slid over her shoulders in time with each careful breath.

That nullity still clung around her, a kind of flex and oddness in the air. She was striking in her emptiness.

"Jewels?"

She looked up. She hadn't been crying. The pastel smudges under her eyes were stains of exhaustion. "Merlin." She reached up to grab the banister, translucent fingers paler than the oak, and pulled herself to her feet. "Thank you for —"

Whatever it was, it was too complicated to fold down into words or approximate with anything but the broadest and vaguest of gestures. Carel nodded anyway, and stepped against the wall, creating a space for Jewels to walk through.

She did it without looking up. As the girl passed, a weight like warm wool settled on Carel, a shadow that nevertheless felt like sunlight, a stern, uncompromising heat. *She will never have power*, Mist murmured, like a mountain whispering into Carel's ear. *She is not the destination, but the path.*

The weight of scalding coils stroked Carel's skin. *What would you have me do about it?*

The Dragon laughed, and did not answer. *The sacrifice is half complete.*

Carel understood. Faerie had been given a Dragon Prince, in Keith MacNeill. A precious animal, born for a task. That task was always the same, within the limits of history. The Dragon Prince came to liberate a fettered people, and he paid for that disenthrallment in innocent blood and his own damnation, as Keith had when he put every Promethean in

Faerie—save one—to the sword, as Arthur had when he—like Herod—sentenced each babe of an age to die.

But that was only half the price. The Dragon Prince also stood to sacrifice: a Summer King, brought low when the winter threatened. And the hand that laid him down would be, always, family, however one defined the term. Arthur had his Mordred and his Morgan and his Gwenhwyfar, Vlad had his Radu, Harold had his Tostig, and Hermann the Cheruscan had his whole damned clan.

Carel had been the Queen's lover for seven years, as long as the Queen had been Keith's wife. As long as Keith had claimed his throne. Surely, that made them—*something* to one another.

Carel could fulfill the geas, become the betrayer, and spare Ian and Elaine.

She let the Dragon feel the frail, mortal force of her rage. *You unforgivable bitch*.

The anger of ants, the rice paper fury of something so small and obscure it barely bears noticing. She was the Merlin, the voice of the Dragon. Interlocutor and *pet*, and while she had a certain influence, a certain power of her own, there was no doubt who the mistress was. The Dragon settled over her, a gentling hand on the collar, and sighed.

Carel, following Jewels into the kitchen, sighed in echo. Keith knew. Keith had known all along what the price was.

Mist stayed silent. The bowed boards creaked under Jewels' footsteps, though she walked ever so lightly and her feet were bare. She paused beside the table where Gypsy sat and cleared her throat. "Reporting for duty," she quipped, as bravely as she could. Her hands kept twisting in the hem of her shirt.

Gypsy peered up at her and smiled. "Have a seat." He swept crumbs off the bare boards with one rough hand, clearing a space. "Do you know what you want to learn?"

She licked her lips and shrugged under her tangled hair. "First, or in general?"

"First," he said, after a thoughtful pursing of his lips. She shook her head. "Well, we'll start with something straightforward, then. Autumn?"

The sound of her name summoned her attention. She'd been trading glances with Carel, who still leaned in the doorway, while she set the kettle on. She knew something was wrong, and she also knew enough not to ask.

"Yes?" She turned with the celadon teapot in her hand.

"Never mind," he answered, laughing. "You anticipated my request. A cup for the young lady?"

Jewels didn't like tea, and she in particular didn't like strong tea drunk plain, with leathery particles of leaf that caught between her teeth. But she drank it, grateful the cup was small, and set it down with a shiver for the tannin.

She was aware that Autumn and Carel had left the room, and she and Gypsy sat alone at the table beside the crowns-of-thorns and the jade plants thronging the window. He leaned forward on his elbows, a little moisture in his beard from the tea, the edges of his mustache caffeine-yellowed. He smelled of garlic, faintly, and more strongly of green Speed Stick.

"So tell me," he said, "what do you see?"

She frowned, and glanced at the sea-green interior. "A dirty cup?" Archly enough that he laughed, making her confident to continue, "You want me to read the tea leaves."

"Sure," he said. "Do you know how?"

"There are shapes," she said, "that are supposed to be symbols. It's called tasseomancy."

"Good. Knowing the right word for something is important. There is power in words, and in names. You'll learn to use them with precision. What do you see?"

"What am I looking for?"

"Energy patterns. Masquerading as pictures or words."

She unfocused her eyes, and tried to look at the tea leaves as if they were clouds surfing an unrippled sky. She tried to unpin herself from her body as she did when she cut, or was cut, to find the rush and ride it, feel the power like a river that she knew had to be there.

There was nothing but clotted leaves in the bottom of her cup, a few flecks stuck to the sides. If she squinted just right, she could almost make herself believe this bit or that bit resembled something—a de-formed face, a lopsided beetle—but she couldn't pretend the shapes were anything other than her brain seeking patterns, as brains do. She didn't see energy, either—just a few drops of thin brown liquid, and the particles of fermented leaves. "No," she said. "I don't see it."

Gypsy bit his lip and lifted the cup out of her hands. He frowned at it, and shook his head. "That's amazing," he said, after a few moments of study.

She climbed out of her chair and leaned over him, cheek pressed to his hair. "What?"

"I don't see anything, either."

"Nor will you," Carel said. She'd stopped outside the doorway again, Autumn just behind her. They had the crinkled look of people who have been talking and have something unpleasant to impart. "She cannot learn."

Jewels snapped upright as if kicked. *"Can't?"*

The Merlin nodded. From the way Gypsy's breathing quickened, Jewels guessed the news before Carel said it. "There's damage. And it's not the sort that can be repaired."

Jewels gasped. The taste of sour tea filled her mouth again as she swallowed frantically. She couldn't deny it. Couldn't even start to deny it. That was the worst: Jewels knew exactly what the Merlin meant, and she was right. *"Damn* him," she said, and knotted her fists at her sides. "Damn him straight to hell."

"If it's any consolation," Carel answered, "I have it on the best authority that he's there."

Gypsy didn't rise. He reached out and put his left hand on Jewels' elbow. She didn't jerk away—too shaken, too stunned. Too *angry* to give any ground to anybody. "He has no power over me," Jewels said, like a mantra, and Gypsy turned to Carel and Autumn, louvered up shaggy eyebrows, and said, "What do you mean, there's no fixing her? That's ridiculous. And *cruel.*"

Carel, merciless with the Dragon in her eyes, said, "You can't reattach a limb that's been blown to pieces. That's a fairy tale for you."

"What do you mean?"

Carel folded her arms. "Unfair, but not untrue."

Jewels nodded. She put her hand on Gypsy's hand, felt a kind of rough affection for the way he'd lurched to her defense, and patted once or twice. "No," she said. "Not fair, not the Fair Folk and not magic. But I know. It's true. And the best part is, I did it to myself."

Autumn stepped into the kitchen and put the water back on, running one thumb across the chipped enamel of the stove while blue flame licked the kettle's sooty belly. This time, she got the cocoa down, and a mug as big as Gypsy's two cupped hands. "Do you want to talk about it? Maybe . . ."

But she let it trail, and fall. Maybe, more often, not.

"If I tell you," Jewels said, "I have to tell you how I started to cut."

"Tell me." Carel shifted her weight. She wore a pale peasant blouse over low-waisted jeans that showed a soft curve of belly, peach cotton catching shadows in its hollows from the darkness of her skin. Neither the girly clothing nor the braids dangling over her shoulders did anything to ease the force of her charisma brought to bear.

The kettle whistled before Jewels found the words. She took the cup Autumn gave her, and stared at it without sitting back down. "I cut myself," she said. "In the beginning. I'd get a razor blade, and I'd pretend very hard that I was cutting off the pieces he'd made bad. And if I cut off the dirty bits, like cutting mold off cheese, what was left would still be fine."

The mug burned her hands. It was still hot enough that she should hold it by the handle, but she didn't.

"And?" Autumn asked, stepping back.

Cocoa slopped onto her finger and stung. She raised the hand to her mouth and sucked it. "I guess I cut off too much."

Amazing how level your voice could be in a hopeless case.

"Stop the bleeding," the red-haired woman had snapped, thrusting a wad of cloth into Don's hands, and Don was doing his best. Don, hands shaking, had eased Matthew onto hastily cleared flagstones before the hearth, while Kit helped the woman — who could *not* actually be Morgan le Fey — rummage through baskets and beakers and the drawers of an ancient apothecary's desk, familiar as if he lived there. Judging by the way her hand strayed to his shoulder, occasionally, and the way he pulled away when it did, he probably once had.

Two dogs as big as Don whined in the corner, under an unshuttered window that framed dripping roses. And Don knelt on the floor, trying to find where the gore seeped from.

Matthew breathed shallowly, drenched in his own red blood. Saturated clothes left daubs on the stones as Don shoved them aside, looking for wounds. The monster had gone for the throat, and the chest and shoulder of Matthew's shirt were shredded.

But there were no injuries. Not on his knee under the torn jeans, where there should have been an oozing, gravel-studded wound. Not on his breast or on his throat, though his skin was pale and clammy and his heartbeat flickered in the hollow of his jaw, thin and thready and close. His nose had healed too, set a little crookeder than before. Don touched Matthew's throat to be sure and felt whole skin, unwounded.

Which is not to say unmarked. Once Don satisfied himself that Matthew was not about to expire on him, checked his airway and breathing and heartbeat and sought—as best he could—for evidence of internal injuries, he had a moment to just *look*.

The bands of tattoos that embraced Matthew's body were dense and dark, some of the heaviest blackwork Donall had seen. Don's fingers prickled where he touched them, although not on the pale flesh between, and the ring on his finger grew warm. There were some scars, older ones, including a knife wound over the heart that must have turned on Matthew's rib cage, because Don couldn't see how he would be alive if it hadn't.

He was reaching unconsciously toward his own chest, to touch cloth over the centipede scar, when a warm hand brushed his shoulder. "May I see?"

She smelled warm and wonderful, like rosemary dried on a window ledge, her streaked braid falling over her breast. He straightened creaky knees and stepped back. "He's not bleeding."

"I see that." Said without harshness. "But he has bled."

"Lost a lot of volume, I think. How can he not be hurt?"

She moved efficiently, swiftly, with a bright focused intelligence that humbled him. "Kit says there was an angel in attendance. Or an angel's agent. He saved Matthew's life, I wot. Just a garden-variety miracle."

The intersection of Ernie Peese and miracles hurt Don's head more than winged demons, legendary witches, or stepping through the looking glass. Ernie Peese, on the side of the angels. *How about that.*

"Damn. And I always kind of thought Ernie was on the take." That got him a blank look, so he shrugged and pointed to Matthew. "He'll need a transfusion. He left blood on the road."

"He needs rest," she answered, stripping away the clothes that Donall had so hastily rearranged. "And building up. Don't worry, my leechcraft involves very little leechery, and I'm not fool enough to bleed a man who's already sucked pale. Ask Kit about my doctoring if you fear it."

"He's not going to get rest," Kit said, crouching with a basin and a rag. He dipped the latter and wrung it out, and she accepted it without looking. "He must be well for the duel, which is tomorrow."

The blood was already drying on Matthew's skin, scaling or caking in strings. He moaned and turned his head when Morgan scrubbed at it. "Warm some broth, Kitten."

Kit made a moue at the nickname, but obeyed.

Morgan just clucked her tongue, and Don faded back against the doorpost to watch, his hands cocked awkwardly in front of him to keep from smearing his clothes. Lily had vanished somewhere. Don hadn't seen her slip out, but the door was open if she shouted. He glanced over his shoulder and saw only rain falling on nodding flowers.

He couldn't stand the blood on his motionless hands. Two steps carried him forward, until he could drop to his knees beside Morgan. "Let me do that."

Wordlessly, she handed him the basin and the rag, then started cutting Matthew's shirt off. Blood washed from Matthew's skin and from Don's hands in the same gestures. Matthew stirred slightly, his left hand flexing as if he meant to push Don away. The handcuff welts on his wrists were healed too, though Don could see the outline of the manacles in clotted blood.

He scrubbed that off quickly.

When Matthew's eyelashes flickered, Kit brought the broth, and Morgan tipped it into the Mage's mouth spoonful by spoonful. It seemed to help; Don caught the cut-grass scent of herbs rising from the mug, and a tang of heated alcohol. He shuddered: brandy in beef stock?

But Matthew didn't complain. He drank like he couldn't get enough, although Morgan rationed him, her knees under his shoulders, her palm cradling his head. The second cup Kit brought wasn't steaming. The fluid was cloudy and straw-colored, pungently sweet.

"Cider," Kit said, for Don's benefit, as Matthew's hand covered Morgan's, tilting the cup and then pulling it away.

He coughed lightly, and pressed a hand to his throat, as if it could soothe the ache inside. "Damn. *What* was I drinking?"

A naked expression of relief blanked Kit's face before he masked it. He was still arranging his folded arms so that nobody could see his hands shaking when Don sat back on his heels and said, "You're all right?"

"I have one hell of a hangover, that's for sure," Matthew said, glancing from Morgan to Kit as Morgan smoothed his clotted hair back, wiping off and discarding a translucent, gelid string. He pointed to the empty cup in Morgan's hand. "Is there more of that? Or water?"

"Your wish," Don said, collecting the cup before he stood. He paused, though, and didn't acknowledge either Morgan or Kit when he said, "I kinda fucked that up."

Thoughtfully, Matthew rubbed his wrists. "You kind of did. Jane's idea?"

"She tried to stop me." The wooden mug was wider at the rim, polished smooth inside. "At least, I think she did. It was the other guy—"

"Felix," Matthew said, rolling his eyes. The exertion of speaking paled him. Morgan's hands slipped to his shoulders and she pulled him up so his head was propped on her lap. "Is that all my blood?"

"Enough of it," Kit murmured, under Donall's voice as he continued, "No, not Felix. Black man, Australian accent—and not the ones you hear on TV—expensive suit. Nice shoes."

"Bunyip," Kit said, startling Morgan. He shrugged her stare aside curtly. "Fae, not Promethean. We met him in New York."

Morgan shifted. "That's a problem."

"They're working with devils too, though I don't think they know. Christian—her apprentice—" Matthew said, weak but clear.

Don's hand tightened on the cup. "A *devil*?"

"Your other friend's channeling angels. Get used to it."

Don said, "I trusted them."

"Oxytocin." Matthew must have noticed the baffled look on Don's face, because he smiled. "It's a chemical. Increase the level in their blood, and people will trust you. Easy enough to manipulate once you know the trick of it."

"You mean Bunyip bewitched him." This time, Kit laid a heavy glance at Morgan. She blushed, like red ink wicked into her freckled skin, and dropped her gaze.

"And probably Jane too." Matthew stared at Donall's ring. "Made any hasty decisions in her favor lately?"

Don said, "You've done that to me."

"You won't cop to liking me on my own merits?" Matthew's mouth pressed thin. He didn't have the strength to laugh. "Anyway, it's well in

Jane's power. How do you think she got elected? It wasn't fiscal policy, I'll tell you what."

Don turned away and went to find the water. Behind him, he heard Matthew struggling to rise.

"I need to talk to Jane."

"Lie down, Matthew." Morgan's voice carried no trace of impatience, but the sound of Matthew shoving ineffectually at his nursemaids did not abate.

Don was dipping the cup in the barrel by the door when Kit spoke. "Where's water?" he said. "Come along, Morgan, warm him a bath. There's no point getting in his way."

"Yes," Morgan answered, crouching, Matthew's arm slung over her shoulders as she pulled him to his feet. The Mage was solid, a limp, muscled weight, but she didn't grunt. Rather, she glared at Kit, who smiled. "I've met the like."

Morgan's cottage is never the same place twice. Always the roses, always the vermilion door. Always the well-chinked, whitewashed field-stone walls hung thick with tapestries and witch-globes and herbs dangling from pegs and always the raven roosting in the thatch, notable for his twisted wing. Morgan's loom dominates the single room, on the wall away from the hearth, and behind it rises the ladder to the loft, a bedchamber tucked between rafters and struts, cozy with all the luxury the downstairs does not pretend toward.

But there are the changes. Things misremembered or reinvented, stories set aside. Sometimes the flagstone slates are gray, sometimes red. Sometimes the mantel stone is granite, gray and uneven and mica-flecked, and sometimes it is silvery schist studded with fire-cracked garnets. Sometimes the thatch is sod.

And on that day, there was a bathtub tucked behind the loom, mostly screened from sight by the tapestry under construction.

Kit drew the water the old-fashioned way, bucket by bucket out of the well. Rain soaked his hair and the borrowed, baggy jeans, but he'd left the blood-soaked shirt on the floor by the hearth. Morgan could burn it. Probably already had.

The rain felt good on his skin, sluicing away sweat and easing the chafes from his borrowed wings. He knew the path to the well and toiled back and forth under a yoke, regular as a pendulum while his boots splashed through puddles.

Lily had been watching him carry water, and finally stepped out of the shelter of a red Japanese maple into his line of sight. "Christopher?"

"Kit," he said, the buckets swaying as he stopped. The motion of the water was transmitted up the ropes, shifting the yoke on his shoulders, and he swayed to compensate. Ripples wiped away the dapple of raindrops on the surface until the raindrops pattered over the ripples again.

She smiled, the last traces of her lipstick smeared on her face. She'd been kissing someone, and Kit couldn't condemn her. "Is he okay?"

"He'll endure," Kit said, and watched her shoulders slump in relief. "The water's for a bath."

She nodded. Matthew's sweater hung to her knees over the vivid darkness of the skirt. "You and Lucifer—"

She saw him flinch. And then he peered into her eyes, and the flinch became a startle. He bent his knees, let the buckets touch earth, and shrugged out of the yoke, which he balanced across their rims.

"They won't let you go," he said. And then he stepped toward her, meeting her halfway as she came to him. "Christ wept. And my fault."

"Your fault?"

"I didn't tell you." He turned, lank hair streaking his neck. The rain rolled in thick droplets across his chest, glossing the scars over his heart and below the curve of his ribs. "You drank."

"I did." She licked her lips at his silence, and then nodded, sharply, as if to confirm it to herself. "And he came."

"He always will," Kit answered. "He will be the perfect lover. The perfect companion. There when needed and gone when you wish to be alone. And the gifts"—he stole a glance, and again could not hold her gaze—"are seductive."

"Where's the bad? And don't tell me *my immortal soul.*"

"The bad? Mean you when he'll break your heart, or when he'll break your flesh? Will you be so sanguine about offering him your body when he wants it for a sacrifice?" He stopped, hard, and clenched his hands.

The rain ran into her eyes when she ducked her head. She reached out, cold fingers and outsized hands, and touched his chest. His scar was as chill as her skin. "He did that to you."

"He arranged it done," Kit said, with a shrug. He caught her wrist, and plucked open her fingers, turning upward her palm so the rain fell into the hollow. "And yet . . ."

"It was him you turned to in New York."

"Aye," Kit said. He stepped back, shaking water off his lashes. He dropped a knee on wet gravel and ducked under the yoke again. But before he stood, he looked at his hands, fingers curled over the bucket handles to steady them, and sighed under his breath. Not a Promethean talent, but—he excoriated himself—an easy enough trick for a witch.

He dipped his fingertips in the water, and when he stood it steamed. Lily stood in the rain, red and violet as the flowers massed behind her, and stared at him over a bitten lip and folded arms. He said, "Did you mean to carry water?"

"Are there more buckets?"

"Aye," he said. "They're over by the wall."

He stepped past her, paused, and waited while she turned. He spoke over his shoulder, not sure if she could hear. Not caring. "It doesn't *work*, Lily. Good girls don't redeem bad boys through the power of their love. Trust me on it, madam: I wrote the play. And you have there a very bad boy indeed."

Lily let her borrowed sleeve brush his goosefleshed arm. "But *you* know it works in fairy tales."

Within, Morgan helped Matthew into the bath. His fair skin gleamed with blue pallor between the ink where it wasn't tanned, but she thought if he had the blood in him he would have blushed to his navel. He managed a tired sort of chuckle, as she steadied him over the lip. "Hell of a second date."

Blood is astounding stuff. It makes its way into crevices and crannies, dries obdurate, discolors pores. Spilled, it can't be gotten wholly clean through any art—bleach, paint, scouring.

Shakespeare was right. The stain lingers.

It stained Morgan's hands and daubed her blouse, and caked and smeared her hair. Don was by the fire, warming cider so that honey would dissolve in it, and Matthew's gestures were already broadening from the brandy Morgan had added to the first mug.

"Second date?" she said, crumbling herbs into the water Kit had warmed. The scent of lavender rose up, acid and strong.

Matthew's eyes were closed, his breathing light and even, slow enough that she reached to check his pulse, callused fingertips stroking his throat. He stirred, but didn't argue. The pulse was steady. She let her hand drop, brushing flesh as it fell.

"Yes," he breathed, lips barely moving. "Five days and seven years ago, you kissed me."

He wasn't handsome. His features weren't so much rugged as prominent, and his jaw jutted and so did his nose—but his body was quite beautiful under the water and the ink that chilled her hands. Mere nudity could not render him naked, not with all the iron worked into his skin, though she watched him shamelessly.

Nudity couldn't. But his face was naked, without the spectacles, and *that* left him vulnerable. Her hands, armed with a flannel, dipped into the water, and she smiled. It could have been much worse.

Eyes closed, he felt her watching. It crept through his chilled body like the heat of the bathwater, drying his mouth. Lassitude weighed his flesh, his arms, his eyelids. Heat, and the liquor, and blood loss and plain exhaustion. He couldn't remember when last he'd slept; his head spun when he tried. Her hand touched his throat again, impersonal and efficient, and then slid across his clavicle, over his pectoral muscle, the rough pad of her thumb brushing his nipple, resulting directly in the catch of his breath in his throat. She laughed, harsh and rich, her braid breaking the surface of the water and coiling wetly on his abdomen.

Her words warmed his mouth. "Shall I kiss you again?"

He couldn't answer. The sound of the rain had ended, but he knew it had not ceased falling. He could no longer hear Kit's and Lily's voices, drifting muffled from the garden, or Don stirring honey into a mug by the fire. Time had stopped; Morgan had stopped it. They would not be disturbed.

Her thumb circled, evoking an electric tickle that furred down his belly to his groin. Fingernail and thumbnail creased flesh hard, sharping into pain. He gasped and reached, blindly. Not for her hand. For her head, her hair, the waterlogged serpent of her braid.

He pulled her mouth hard against his own.

The blood tightening his mouth was probably his, smeared on her lips, carried on the splash of bathwater between them. She bent double over the edge of the tub, the rim indenting her soft belly, one hand twisting his nipple—pulling until she pulled him away from the end of the tub, hauling him into the kiss—while her free hand skinned her jeans off her hips. A brief struggle followed while she kicked out of boots and trousers. She slithered into the water as Matthew opened his eyes.

The blouse pinkened as it adhered to her. From his blood in the water, it must be, because her skin was too white to lend the color. Her fingers twisted deftly one last time, her thighs soap-slippery and yielding against his hips as she glided into the water. In his blurred vision, a rainy light limned her: the silver-streaked braid knotted in his left hand, the steamy droplets condensing on her lashes. Her shoulders and baby-kissed breasts trembled under the gathered second skin of her blouse. Changeling eyes locked his as her hand wrapped flesh no hotter than the bathwater, twisting until he keened like a fox. "Morgan!"

Her tongue flicked, and all he could see was the way it skipped along her teeth.

He could lift his right hand. He pressed it against her chest, reaching for her breastbone, found it pressed against her breast instead. She didn't flinch from the scar or the twisted fingers, but moaned through her teeth and rubbed against his hand, cushiony flesh and cotton gauze, her nipple peaking. She leaned forward, fingers rippling as she lifted him, slid over him. Water lapped his throat in time with her tongue, slopped over the lip of the tub, scattered the flagstones. He *ached*, like cold fire drawn along his bones.

Her skin brushed his, throat speckled like a trout, wet curls skimming his glans. "Morgan," he said, between his teeth. "Stop—"

"Shh." She lifted herself from the water, gleaming, her breasts level with his mouth for a moment as she leaned back. Off-balance.

It didn't matter that he didn't have much strength. He had enough for one quick pull, a sharp yank on her braid that sent her crashing back, yelping like a much younger girl. She smacked against the side of the basin, water flying, and slid down while he hauled himself to his knees, his hand on the tub rim the only thing holding him up. His arm trembled, his whole body shaking, sick need and adrenaline twisting in his guts. Something ugly down there, something primal and flayed. He stepped on that hunger before it could make him reach for her again.

"Morgan," he said. Third time, voice rattling against his teeth. "God damn it, *listen* to me when I tell you to stop."

She pushed herself up, back against the sloped side, drenched lavender blossoms flecking her cheeks and breasts. "Can't blame a girl for trying," she said, and stripped her shirt over her hair. "I've got your blood all over me anyway, and Kit and the other will need to bathe too. As long as I'm here, would you mind passing me the soap?"

Wordlessly, he did, and found the flannel on the floor beside the tub.

"I thought I had you," she said, evenly, unbraiding her hair to scrub it in the still-steaming water.

"So did I." His skin prickled, and it wasn't the heat of the bathwater or the lavender oil.

"Well, good to know I haven't entirely lost my touch. So. If the direct approach won't work, answer me this—"

He lifted his chin. She was offering the soap, an odd-shaped yellow bar curved in her magnificent fingers. He took it, and lathered the flannel. There was a lot of blood to work loose from the creases, and he ordered himself to remain unself-conscious that he was scrubbing at it in front of a naked woman whose legs were laced between his own. His own recent inability to obey orders notwithstanding. "Yes, Morgan?"

"If I can't seduce you, Matthew Magus, then what will you take in trade?"

Faerie plays tricks on occasion, with space and with time. Kit and Lily, buckets slung over their shoulders, returned to the house to find Matthew—dressed randomly in hose and a bulky, borrowed sweater—drinking yet another mug of warmed cider and nibbling cold chicken, while Morgan combed out her water-dark hair. The tub had been emptied, a wet oblong surrounded a drain through a gap in the foundation. Don stood beside it, scrubbing blood spots on his jacket with cold water, his sleeves rolled up over thick, sinewy forearms and his collar

open far enough to reveal his powder-blue undershirt and the black
nylon edge of the ballistic vest he hadn't removed. His holster stretched
across the pale blue cotton of his shirt, creasing the fabric in his
armpits. The shirt was clean; blood hadn't soaked through his jacket,
and his face looked freshly washed. Kit set the buckets down with a
clunk and turned to help Lily, who didn't need it, but he wasn't about
to permit Morgan a look at his face until he was certain his expression
was mastered.

"Get lost?" Don said. He gestured to flannels and soap when Kit
looked up.

"A wrong turn between here and there, apparently," Kit answered,
while Lily stared at him, befuddled. He rubbed at his face, flaking away
blood, and unhooked one steaming bucket from the yoke. "I shall use
the tub if you'd like the basin."

Her attention followed his to the washstand by the stove. She took
the toiletries he handed her, collected the second warm bucket, and
went, struggling out of Matthew's rain-soaked sweater along the way.
Morgan stood as she passed and took it away from her, spreading it on
the hearthstones to dry. The dogs were out in the rain somewhere, so
there was no competition.

"Kit," Morgan said, without looking up from the wet cotton she
fussed into shape, "I've put some clothes you left behind on the loom.
Trews and boots, shirts and coats. Once you're clean."

He grunted and rubbed soap through his hair, bent over the edge of
the heavy tub. The rain had rendered him halfway clean, and when he
upended the bucket over his head and shoulders, the worst of the rest
sluiced away. The blood under his nails would have to wait.

Matthew was still looking at him, speculatively, when he straightened. Kit glowered and turned away. He had no more right to condemn
the man for falling to Morgan's charms than he had Lily for falling to
Christian's. But it remained a peculiarly unsatisfying satisfaction to observe one's errors repeated.

He toed out of soaked boots. Peeling off the wet jeans could hardly
have been more unpleasant. Harsh fabric scraped his skin; he left them
in a pile and stalked nude and shivering to the loom. "There are two
suits of clothes."

"One's for Lily," Morgan said. She gave the sweater one last prod and rocked back on the balls of her feet, satisfied. "I thought your things would fit her."

Of course they would. She was nearly his height, only a bit heavier in build. The hose would set off her legs. He stole a half-covetous look under his arm, eye drawn to the edge of her shoulder blade whitening skin as she lifted her arms, the nubbed arc of her spine. "Green," he called, "or black?"

She turned, hands in her hair, the stretch of her pectoral muscles lifting her breasts and a thread of water sliding down her nose. "Black," she said, keeping her eyes fastened on his face. More or less.

He grinned, and she blushed—sharply, for a girl who wasn't very fair. The heat slid up her face like warm, rising water. He was as naked as an angel, and as untroubled by it. And he had an entire wardrobe here, in this witch's house.

Mind your manners, Lily. "Except shouldn't you choose?"

"It matters not." Both shirts were white lawn, one ruffled and frilled and one with falling collars. The green coat was moiré silk, the fashion of a few hundred years back. The black doublet was older, dusty glove-soft velvet slashed with emerald taffeta, embroidered with emeralds and peridots on silver thread. He'd forgotten he'd ever owned it, but there was no mistaking it now. It was sewn when Elizabeth was queen, and Will had mocked him for it—

He sighed, and picked up the coat in Faerie green. It would serve. He wondered if Morgan would loan him a sword.

After they were dressed—Kit efficient, shameless, and Lily with her back turned, in hiding behind the loom and its half-completed tapestry—Morgan chided them onto the benches beside her table and brought platters from the pantry. "You may eat without fear," she said. "Of my food and drink, in any case."

"Too late," Lily murmured, but only Kit heard her.

Matthew crossed the floor gingerly and sat down—next to Kit, surprisingly, and not Morgan.

"Bunyip," Matthew said, accepting the slice of bread and jam that Morgan pressed on him and setting it down on the table, untouched. "Tell me about him."

Unlike Matthew, Kit was eating with a will. Not untidily—his table manners were very neat, though he ate mostly with his hands (and occasional resorted to a knife)—but rapidly, small bites of bread and cheese and onion jam, torn loose and tucked into his mouth with gestures like a squirrel's. He washed the current mouthful down with a gulp of ale and licked his lips. "A water spirit, I gathered. He claims he has the Dragon's dispensation to usurp Kelpie, if he can."

"And he's allied with Jane."

"So it would appear," Kit answered, with a nod to Don for confirmation.

"Dragon?" Don said. He turned a knife over in his hands, ignoring both the butter and the bread it was meant for. "The Times Square Dragon?"

"The same," Matthew said. "They're all one beast."

"Except Bunyip calls her Rainbow Snake," Kit said. He glanced around; the men's eyes were on him. Lily studied her hands, and Morgan was smiling her slight, unkind smile.

Don sat back hard enough that his bulk rocked the bench. "Aida-Wedo," he said. "Rainbow Snake?"

"I don't know her," Kit admitted. "Is that her name?"

Don set the knife aside. "My mother follows Obeah, and she's the loa my mother serves. Aida-Wedo, which is one of the names of Erzuli. *She*'s your Dragon?"

This time, Matthew happened to be looking at Don when he said the name, and saw the wavering awareness like the flicker of a snake's sensing tongue. "Apparently."

"That's not right," Don said. "The Dragon's a monster. Aida-Wedo is not."

Morgan smiled. "You misapprehend dragons. Mist is not a monster. Mist is *Mist*, and—not unlike the Devil, or the witch Morgan le Fey—everything about her that you can imagine is true, or has been, or will be. The Wyrm is the mother of us all. She gnaws at our hearts and at the roots of the world and at her own black tail. She guards the treasures of the unknown heart, and you must win past her if you would be a hero, and she is the death of heroes and cowards both, in the end, aye, and poets and pretty maidens too—and out of her they are reborn."

She paused and sipped her wine before continuing. "Rainbow Snake is no more nor less true than Fafnir in his lair. Part of becoming a Mage—or a witch—lies in that understanding, to hold the contradictions at heart all at once."

"And her servant is talking to Jane? What about the Merlin? Isn't she on *your* side?" Donall turned away from Morgan, seeking Matthew's gaze. But Matthew's eyes were dropped behind a blunt wedge of hair released from its ponytail, elbow on the table and his forehead resting on the edge of his hand.

"She's on all the sides," Morgan said. "That's the bitch about dealing with gods."

"And then there's Christian to deal with," Kit said. "Whatever he wants. Which could be just causing trouble, or he could be using the Prometheans to keep us off-balance and us them, in service to some larger intrigue."

Lily looked down, silent.

"I was right," Matthew said. "I need to go talk to Jane. Before the duel." He looked up at Kit, starkly, and just as quickly dropped his eyes again.

Morgan grinned into her wine, her gaze never leaving Matthew's pale bowed head. "You know," she said lightly, "I knew the Bunyip's name, once upon a time. There's always the chance I could remember it. If you *really* cared to know."

Black swans fly by night. They travel in secret, in darkness, and during the day they rest along their migration routes, in brackish tidewaters and wide rivers, their long necks curving valentine hearts reflected in smooth water. During the breeding season, they are the most social of the swans, filial and devoted, their gatherings teeming with cygnets, cobs, and pens. They nest in tribes, whole villages of swans, coal-black but for the flight feathers, peaceful under the sun.

This is because they remember their ancestors and the punishment Bunyip wreaked upon them when they were men. And that he charged an entire village for the offense of one young man. Prejudice breeds a certain unity in the face of misadventure.

Swans remember. Cities remember. Events, and lessons learned. The slow accumulation of wisdom piled stone upon stone, as experience accretes like verdigris and smoke stains in stonework creases and on facades. Cities remember every hand that touches them, though the touches seem fleeting to stone, though subsequent inhabitants strive to eradicate the marks of their predecessors. London recalls Londinium. New York recalls New Amsterdam.

Swans and cities are wiser than Faeries and men. Because where men remember, they often do not learn. Men haul their rancor down generations, bequeathed father to daughter, mother to son, until—the causes beyond recollection—a grudge becomes a nationality, and a quarrel becomes a war.

By the emerald heart set in the filigree streets of New York, Matthew Szczegielniak stood under bare trees, looking up through the scratched lenses of a spare pair of glasses, and remembered a quarrel.

It was a cold Saturday afternoon and no one else was standing. They hurried past, heads ducked against the wind, hands balled in pockets. Paper cups skittered over oil-stained sidewalks and plastic bags enshrouded the bases of sign poles. A few thousand starlings preparing to flee the winter rustled and chattered like self-propelled leaves in a stand of maples, bending exploratory parties—black solar flares—out, and back into the body of the flock.

Matthew pulled his hands from his pockets, grateful to be back in his own clothes. He crossed against the light. The cop on the corner happened to look in the other direction. No taxicab came close enough for him to feel the wind of its passage.

He was sick, wobbly. Recovering—it hadn't been *that* much blood, a pint or two, by the angel's mercy—but not his best self. He was a fool to walk into Jane's tower unaccompanied, when the wards she had wound into it, stone and iron, made his heart race over his breathing from across the street. He was putting himself in her power.

And he was charmed.

Again.

His own power answered Jane's incumbency, a cold sea surging in his belly, his fingertips fizzing with energy. The thing awakened in his anger at Morgan had not ended. It crouched under his heart, blinking like a great mad cat.

He knew it by its eyes. *You are too much surrendered, Matthew Szczegiel-niak.*

He turned away and brushed past the doorman, unremarked.

There was a code pad by the penthouse elevator. Jane had changed the combination, but this was within Matthew's damaged abilities. Technology wouldn't keep a Mage out. It told him its name, whispered when he stroked his fingers across the keys, and he whispered it back.

The elevator doors whisked open. Jane would know he was coming. He had entered her lair. He put a hand on the walnut paneling and listened to the cables, the motor, the simpleminded computer that controlled it all, eavesdropping for a Mage's voice whispering of metal fatigue, failure, slipping gears. He didn't think Jane would drop him. But if she surprised him, he might still convince the elevator to let him down softly.

It was a long enough fall for a little fast talking.

If he wasn't so damned wobbly, he would have taken the stairs. Instead, he was gambling that Jane wanted to talk to him even more than he wanted to talk to her—perhaps *wanted* wasn't precisely the right term?—and that she would stay her hand.

The doors opened again, and he entered an atrium so freshly remodeled that he could smell the mortar under the marble tiles. They were finely laid, but not yet resigned to their fate, and the mutter of their discomfort made him step quickly. Their voices would mellow in months and years, as they made their peace with the building, and their voices merged into the choir that was the city: Italian marble, Connecticut brownstone, Pennsylvania iron, Japanese bamboo, the yellow bricks paving Stockholm Street from the Kreischer Company on Staten Island.

For now, Matthew stepped quickly across the floor. And stopped, his sneakers squeaking on the tile.

The door across the atrium was open, the space all white beyond a silhouetted figure. Jane did not await him. But Felix Luray did.

"Hullo, Matthew. Are you here on behalf of Kit?"

"I'm here to speak to Jane, actually."

"She's out. Any business can pass through her second." He paused, coyly. "It is business, I presume?"

"Still so jealous? What is it, Felix? Sibling rivalry?" Matthew shrugged and drew his foot across the floor, provoking a wince-inducing squeal. He set it, and began to turn, only to be stopped by Felix's voice again.

"Matthew."

He turned back.

Felix could have been his calculated opposite. Matthew wore sneakers, jeans, a plain white T-shirt under an unconstructed fawn corduroy jacket. Felix hadn't even unbuttoned his suit. His hair was slicked in polished waves, fine silver coils woven through a blackness as glossy as the toes of his shoes. Matthew hadn't bothered with his ponytail; his hair swung against his jaw, narrowing his field of vision to the waiting Mage.

With a certain exertion, Matthew avoided folding his arms.

"Come in," Felix said. "Maybe we can have a conversation without insulting each other."

He stood aside. Matthew walked past him, into the enormous room, and managed not to flinch when Felix shut the door.

The twisted iron hulk in the center of the room dominated Matthew's attention. He went to it slowly, past plants and artfully grouped furniture as if he did not see them at all. His shoes fell silent now on inlaid wood and scattered carpeting.

Felix waited by the door, feeling foolishly as if he should be stamping his heel.

But Matthew's reverence was hypnotic.

He paused arm's length from the ruined stair, and reached out to it with his ruined hand. His thumb extended, the dinged and chipped ring of rowan wood clicking dull iron. The metal was not cold. Its warm surface was rough, pitted. He ran his hand up it, to where the banister ended, sheared off and twisted, at the height of Matthew's head.

He stood for a moment and held it, as best he could, arm raised like a child holding its mother's hand, until the silence stretched too sharp to bear. Felix chuffed like a lion. "Don't you want to know how it ends?"

In the big room, it echoed. Matthew waited until it died. Still gripping the rail, and said, "What makes you think I want it to end?"

"Not in it to win it? Good news for the good guys, that."

Matthew let his hand fall. He turned to face Felix and leaned against the stair, crossing his ankles. "I don't believe it's ever over, is all."

"What do you want, Matthew?"

"You asked *me* in."

"Come back to us."

"You don't want that."

"No," Felix said. Matthew's presence by the stair was a weight in the room, a gravity well. He struggled against it, walking upstream, until he reached the bar cart. "Jane does."

Matthew's silence hung like the moment between the lightning and the crash. It hung there while Felix poured whiskey and doctored it, a few drops of water in the glass.

"Oh, Felix," he said, at last. "Loyal as a dog. I'd hope she'd treat a damned dog better."

Felix shrugged. He didn't drink, just came back with the glass in his hand: a frosted crystal tumbler, heavy as a stone, the surface textured with knowing owls. Lalique, and suited to Jane's whimsy. "She has what I want."

"It could be Kit." He uncrossed his legs and straightened. "What if you left Jane?"

"Christian would stand her second."

"Christian's no Magus," Matthew answered. "He's a devil. Answer me."

"No."

Matthew wasn't sure which question Felix was answering, unless it was both of them. Felix climbed, and sat down on the fourth step, two from where the hulk ended, kitty-corner to Matthew. Shoulder to shoulder, but not side by side. "That's not what we're for."

"What we're for is *over*—"

"And who's at fault for that?" He sighed. "Reinvented, anyway." He set the tumbler down, lead crystal clicking iron. "Are you sure you don't want to know? I can tell you. There's a lot Jane didn't teach you."

"*Worlds*," Matthew said. He was grinning, painfully. Felix didn't see. "At least I'm not the one who has to fight her. I'll give you the damned city, Felix. I can do that—"

"You cannot."

The Dragon twisted in Matthew's breast. *Bitch. It was your idea.* "Which one of you is working with the Fae?"

Felix sipped the drink. Lagavulin. Not his favorite. "You can't *give* me New York."

"Why not? You blamed me for taking it for long enough. Fine. Fuck it. I'm giving it back."

"Oh. If only. What would it cost me?"

"Leave Jane. Save her life. She can't duel without you—"

"Save Christopher's life, you mean. If Jane doesn't default, she'll destroy him. It's *Rossville*. What's an Elizabethan poet going to do with that?"

"That too," Matthew said. "What do you owe Jane?"

"Nothing. What do I owe you?"

"Nothing."

"Well then," Felix said. "Thirsty?" He held the whiskey up beside his head. Matthew didn't take it. Felix sipped again, and let the silence hang.

"Why?" Matthew said.

Felix thought it over, rolled the question like a jewel in his hand. "Because I believe in humanity," he said. "Because Faerie and magic are about being *born* special, being born gifted, like you. Being chosen. Not about what you do, but who you are."

"I wish it wasn't," Matthew answered.

"And Prometheus could be the opposite," Felix continued, rolling over him. "And Christopher won't make it that."

This time, Matthew took the glass out of Felix's hand.

The whiskey tasted of ancient waters and thoughtful decay, rich, sweet, fiery all at once, layered with smoke and mist and soil and life and the faint tannic tickle of bitterness. He rolled it over his tongue, and drank it down.

"Don't worry," Felix said, getting up to fetch another glass. "There's more where that came from."

"Believe me, I know." Matthew breathed out across his tongue. "All right. How does it end?"

Felix unstoppered the decanter, which did not match the glasses. " 'And they all lived happily ever after.' "

Matthew snorted into the tumbler. His breath rang like wind through a bell. "Right, Felix. You, and your little dog Toto too. Seriously. You wanted to tell me how it ends. I'm asking."

Felix turned around, the whiskey in his glass glowing like amber in the sun. Aeons, trapped in resinous light. Ancient history in his hand. "Have a pen?"

"Not on me."

"I've got one, then."

Matthew watched Felix set the glass on the bar cart and carefully uncap his fountain pen. It was a Waterman, not very expensive, a practical rather than an ostentatious choice. It wrote like gliding silk across your hand.

He dipped the nib in the whiskey, slowly, and lifted it from a translucent blue coil as bright as a swirl in a blown-glass ornament. Matthew came to him, put his glass down, and stretched out his left hand to take the pen, careful not to shake it. A thick cobalt droplet shivered at the tip. His handwriting was awkward now.

He wrote his name on a card, while Felix struck a light. A white candle's wick flared against the match, and then Felix shook it out. He took the Waterman from Matthew's hand and signed his own name before capping the pen. The ink was pale, diluted, wetly feathering into the card.

Felix poured half the tinted whiskey into Matthew's tumbler. Together, they took up the card—Matthew pinching a corner painfully, Felix supporting his hand—and set the edge in the flame. They held it up, rills of brightness lapping the paper as the edge curled into soot, and each hefted his glass. Matthew's eyes never left Felix's face.

"May you be in heaven half an hour before the Devil knows you're dead," Felix said.

"If you must use morbid invocations, why not go whole hog?"

"Pardon?"

"Oh, how about—here's to us and those like us. Who's like us? Damn few, and they're all dead!" Matthew answered, and clicked Felix's glass.

"That's Scottish."

"So? You're not Irish, either."

They drank together, the whiskey unpleasant with a chemical tang, the orange flames searing their fingertips. Matthew swallowed and rattled his head to shake the taste of the ink off his tongue. Feathers brushed him when he closed his eyes.

Feathers. His ears were deafened by the beat of wings, his skin assaulted by the rush of pinions. Green wings, white wings, wings of gold barred black as an oriole's. Swan wings and heron wings and the wings of sparrows and of sparrow hawks, and behind them all, like thunder, the broadest blackest wings of all, the primaries tipped white, hammering the sky like fists hammering the bars of a rusted cage. An assault of angels.

And the sky rang like a gong.

Matthew opened his eyes. Blisters swelled on his fingertips as Felix snatched back his own scorched hand. They stared at one another, and Felix dropped his chin. "Well, that was ambiguous."

Matthew leaned forward and set his glass down on the bar cart. "Right." He swallowed again, the astringency lingering. "Thank you, Felix. Good luck. I'll see you at the war."

Chapter Twenty-one
Dirty Water

The Queen of the Daoine Sidhe held out her hand. She beckoned her page, the bow of her mouth stopping just short of a smile, and he placed a goblet in her grasp.

"Thank you, Wolvesbane." Water bulged over the brim. "Now leave us."

He scraped, and scampered. She palmed the moist silver weight of the cup and watched him go.

She did not sit upon her throne. *That* bloodthirsty animal glowered over her shoulder, sharp-clawed and ready to lend her its strength whenever she might be moved to pay the cost. That power—be it ever so fleeting—had won her her very first war.

She turned the goblet over in her hand and cast the water on the stones. "Uisgebaugh."

He answered. Just a little precious fluid—and his name—and he rose from the floor in a pillar of water, filling her throne room with the tear-sharp scent of the sea. The column crested like a breaker, threatening to splash, but when it toppled, all that washed the floor were Kelpie's flowing hairy feathers. His fetlocks left scarlet brushmarks in their wake; he was crimson from hoof to throttle, and dabbed with blood all up his face. "Mistress," he intoned. "You rang?"

Painful, but it made her laugh. "The court needs a jester, Whiskey. Are you auditioning?"

"If that is the only use you can think of to put me to." He braced his legs and shook out his mane, spattering blood like a wet dog spattering mud, and then arched his neck at the resulting mess in satisfaction. "Ask me what I killed."

His gratification was a chill stone on her breast. "Jane Maga," she said, her voice as level as it should have been.

"A peryton named Orfeo." He spat a bloody feather on the stone. "In New York. And who do you suppose held his binding?"

"Fetch me my Merlin," she said. "And my Seeker as well."

He began to bow again, halting when she held out her hand, the empty goblet swinging loosely from her fingers. "Who do *you* suppose, little treachery?"

"Madam," he said through red teeth, "I know you don't truly care to have that answered."

"Indeed." She let the cup slip through her fingers. It rang down the steps of the dais, denting as it bounced, some half-precious stone set on the rim cracking like a shot. "Go on with you, then. Oh, except one more thing —"

"Mistress?"

"Keep the monster's shadow for now, if you like. But I want it back. Eventually."

Queens in Faerie do not mourn. So it is storied; so it must be true. As is the way of things.

So Àine of the Unseelie Fae could not be walking the strand with burning eyes, the windblown petals of embroidered sunflowers trailing the green sleeves of her gown, her hands folded inside them, her long black hair all tumbled down her back. Sand nor stone was suffered to touch her dainty foot. Her brocaded slippers floated a finger's width above.

Once in a while, a breaker taller than the rest would comb the beach under her feet, overturning shells that glinted like chips of skull among the stones. She took no notice. She was following the rain-fine tracks of cloven hooves.

The sandy margin soon gave way to tumbled cobbles, and a bluff — a cliff, nearly — humped itself up beside the sea. The rocks she set no foot upon were slick with rime, as if colder air pooled here, trapped by some trick of the wind.

Atop the cliff perched a cottage, no more than one room or two and dark behind window shutters. Àine drew her sleeves tight against the wind. The air carried no warmth, no homely breath of peat or coal smoke: just the tang of the sea, and a distant peal of whinnied laughter. The house was shut up tight and cold. Its mistress had business, and did not know when she'd return.

That whinny echoed from the cliff, which faced the sea. Whatever voiced it did not walk on land.

The boulders heaped at cliff-bottom were slick and gritty underfoot when she let her shoes find them. She picked over rocks mucous with algae, festooned with rubbery green-black tentacles of bladder wrack that popped underfoot, adding their own fluids to the mix. Àine hiked her skirt about her thighs and crouched amid the folds.

Among scattered tide pools, she found what she hunted: scraped rock, bare and scarred white with fresh marks the sea would wash dark soon enough. The marks of something running, over stone and moss and terrain that would be a gamble for a mountain goat. Not her cloven-hooved quarry. This was another beast, much heavier and without the thoughtless grace.

Àine dipped a finger in the sea and tasted: brackish water, acidic and musky, a taste so concentrated that it filled her sinuses and clung to her palate, overwhelming.

Every drop of the ocean lives. To say it *teems* is insufficient. It is an ecology, an orchestra, a cosmos unto itself, thick with algae and bacteria, luxuriant with amoebas, populous with diatoms cheerfully engaged in the biogeochemical cycling of carbon, oxygen, phosphorous, iron, and silicate. Every sea is alive, and every man is a sea.

"Nuckelavee," Àine said, her fingertip still pressed against her mouth.

The water lay flat as a sand garden, only rippled by the wind, as the Queen rose and put her back to the bluff. The wind flattened her gown over her hips, flagged the skirts in long streamers behind her, unsettled her on the stones. Cold like a film of ice crept between her scalp and her skull, and she reached into her sleeve for a comb.

Satiny wood, sweet with absorbed oils, slipped through her hair. She sang into the sea breeze as she combed and waited. Her hands paused, uplifted, when the ocean again lapped her toes. Spray polka-dotted her flower-colored slippers.

Crimson and horrible, Nuckelavee rose.

The monster looked peeled, yellow putrescence forging through manifest veins, a sheen of lymph glossing its flayed surface. It might have been a chimera stitched from half-dressed carcasses, bits of a man sewn to bits of a horse and a sheep and some fin-footed benthic behemoth; it stood with arms folded over its pulsing chest, bony clawed fingers wrapping its biceps.

The lower head—projecting from the monster's abdomen on a ewe's neck frilled by a stingy clotted mane—could have been a horse's skull, the flesh desiccated over the bones, a single great rheumy red eye leering in the center of its face. Long yellow teeth met at a chiseled angle in the lipless maw. Àine could hear them grinding like rocks in the surf from her place on the shore.

The upper head was a round glaring thing with gnashing teeth and a nose no more than two flat holes in its center, so huge it rolled from one of Nuckelavee's raw shoulders to the other, trailing mucilaginous strings. Steam bellied from its nostrils before it spoke. "Had you waited," it said, "I would have come on my own. Winter is on us, and I run free."

She did not speak, or lower her comb. The wind brought its scent like a dying ocean, thick enough to make her gag, though she was a Faerie and a daughter of Manannan, though she wore no dread for any devil of the sea.

"Speak," Nuckelavee said. "Little queen."

"*Dàcheannach,*" she said, knotting its name into her hair.

The house was already filling with the good smells of Gypsy's cooking when Carel heard the familiar rap on her front door, so when she opened it to reveal Kelpie on the porch she sighed in resignation. "She wants me?"

"Why else should I come?" His grin bared all his teeth. He glanced at the horseshoe nailed over the door. "Unless you care to invite me inside."

"Wait here." She vanished within, to fetch her jacket and boots and tell Autumn where she was going and with whom.

Autumn just paused over her cutting board, not even laying her knife down, rolled her eyes and said, "You have your phone."

Carel kissed her on the cheek and hurried out the door. Earning Autumn's forgiveness was half the fun.

"Up on my back," Kelpie said, when she joined him by the steps. He'd shifted to equine form, and now dipped his head to meet her eye to eye.

"You promise to put me back down again on dry land, on my own two feet, legs unbroken?"

"My lady Merlin," he said. His tail slapped his flank. "Legs nor anything else, neither."

He dipped a leg so she could mount, and she grabbed a hank of mane and swung onto his back. "There's blood in your mane."

"Is there? I thought I got it all out."

She clung with both hands. "Maybe it's catsup."

He gathered himself and sprang. A gentle canter through the tree line took them downslope. There was a stream at the bottom of the property. Not big, but big enough. He splashed into it, fetlock deep, feathers belling about his ankles as the chill water numbed his hooves.

He dropped away under her like falling water, like an amusement park ride. She knew better than to brace for the thump of striking the ground, and couldn't prevent it, anyway.

And so they came to Faerie.

He arrived in the courtyard fountain and clambered out unceremoniously. His hooves had long eroded the beveled stone rim. When his shoes clicked on the paving stones, she slid down. "Thank you, Whiskey."

" 'Twas nothing," he said, and meant it. "She's in the throne room. I go to fetch the Seeker now."

He bowed his horsey bow, and stepped into the fountain. And Carel retucked her shirt, straightened her collar, and went before the Queen.

The Queen was waiting, and Carel almost didn't recognize her. She wore a simple shirt and ice-gray corduroy trousers, Western-style riding boots to match—nacreous gray, with ivory stitchery—tucked into the cuffs. And her thick mahogany hair, which had not been cut in seven years, and had trailed about her like a cloak of secrets . . . was gone:

clipped tight up the back of her neck, softly shadowing the pale sunless skin of her nape, revealing the delicate and beautiful hollows between the muscles. Carel could have reached out and laid her hand on the Queen's neck, felt the stretch of the *longus capitis*, arising on either side from the third through the sixth cervical vertebrae, inserted under the inferior surface of the occipital bone. If Carel peeled back the skin, she could have seen the pearly tendons hand-clasped on bone, the long muscles relaxing as the Queen's chin dropped forward and clipped bangs brushed her forehead. The stretch of her neck revealed ice-needle scars that marked the blood she'd fed, over and over, to Faerie and her throne.

So Carel laid her hand on the Queen's neck, and soft hair shirred against her palm. "You cut your hair."

What could she say that would be less necessary? But the Queen smiled at her and pressed into the touch, tilting up her chin. "I always hated it." She carded fingers through the remains, stepping away. "Think of it as removing temptation," she continued. "What did you expect to see?"

Carel let her hand fall to her side and scrubbed the palm on denim. "A woman grieving in a chair."

"That's over." The Queen clasped her hands and smiled, strong and straight, her big capable fingers rippling against each other. "Seven years is enough to mourn. Tell me, Merlin, how to kill the Summer Queen."

"*Áine?*"

"Was I unclear?" Arch and merciless. "My predecessor took her own life. I've never had to kill a Faerie Queen." She turned and gestured to the heap of bony knives that was her throne. "We're not so easy to kill, you know. I could ask Morgan—"

"Yes," Carel said. "Everybody asks Morgan. I suspect that's how she knows all the answers. Every question is the answer to someone else's dilemma. What's Morgan got that you haven't?"

"Magic," the Queen answered, pacing slowly. "Beyond the willmagic I won't use, and the glamourie that any fool can see through. And experience. Fifteen hundred years of that. Age and treachery, so they say—"

"Morgan le Fey is the woman who has mastered her own stories,"

Carel said. "She's alive and herself, after all these years, because she's taken charge of it. Tended her myth like a garden, pruned and fertilized. A good trick. Takes a thousand years. Live that long, and they'll say the same of Elaine."

"Damn me, I'd better. There's not much to choose from when it comes to Elaines. And *you* didn't answer my question."

"Because I don't know the answer. A silver bullet?"

The Queen actually laughed. "A silver blade. Perhaps Keith would kill her for me."

"If he weren't in Hell."

"There's that little problem. Silver then. Self-sacrifice."

"Why Àine? Why all of a sudden, now?"

"Whiskey killed her pet in New York," the Queen said. "And something else."

"Something secret?" Kadiska asked, appearing from the shadows near the throne. "I'd better run along then." Teasing, her narrow braids held off her scarred cheeks with one hand.

"Where's Whiskey?"

The Seeker shrugged, and tossed her hair over her shoulder. "He went on. You cut your hair. Where's Gharne?"

"I was getting to that. I set him after Cairbre."

"And?"

"Cairbre went to Àine," the Queen said, pushing Kadiska's braid off her forehead. "Straight from Hell. And has not left her palace. What fate befell him, I have no idea. Go keep an eye on Ian for me, Kadiska?"

When the Seeker smiled, her teeth resembled the blade of a saw. Her shadow flared and swayed behind her, so the Queen almost heard the hiss. "Do you want the bard dead?"

"No," the Queen said. "But I may yet change my mind."

The house seemed more hectic in Carel's absence. You wouldn't think removing a person from the group could make a place seem *more* crowded—but so it did, and there they were. As if Carel's calm enlarged the space around her, like the calm of ancient trees.

Other than Jewels and Gypsy, Jason had been the first to arrive. Autumn hadn't reached Lily, but Christian had said he'd get in touch and pass the message, so Autumn let it lie. Kids had so damned much energy for falling in and out of love.

Autumn had pretty much given up on falling out of love, anyway. She was still grinning to herself over that when Moira rang the doorbell. It had to be Moira; anybody else would either let herself in or come around to the kitchen door and shout through a window cracked to let the heat out.

"Coming," Autumn called, and set her knife down again. She dried her hands on a kitchen towel as she walked down the hall. Moira usually had her hands full.

Today was no exception. Four bottles of sparkling cider and two of Pellegrino jostled for space in her arms, and she'd pushed the doorbell with her hip. Autumn hastened to unload her. "I'll put these in the fridge," she said, as a blue Honda crunched over the broken asphalt at the top of the drive. "And that's the last of the stragglers except for Michael, I think. Come on. Everybody's in the kitchen."

Christian parked while she was getting Moira settled in with Jason and Jewels around the big table, so they could heckle Gypsy while he cooked. He took it good-naturedly, his grizzled ponytail swishing across blue flannel–covered shoulders as he stood at the stove and stirred, and shook his head from side to side. The beard couldn't hide his grin.

Jewels had gone very quiet, smiling shyly while Moira tried to draw her out. Interview questions, as if Jewels were applying for a job, and no matter that Autumn had already told Moira that Jewels had thought better of joining a coven just now. Autumn sighed, and intervened with cookies.

Just in time. As she was turning around with the plate, the back door clattered open and Christian and Lily came through the mudroom. Christian seemed his usual self—bright-eyed and blue-jeaned—but Lily, raised beyond the usual extravagance of her clothes, might have been a prince from a forgotten land. She wore a Renaissance fantasia of black velvet and beaded embroidery with tights that showed her legs to advantage.

And she blushed and stammered when Autumn said, "Well, look at *you*," and then introduced the two of them to Jewels.

"We've met." Christian brushed past Autumn, two cookies vanishing

into his palm, paid for with a kiss on her cheek. Tension quivered be-
tween him and Lily, and Lily watched him, big-eyed and guarded, until
Autumn broke the circuit and handed her a cookie, half by force.
"Peanut butter," she said. "You look like you can use it."

Lily's fingers were cool where they touched Autumn's. But the cookie
was warm, and she nibbled it while she let Autumn steer her into the
seat next to Jewels. "Tea or something?"

"Tea would be great," Lily said. She should do something to get Jewels off Moira's hook, she knew. She couldn't quite muster the where-
withal, though. And thus the stage was set for Jason to charge to the
rescue.

He had been nursing his tea, monitoring Moira's questions and Jewels' answers without commenting much. Now, he put a hand on Moira's
arm and stopped her midsentence, rising from his chair as she turned to
him and tilted back her head. "Why don't we move this into the living
room," he said, "and give Gypsy a little peace in the kitchen?"

"Why start a new trend?" Gypsy said, provoking scattered laughter.
He didn't interrupt as they rose and went, but he did turn far enough to
catch Jewels on the edge of a wink.

She smiled back, uselessly. Whatever confidence came to her when
she gripped a knife didn't serve her here. She stepped closer to Lily as
they walked down the hall; she at least was clad in the virtue of familiarity, whatever the history.

But a glimmer of light distracted her, a flutter of something in the corner of her eye, and it wasn't Lily she bumped into. Instead it was the
red-haired devil Jewels had seen at the ball, dressed just in a T-shirt
now. He steadied her with a hand on her elbow and squeezed, then
ducked his head and murmured into her hair. "Now, Juliet," he said.
"What on earth are *you* doing here?"

She looked at him, surprised, and from her options selected stupidity. "Nothing," she said, and arched her brows to make her eyes wide.
"What are *you* doing here?"

"Chatting with a pretty lady." He raised his voice as he drew her
aside. "You should see Autumn's trees before the light's all gone. We'll
catch up in a minute."

Christian led Jewels toward the front door, and Lily followed them like a ghost, the puffed velvet sleeves of her borrowed doublet hissing against her ribs. "You can go sit down," Christian said over Jewels' head, as Lily reached forward and prevented him from closing the door between them. Warped wood abraded her fingertips, but she held on tight and didn't look at Christian at all. Jewels' eyes were clear and pale.

"I should probably tell you that he's the Devil, you know."

"I know." Jewels nodded, curtly. "No one else can help—"

"Look," Christian said, not unpleasantly, "if we're going to have this conversation now, can we please have it outside?"

"Sure," Lily said, and didn't slam the door behind her after she pushed them onto the porch. "Well?" She waved the back of her hand in the general direction of the yard, fingers gray in the gloaming. "Are you waiting for the fireflies? They're not out this time of year."

"Believe me," he said. "I know it." When they had descended the stairs, he turned to Jewels and brushed her cheek. "You're not scared of the Devil?"

"On the contrary." She accepted the touch like a statue, unconvinced and unconcerned. "He might be just what I need."

"Jewels—"

"Jealous, Lily? I won't steal your boyfriend."

Lily grabbed Jewels by the elbow and spun her away from Christian. Lily wasn't any taller, but Jewels was cagebird-frail, and Lily had solid bones. Sere grass splintered under Lily's feet as she twisted. "Yeah," she spat. "That's what you said last time. And look what that got us. Bitch."

For a minute, Lily thought Jewels was about to bust her nose. And then Jewels settled back in her sneakers and frowned. "So he was stupid about me," Jewels said.

"Yeah, and you weren't the one who had to watch him die."

"I'm doing this for *him*." Jewels stared at Lily, pale in the failing light, ridiculous ear-tips poking through her wavy hair. She jerked herself free of Lily, and turned back to Christian. "Teach me."

"I can't," he said. "You know that—"

"Yeah." She rubbed her forearms and glanced at Lily, quickly, and then just as quickly away. "I'm *broken*. Gypsy told me. So what the hell do you want me for?"

"You don't have your own power," Christian said. "But there's a power you could put on for a while. Long enough to start the job, and enough to finish it. But you'd not be the only one who wanted it, and was willing to do what it took."

The tilt of Jewels' head was a command.

"Matthew Magus," Christian said. "He's carrying a powerful gift. And the first one who has him—"

"Fuck!" Jewels hopped back a step, her hair falling around her like a collapsing parasol. "But he's so—"

"—old," Lily finished, and they looked at each other and burst out laughing.

Christian waited them out. "Jewels?"

"I don't think he'd want me," she said, tucking her hair behind her ears. "But I'll do what it takes. Why should he have all that strength, anyway, and me nothing?"

Lily stepped closer and murmured, "Let me. You don't need to do this. I have power." She glowered at Christian. "You tell me it's not enough."

"More when you dress like that," he said, with a little grin. "Gender-fuck is your mojo."

Jewels gave Lily's wrist a quick squeeze, scraping her skin with un-painted nails. "Together."

Lily nodded. *All right.* "I'll be right back," she said, her glare never shifting from Christian, who watched her with calm mockery. "I need to give Autumn my keys, and see if she'll take care of my cat."

She was just about to step back when a headlight painted them, pre-saging the purr of wheels on the driveway. They all three looked up as a red vintage Vespa glided onto the narrow line of grass between Gypsy's Jeep and the walkway. Michael propped it up between her thighs and pulled her helmet off, her bangs tumbling into her eyes. She wore a denim jacket that wasn't nearly warm enough, unbuttoned over a white T-shirt emblazoned with a falling red rocket ship and—in small, plain type—the words SCIENCE FICTION IS DEAD.

"I'm sorry," Michael said. "Am I interrupting an argument?"

"We were just finishing," Lily said, and ran inside.

Michael didn't dismount. She sat there, her helmet in her hands, and frowned at Christian silently until Lily came charging back down the stairs, caught Christian's and Jewels' hands, and led them past the angel, down the drive.

Michael watched them go. When they vanished in a shimmer of twilight she shrugged, and hung her helmet on the handlebars of the scooter, and stalked up the stairs.

Chapter Twenty-two
Hoist That Rag

Ernie Peese had the armor of his faith to protect him. Which was as well: explaining to a street full of patrol officers how he came to preside over the mutilated body of a Fae, the corpse of a boy who was one of the damned witnesses in *another* ongoing case, a good-sized puddle of human blood, and absolutely no trace of a white horse and the three or four people spotted leaving the scene . . . had been a near thing.

The good news was that it wasn't his case anymore. This was indisputable evidence of Fae involvement, and it went to the FBI now, and from them to Faerie. The bad news was that Peese was on administrative leave, having discharged his firearm *and* gotten into a brawl involving supernatural creatures—and that there was not a hope in heaven of keeping the shredded remains of the peryton out of the press and off the evening news. The *Post* would have the best headline. Ernie's money was on FAIRY WAR!

He went home, took a nap, had dinner on the table to soften the news when Lucy got home from her shift at the hospital, and fell asleep on the sofa in front of a videotaped episode of *Columbo*. He needed the time off. He might as well enjoy it. There'd be enough catch-up to play in the cold light of morning.

The phone warbled at five to nine. A thrill chased the sound along his nerves; he woke with a startle and snatched the handset off the end table before it finished ringing. "Got it," he called, in case Lucy had been hurrying for another extension, and put the phone to his ear.

"Detective Peese?" Her voice was familiar from several years of news bites and local television interviews. "I hope I didn't wake you."

"Only a little," he said. He rubbed the back of his neck, which didn't ease the pain strapped around his head from skull-base to temples. "Mrs. Andraste?"

"Very good. I'd like you to come visit me, Detective."

"I'm on leave. You'll have the call the lieutenant —"

"This is personal." A creak of plastic carried over the line, as if she were twisting the cord in both hands. "One does not call down archangels in my city, Detective, if one cares to go unnoticed."

A tongue like sandpaper clove to the roof of his mouth. He cleared his throat and coughed. "Your city, ma'am?"

She let it pass. "I need to get a message to Michael."

"Have you tried prayer?"

"Mr. Peese," she said, *"come."*

The phone clicked dead in his hand, empty cables echoing his own breathing back to him. A restrained *tick*, the press of a forefinger rather than a slam. He rubbed at his face.

There might still be cold coffee in the coffeepot. He dropped the handset in the cradle, heaved himself to his feet, and staggered toward the kitchen, wondering what the hell Lucy had done with his shoes.

Felix didn't need a devil to show him the way into Faerie twice. Having Kadiska's trail to follow didn't hurt, either; the scent of her was like roses baked into the stone.

She herself might flit in and out of shadows, the Seeker's power, a thing of half-light and memory, while Felix was forced to find a rise in the Ramble crowned with thorn trees, and step through like any magician would. But once in Faerie, on a yellow-green hillside, he dug a compass from his pocket. "Kadiska," he said, and watched it twitch and waver before settling on a left-hand path. He told himself that it was not possible for him to *smell* her when he faced into the wind.

He'd dressed for a tramp: country tweeds and stout boots, a pistol in his pocket and a knife thrust up his sleeve. Those last threw him off-balance, the gun in particular bumping his hip with every stride, but he wasn't brave enough to venture into Faerie without a touch of iron above his ring.

The trail led him down the slope and beside a river that ran dark red, and suffused the air with a meaty, iron-rich smell. Many feet had worn the path bare before his.

His ring grew colder on his hand. The path diverged, and again he studied his compass. The needle shivered like a spaniel on point, directing him away from the crimson river, thankfully—all very picturesque in a ballad, but unpleasant to walk alongside—and over the flanks of hills, down dells, and through pasturage with never a sheep in sight.

She found him before he found her, waiting in a beech-roofed meadow for him to step around a low-lying branch.

Here in Faerie, she made no concessions to mortal dress. The light through beech limbs dappled her long indigo-black torso, leafy translucence creating a diffuse green glow broken by dancing, radiant shafts. Loose crimson trousers wrapped her lower body, her bracelets and necklaces tinkling like glass bells as she breathed. Her shadows lay about her, each one a promise: wildcat, cobra, spider, and broad-eared elephant.

He paused at the edge of the glade. "You came looking."

"The shadows tell me plenty. But not why you're here."

He kept his hands out of his pockets, the compass folded in his palm. "Maybe I wanted to see where you were from."

"Maybe you wanted to track me down," she answered. "What, hunt the Queen through me? I won't take you to her, Felix."

"I only wanted to see you." True enough. Truer to say he didn't want to be here at all. "I have something to give you. Something important. Now."

"What's in your hand?" She closed half the distance, imperiously reaching.

"Just a compass." He held it out. "The needle's iron."

He cupped it in his left palm. She stepped nearer, leaves rustling under her feet, and bent to look. Her braids slid over polished skin, caught on the round nubs of her scars. He knew what they felt like, beads rolled under his palm.

"This isn't what you came to bring me, is it? I must hurry you, Felix; I'm away from my task."

He wasn't fool enough to think he'd get a second chance. The only thing buying him the first one was that Matthew never would have done such a thing—and that Felix and Kadiska had been friends. Once, of a sort.

A twist of his right hand freed the meteoric iron knife from his wrist. The hilt warmed Felix's palm, clicked against his ring. He folded his fingers over the compass, and let his left hand fall. When Kadiska lifted her head, turning from the waist, he placed the point of the blade below and inside her left breast, between the fourth and fifth ribs, angled up, and pushed it in.

Obscene, how easily and how irrevocably it glided home. There was very little gore; the black ensorceled blade itself kept her heart's red blood inside even as it perforated her left atrium, punctured her left lung, and severed the pulmonary arterial trunk.

She was dead before he caught her under the arms and lowered her tenderly. The brain, they said, kept functioning for long seconds after the heart was gone. He sat on the leaves beside her and held her hand, to be sure she didn't die alone.

He didn't try to close her eyes. In funeral parlors, they sew the eyelids down; the trick of smoothing them with a palm only works in the movies.

The atmosphere of money enfolded Peese like cling film when he entered Jane's apartment. It coated his skin, thick and silken; it slid down his throat like buttermilk. It intimidated.

It was meant to.

Jane greeted him with tea and cookies, which he accepted, but didn't taste. He sat stiffly upright on the sinfully comfortable love seat, staring past his folded hands at the teacup on the coffee table while she nibbled a cookie and watched. She got bored first.

"I am instructed to talk to you about Heaven," she said.

He laughed. "I've never been." When he looked up, her eyes were on him, clear and thoughtful under soft, pale hair. "Instructed by who?"

"Whom." She sipped her tea, golden Ceylon in a tall white pansy-painted cup, a wheel of lemon bumping her lip. Oils seeped from the rind to bead the surface, the aromas consoling. "A Wild Fae. Who has no love of the Lord of Hell, or the Daoine, either. He thought we might make an alliance."

"Archangels do not bargain. Besides, Fae. They'll deal with devils, and any other thing."

"He *cares* to deal with you. Or with your master."

"I prefer to call him a guardian angel. So to speak."

"In any case, Prometheus is in the process of reinvention. I'd like to plead our case. Look." She put her cup on the saucer and the saucer on the coffee table. "Would you just call him? I'd rather not explain it twice."

"It's not quite that simple."

"Angels," Jane said, "know when they are named."

She leaned forward and laid her cool hand on Peese's wrist, her marcasite bracelet sliding low over blue veins and bones. He shrugged and covered her fingers with a brief pat.

"Michael?" Peese pulled his hand away.

The angel appeared without fanfare, wearing blue jeans ripped at one knee, eight-eye Doc Martens with a Union Jack toe, and a white T-shirt with a line drawing of a frazzled-looking cartoon bunny making a particularly American gesture on the front. "I was listening. You were Hell's ally not so long ago."

Jane Andraste smiled. "That was in another country—"

"And besides, those men are dead?" Michael uncrossed her arms. "You know Lucifer sends messengers pleading forgiveness."

"That displeases you."

"I have no quarrel with him until I am assigned one. But I take an interest. Of course."

"Bunyip seemed to think Heaven had more than an interest."

"There are a lot of devils in Hell." Michael's eyebrows rose. Otherwise, she might have been a statue.

"So it would seem. I'll tell you the truth, then, as plain as I can make it. I fight a duel with Christopher Marlowe—late of England, Prometheus, Faerie, and Hell—"

"I know him."

"Just so. In a very few days. He has the very Devil on his side. Witchcraft. And I need wards against it."

"And you want to bargain with God for those protections."

"I wish to *remind* you that Marlowe is allied with forces that have no love for Heaven. That to combine Faerie and Hell with Prometheus would subvert—reverse, even—the task that Prometheus was founded to fulfill."

"Prometheus is a shadow," Michael said. "A cracked vessel. It holds nothing."

"No," Jane said. "But it will. Ally with me, and I give you the Prometheus that will follow. I give you a more tractable Faerie . . . perhaps. If everything goes according to plan."

"If I loan you my power to destroy Christoferus Magus."

"Bring him to heel."

"Oh," Michael said. "*Whatever*. I won't fight your duel for you." Great wings unfolded from her shoulders and fanned the still air softly, rustling silk flowers and flexing the rice paper squares in the shoji screens. "I have one of my own. Not to mention whatever the Morningstar's plotting." One wingtip flicked in eloquent dismissal: *and he is always plotting*.

"A duel of your own?" Jane picked up her tea. Steam flowed over the side of the cup, bent by Michael's agitation.

"Yes," Michael said. "The Daoine Prince has challenged me as Hell's champion, to prove the Morningstar's innocence in the eyes of Heaven." Her perpetual frown curved deeper, creasing her face from lip to chin. "Trial by combat. He'll be slaughtered."

Jane would have turned, just then, and stared at Felix under one peaked eyebrow, if he had not been gone. Peese was no help. He sat, head bowed and hands folded, as wordless as he had been since he first said Michael's name.

"I'm not afraid to do the work, Michael. But it's our souls that stand at risk if Marlowe's allowed to win, and Matthew's and his I'll save for you if you help bring them to the light."

Jane did not rise, and the angel did not settle. But the silence dragged taut between them as if they struggled over a rope, and in Michael's eyes Jane saw all her sin and malfeasance, the small selfishnesses and the hubris that had nearly wrecked the world, reflected. The chill settled into her, hard and sharp as swallowed glass. She had failed and failed again, and all her failures were naked in the angel's eyes.

She drove her nails into her flesh, and lifted her chin, and did not blink. And the angel looked down first.

"Yes. It's a good reason. All right. You have our help. But see to it that you do not fail. And I will have none of your Promethean trickery."

"No tricks," Jane promised. "So, tell me, Michael. If we're to be friends and allies, have you any fear that Lucifer will regain God's grace?"

"Fear? Not much."

The archmage sipped her cooling tea. "And if you had a legitimate means of keeping Lucifer in Hell? Would you use it?"

"I am an angel, Mrs. Andraste."

"I know," Jane said. "That wasn't what I asked."

Chapter Twenty-three
The Arrangement

"Well," Matthew said, hiking up the bank between the wood and the walls of the palace, "that got me nothing but bloodied."

He spread his arms and flopped on the resilient turf, bouncing on his left hand before settling into the grass beside Kit. Kit, sprawled under the sun of Faerie like a smug green lizard, did not open his eyes. "Thought you to obtain any satisfaction from her?"

"I didn't even get to talk to her. Just Felix, that rat in a bespoke suit. And he was no use either."

"You tried," Kit said, complacently. "You failed."

"And now?" Matthew propped himself up as the shadow of a passing bird flickered between them and the warmth of the sun. It was gone by the time he glanced after it.

"And now we fight," Kit said. He pressed his elbows against the yielding lawn and pushed himself upright. He looked past Matthew, frowning across the garden. "Your prodigals return."

"Mine?" Matthew rolled onto his back and turned his head to see, the sun on his face warm and firm as a caress. Christian walked up the curved road to the palace, Jewels on his right side and Lily, still in Kit's castoffs, on his left. Matthew met Kit's frown and matched it. He hadn't been sanguine about letting Lily go with Christian to take Don to New York—but she'd insisted, and it seemed unfair to leave Don alone with the Devil without the buffer of somebody halfway trustworthy. Lily and Christian returning having exchanged

Don for Jewels wasn't any more reassuring. "I'm responsible for the lot, huh?"

"They have not the art for it themselves." Kit grinned. "And nobody entrusts his children to me." He heaved himself to his feet and held out his hand. Left hand, for Matthew's ease. Matthew accepted, and hauled himself to his feet using Kit as an anchor. "Here's a more immediate concern. Can you think of a way to pry that name from Morgan's lips?"

"Bunyip's?"

"Aye."

"I could give her what she wants—"

Kit unclasped Matthew's hand and snorted. "Aye, and enjoy it. For a while. But you don't want that."

"As long as I'm carrying this . . . thing around with me, nobody who thinks they have a chance with me is going to give me a rest. And it's not as if I can use the power myself, or even know what it's *good* for."

"Well," Kit said, "I could—that is, you might—"

His voice trailed off. He stared at Matthew wide-eyed, blushing until his eyebrows stood out in pale lines against his skin, abashed as any ten-year-old. Matthew looked down. "Ah—"

"No," Kit said. "Stupid thought. Never mind."

"Dammit, Kit. What am I supposed to *do* about this?"

Kit didn't mean to. But in four hundred years, he had never once been accused of being at the mercy of his better intentions. "Close your eyes and think of Manhattan?"

Matthew stared at him, stricken, while Kit's face burned even hotter. And then Matthew threw back his head and started roaring, great, belly-shaking howls that knocked him on his ass, back in the grass, leaning forward with his elbows on his knees and laughing until he had to stop for want of air. He slumped onto the turf, panting, and shaded his eyes with his hand as he grinned up at Kit. "Thank you," he said. "And thank you for the other offer, um. . . . But—"

Kit winked. "Surprise you though it might, that's not the first time I've been refused."

That started Matthew laughing again, more weakly this time, the clipped grass poking his neck and blades worming through his hair to tickle his scalp. "Kit," he said, and hesitated. But what the hell: the poet was a product of another age, and he'd know what Matthew meant if he said it plainly. "Damn," he said, planting his feet and rolling onto them again. "It's been a long time since I had a friend."

Jane, but he didn't say. He hoped his taste had improved.

Judging by the smile that transfigured Kit's face, it hadn't been the wrong thing. "And you've given me an idea." He glanced over his shoulder. "Which I shall explain to you after we dispense with these."

Because apparently Matthew's hysterics had carried, and Christian and his entourage had left the road and were toiling up the soft bank now. Christian walked in the lead, Jewels flanking, but it was Lily whose pallor drew the eye. She looked unwell, wobbly and sick, and when they stopped she walked the extra step to catch up, then reached out to steady herself on Christian's elbow. He patted her fingers, encouraging.

"Matthew Magus," Christian said, courtesy wrapped in a smile. "Kit. May I ask a favor of you?"

"Of course you may ask," Kit said, while Matthew tried and failed to catch Lily's eye.

Christian smiled the sort of smile that vampires might affect, to hide their fangs. "Would you deliver Miss Gorman here to His Highness in good health? She's chosen not to pursue the study of witchcraft, and I offered to return her to Faerie."

"And here she is," Kit said.

"And here I am." Jewels stepped forward, rubbing her arms.

Christian glanced at Lily. "But my other companion is unwell, and if I might prevail upon you gentlemen—"

"You're back quickly," Matthew interrupted.

"I have no *aptitude* for witchcraft, it seems." Jewels glared at him as if he bore some responsibility. "Do you remember when you told Geoff and me that there are seven kinds of magic, and only named six?"

His head jerked reluctantly.

"What's the other one?"

"What are the six I named?"

She paused, tongue-tip protruding from her mouth. His expression remained unforthcoming whether it was a test or an honest request for information. " 'Magic of symbol,' " she parroted, " 'to which almost anyone can be trained.' Except for Juliet Gorman, apparently. Magic by gift"—she shot a dire look at Lily. Lily, wiping cool sweat from her forehead onto the back of her velvet sleeve, never noticed—"and magic by sacrifice. The opposite of my problem, apparently."

Matthew didn't flinch from her stare. He'd met the eye of wilder things. "That's three."

"Magic of the will." She glanced aside, at Kit this time, uncertain in her defiance.

Kit nodded. "Continue."

"Names and bindings. Magic by blood. That's five. And illusion was six. So what's number seven?"

"Magic by deception," Christian said, and smiled in the face of Matthew's black scowl. "Morgan le Fey's magic, and Lucifer's magic, and the Dragon's magic—and the most secret mysteries of the Prometheans. The only magic that can change history and make false things real."

"Yes," Matthew said, unwilling. "And hell to meddle with."

Jewels didn't think he meant her to see it, but she noticed the way his right hand tried to clench, and failed. "And I can't learn any of it," she said, with sulky satisfaction. "I'm a cripple. A one-eyed freak." She looked down at her hands. "But I can give other people power, can't I?"

Christian nodded. "I think you can."

She ignored him, staring at Matthew. And Matthew, watching the way all Faerie's sorcery sheeted around her like water running off oilcloth, nodded.

"Thank you," she said. "Then I have something to offer Ian. Will you bring me to him?"

As it turned out, Matthew couldn't. Ian was nowhere in residence, and even the pages could not say where he had gone. After a few fruitless inquiries, they determined that Matthew would escort Jewels and Kit would speak to the Queen.

Escort was the generous term for his role. The page girl Monkshood guided them, her broad hare's feet thumping as she ran, because neither one of them knew the way. Matthew would have left Jewels at the door if she hadn't looked at him, small and shivering, and said "Please. I don't want to be alone."

"For a little while," he said, and followed her into the room. He left the door a little ajar, though. Just a crack, enough for air and sound to filter through. "I'm sorry about Geoff. If I could—"

Whatever he expected, it wasn't her cracked, harsh laugh. "Would you? What? Take his place? Lily told me what happened." Jewels snorted, and threw herself down on the bed.

Matthew sat beside her, trying not to loom. "I'm sorry. But I can't make you believe that."

"Oh," she said, "I believe it all right." She reached out blindly, without lifting her face from the veil of hair puddled over it, and groped his knee. He took her hand between his own and squeezed gently, then let it fall back on the covers. "But it doesn't change anything, does it?"

He opened his mouth, but let the words die unuttered. "He didn't want to be there," he said, when he'd had a chance to find a way to say what he meant that sounded less like a condemnation. She was a *child*. She didn't need to carry Geoff's death around for the rest of her life. "I don't want to be here either, you know. But we don't always get what we want."

Platitudes. Good work, Matthew.

Jewels stirred against the bedclothes, pressing her cheek to cool satin-woven silk. "No." Her voice came out half a mumble, distorted by the cloth and hair against her mouth. She sat up, shook her ash-colored tangles from her face and held them back with one raised hand, her elbow and upper arm a spiky angle against the sunlit window behind. "You want everything I've got, don't you? You want to be a normal person and have a normal family—"

"You have a normal family?"

Meant as a joke, but it fell between them like a stone. "You mean my mother the drunk or my father the child molester? Yeah, I've got a normal fucking family, *Matthew Magus*. And you?"

"Dead parents," he said, in a colorless voice. "And a dead brother too, who got kidnapped by Faeries and driven mad along the way. And an adopted mother who turned out to be the devil incarnate. You know. The usual. I'm sorry for your pain."

He stood. It was grief, and she had every right to her grief. But he had every right to *his* too, and the fact that hers was fresher didn't make it right for her to claw his scabs.

"If I had your power," she said, "you had better believe I'd use it. If I . . . Geoff wouldn't be dead."

"I believe you." The door was five steps away. He stopped with a hand on it. "I'll send someone for you when Ian returns."

"Wait."

He waited. She stood, footsteps scuffing on carpet, and came up behind him. One hand pressed the small of his back. "But we're not so different, are we?"

He turned, aware that her hand slipped to his hip, while the other one crept past him and pushed shut the door. "Juliet," he said. "You're half my age. Have some wine and go to bed."

"What's the legal drinking age in Faerie?" She didn't step closer, and he folded his arms over his chest to keep her away. "You have all that power and you won't use it—"

"Can't." He snapped his fingers. "It's like trying to thread a needle with a Mack truck."

"There's a mental image." She laid her hand on his barricaded arms, wrapped her fingers around one wrist, and tugged. He permitted her to move him, unfolding his arms until his hands hung by his sides. "So what would you give me if I could give *you* your magic back?"

"*Give* it back?"

"Sure." She tapped his chest with two firm fingertips, wrinkling her nose at the face he made. "I haven't any power of my own. But I *can* initiate. I cut you, give you back what the unicorn took away. Christian told me," she said, answering the question before he'd quite gotten his tongue around it.

"And what did Christian tell you to trade it for?" Wary, a little amused. But, she thought, intrigued. Men were fascinated by her: her scars, her ink, the metal lacing her flesh. And he had a lot of ink of his own. She'd like to see it too.

His breath was warm on her face. A little sour, but she hadn't had a chance to brush her teeth recently either, and he smelled good, for a sweaty man. His skin was sweet. The careful diet that went with those muscles, no doubt.

She stood on tiptoe, captured a fistful of his hair, and kissed him on the mouth.

And he kissed her back, his bad hand a warm knot in the curve of her back, his mouth soft and hesitant. And then he put his other hand on her waist, straightened up, and gently and definitely set her back two steps and a half. "Been kissed by more girls this week," he said. "You know, I think I should stick to this cologne."

"You *son of a bitch*."

"If you like. Whatever Christian offered you, no."

She stared at him, and bit her lip. She stepped forward—or tried. She'd have had more luck pushing a parked car than shifting him. The *car* might have rocked when her weight hit it—and he was only holding on to her with one and a half hands.

"Crap," Matthew said. "I should have taken Kit up on it."

"What?"

He sighed and straightened his arms, pushing her back another half step. He flinched when her fingernails sank into his wrists. "No. Just—no, okay?"

"You have power and you don't even *want* it. And I've got nothing. It's not fair!"

"No," Matthew said. "No, it's not. Now back the hell up."

Matthew caught Kit by the elbow as he left the throne room, and swung him to one side. The suits of armor—Matthew couldn't even hear a breath to confirm they lived—on either side of the doors did not shift their stance. "Fucus, Matthew?" Kit said, and brushed a fingertip across the pink slickness unevenly coloring Matthew's mouth.

Matthew frowned at Kit's finger when he held it up, then snorted and turned his head, unrepentant. "Juliet."

"And wert thou her Romeo? No, I see not—"

"Come on." Matthew held on to Kit's elbow and hauled him down the corridor, Kit stumbling in his haste. "Pick on me later. Talk to me now. You mentioned a plan."

"Oh, aye. But not in these halls, I think. Come with me."

Then Matthew was hustling to keep up with Kit. "Where are we going?"

"Hell. Where we can be assured of a little privacy."

"In *Hell*?"

"The Devil does not eavesdrop," Kit said, with a wry half scowl. "He thinks it rude. And anyway, we'll need his help."

" 'The prince of darkness is a gentleman.' "

The scowl went to a smirk, as Kit paused before a parlor. "Once there were no mirrors at all in Faerie, you know, but things have changed since I've been gone—ah! We are in luck." He held the door aside, and waved Matthew within. Matthew obeyed, pausing in the center of a baroque and gilded room. "Sunday parlors always have mirrors, don't they? Ready for your voyage, Matthew Magus?"

"Did you learn anything from Elaine?"

Kit held a finger before his lips, and gestured to the mirror. Matthew stepped up beside him, allowing Kit to clasp his right wrist tightly. "I am at your disposal, Master Marlowe."

Kit grinned at him. " 'And when he falls, he falls like Lucifer, never to hope again.' "

"You?"

"Will. Some teacher of literature you are—"

"I don't know the play."

" 'Tis not surprising," Kit said. "*Henry the Eighth*, and not one of his best. I think he wrote it only to complete the set—"

"Jealous?"

"Envious." As Kit faced the mirror, it revealed the smile playing around his lips, half hidden by the beard. "I'd be twice the fool I am to be *jealous* of poetry like that. Come along."

They stepped through, and fell. Matthew might have panicked, but Kit's grip was strong. Darkness rushed past, whipping his hair and stinging his eyes, and he reached up left-handed to be sure he hung on to his glasses. He couldn't see the man who clung to his wrist, or his own hand in front of his face. "*Kit?!*"

"You needn't shout."

Almost prim, so that Matthew laughed—which was good. The oxygen settled his nerves, and if he pretended he was skydiving, that the free fall was a controlled and chosen thing, the scrape of adrenaline through his veins became a focus rather than a panic-inducing blur. "How long do we fall?" Without shouting this time, though he pitched his voice to carry.

"As long as we need to. Don't worry. There's no bottom."

"No—oh!" And suddenly, in the darkness, they were caught, an unanticipated yank that straightened their spines and banged them together, bruising ribs and elbows. Warm arms wrapped them, revealing their features dimly in a pale, moonlight glow.

:Kitten, I have told thee before, thou shouldst send ahead that thou art coming.: Lucifer chuckled, the hard warmth of his velvet-clad body bearing both Magi up.

Matthew and Kit felt the pump and stretch of the starlit wings through the angel's body, felt the muscles on his chest flex with the rowing rhythm of the pinions. The strength of those arms and those wings was incalculable. They could not have said at any given moment that they stopped falling and started flying. But they knew, and a dizzy exaltation took them both.

Too short, the flight. The Morningstar set them down on a stone disc furnished like any lamplit, comfortable sitting room in existence, except it had no walls, and hung softly in a yawning black abyss. He lowered first Matthew and then Kit lightly to their feet, his great wings pounding while he hovered, the wind making mare's nests of their hair.

Matthew ducked low until Lucifer settled beside them, debonair and perfect in a brushed black velvet doublet, picking a hair that was Kit's, by its color, off his breast. He smiled at it, pursed lips as rich and soft as any woman's, and blew it off his palm.

A cross-breeze swept it from the light, into the abyss.

Kit said not a word nor made a gesture as he watched that little ceremony, but the nameless emotion that stilled his face pierced Matthew's heart and silenced his tongue. If he could have moved against it, Matthew would have reached out and brushed the back of his hand against Kit's, as if by accident. But he could not even draw a breath.

And then Lucifer turned back to them, and smiled like a budding rose, and Matthew's heart as much as stopped beating again. :Gentle-men,: the Devil mocked. :However may I serve?:

"Matthew," Kit said, thinly, "please remove your shirt, so that Lucifer can see your marks."

Matthew untucked the hem slowly, ducked his head and yanked the shirt off over his head without thinking about it too much. Eyes down, looking at the floor. When he glanced up, he found himself looking in Kit's eyes, the right one glimmering brighter with reflected light.

:Yes,: Lucifer said, the backs of his fingers pressed against his jaw. :I comprehend. Show me the rest, Matthew Magus.:

Matthew let his shirt fall to the floor and glanced at Kit, who shrugged. Lucifer's hand snaked down in an abrupt gesture, counter-weighted by the flicker of the opposite wing. :Hast anything God gave not Adam?:

Matthew coughed. "Not that I know of."

:Then I've seen it. But I have not seen the spells inked in your human hide, and you must have taken your trousers off for the sorcerer who wrote them there. *Strip.*:

Matthew squatted to unlace his boots. Stood, and unbuttoned his jeans. Hooked his thumbs under the waistband and shoved them down, boxers too, leaving clothes slouched around his feet like Christmas wrappings. "Happy?"

"Ecstatic," Kit said, with the sort of leer that would have begged a slug on the shoulder if Lucifer hadn't been standing between them.

:Turn,: the Devil commanded, and Matthew turned. Slowly, stepping out of his jeans first so he wouldn't trip. Forked tongue-tips wavered from the Devil's mouth a moment, and he turned to Kit. :Yes. I recog-nize them. As do you, no doubt?:

Kit inclined his head in the Devil's direction. "We'll talk of it some other time."

:You wish them removed?:

Kit smiled. "I wish them duplicated."

Later, while Kit reclaimed his clothes and dressed, back turned to Matthew and Lucifer in a show of modesty, Matthew paced the edge of the room over the abyss and trailed fingertips along a tabletop. The

Devil's attention was patent; he looked up to meet those transparent azure eyes. "Do you suppose it's jealousy?"

:Matthew Magus?:

"Michael. You and Michael. Is that what's between you?"

Lucifer's amusement curved his mouth gorgeously, his hair disarrayed in ringlets against his cheek, over his collar. *"Oh, what a goodly outside falsehood hath."*

:Angels do not suffer envy, Matthew Magus.:

"I've heard stories that differ."

But nothing Matthew could say would shake that smile.

:Then they must be true.:

ᘓᕤᑕᐧ Chapter Twenty-four
New York City, King Size Rosewood Bed

Wolvesbane opened the throne room door, and Ian stepped forward, conscious of his carriage: chin up, hands at his sides—the apple he'd been eating while he waited palmed in the left one—and straight-spined. He entered the throne room not along the promenade, but from the head, alongside the dais. Less far to walk, and less sense of marching to his execution.

He should thank the Queen for that.

Measured paces brought him before her soon enough. His mother awaited him not on her chair of estate, but on foot before it, clad in the sort of iron-world clothes he hadn't seen her in since she was Seeker and not Queen. He'd *never* seen her with her hair shorn, but he expected he understood.

The Merlin stood beside her, hands on her hips, looking more tired than upset.

"My royal mother," Ian said, bowing low.

"Stand up," she said, and touched his chin to make it so. Her fingers flexed, as if they could hook him, and then relaxed and fell away. "Tell me that Cairbre wasn't on your errand, Ian, at the court of the Unseelie Sidhe."

"I can tell you more than that," he answered. "If he went there since Lucifer's ball, he went there against my orders."

She was watching him, staring into his eyes with her grayish ones. Not an attractive color, but a changeable one, and Morgan had it too. So had Hope, who had died.

"I am not lying, mother."

"No," she said. "I can see you're not. So he acted without your knowledge?"

"I discovered his plotting at the ball. The outline of it, anyway. I did not find it necessary to bring it before you."

"It's you he serves."

Ian shrugged. A revelation to no one. "And he went to Àine? And has not come back?"

The Queen made a gesture that was rude in any language. "I hope she turned him into a frog."

The Fae did not often resort to execution. They had no souls; their deaths were final. More often, they would transform and imprison rivals—changed into swans, harts, trees.

Carel put a hand on the Queen's sleeve. The Queen leaned into it for a moment and then nodded, yielding the floor. She actually walked backward, one step and then two, and Carel moved into her place. "So, say that's settled—"

"Is it?"

Carel smiled. "We can say it is."

"And yet," Ian said. He arched a brow at her, and cocked his head, and smiled.

"And yet," Carel answered. Behind her, the Queen folded her hands and bowed her head, twisting a toe on the stones in a most unqueenlike fashion. "There's a little matter of a duel."

"Oh," Ian said. He shrugged. "That."

The Queen raised her head. "Ian, your father—"

"Father," he said, "will stand as my second. Unless, of course, you should die or abdicate before the combat, whereupon I would no longer be subject to the challenge, as a monarch."

The Queen paled. Ian smiled at her and bit into his apple, prying off a crisp red chip, the tart ivory flesh waxy and pink-veined within. "Don't take it so hard, mother," he said. "You and the Mebd both taught me well."

A drop of juice ran down his chin. He reached to wipe it onto the back of his sleeve and startled as the floor jumped under his feet and the drop jiggled loose and fell, spotting his doublet dark on dark. He turned with Carel as the floor shook again, the glassed Gothic windows cracking in their frames. The Merlin spread her hands at hip level, fingers outstretched like an alert spider's legs, and the shaking stilled, though a faint tremor like the echo of a finger run round the rim of a crystal goblet tickled up their nerves.

Ian unbuttoned his doublet, slipped out of his shirt. He tossed them to the floor and reached for the waist of his breeches. If battle had found them, he would face it as a wolf.

He froze like that wolf at the figure revealed in the doorway, a flensed and stinking creature like the corpse of a horse dragged from the bottom of a loch with a drowned man sat upon its back. The shattered armor of the door guards clattered about its feet, kicked cans, as it shambled into the throne room with a silken bag slung over one peeled shoulder.

"Unseelie," Ian said.

His mother's chin jerked. "Nuckelavee."

It lifted a green pine bough in its malformed claw and curtseyed low on awful limbs. "To the Usurper Queen of the Daoine Sidhe, from Àine of the Unseelie Court, Queen in Faerie, defiance. I bring a message for your Merlin."

The Queen looked at Carel. Ian did not take his eyes from the messenger. "Speak," Carel said.

With a flourish, the messenger upended its bag on the checkerboard floor. The contents bounced and scattered: a human head and human hands.

Carel stepped between the creature and the Queen. She wouldn't look. Not now. "Is that your message?"

"Her Majesty Àine wishes you to know that your lady Autumn is her guest in the White Castle. And there she will remain, along with the Daoine bard."

Carel's hand moved.

What she hurled was chthonic, draconian fury: not precisely lightning, and not precisely fire. It crackled like electricity and it stank of ozone, and it spattered, violet-white with power, against the air in front of the Unseelie, blocked by some powerful ward. The Nuckelavee bowed and withdrew, sliding back through the vast double doors, while Carel was still framing her second curse. Ian recovered first, running forward shirtless, his sword in his hand, shouting to rouse the castle—as if the thumps of the thing's club dispensing with the armor hadn't been enough. The Queen called for Whiskey as Carel walked forward. She crouched inside the door, wrath crackling around her hands.

It would wait. This wasn't the building she meant to bring down with it. Because she knew before she touched the grisly trophies what she'd find: the gray head and work-rough hands of the hedge-wizard who called himself Gypsy, who must have gotten in between the Nuckelavee and its prey.

She touched his saturated hair and recoiled from the loathsome mats, sticky-flaking with dried blood. And then she forced herself to stroke the hair back, to touch his face, his cheeks, his half-closed eyes. She knew his life in his blood, his name, his path.

"A long life, and a merry one, and a quick death, and a painless one," she said, and touched the back of her bloody hand to her tongue, a kind of promise. "Gypsy, you gallant fuck."

The blood was bitter in her mouth. She clenched her useless fingers against her palms.

When the dogs lifted their heads, Morgan set aside her knitting. She dropped it into the basket beside her chair, taking pains with the needles, and stood. By the time a blond head peeked over the sill of her window, she had the kettle on.

"Matthew," she said.

He folded his arms. "Have you heard from Don?"

"The raven's not back. Have a drink. We'll wait together."

"Could be a long wait." But he came around to the door and let himself in, pausing between the peeled boles that framed the entrance. The dogs swung to their feet to greet him, and he trailed his cramped right hand over each wiry-browed head, rubbing coarse coat between his thumb and forefinger. Their noses were cold, their muzzles almost silken. He crouched and fondled their tulip ears. "I'm not just here about Don."

"I didn't think you were. But drink, and we'll talk."

"I might prefer to skip the talking." He stood while she poured water. "You know the Bunyip's name."

"I know everyone's name." She paused, elbow and wrist bent, head half turned, the iron kettle raised as lightly as a spoon in her flannel-armored hand. "Well, nearly everyone. But his for certain. I wouldn't recommend you try to bind him with it, though. Elaine might be strong enough for that. But it's not your métier, Matthew Magus."

"There are other uses to which a name can be put."

She smiled through her hair and poured the water into a speckled blue and gray pottery teapot with grooved sides. "Hm. But I can't just give these things away, you know."

"Bad for business?"

"Bad for the magic."

She rehung the kettle on its arm and set the lid on the teapot, trapping the steam within. One thin tendril curled from a spout shaped like a curious elephant's trunk. She swaddled the body of the pot in cheerful yellow and red linen napkins before she looked up again.

"I thought it would take longer to wear you down." She poured a cup and pressed it into his hands. His fingers curved into grooves that matched those on the teapot. "It might be a little weak yet."

"Second cup is the best," he said. "Like yesterday's soup."

"I didn't know you were a tea drinker."

"Jane is." He toasted her and raised the cup, lemon verbena and mint steam curling against his cheeks. "You learn to cope."

"Truer words," she replied, and tasted her own cup. Of course she could have poisoned his despite that, or drugged it. Pouring two potions from one pot is no handicap to a witch.

He drank anyway. "I might be tired of everybody waiting to see which way I'm going to jump."

"Your sex life as spectator sport makes you uncomfortable?"

"It's not my power to use, is it? It's my power to give. And then I have no control over what happens next."

She smiled. "How does it feel to play a woman's part?"

"Is that what this is?"

"Historically speaking."

He frowned into his cup. "I'm sorry."

"Don't worry," she said. "I have more deserving targets to blame for the patriarchy."

He chuckled as she took the empty cup out of his hand, rough warm pottery brushing his fingertips. "I suppose I could swear to die a virgin—"

"That," she said, "would be a very great loss." She put her hand against his cheek. She was taller than he, her breath warm and lemony across his face.

"What will you use it for?"

"Could you trust me if I told you?"

"Very well," he said. "The name."

"You'll laugh."

He leaned close and drew her into his arms, against his chest. "So let me laugh."

She closed her eyes, lips moving against his. "After." Her hand slipped up his shoulder, behind his ear, through buzzed prickles and into the longer, nylon-slick cap of yellow hair that swung blunt-edged against his cheek. "You've got some gray in this, Matthew."

He pushed a silver-streaked lock of red off her own face. "I'm not the only one."

She grinned, and pulled his mouth against her mouth.

Climbing the ladder to the loft was such a profound statement of intent that it made his hands tremble. She took his glasses away and set them beside the bed on the window ledge. Her mattress was deep and soft, rustling straw-tick under springy sheepskins, and over those a feather bed like the ethereal warmth of spring. The ropes creaked; he flinched and Morgan laughed. "You'll come to no harm."

"Do I seem intimidated?"

"You wouldn't be the first," she said, and slipped under the covers too. Her long ivory body was covered in speckles—darker where the sun regularly touched, paler on her legs and shoulders and the white curve of her belly. She laid her right hand on his chest, fingers together and thumb spread wide, and framed the scar over his heart in the reversed L. "Wasn't it better to come to me willingly?"

He arched an eyebrow at her. "Better than what?"

"Better than being clawed to scraps by the Maenads, for one." She kissed him and he kissed her back, gaining confidence.

"I hope you don't carve notches on your bed frame."

"Do you see any?"

He craned his neck. She laughed and struck his chest with the heel of her hand, her hair sliding over their shoulders. "It would take a room of bed frames, Matthew. Fifteen hundred years I've been a woman. That is no short while."

"Ah, there's the intimidation—"

"I'll teach you."

"That's supposed to soothe me?"

"Fair enough," she said, when she stopped laughing. She flipped the covers over their heads. "Let me feel your hands."

He touched her, breath swelling his chest when his palm skimmed over her breasts, his misshapen right hand steadying her hip. She outlined the ink on his skin with the pads of her fingertips and straddled his hips to kiss him again. Her thighs caressed him as she leaned forward, warmth trapped between them, the down coverlet tented over her head filtering light from the window under the eave into bright transparency.

Her bones made sharp relief under the skin, shoulder blades elegant as vaned wings, spine like a string of baroque pearls. He touched them, stroked each one, warmed her pulse with his open mouth while her nails skittered across his abdomen and thighs. He let her make him want her. It was easier that way.

When she wrapped her fingers around his shaft, running her thumb over taut, crepey skin, he closed his eyes and hissed through gritted teeth.

"Don't do that," she said. "Open your eyes."

He did, focusing on her face, reaching one-handed to steady her as she lifted herself over him, drew a sobbing breath, and pressed herself down, enfolding his sex in her own. He watched as she took him in, her eyes, her mouth, her hands first cradling him and then spread on his belly, fingers flexing as he tightened his abdominal muscles and arched his hips, rising to meet her, gasping as she caught his wrists, pushed them against the bed, and bore down until their bodies locked tight as mortise and tenon. She smiled at him, and he drew a deep breath in and let it out slowly, relaxing under her weight.

She nodded, her hair all around them under the bedclothes, her fingers rippling on his wrists. "He is the saltwater oldest brother; Garndukgu-Wurrpbu is his name. Can you say it?"

He tried, and failed. She coaxed; on the third time, he got it, but she made him repeat it twice more. "And you don't think I can bind him?"

"I don't care if you can bind him. And another thing. All you damned men are the same, but *I* am not Ygraine." She released his wrists, rocking back on her heels. And then she slapped him across the face hard enough to turn his head and leave the shadow of her fingers on his cheek. She shook her hand, blowing on her fingers, and twisted her hips savagely. The quilt slid from her shoulders to slump across his thighs. "And I will thank you to come to my bed wearing your *own* face in the future, Master Marlowe, unless you fear to be turned away."

He covered the welted cheek with his palm. "You knew."

"You're not the player Will was." Scornful dismissal. She braced herself against his shoulders as she rocked in an oceanic rhythm. "That's not how Matthew folds his arms."

Her hair covered his face. Her waist lengthened and relaxed under his palms. "And the name?"

She leaned back, locked her left hand in his reaching one, and slid the other between his thighs to squeeze and seek in the moist warmth there. He groaned and turned away. "See? I've not forgotten all. Would Matthew like that, Christopher?"

He pushed himself up, the left hand still in her own, now encircling her waist, pulling her arm across her body as he pressed his face between her breasts.

She shook her hand free of his, laced it in Matthew's blond hair, and pulled Kit to her, rubbing her sweat into his skin. "I like his strength on you."

Kit flinched, but insisted: "And the name, why give me that? What does it gain you?"

"You find it easy to forget that Murchaud was my son too."

"Madam," Kit said, kissing her collarbone, "you do not make it easy to remember."

The Western Isles do not exist on any map. They are a wild and untrammeled country, England when England was young and the

wolves roamed her dark forests, Ireland when Ireland was trod by
the feet of warlords and queens. They are a measureless land, one
that brushes against the iron world where the iron world rusts thin:
in the marshes where the witchlights burn, on the hills crowned with
kingly thorns. They are boundless in that; they can be reached from
America as easily as England, from Mozambique the same as Viet-
nam. And yet they are a land circumscribed on all sides, a green jewel
set in a bone-white ring of sand adrift on a nameless tide, a handful
of jade hills with their feet washed by the sea, and bigger on the inside than around the edge.

Matthew walked the beach below the palace while he waited and
wondered how far he'd have to walk before he would find his own footsteps in the sand. It was a project for an afternoon, anyway. One lap
around Annwn.

He needed the exercise.

And it kept him out of sight of the castle; he couldn't afford to be
seen. Maybe Bunyip would lurch up out of the deeps and eat him, and
he would be quit of all the ridiculous plans and demands, the claims and
counterclaims. There *had* to be something better he could do with his
life.

A mile and a half later, he broke into a trot. The beach had more of a
Pacific than an Atlantic character, the sand fine and hard-packed
enough to run on, and he made the most of it. Blue jeans and boots
weren't ideal clothes for jogging in, but they weren't the worst, and he
managed a pretty good two or three miles counting breaths until his
progress was slowed by a bouldery stretch. The tide was rising, but the
high-tide mark was well below the tops of the rocks, so he clambered
up. It was tricky climbing mostly left-handed, balancing with his right,
and the rocks were spray-slick when the sea hissed in and out under his
feet.

At least the scramble took enough concentration to distract him from
the endless replay of his last conversation with Kit. *You hate her*,
Matthew had said, as Kit was buttoning his collar over the faux tattoos
painted black on his chest. And Kit had smiled and stared at himself in
the mirror as his hair grew paler and brighter and his shoulders broad-

ened to fill Matthew's shirt, and said, *Hate is a strong word, Matthew. We need that name. And it's nothing I haven't done before.*

And he'd let Kit have his way, when what he should have said was *More reason you shouldn't have to do it again.*

Mist was right about him.

He paused at the highest point of the sea-swept boulders, in the shadow of the red cliff behind, and watched the tide surge through the stones underneath. Spray wet his cuffs and splashed his boots, tall curtains of fountaining surf flashing like chains of pearls and diamonds in the sun. He could pick his way forward ten steps, or a dozen, and stand right beside it, feel the tremble of the angry sea under his rubber soles converted to a roar, be deafened by it, be ravished. If he slipped, the sea would kill him in an instant, dash him on the rocks without a breath of thought, cave his rib cage and crush his skull. *And we think we bound that,* Matthew thought, and twisted the rowan ring on his thumb. *Only inasmuch as it ever permits itself to be bound.*

He turned away from the sea and continued.

He had to look down, watch his feet, calculate his balance as he hopped. Wavelets slurped in the crevices, washing strings of filamentous seaweed cemented among wet black snails and mussels showing anoxic violet lips. Chalky barnacles flicked feather dusters and one grim red sea star grappled a doomed shellfish near where Matthew skipped down the last few rocks.

The sea ran softer here, rolling up a slow shelving beach rather than hurling its wrath at the stones. He splashed through swirling water that drank his footing and clutched his ankles to gain the firm sand near a withered high-water mark. The waves weren't all the way in, and the needle-fine outlines of seabird tracks still embroidered the margin recalled from last night's tide. The tracks were beginning to crumble at the edges, where the sun baked the water from the sand.

Matthew dropped to one knee: the same knee he'd skinned. Water wicked through his pants on an instant. With his right forefinger, he traced the hoofprint that had caught his eye, just above where the waves now washed. Two toes, like a deer's, trailed by the fine feathery brushes of her fetlocks. One hoofprint, and another. There were more, where the water had not yet crossed, meandering in and out of the sea as if she had galloped, playing tag with the waves.

He lurched to his feet and began to run again, flying along the border of the sea and shore.

The sun grew high, though, and his hair slipped loose from his ponytail to adhere to his face. He hadn't brought water. Going for a little walk, that was all.

The unicorn's hoofprints veered away from the sea.

He hadn't seen her yet, but she couldn't be too far. She was running along the wave-tips, and the wave-tips were rolling in; if she'd been much ahead, he never would have seen her writing in the sand. As she undoubtedly meant him to.

There would have been no tracking her over salt grass, but there was a path, the sand freshly scuffed, and Matthew followed it between bordering tangles of dog roses though it gave way to pebbles and then clay. The grass became plain grass, a meadow, and the roses no longer hunched with salt and constant wind. A long silver thread winked from one thorny briar, thrumming like a spider-strand.

Matthew jogged past. *Kit must be looking for me by now*, he thought. He dropped from a run, pulling off his spectacles, and mopped sweat onto a sleeve before it could sting his eyes. His skin felt papery hot. He'd gotten burned. Maybe not too badly, though; it didn't hurt yet. Still, beaches and blonds. His own fault if he blistered like a crème brûlée.

He'd turn back at the top of the next hill. Which, of course, was when he spotted her. She posed like a coquette in the vale beyond, hind hooves on the bank, forehooves in a chuckling brook that glistened like a thread of mercury. White as an egret, her horn sword-blade blue. And waiting.

The briars grew close across the path at the hilltop. He saw more strands of mane or tail scratched from her hide, some straight and silken, some knotted into bobbin lace, snarls snagged and tugged free. He'd have to push at the rose canes to climb down, and they were *scaled* with thorns.

He reached out with his right hand, because it mattered less if he hurt it, and brushed the briars aside.

Rose tree and thorn hill, and you would have thought he might have learned by now. The plant pricked his thumb and he jerked his hand back. Too late. For he was somewhere else.

Not a hilltop in the sun, but sweat chilling his neck in the shade of weedy locusts and live oaks, while brambles sticky with overripe fruit and buzzing with greedy hornets dragged at his thighs. It was cool, the gray sky high and misty, and the woodlands reclaiming it all.

But it had been a graveyard once. Amid the verdancy, viridian and chartreuse, emerald and olive, the vines and poison ivy and Spanish moss dripping thick from laden boughs, five or seven tombstones struggled under the briars. Berry stains marked weathered sandstone, and bird stains too. America and the South, not Faerie anymore, by the smell in the air. And summer, not November. No, he did not want to be here. The hiss of the sea in the distance and the tang of salt were echoed in the slipstream hiss and ozone tang of a nearby highway. Not too far, just behind the screening vines.

There was a snowy flash in the shadows beyond the graves, but he stepped forward before he saw that it was the white of swan wing feathers and not of a sea-combed mane.

Brambles snagged him, and he was somewhere else again.

Frosted leaves crunched underfoot, and he knew this air better than any air he could have breathed. New York City, with her white and yellow lights staining the graying sky beyond the meadow. Central Park, a clearing in the Ramble, and no thorns touched him this time.

No safe place for a lady alone at dawn.

But there she was, gray hair snarled and knotted in front of one eye, her hands clutched tight and swathed in the folds of a red velvet cloak heavy and soft as snow. It was torn from one shoulder, snagged on the winter-ragged brambles caging her, and icy light limned the flute of one fine collarbone. Her bare toes curled for balance in the mossy ground.

Three beads of blood swelled in the hollow of her ankle. Another scratch decorated her cheek. She couldn't move from where she stood; the thorns would see to that.

He knew her face, the unplucked eyebrows, the breathless expression, the wild fathomless eyes.

And she was barefoot in the frost.

"I saw you in Hell," he said. "With an angel."

"Fionnghuala," she said. "Nuala. Daughter of Llyr."

"Fionnghuala," he said. "You're dead, in the legends. Baptized a Christian and fallen to dust."

"So was Arthur, Matthew Magus." She smiled.

"Everybody knows my name." Understanding pierced his throat like a swallowed needle. "Where is your cloak today?"

She raised her arms among the thorns and opened her velvet wrap. She was naked underneath, and the inside was white as shattered quartz when she spread it wide, the feathers ruffled where they had brushed her skin. "Shape-shifter," she said, shaking her hair out of her eyes. "The cloak has two sides."

"You must be cold." His eye sketched her breasts, her belly, her thighs and the shadows between them. Her nipples were silver in the half-light, the curls at her groin and underarms pewter, her skin like more frost against the frost that melted under her feet. Steam drifted from her nose.

"I have my feathers." But she didn't fold them around her. She let her arms drop to her side, cloak draping her shoulders. "I gave you something. Seven years ago, and seven days."

"You want it back?"

"You needed it then. And now someone needs it more."

A distant siren gyred over the city, thrilling the length of Matthew's back and neck. "Then come and take it. Or are there just too many thorns?"

She walked through them. They inked bright lines on her body—her arms, her thighs, her breasts. She never flinched, and her eyes never fell from his face, but he could see how they tightened about her, tugging, catching, piercing—

"Nuala, *stop*."

"Your city." Her shrug welled crimson down her breast. "Though her love is unrequited, she knows you pursued me, and so binds me. Wilt free a swan, Matthew Magus?"

"Does it bite?"

"Well, yes."

He came forward and peeled the grasping thorns from her flesh, careful as could be. She bore it in silence, but shivered like a horse snagged on barbed wire when he plucked them out and smoothed the shining drops of blood. "I'm sorry. I haven't got a spell for this."

"Haven't you?"

He unwound the last briar from her body and lifted it away. While his arms were raised, she stepped forward and wrapped him in hers, throwing her cloak over his head.

She might be slight, but she was strong. Her fingers threaded his sweat-clotted hair, yanked the elastic loose roughly enough to make him gasp, and pulled his mouth to hers before he managed to close it again.

She was not young. All her youth was spent as a swan, Llyr's daughter, and all her beauty wasted with a curse. But she was warm and she was lithe, and she was naked in his arms. She kissed his lips, his jaw, his throat, and left the red marks of her teeth upon his skin, and pulled his hair till tears seared the corners of his eyes, until he clutched her shoulders and shoved her back.

She didn't go. He got some air, but she hung on, his hair spiked through her knotted fingers, their breaths hissing into the warm narrow space between their mouths. She leaned into him, her thigh wedging his, her belly molded to his groin. "Take off your clothes."

"In Central Park?"

She grinned, more wolf than woman. "Could be Times Square."

Her forehead pressed his, smudging his spectacles, her nose on his nose. He swallowed, hard, his throat so dry it hurt. And reached between them, breath catching when the backs of his hands brushed her nipples, and unbuttoned his collar.

She caught at his mouth again, nipping, nursing his lower lip almost painfully hard—until he bit back. She moaned and melted against him; encouraged, he sucked her lip between his teeth and nibbled. Her hands yanked harder at his hair. He shrugged his shirt down and dropped it. She kicked it aside.

She knocked his glasses askew. He swore and fumbled after them, so she pulled them all the way off and tossed them—lightly—away. There was no witchcraft at all in unraveling a couple of laces. She crooked a finger and it was done. "Boots."

A flat order he obeyed, kicking them loose and barely catching his balance before she dropped to her knees within the cloak's drape, ignoring the tug of his fist in her tangled hair. She pawed at his belt, stabbing her thumb on the tongue, and wrenched his jeans open. "*What* were you wading in?"

"I was following *you*."

"Hah!" She grabbed and yanked, jeans and paisley cotton boxers trapping his thighs, the belt buckle bouncing off her biceps and slamming her rib cage. "Ow."

"Ow yourself." But he started to work his fingers loose from her hair.

"Hang on to that," she said, feathers tickling her back, broken thorn canes bloodying her knees. "You might want it—"

"Fucking Christ—"

She flinched. "Interesting choice of oath."

"Please," he said, fervently, and she laughed at him and kissed again. Until he interrupted her. "Nuala. That's, ah—but I'm not entirely sure that's symbolically adequate. And—"

"Men," she snapped, and hauled his pants the rest of the way down. He sprawled half atop her when she pulled his wrist, then caught her hand in his and pressed it down.

He laughed. "What?" she asked.

"We're probably the only heterosexual couple in this thicket."

She lifted her hips against him, heat and plenty that made him shiver. Her hand snaked down and *squeezed*, and he groaned against her throat. "Why did you wait for me? Once Jane let you go, didn't you have a lot of living to make up for?"

"I thought the unicorn—I thought *you* might come back. I didn't want to . . ." He shrugged. *Lose my chance.*

"Don't flatter."

He stilled like a stag at a twig crack, and turned his head as slowly as that hart to meet her gaze. "Don't call me a liar," he said. "Just because *you're* a unicorn."

"I never said I wasn't." Mild and reasonable. "Weren't you in a hurry?"

"I thought—" He paused and kissed her throat, his bad hand skimming her thigh as he blushed to the roots of his hair.

"Just this once, it's all right." She shifted, hooked her legs over his hips and pulled herself up with both hands on his shoulders. The cloak had fallen open and he shivered, but she was warm against his chest, in the shelter of his arms. "Ready?"

"Not on your life."

"Might as well get it over with, then," she said, and sank her nails into his ass.

His skin rippled with gooseflesh. Thorns gouged his wrist and forearm. A sharp-edged stone had lodged under his kneecap, wedging deeper with every shift of his weight. But for a moment, all he could feel was the thunder of wings in his head and his breast, the holy resilience of her rising to meet his, the long, dulcet glide of his body into hers.

She clove to him, tight, hard, fingers in his hair and nails in his shoulder, legs a wicked vise, breasts soft and fluid against his chest, and stilled him with her body so he lay against her shoulder and panted. The iron-laced ink in his skin prickled her with needles and with pins. His glasses were over *there* somewhere, but he was close enough to see her without them, the edge of her jaw, the fine lines in the crease of her eye, the softness under her chin.

"Breathe," she murmured against his ear, and somehow he managed. She pushed and pulled him back, hands in his hair and against his chest, until he lay over her stiff-armed and propped on his knuckles. She ran her fingers down his chest, over the coolness and heat of his tattoos, and paused with her fingertips resting over the fine scar she'd marked him with.

"Think about the sensations," she said. "Concentrate on your body. It works better in the long run, and we might as well set a good precedent."

Amused, he kissed her hair. "You know, *virgin* means *with anybody else*. I've got a *little* practice."

"Yak, yak, yak. Trust me. Hold still. This might hurt a little," she said, and tightened her legs around his waist as she pushed her fingers into his scar.

It hurt. Like a blunt knife worked under the skin, and neither his teeth sunk in his lip nor the warmth of her around him helped at all. He locked his elbows and let his head drop until his forehead rested on hers again, and tried to watch.

And first, she tore him open. Right at the scar, fingers burrowing like snakes, pulling him apart at the center seam. His flesh stretched. He expected showers of blood over her fingers, red meat and white sinew behind.

But there was no blood, only the extraordinary pain, the sensation of being on iron hooks, shredded and pulled open. Not just his skin: his ribs, his heart, his lungs. He fancied he heard bones cracking as she spread her hands, her face tight with effort, braced by his own weight and her legs pinning his hips. She glanced up, caught his white-faced agony, and flinched. "Feel it," she said. "Trust me. Nothing else helps."

He licked his lips, closed his eyes, and *felt*.

He felt her peel him, felt every nerve and fiber between skin and flesh yanked loose, from neck and back and thighs and halfway down his arms. Felt her lips on his lips, warm and soft as she reached up, her breasts rippling where they brushed his chest. Felt her clench around him, the deep pulse of contradictory sensations that burned his sinuses and sent salt water dripping down his nose in a slow continuous stream, the distillate of pain, so pure it didn't even have a name.

She relaxed, her hands slipping down his ribs, stroking his shoulders, brushing his nipples and his throat. "Open your eyes," she whispered, kissing his face, licking up his tears, pushing aside his filthy hair. "It's over, Matthew. You were brave. It's over now."

He opened his eyes. And greatly daring, glanced down.

To find himself bare.

The ghosts of his ink lingered on his skin, pale brindled on the gold of a late-autumn tan, but the ink itself was gone. Or not gone: wadded in her hand like a camouflage net. She squirmed under him and made him gasp, hauled at the edge of her crumpled cloak, and picked open a basted seam and shoved them inside. "I think you'll feel much better now."

"What was it?"

"What was what? The tattoos?"

"That you gave me," he said, "and took back."

"Absolution," she said, and folded away the pocket of her cloak. She touched the center of his chest, where the scar had been. "Your sins are your own, Matthew Magus. From this moment on." And then she put her hands on his shoulders and pulled him against her until they lay, warm skin on warm skin.

"I'm not a Christian."

"Funny thing, that. Make it a good sin anyway. For my sake."

His head still sang from raw white pain static and her warm, demanding scent. "Lady," he said, "I can only try."

◦∿⊃ Chapter Twenty-five
Why Did I Leave South Boston?

Max's ecstasies when Lily staggered through her front door were unparalleled. He twined her ankles, scolding, scorning Christian with his tail. Lily crouched to scoop him up and wobbled, her right hand tented on the floor, her head dropping between her knees. She grounded the other hand, her caduceus clicking wood. Chills rattled up her spine, clattering her teeth. She gritted them and tried to breathe evenly through her nostrils, to not feel the aching joints, the nausea slithering through her gut. "I need . . . hospital. Shit, it's Sunday—"

They'd think she was an OD if she staggered into the ER jittering and hyperventilating, Medic Alert bracelet or no, if she couldn't reach her endocrinologist and have him call. She fumbled in her handbag. Her phone, the Solu-Cortef. "Christian?"

He stood beside the unclosed door, one shoulder on the upright, watching her. "I forgive you," he said. "Take my hand."

"I don't need your hand, I need my goddamn shot." She couldn't find it in the bag. Max reared up like a meerkat and pushed his face against her cheek, whiskers prickling, fur like black satin. He smelled like rancid tuna fish; Autumn had been by to feed him. "PrRau?"

"Dammit, Max—" She couldn't blink the headache back. It filmed her vision, sloshing back and forth like hot liquid when she shook her head. She lost her balance, slammed her elbow, and fell, spilling the bag on the floor. "Ow. Damn, damn."

Christian was crouched beside her without her ever having seen him move. He brushed her hair off her cheek as Max shoved his ears into her palm. "I can heal you," Christian said. "I know you're jealous of Jewels. I know. But she's not what you are. No one could be more special to me. You know that, Lily."

"Not jealous." Her teeth chattered. She pulled her palm off Max's warmth, batted Christian's hand away, and groped among the spilled contents of her handbag for the shot. A plastic cylinder, light, neutral in temperature. She brushed cool tubes of lipstick, a fluff of tissues, glass beads on a hair elastic. No cased syringe. Her arm trembled with the exertion of holding her weight off the floor. "*Help* me."

"I'm trying to. You're a witch, Lily. You don't need that."

"Get out." She strained, heaved herself onto her stomach. Both hands. She could push herself up with both hands. If she could just *see*.

The syringe wasn't there. She wasn't missing it, wasn't reaching past it. It was gone, and so was her phone, and so, in fact, was the silver snuffbox that held her pills. She didn't even have those. "Christian," she said, forced to stop as her stomach spasmed and she retched, a stringy thread of yellow fluid gliding off her palate and splashing the floor. Her words panted on racing breaths. "If I don't get my shot, I will die."

"You'll live forever," he contradicted, stroking her cheek with the back of his hand. "You'll help me stop Lucifer. And you'll rule by my side."

God in Heaven. "I'll die."

"Die unshriven." His hands were so gentle, so kind. They soothed her neck and shoulders, pulled her away from the pooled vomit. He enfolded her in warmth. "Die and be damned. Or live and be a queen. Your choice, Mary Theresa Wakeman."

No choice at all. "I liked the way you kissed me," she said, or mumbled, pressed against his shoulder. "I wish—"

"I know," he said. He smoothed her hair over the doublet's velvet shoulders. Max climbed up Christian's knee and head-butted Lily, rumbling worry and affection. "It's a good wish, love. It can still come true."

In the musty hallway of Peese's apartment, Don paused at the top of the stair and turned to regard the raven. "I'm not so sure this is a great idea."

It blinked one black eye shiny as a sequin and cocked its head. The irony transmitted without words, and Don gasped and shoved his vest down. It was pinching his armpits. "I know, I know," he said. "I should wear the damned thing looser, but then my backup gun slips down and pinches my fat."

Another voice interrupted. "Now I've seen everything. You're talking to pigeons. And another thing. If you lost a few pounds you'd fix those problems and you wouldn't huff like a fire truck climbing my stairs."

"It's a crow," Don said, ignoring the hairy eyeball the raven shot him. "And I'm in better shape than you are, Ernie. You could have told me you were working for an angel."

"You could have told me you were working for a sorcerer."

"I wasn't until this week."

They stared at each other, Don shifting restlessly from one foot to the other, Ernie leaning on the rail at the far end of the stairwell. "Look, Don. I don't gotta like it."

"Don't gotta like what?"

"Michael." He blinked and pulled his arms off the rail. "Shit, you didn't know. I figured that you were here because . . . Christ, I'm such a bonehead."

"No, I just came by because a little bird told me." Don jerked his head at the raven, which clutched the banister and beat uneven wings. "And you just told me something else."

"I didn't tell you nothing."

"No. Just enough. Is it too early for a beer, Ernie?"

He scratched his elbow and shuffled away from the rail. He was wearing creased trousers that looked like yesterday's, and fuzzy monster slippers. "Not if you ain't been to bed."

Kit woke in his own skin, to find Morgan leaning over him, the morning flashing hammered highlights from her hair. "I'll tell you for free who's got the power to do what you need."

He touched her cheek. "Who?"

"Lily Wakeman. And I'll tell you how to find her."

"If?"

"If you bring her back to me when you've convinced her, and taught

her the binding. It's been long since I taught someone. And she'll be a
witch, that one. She's three times Matthew. Twice Elaine."

He swallowed. He'd shaved for the disguise, and her breath felt soft
on naked skin. "Tell me how to find her."

"*Kit.*" Disappointment, or mere mockery? "She's wearing your
clothes."

Lily didn't like dying. It hurt, and Max wouldn't stop pestering. She
couldn't stop heaving and she was cold, so damned cold, and Christian's
warmth didn't penetrate her skin, did nothing to ease the shakes. She
would have begged, if she thought it would have done any good. She
had no pride.

Something was shaking. The old house. Someone climbing the
stairs—*running* up the stairs—but Christian lifted her off the floor and
swept Max away carefully with the side of his shoe. "Psst, kitty," he
said, pulling Lily against his chest.

She squirmed. She didn't want to go with him. She wanted to call her
doctor. She pushed at his chest, her bracelet pinching her wrist, the
medallion banging the side of her nose. *"No!"*

He turned, cradling her, as the door banged open and rebounded off
the wall with an unresonant crack. Max bolted under the fainting
couch. The doorway framed Marlowe, a too-big shirt stuffed hastily
into black trousers, his bare feet balanced in a swordsman's pose and an
extended rapier bisecting his face.

He smiled, and blew a lock of hair out of his eyes. "Unhand the lady,
Christian."

Christian shifted Lily's weight in his arms, her fluttering breaths loud
in the dusty room. Sun seeped in fingerling rays through the curtains,
haloing Christian and flashing in Kit's eyes. Kit squinted and slipped a
half step aside. The sun could also dazzle off his blade. It might be an
advantage.

"Back licking the Morningstar's boots, I see. She's mine or she's
dead."

"We'll see." Kit advanced, shuffle and stomp, his weight behind the
line of his rapier. "This isn't a pistol. A hostage won't save you."

Christian snorted. "A rapier won't hurt me."

"I dueled Lucifer once. And I won."

"*Those* 'swords' don't count, warlock—"

"Hah!" Kit, shouting, lunged. A little banter, a little distraction. He *couldn't* hurt Christian. But perhaps he could get him to let go of his prize. He'd deal with whatever the Devil had *done* to her after.

But Christian stepped back and aside as smooth as a dancer, dodging Kit's feint. Lily whined against his neck as he hitched her up. He'd sling her over his shoulder if need be. "Much as I hate to cut this short . . ." he said, and allowed himself to fade.

He was taking her somewhere. And Lily did not want to go. She didn't like dying, and she liked this even less, being swung around like an overstuffed duffel bag. She pushed, but her hand was shaking, her elbow and shoulder ached. Her fingers slipped on Christian's denim jacket, and the bracelet banged. "Ow."

She couldn't focus through the pain in her head, the ringing in her ears. Her vision blurred, her skin chill and wet.

The enamel caduceus on her wrist burned like a cherry-red brand against the anodized disk. Caduceus. *Kerykeion.* Tiresias. Tiresias' staff, bound by copulating snakes. Symbol of Hermes. *Mercury, Hermes, Trismegistus, Thoth.*

Good Goth girls knew these things. Good comparative religion grad students knew them too.

Mary Lily Theresa. Think.

Tiresias, who was transformed into a woman when he separated two copulating snakes with his staff. Who was blinded by Hera, or perhaps Athena, and gifted with prophecy by Zeus—or, perhaps, Athena. Hermes, the god of healing. The god of messages. The god of between-things, transmutation. Magic.

A handmade bracelet. A life-saving insignia.

A gift from an angel.

Lily pressed her lips against the anodized design, blurring it with her lipstick, and whispered, "Michael, please."

The room faded and Kit dove toward her, dropping his rapier to clutch Lily's collar and hair. Darkness flashed. Stuttered. Failed. And dissolved into choirs of glorious light for endless moments, before that too faded, having dazzled.

*   *   *

When the light dimmed, Kit found himself kneeling in a sere, wintry meadow at the edge of an iron-black tarn. Lily's fever-papery skin clung, fragile, against his fingers when he rolled her over and pulled her into his arms. Her lips swelled, branded deep with the coiled outline of two snakes. It seemed like the least of her problems.

He glanced over his shoulder, left and right. No sign of Michael. No sign of Christian, more to the point. Kit tossed his hair off his forehead. His hands were busy with the girl as he spoke to the absent devil. "It was a fireplace poker. *Coxcomb.*"

There must be something Morgan can do. Kit lifted Lily as gently as he could, his knees aching under the weight. He strained up, staggered, caught himself and cuddled her to his chest. She wasn't light for her size, and whatever strength she'd used to cry Michael's name had been her last. She was limp as a corpse in Kit's embrace, her eyes dully wet behind slitted lids, and the only assurance he had that she lived was the racing pattern of her breath and the heat soaking from her skin.

The lake would serve for a mirror. The bank was turfed and didn't look too bad. He stumbled toward it, balanced as best he could, sliding on the wet grass. Mumbling a little prayer of thanks, because it never hurt. And it kept him from chanting *Surely Morgan can help* over and over like a damned rosary.

The shape that rose from the water was as black as the water, and sparkled in the sun. Its vast eyes whirled with opal colors in the crushed velvet of its face, and the great scale-sequined claws *sucked* in the wet earth of the shore, releasing the cold, rotten reek of waterlogged mud.

Kit paused.

Morgan said he wasn't strong enough. Morgan was probably right. The world was full of better Magi, stronger warlocks, cleverer sorcerers. He was a dabbler. A dilettante. Northampton had said as much, whilst Sir Walter laughed.

There was nothing else he could do. "Garndukgu-Wurrpbu," he said, in his clearest, most carrying voice. "Let us pass."

Bunyip grinned through a mouthful of swords and daggers. "As you wish," the monster said, and with a negligent wave transformed them both into black swans.

Matthew wasn't young enough—or fool enough—to call this love. But that didn't ease the wistfulness that ran sweet fingers up his neck as he watched Fionnghuala, wrapped in a knotted towel, sit on the edge of his bed and comb her wet hair. His skin still tingled with remembered pain, and his own turn in the shower had presented him with an alien body, nude and vulnerable, marked with strange, golden lines across his torso and arms, white and bare elsewhere.

"The duel's tonight," he said, to fill the silence. "I need to find Kit. Since I abandoned him to chase a unicorn."

"We'll go together." She laid his comb on the bedcovers. "Get dressed. You'll want your coat. It's supposed to snow."

"In Faerie?"

"In New York."

He laid out the red coat—because it would annoy Felix—and a white button shirt, and then stared at them for thirty seconds before returning to the closet, knowing what he was looking for but not quite where to find it. The steamer trunk under a pile of old shoes seemed likely, though, and he pulled it into the light to go through it.

The jeans he wanted were on top of the pile. Vintage, soft denim worn thin, embroidered with dragons on the side seams, boot cut rather than the bell-bottoms the garish decorations would suggest. They'd been a gift from Jane sometime in the mid-1990s. That would mean something too: the dragons, and the gift, and the acknowledgement of Jane.

He lifted them out, and found something else underneath. Another pair of jeans, torn, bloodstained, mud-stained.

He'd forgotten to empty the pockets. He shoved his hand into the left-hand one and found something that rattled like a handful of change. Once upon a time, he thought, when coins were silver, they really would have jingled, and not *clanked*. He contemplated the cliché for a moment, and pulled a handful of base metal out of the pocket.

It wasn't coins. It was twenty-one cold iron rings, seven times three: ten for fingers, eleven for ears.

Another chain disguised as armor. "How many ways did she have me bound?" he asked, without looking over his shoulder.

Warm, horny-callused hands touched his neck, and small knees pressed against his back as Nuala bent over him, her hair dropping forward. "You'll be finding out for years. Every so often you'll turn a corner, and there it'll be. Another chain you didn't know about." She clamped her fist in his hair and pulled his head back, staring upside down into his eyes. " 'Twas I who killed your brother."

He reached up and pressed the back of his bad hand to her cheek. "You did what I should have done. What he wanted. What was merciful. And you didn't do it for Jane, did you?"

"Jane thinks she controls many things she may not." Fionnghuala kissed Matthew's mouth and stepped away. "What will you do with the rings?"

"Keep them." He stood with the dragon-embroidered jeans in his hand. "They may come in handy, someday. I wish I could fight her myself—"

"Another thing you could blame me for."

"I could." He threw the rings on the bed, and started struggling into the jeans. The zipper was a pain in the ass. The flap was on the left, and his right hand wasn't strong enough to keep a grip on the tab. He managed, though, and stuffed the rings into his pocket and reached for the shirt before he finished speaking. "But I won't. There's other things I can do."

"Matthew—"

"Lady," he said, tucking in the shirttails, "let alone."

She bit her lip, and picked up the comb. "Let me fix your hair. A favor from a lady."

So he sat on the edge of the bed, and it was done.

He looked strangely gallant when he shrugged the coat on and stomped into steel-toed boots, and hid his right hand in a leather glove. Strangely gallant, and strangely whimsical, a pony-tailed patchwork sorcerer with his steel-rimmed glasses glinting clemency from the bridge of his nose. "Would you like to borrow a shirt?"

"Thanks," she said. "I have my cloak." She flipped it around her shoulders, drawing the velvet against her skin. "I've clothes in Faerie."

He didn't smile, but held out his hand.

Through the mirror in the bathroom, now that Kit had showed him the trick of it, they stepped into Faerie.

"Something's wrong," Fionnghuala said, before their feet were even firmly on the stones. Matthew nodded. He could smell it on the air, tension and blood, a crackling fury that shivered the palace foundations.

"Go get your dress. I'll meet you wherever Elaine is."

"Can you find your way?"

He touched her nose with a fingertip. "I can find a page."

Foxglove found him first, actually, as he raced down a spiral stair. The ground floor seemed a logical place to commence his search, but he was grateful to the voice that piped, "Matthew Magus, this way!" and the spindly figure in livery that presented itself.

"Fionnghuala is with me," he told the page as they hurried to the throne room at a pace only a few scraps of decorum shy of a run, Matthew's boots thudding and his coattails sailing behind him, chains and charms jingling with every stride—until he drew up in front of the throne room doors. "Oh, my."

The marble floor was shattered before each door, scraps of dented silver that had once been armor scattered this way and that. The doors themselves were scarred, delicate spiral and triskelion carvings chipped and broken, as if something had slammed into each one. They stood open, and the throne room was even halfway crowded, beyond.

Elves and fairies, gnomes and sprites, Tuatha de Danaan tall and fair and creatures without a trace of human shape—or even bilateral symmetry— thronged beyond, clumping and chattering and making small, desultory gestures of grief and disbelief that he knew all too well.

The throne on its dais stood empty at the other end of that mob, and he would wager the people he needed to see were by it.

"Thank you," he said to Foxglove, but the page was gone.

Morgan's shoulders, her hair, her height and her unmistakable carriage caught his eye as she moved through the crowd, speaking to one, touching another, gentling and moving on. Some shook their heads—some horned, some leafed in green, some hung with black and rose and silver pearls—at her words. Some nodded hesitantly. Some murmured a quip with twisted mouths. But all stood a little straighter when she had passed.

Matthew squared his shoulders, braced himself, and hurried to catch up to her. She spoke before he said her name. "I hope for your sake that was Master Marlowe's plan."

"I hope for my sake that you haven't killed him and buried the body at a crossroads."

"I gave him the name." She lifted a hand adorned with a silver ring and pressed the fingertip into the notch of his collarbone, stroking the bare skin there. "And I see I've missed my chance to collect on your gratitude for my munificence."

"Does it show?"

"It might be written on your face with a pen." She tossed her hair behind her shoulder. Not a coquette's gesture, but a queen's. "Have you left your fear on the bedsheets with it?"

"It was easier before I met Geoff." A nauseous admission. "If I had walked away from Kelly and Jane twenty years ago—"

"Matthew."

Her voice stopped him. He pulled his gaze from the toes of his boots and looked at her.

"Which one of you is dead?"

"Me or Kelly?"

"You or Geoff."

He stepped back and shuddered. "Thank you for throwing that in my face, Morgan."

"My point is merely that you might not be so quick to grasp after his choices. If you thought things end to end."

"Touché," he said, with a tip of his imaginary hat.

The witch clucked her tongue. "Were we fencing?"

He stared at her for seconds before he shook it off, and waved around the room. "What happened here?"

"Matthew," Fionnghuala interrupted, appearing at his shoulder in a sweep of red velvet and airy feathers over a plain green gown, "Wolvesbane says Kit's not in the palace, and hasn't been since he left it with you."

That would be true and accurate; the pages always knew.

Morgan coughed. "He went to fetch Lily from the Devil."

Matthew turned on instinct, brows arching behind his glasses, and met Nuala's frown as she looked too, and said, "I'll go."

"*I'll—*"

"*You'll* stay here. Because if Kit's in trouble, you can't fight it. And when was the last time you slept?"

He opened his mouth and closed it. The murmurs of the jostling crowd around them gave them a kind of privacy, combined with the space the Fae accorded to both Morgan and to the iron on Matthew's coat. He glanced to Morgan, reflexively, for support, and found her grinning at Fionnghuala. Morgan shook her head and held out an even older spare pair of glasses: the ones he'd loaned to Kit. "By the way. I understand these are yours."

They warmed his hand. He slipped them into his breast pocket. He turned, casting over the crowd. "Has anyone seen Jewels? She might know how to find Lily."

"She's over there."

"Matthew?"

He concentrated on the back of Jewels' head, feeling the power running clean and unfettered through him in ways it hadn't . . . ever, he realized. As if Fionnghuala had broken down a dam with ringing hammer-blows when she peeled the iron cage off of his skin. The shiver left him light-headed, dry-mouthed.

He put his hand on Fionnghuala's shoulder as soon as he got the shaking stopped. "Go," he said. "Get Kit. Bring him to Rossville if you find him. Morgan, where's Carel?"

"That would be the other problem." She told them quickly about Nuckelavee and the message from Àine, and that the Queen and

Whiskey and the Merlin had gone to deal with it. "And there's no sign of Kadiska, either."

"The timing on this was not an accident."

"No. I don't believe it was. You know Ian's supposed to fight Michael tonight, as well?"

"Fuck, nobody tells me anything—"

"Going," Fionnghuala said, and melted into the crowd—just as Jewels responded to the pressure of Matthew's stare, looked up, caught sight of them, and winced. She didn't pull back, though, when Matthew crooked his finger at her. She shook herself together, tucked her hair behind her ears with a nervous flinch, and closed the distance with crab-quick steps that took her around the knots of conversation between.

"Matthew, I—"

"You need to choose," he interrupted. "Pick a side. Right now."

"What do you mean?"

"You took service with Ian. Did you mean it?"

Her tongue eased dry lips. She nodded.

"Then I won't tell him about you making deals with Christian. Unless you give me another reason to."

Her eyebrows drew together, and she folded her arms over her chest. "What have I got that's worth blackmailing me?"

He hadn't even thought of it. And from Morgan's reaction, it was plain on his face. The truth was probably the most dismissive thing he could have said to Jewels, and he considered it for thirty seconds before he said it anyway, because it *was* true. "I did dumber things when I was your age, kid. And I've lived with them. So I guess you ought to get the chance to live with your dumb ass too."

She rocked with it, took it like a blow, but she didn't snap back at him the way he would have at that age, and she didn't look down. Matthew gave her a break, and turned his own attention to Morgan. "If something's happened to Kit, then Jane's my problem tonight."

She grabbed his wrist. "You can't *fight*, you idiot."

"I know." He shook her hand off, gently, and peeled down his glove. "It's a pisser, isn't it? Can you ask Don for me, if he'll stand my second? He went back to New York."

"Wait." Jewels, her face very hard in the light through the crazed windowpanes. "I can help."

Her knives were in Boston, but Morgan brought her what she needed, and a small, quiet room wasn't hard to find with the entire castle assembled in the throne room, clucking and ruffling about the smashed doors. The one Jewels was given was about ten feet square, now stripped of whatever furnishings it had previously contained. The naked floor was tiled with black portoro marble shaded with saffron and ochre veins, the surface so polished that reflection gave it the illusion of depth. The air was cooled by tall windows and brightened by sun and candelabras, with four dozen beeswax tapers giving forth golden light and a honeyed scent in the crystal chandelier.

Reflected in the center of the mirror-bright marble stood a single armless silver chair, fluted and filigreed and seemingly fragile as an eggshell. Matthew regarded it impassively. "You can't give me a weapon."

Jewels shook her head. She dropped down by the door, beside her tray of implements, and unlaced her shoes with bird-deft hands. "I can give you a shield."

She stood and kicked her feet bare while Matthew closed the door. Morgan would have come with them, but Matthew—surprising Jewels—had demurred. "Thank you," he'd said. "We'll do this alone."

He folded his shirt and coat onto the tile, piled his jeans on top, and weighted them with his boots before seating himself straddling the back of the chair.

"Nice boxers."

"Fuck you." He turned to grin at her, hollowing the muscle in his shoulder, tautening the line of his neck. He tapped the back of the chair with his bad hand. "If I start raving, go and kill the first wicked queen you run across."

"Sorry?"

"Forget it. I'll send you some books when I go home."

"I'll drop you an e-mail. So what do you want?"

He pulled at a rung of the chairback, thinking. He'd thought she would have something in mind. "Fortitude," he said, on the theory that the snap decision is usually the best one.

He'd also expected her to answer snidely. *Well, I don't have any idea how to draw that.* But she *hmm*ed and stroked his back lightly with something stinging cold. Alcohol. The air peeled it off his skin and left a reeking chill behind. "The lion?"

"Yes."

"You're sure? You'll wear it the rest of your life."

The more he thought, the more it pleased him. If anything meant home and strength and heart and culture more to him than the New York Public Library lions, he couldn't have named it. "I'm sure."

"Should I leave room for Patience later? If you want him?"

The chair was cold, edgy against his thighs. He hadn't expected kindness, either. "Sure, Jewels. That'd be nice."

Her hands left his shoulders, returned long enough to deliver a reassuring pat, and lifted again. He watched her reflection in the floor as she went to collect the tray. "I didn't expect you'd trust me. After"—*Christian*—"everything."

"It's your way of getting something back for Geoffrey, am I right? And maybe Lily too?"

"Lily and I never got along so great." The tray was lacquer, gold cranes on white. It had little feet that clicked when she set it beside the chair.

"Oh."

"But she tried to warn me about Christian. He killed her for it, didn't he?"

"Honestly?"

"Yeah."

"Honestly, yes." Something firm but not sharp moved over his skin. A felt-tip pen. "Probably. So why, if not for them?"

Her hand stayed steady. It was her breath that caught.

"Jewels?"

"Gypsy," she said. The pen slid smoothly along a sweeping line. "Gypsy told me the truth with a straight face, and he didn't act sorry for me. So I help you, you help Carel, Carel tears the Cat Anna's head off and stuffs it up her ass."

Admiring: "Simple."

"Yeah."

He shut up and let her draw in peace.

Matthew's skin was flexible under Jewels' finger pads, the grain fine for an older man's. She caught herself stroking the tigery streaks where the bars of his tattoos had been, and pressed her fingers against her palm with the heel of her hand.

The lion formed quickly. There was a trick to it: negative space, and a simple, deliberate line. Suggestion rather than detail, the drowsy eyes, the Byronesque curl of the mane. A hint of a knowing smile.

"There." She dropped her Sharpie. "Want to see?"

"You're the professional. I'll trust you this time."

She snorted and picked up a knife.

"Aren't you supposed to reassure me now?"

"Man," she said, "let me reassure you. This is going to hurt like hell."

Heat followed her blade like a line of alizarin crimson following the stroke of a brush. That was all, at first. Heat. No pressure. And then the sizzle of insulted flesh, distinct and meaningful. He closed his eyes, pictured the line as if on a canvas, drew it with his mind. A cheek? A shoulder? The heavy drape of living mane? Flesh made symbol, carved in stone. Stone made symbol, carved in flesh. He hissed. Jewels steadied him.

"Shield," she said. "Good. Again. If you want it to scar pretty, scrub it out every day. It has to granulate, not scab."

"Not the easiest spot to reach."

"What, pretty boy doesn't have somebody to do it for him?" The blade retraced its path. Worse, this time. Scorching over already in-flamed skin like a toothpick across sunburn. Maybe easier if he watched. Her reflection in the floor was gawky dis-grace, bony elbows on walking-stick arms upthrust like she was tossing a salad.

She moved the towel to catch the slight ooze of blood that splayed along his ribs, sticky threads like faux tears drawn on a clown's cheek, rays diverging from an arc.

"Same line?"

"You get a better scar if you pull out a wedge."

Of course you did.

He closed his eyes again as she peeled the wasted skin away. He drew the next arc with her, in his mind, a fraction behind the knife. It hurt no worse than the ink had, and he knew his body's kinks well enough by now not to be shocked when he responded. By the fifth stroke, he sobbed through gritted teeth. By the seventh, the buzz took hold: he floated watching over her shoulder by the time she was done.

She had line like a Chinese calligrapher. It was Fortitude, no mistaking: the weight of his paw, the arch of his brow, the somnolent fearlessness, suggested—*rendered*—in a few dozen lines. "Beautiful," he said, forgetting he wasn't standing behind her.

"How do you know?"

"I know." The ink hadn't been gone a day. *Some of us are not meant to go through life unbranded.*

She bandaged the pattern with clean gauze and something that burned as much as it soothed. She washed the blood off his back before she kissed him on the forehead and left him alone with his pain, to take what rest he might before the war.

Chapter Twenty-seven
John Barleycorn Must Die

Lands that know the sea, know the sea is hunger. Salt water is entropy, the antithesis of space, that great preserver. Water, the universal solvent. Water, the end of all things. Water, the grave of time.

Between Staten Island, New York, and the coast of New Jersey lies a tidal strait called the Arthur Kill, which links Newark and Raritan bays. The Arthur Kill is ten miles long and six hundred feet wide, dredged to forty-one feet. It is the artery through which lifeblood feeds the dragon's greedy heart, in the shape of container vessels vast as unpeopled cities, ships with names like *Sovereign Maersk*, *P&O Nedlloyd Rotterdam*, *Atlantic Compass*. Three bridges bind the Arthur Kill shore to shore: the Bayonne, the Goethals, the Outerbridge Crossing.

It is clotted with dead ships like the dragon's broken dreams, sorrowing hulks deliquescing into a voracious sea. Not one, or two, or a dozen scattered cadavers groove the tidal mud, but an oceanic necropolis of tugs and ferries, of submarine chasers and tramp steamers: proud hulls staved, hatchways yawning open, decks pitched and listing. And the Whitte Brothers Marine Scrap Yard is the elephant's ossuary at its heart.

Matthew stood on the oxidizing deck of *PC-1217*, the wind sliding icy hands under his collar, and watched the sun set behind New Jersey and the massed cold corpses of things that sailed, and sail no more. The snow Fionnghuala had promised drifted down halfheartedly, chill shavings from a leaden sky, but the clouds ended with the city and the narrow band beyond the overcast burned like smelted ore.

The wind was cold enough to sear, but it didn't dull the ache of Matthew's shoulder. "Man," Don said, from the lee of some slanted debris, "wouldn't it be nice if she didn't show?"

"It would answer some questions about where Kit is." Matthew snaked his right arm under his left, taking some of the weight off his shoulder, easing the stretch of the skin. "She'll show. The sun isn't down yet. And Felix wouldn't let her miss it, just in case."

Àine's castle gleamed in the evening light like a jumble of bones weathered white on the strand, the curled tip of a finger extending. Behind the surrounding ocean, the sky shone lustrous pewter. Whiskey stamped to a halt atop the rocky isthmus, his hide steaming gently in the evening chill; he set his hooves abruptly enough that Carel clutched the Queen's waist.

"She's changed it."

"If by *changed* you mean *relocated wholesale*, then yes, she has." The Queen knotted her hands in his crest and drew herself up his neck. High enough to see clearly; not high enough to escape his acrid, horsey sweat. "The sea's to our advantage."

"She has allies of her own."

"And Autumn," Carel added. "And Cairbre."

"I shall not treasure his safety," the Queen answered. Ian had told her enough. "I wish Kadiska were here."

Whiskey snorted, dropping his muzzle toward the stones. "If wishes were horses—"

The Queen kicked him in the ribs; he forbore bucking for Carel's sake. The Queen would have stayed on, anyway. The Queen wasn't much of a warrior, but she could ride.

Long, curling combers broke against the headland and rolled down the sides in a V made ragged by the rocky seabed. Whiskey kicked a round black rock down the slope. He pricked his ears and lifted his head into the wind, letting it tease his mane, and watched the black shapes drifting against the sunset: albatross, pelican, tern. The largest among them detached itself and soared landward above the white towers, where the white silk banners cracked in the stiffening breeze.

The shadow rippled over gold like a fistful of sheer gauze veil. It banked past them, turning to sail into the wind, and shot over Carel's head as the Merlin ducked to one side; it settled on the Queen's shoulder with a flare of membranous wings. They vanished against a slender black body as the tail looped the Queen's throat, and Gharne rubbed his velour cheek against the coarse chop of her hair. "It suits you."

Carel sat back up as the Queen dropped her seat-bones on Whiskey's back. "The whole world rides my back," the Kelpie said, shaking out his mane again.

But he might not have spoken. "Gharne," Carel said. "Have you seen her?"

"In the tower," he answered. "Your lady is not dead yet."

He could not rouse her. She sprawled on grass, one wing folded but the other reaching, flight feathers splayed like a woman's white fingers from the black point of her sleeve. He prodded with his bill, rolled the weight of her head on her ribbon-limp neck. She breathed, at least—but she breathed, and that was all.

At last, he settled in the cold grass beside her and draped his own wing over her body, his chin upon her shoulder, flank to flank as if the echo of his heart could steady her racing one. At least he could keep her warm.

The magic of men is not for swans. They are not poets and they are not witches. They are not Magi. They have living wings; they have no need for metaphorical ones. So he waited by her until the day was failing, until blue evening stole over them and the only sound was the lapping water.

The fading light made him restless. There was somewhere he was meant to be. He and she, together. There had been something they were sent to do.

But it was peaceful here by the water, and there was no way for a swan to carry a swan.

The plop of feet in mud lifted his head. It rose on a curve of neck, bead-shiny eyes blinking. He could bite; he had wings like iron bars. If the monster was returning, he would fight.

But it wasn't. Something white and shining climbed out of the pond, duckweed in her wet mane, water lilies garlanding pale shoulders. She placed tiny hooves in the Bunyip's furrowed footprints, a child trying on a big man's shoes, and stepped onto the bank.

A fragile thing, fine as porcelain . . . until she dropped her steel-horned head and shook like a dog, rolling from the tip of her nose down neck and shoulders and haunches, shedding muddy water and vegetation onto the bank and into the air. She finished with a satisfied shiver, arched a doe-slender neck, and minced one step toward the swans.

Silently, he folded his wings and withdrew.

The unicorn dropped beside the stricken swan, grass bending under her knees, and nosed the extended wing. Seashell nostrils flared in an ash-soft muzzle, riffling the swan's plumage to reveal smoke-colored down. She sighed, and laid the rapier edge of her horn across the bird's broad back so that her beard and mane darkened the shining plumage with water, and shut her eyes.

And maybe the swan's breathing eased, and the hammering of her small heart slowed. For such is the virtue of unicorns.

The male swan watched, and when he heard the other swan sigh and her straggling wing flicked closed, he spread his own feathers wide and bowed to the unicorn. She didn't raise her head, but she winked at him, the droop of silent-screen lashes against a satin cheek.

The sun was just settling its last curve under the edge of the world when he beat an ungainly path into the air.

Black swans fly by night. But he had a long way to go.

Autumn would not drink, but she had washed the blood from her hair and her hands and cursed her mistakes. After Jason and Moira had left, Christian had returned. Returned, and when she'd opened the door to him, he hadn't been alone.

No.

She bit her lips, shook her head violently and swallowed two short sips of air. She wouldn't cry for Gypsy now. She wouldn't worry about the cat.

She'd survive, and she'd deal with it later.

The Devil had left her a basin, a pitcher, a tray with cold frothy milk and sharp-smelling cheese and fruit piled high in a bowl beside a silver knife. A knife sharp as a razor: she tested it before she slipped it up her sleeve and bound it there with a fillet torn from a sheet.

Of course, if they gave her a knife, they did not care if she used it.

The hearth lay cold. The long curtains rippled at the windows. And when she leaned out, her hair falling over her shoulders like Rapunzel's bobbed four stories shy, all she saw was the sky, and the stones, and the long relentless sea. Salt air wore at her throat, wet curls coiling along her temples. The water she'd soaked with was cool and smelled sweet, and the pitcher never ran dry no matter how she poured it. If she could taste, just taste—

—but no.

So she watched the gulls, her back to temptation, and tried not to think of thirst, or Gypsy's blood on her shirt, the spots she couldn't wash out. She was standing there still when the piebald horse appeared and paused at the top of the beach.

From the vantage of her tower, she saw, before he did, the beautiful monster that rose out of the sea. She shouted a warning, but it was ripped from her lips by the wind.

Whiskey heard the sound of hooves before any of his riders, and turned his back to the wind. It cowled his mane between his ears, furled his tail along his flank. He did not bow to those who cantered down the bank in single file, mounted in order upon a black horse, a bay horse, and a red, though their hair glowed gold, and blue-lit black, and red in the half-light, and so he knew their names before he could see their faces or catch their scents with the wind at his back.

He didn't bow, and neither did his Queen. Carel slid down his side, however, to greet them on her own two feet, her boots in solid connection with the flinty ground.

The Morningstar spoke first, granting pride of place to the Queen. :Àine is host of the duel,: he said. :And no. The timing is not a coincidence, Your Majesty.:

"Have you ears everywhere?"

He smiled, his hair writhing in the breeze, under the shadows of his crown. The velvet he wore was as black as his mare, and his wings were folded tight in shadows, barely visible in the gloaming. :I am the very

Devil for it. Will you observe the duel, Elaine? And you, Lady Merlin? As my guests? I'm entitled to a few.:

"Can I forbid it?" The Queen spoke to Ian, who avoided her eyes.

So her attention went to Keith. He smiled and kissed his gauntlet to her. "Fear not, lady. Trust a wolf to know."

"It gets us inside," Carel said.

The Queen frowned. Whiskey shifted under her, restlessly. "It gets us inside," she said. "Very well."

They fell in line with the Devil, behind Ian and before Keith on his blood-bay warhorse, the Queen riding Whiskey and ridden in turn by Gharne. Carel walked at the piebald stallion's off shoulder, her hand on the Queen's knee to guide her as she studied the white towers looming overhead. The causeway was wide enough for a carriage, but they rode it single file.

"I see Autumn," Carel said. "She's pointing—" The Merlin squeezed the Queen's knee, and pointed as well.

"Mistress," Whiskey said, as Bunyip heaved himself from the sea, "light down."

When the sun set, it grew no darker. New York City's head was in the clouds and wreathed in light. It refracted through water vapor, the city-glow a pink translucence that rendered everything soft and plain, even on what should have been the dark waters of the Arthur Kill.

The tide had begun falling, as if in pursuit of the last light of the sun, and the moon—a dying crescent—had set in the afternoon, before the clouds rolled in. The hulk of the submarine chaser rested in mud—the ship was no more seaworthy than a brick—so the water slid down her hull without affecting the pitch of the crumbling deck, and echoed strangely when the wavelets tapped her hull.

PC-1217 was trapped alongside a derelict tug, between two crumbling floating cranes, a possible jump from deck to deck, but she was not their kind. She was born a warrior, a defender of shores and shipping whose career was brought to a close not by a U-boat torpedo, but by the sea and its storms: a September hurricane met off Florida in 1944 had doomed her.

She told Matthew as much, while Don paced her perimeter and

Matthew crouched on her cluttered deck, stuffed his glove in his pocket, and let his fingers stroke her tired skin. An old lady, long forgotten by the suitors of her youth—an old maid now and fading, her armaments stripped, her crew scattered, even her railings salvaged, leaving only the empty sockets—but her gaping hatchways and welded doors recalled what she had been. She told him of high seas and hungry men, of devil boats cutting the dark wave bottoms. She told him of purpose, the percussion of her guns and the wild song of sonar thrumming her, and the deep frustration engendered by the mocking touch of the sea stroking the length of her engineless hull.

She was not made for this. But everything of worth had been stripped from her when she was scrapped. They had not even had the decency to scuttle her. She who had shone in her battleship livery stank now of mildew, rotting metal, guano, the urine of trespassers who would not understand her service or her sacrifice. All she had left was to wait for the mercy of the sea. And in a manner he might not have, not so long ago, Matthew understood, and he wept for her, trapped by her wounds in the harbor that is not what ships are built for.

And then he lifted his hand from her deck—his cheeks freezing with moisture, damp flakes of paint clinging to his fingerprints—and raised his head. Through the pastel light and the drifting snow, he heard the purr of an outboard motor.

The last light of the sun stained the underbelly of those western clouds. Jane, damn her to Hell, was right on time. And equipped with a rope ladder, apparently, because a moment later, the thump of the motorboat brushing the derelict's hull was echoed by the thump of grapples striking her deck and then the creak of cables taking weight, and Felix hauled himself over the submarine chaser's stern and turned to offer Jane a hand.

She joined him gracefully, as if her years were no more than a decoration. Her eyes widened in the rose-colored glow, as she looked from Matthew to Don and back again.

Matthew shrugged cold shoulders in his coat. A mistake; he felt scabs crack. "Remember when I said I'd follow you to the ends of the earth, Jane? Well, here we are—"

She glanced succinctly at Felix before turning back. "Where's Christopher?"

"I was hoping you'd know."

"Oh," she said, her bracelet glittering black, sliding the length of her forearm as she pressed at her mouth. "Shit."

"Mmm." He should be worried that it wasn't Jane behind Kit's disappearance. He shouldn't allow himself this sharp surge of vindication at her shock. "So. How does it feel when *your* allies turn on you?"

She looked down before she moved forward, studying the footing. Debris cluttered the old ship's deck. *PT-1217* was 173 feet in length; Matthew had room to step back, if he needed it.

But he was not yet ready to give Jane any ground.

"Why think my allies had anything to do with it? Why not your man's own cowardice?"

"I think your allies because I think *you* would follow the forms, Jane. To the letter."

She smiled. "I always do. So it's you and me, then?"

"Yes." He turned to make sure Don was ready. "So it's you and me."

"Good." Despite the cold, she shrugged off her coat and handed it to Felix. Matthew hung on to his own. She wore painter's pants, laced boots, a man's white shirt that hung like a smock even tucked in and with the sleeves rolled up. It had been her husband's. Jane, like Matthew, had chosen symbols all her own. "Let me know when you're ready to yield, then. Are you ready, Matthew Magus?"

"Yes," he said. "I'm ready."

"Good. Let us begin."

The causeway leading to Àine's castle had been cut by a channel deep enough to give horses pause at high tide. There was a bridge, a horrible rickety thing that looked deserving of an underfed troll. And the bridge was guarded by the Bunyip.

"The duelist," Lucifer said, indicating Ian. "His second. His patron, and family guests. We are invited."

"I have business with the Kelpie," Bunyip answered, conical neck swelling with his voice. "The rest may pass."

The Queen had rested her hand on Whiskey's shoulder after dismounting. It remained there, warm on warm hide, sleek hairs scratching her palm. "You speak of my servant," she said, and stroked his withers absently.

"Will you stand his champion then?"

"Mistress," Whiskey said, arching his neck like a drawn shortbow, "this is mine."

She knew the tone. It wasn't all that foreign a visitor in her own voice. She knotted fingers in the root of his mane and tugged, hard enough to flex the meaty crest of his neck back and forth over the bone. "See to it, then," she answered, bored and bland, and scratched him with her nails as she took her hand away. She joined Lucifer, leaving Whiskey behind. Bunyip's eyes were half the size of her head, vast fires glaring through black glass. "Let us pass." Gharne, who had been still as a silk stole around her shoulders, lifted his poison-arrow head and smiled.

Bunyip stepped aside, and the Queen stepped with him, eye to eye. The others filed across, three horsemen and Carel on foot, and the Queen did not turn away until their feet were dry on the far side of the narrow bridge. And then she walked past Bunyip, leaving Whiskey alone, and behind.

She paused over the water, before her feet left the wooden bridge, and spoke without turning. "Whiskey."

"Mistress?"

He couldn't see her smile as she started walking again. "Come and find me when you're done."

Four hundred years Prometheus labored to lay magic in chains, protect the fragile cult of science, nurture its programs and its principles. Their age of power bound the earth and sea in girdling chains, tamed magic into technology, brought Faerie and all its wilderness to heel.

Their own great work crippled them. The wild unkind magic could not be captured without limiting the Promethean magic too; every link of a chain that binds is also bound. The elevation of technology, the transmutation of medieval alchemy into the ascendance of the age of reason, the creation of what was to have been a truly human millennium accomplished what the Fae could not, and bound the Promethean magic as well.

When the Dragon shattered her chains and Faerie took back its place, science—the arts of technology—was too firmly rooted to be much perturbed. But the Promethean powers remained channeled, a river turning a shattered waterwheel.

Matthew, facing Jane, rubbed his hands together. The right one prickled pins and needles; the left felt raw across the knuckles, where the cold nibbled his skin.

"You've lost your shield," Jane said. She stepped left, a fencer's sweep of foot and change of balance. Matthew echoed the gesture, orbiting their common center.

Matthew adjusted his glasses. They misted in the chill and damp. "If that's what you want to call it." He stepped this time, and she echoed. His boots crunched strange objects, scuffed aside a rotting square of drywall. "Does it worry you not to have control over me?"

One more step brought Don into his peripheral vision. Don leaned forward, waiting, straining like a greyhound in the gate.

"When did it ever?" Jane answered. But there was a flash, an edge of bitterness. He'd gotten a nail under her skin.

She *had* controlled him. Down to the breath he drew. He'd thanked her for it, and it hadn't been enough for her. Fair enough. He had, after all, defied her in the end.

Her tests glided over his boundaries like a seeking hand. Charisma like a furnace, backed by Magecraft, urging him to lower his barriers, accept her again. It would be easy. She'd help, advise, protect—

Now his back was to the stern. Treacherous. If he didn't turn and look he could slip off the deck, flail into the Arthur Kill and strike deep through the falling tide. He'd break both legs when he hit, and the mud of the tidal flats would bind him until he drowned—immediately, or with the strait's return.

He laughed. Distract with the expected suggestion, then feint for a presumed fear. She could do better, even if that was an attack he couldn't match. Influence, persuasion, those were within his powers, if he didn't intend to *hurt* her. When he even thought of a straight assault, though, he felt his magic gutter. "You should have stuck with Felix."

"You know, I think you're correct?" She looked at Matthew when she said it, though. "He wants the right things."

They had come three-quarters of the way around the circle now. Matthew paused, scuffling his boots against the deck. The sub chaser yearned after him, all 173 feet of her shivering as the sea drained from her hull. The tide was falling faster now, and she told Matthew about it, giving him the knowledge through the rubber of his soles, the bones of his ears. She had slept long and deeply, while the world grew strange around her and her bones weakened from too much rest. He had awakened her with a kiss.

He petted her deck with the sole of his boot.

Jane struck: a straight-out blow he thought was a feint, a wedge of fury with all her weight behind it. Unsubtle, and he batted it aside without effort, felt it splash and scatter around the shield that was Fortitude. Now, when she was extended, would have been the time to hit her.

If he could. He reached for her, but couldn't make it a blow. He twisted it, though, and caught her eye, and reached in with a tickle of trust and old friendship. Her expression softened as he said, "That wasn't your best effort."

"Lucky for me."

"Improves your chances." Said with a lighthearted shrug, as if they sparred in practice.

He felt her agreement, pleasant surprise at his tractability. Yes, this was how it should be. One of them should suggest, the other respond. It wasn't about Felix. It wasn't about the war. It was about Jane and Matthew, who had been friends, who could be friends again if Jane would just agree to see things his way, to compromise.

She laughed, and clapped her hands. And just as he was drawing a relieved breath, the submarine chaser groaned apology. Prompted by the Magery that Jane had worked while Matthew was preoccupied with his own seduction, the ship's brittle deck unraveled under Matthew's feet, and he broke through.

Carel Bierce, Merlin the Magician, walked into the palace of the Cat Anna sheltered under devil's wings, the Winter Queen on her right hand, the Dragon Prince on her left, a Prince of the Daoine Sidhe at her back. They came under an archway that stood open, inviting all within. The tunnel beyond was portcullised and roofed in murder-holes, oil stains alien against the white translucent stone. Carel spared them not a glance as she walked under, her power around her like a dragon's fire, and paused at the courtyard gate.

She and her companions found an angel waiting.

Michael sat alone in a pearl-cobbled courtyard that was walled only on three sides, polishing her sword upon a stone. The whetstone was a rough gray thing, a haggled bit of pumice, and it scattered bits across her jeans and the ankle of the boot she had propped on her knee, the flat of the blade braced against the arch. To her left rose the sweep of a grand stone stair. To her back, the walls of the palace flared wide, cast open like arms embracing the sea. They were built right out into the water, so the tidemarks stained white stone, and they marched in serried descent some hundreds of feet out to sea. Torches burned in profusion along the battlements, lighting the sea and the waves below, and under the dark waves more lights shimmered, green and amber and blue, a hint of windows open on the deep.

Michael looked up when the Merlin strode through the castle gate, but crushed her whetstone in her left hand when Lucifer rode into sight. She stood and bowed, a frown narrowing her face. She kept her focus on Ian, though, as he swung a leg over the bay and slid down her side, and not on the Devil at all.

Lucifer dismounted without fanfare, half a beat before Keith, and took both Ian's and the Dragon Prince's reins. He led the horses to the highest corner of the courtyard and busied himself looping their reins through the iron rings of a hitching post that hadn't been there before.

Iron rings in a Fae Queen's castle; Lucifer had not tempered his arrogance.

"If I'd known you were coming," Michael called, sheathing the sword across her back, "I would have brought the family."

The sounds of the sea echoed within the sheltering walls, and waves mellowed by the palace walls lapped a crystal-pale, sandy beach that sloped up to the cobbled court. The echoes drowned sounds beyond the whimper of the surf, but Keith and Ian shared a glance over something they heard that no one else seemed to, and Ian nodded slightly. Faintly, over the breakers, he'd heard a stallion's cry of rage.

Lucifer stared past Michael at the glow-speckled sea.

:What need I more, when my favorite brother attends?: He turned, and gave Michael the smile that Michael would not answer. :I come as a guest. Here are your challengers. Where is our hostess?:

As if she had been waiting for her cue, the double doors at the top of the stair opened wide, and Àine, clad all in green with her dark hair swept up on her head, said, "Here."

As one, they turned: Michael and Keith and the Morningstar, Ian and the Queen and Carel. Carel most of all drew the eye, stern and impassive, broad at the shoulders, and her head proud on her elegant neck. She didn't fold *her* arms; her hands hung naturally at her sides, and her braids spread over her shoulders like the veil on an empress' crown. But she had weight, and the torch's shine bent around her. Every shadow stretched away, flickering and black, as if she glowed with an ember's heat, and the hands that hung by her sides were veiled in a gauze of sparks so dark they were almost violet.

"You have something of mine," she said, in a voice that belonged less to the woman, and more to the half-seen, batwinged vastness hanging over her.

And Àine smiled. "So I do. And I'm willing to bargain for its return."

She descended, shimmering with teal and lime and emerald sequins, the robe beneath rich greeny-gold as olive oil. The Nuckelavee came behind her, its rotten head rolling on its shoulders as it headed a procession of lesser monsters, redcaps and Leannan Sidhe and the flesh-craving courtiers of the Bone Court. Carel clenched her hands.

"After the entertainment," Àine said.

The brush of the Queen's fingers on her elbow brought Carel back. Carel turned, so slightly, and looked in Elaine's changeable eyes. *Cold*, they told her, and Carel took a breath and gentled the Dragon within. Cold as Fae. There wasn't a thing she could do for Gypsy. And Autumn was still alive.

"By all means," Carel said, as Keith and Ian silently came up beside her and the Queen. "Let me be entertained."

Carel didn't see it, but the Queen did: the tilt of the Morningstar's head, the quick purse of lips, an eyebrow arched. :By all means,: he echoed, :let us *all* be entertained.:

Àine paused, and gave him a curtsey with a mocking twist of her heel and no more than the flick of her wrists raising her hem. He answered with a bow that swept one hand to his heart, one wingtip across the nacreous cobbles and over the sand to point at the rim of the sea, a hard silhouette against the radiance that heralded a not-yet-rising moon. "We all dance, when devils call the tune," she said, showing him the fangs indenting her berry-ripe lip.

The folds of her cotehardie slipped from her fingers and puddled by her feet. Her hands rose and summoned into being two galleries of boxes and two stands of bleachers along either wall of the palace, bright with banners. On the right side, the cerulean and silver of Heaven. On the left side, the *gules simple* of Hell, and under it, Keith MacNeill's red wolf on snow, reversed with the crimson dragon. Over them all flew the white banners of the Bone Court, the Unseelie Fae.

"No," the Queen said, with a quick glance at Ian. His head down, his hands folded, his flank to Carel, he seemed all but oblivious. "Pull those down. If my son fights, my son fights under the Daoine banner."

"I'm sorry," Carel said. She reached out and brushed the Queen's elbow as the Queen had hers, but she looked past the Queen, to the Dragon Prince. As if Keith felt it, he turned, and frowned at her across the Queen.

"Sorry?"

Carel smiled the Dragon's toothy smile, tears stinging her sinuses as the shadow embraced her. She let go of the Queen's arm, allowed her hand to be slid into her sleeve, found warm curved wood and a knob of bronze and silver. "Your son doesn't fight," she said, and plunged the blade into Ian's back, below the ribs, beside the spine.

Chapter Twenty-eight
Whiskey, You're the Devil

Matthew fell.

He reached reflexively and caught at the edges of the gap. The left hand gripped; the right hand struck flaking steel and bounced away. Rust cut his palm, purchase crumbling, metal like stretched cloth under his fingers. He caught himself, one-handed, and swung, the red coat bellying about him.

The ship herself tore under his hand and he went down into darkness, magically unsnagged by ragged metal. Maybe the coat protected him from cutting edges; he vanished like a magician through a trapdoor, out of the city-lit night and onto the deck below, where he struck unevenly and rolled.

The pop when his right knee buckled was loud enough to echo in the confined space into which he'd fallen. Pain followed, twist and shred, new injuries reawakening old.

He rolled onto his back, panting, waiting for a shadow to cross the peach-colored sky behind the irregular hole in the decking. Footsteps echoed more than the lapping water; he couldn't tell where they were coming from. The decking was oxidized slime, soaking through to his skin. He rolled over and tried to stand without allowing time to think.

The back *could* be made to support him; the knee gave way with an appalling short circuit of pain. He'd torn the anterior cruciate ligament. He wouldn't walk on it tonight.

It was too dark to hop. He'd have to crawl. Not that he had any idea where he was crawling to, or if the ship's ladders were still in place. He might find a hatch and discover that the only ascent was via more empty sockets and unscrewed fasteners.

His fall had damaged the sub chaser's delicate equilibrium. The hulk groaned under him, settling, half-liquid mud and seawater gurgling in her rocking hull. She stank like a tide pool, salt and trapped rot, the rusted metal gritting into his palms and sliming the knees of his dragon-embroidered jeans. He had to crawl with his right leg pointed out behind him, the unsound decking scarring the backs of fingers he couldn't feel. He might wear down to the bone. He'd never know.

The hatch in the middle of the foredeck was open. The hatch cover had been torn off, and it or possibly some other piece of debris lay across the opening kitty-corner, but anyway, Matthew could see an irregular patch of light. He slowed his breathing—he could hear it echo—and listened to the ship, to the night. *Where?* he asked her, and felt her wriggle at the attention, like a puppy daring to hope it might be forgiven so soon. He couldn't do Jane's trick with the floorboards—not *wouldn't*: it was as impossible a task as if he tried to reach out with his third hand and pick up an apple. The potential for violence simply was not there—but the cold iron rings jingled against his thigh with every painful, stiff-legged inch he dragged himself, and that brought an idea of what he might do instead.

The light dimmed, what little there was. It hadn't been helping him avoid the peeled seams and popped rivets slicing his palms. He'd need a tetanus shot. He corrected: presuming he *lived*, he'd need a tetanus shot.

"Matthew?"

A tentative voice. Jane's, not Felix's, as she leaned over the hole she'd punched under his feet. Then she wasn't ready to declare the duel done. Not that he would have let her.

The echoes could help as well as hinder him. He'd been listening to them. He turned his head, pitched his voice into a nice bouncy corner, and called up, "Do you yield?"

Her laugh jostled drips into his hair. "Do you?"

A knee-knocker divided the corridor between him and the sharp patch of brightness overhead, the sort of thing you'd step over almost without thinking. His reaching hands found it and he bit his lip so as not to sob.

"I'm just getting started."

Elbows up on the lip of the knee-knocker. His coat had fallen closed across his chest. He slithered over like a crocodile slipping off the bank into a storm, just as muddy and on just as unforgiving a night.

"Are you too stubborn to yield, Matthew? It wouldn't go badly for you."

"Jane," he said, as his fingers closed over the cold, blessed bar of the ladder that he'd been praying for, "you're going to have to kill me."

That won him a longer pause. He wondered how many languages she was counting to ten in. "Hell of a thing to say in front of a cop," she answered, when she had her voice arranged.

"I mean it."

"I'm sure you think so." So smug. He imagined how her lips would curve if she thought no one was looking. "You were the most talented apprentice I ever taught. The strongest Mage. It doesn't have to be over yet."

"It's been over for years. And anyway, talent's not everything." She was still circling the gap where he'd fallen through. He clung to rusted steel with one and a half hands and one useful leg and—whispering *Lie for me* to the submarine chaser—he began to climb.

Carel caught Ian as he slumped. Strained cloth in his doublet popped threads; she dug her nails in and lowered him gently. The Queen's reaction was automatic, defensive. She turned to Àine, Gharne flaring a hood of menace around her head, and only Keith's hand on her sleeve restrained her.

"Carel," he said, and winced.

Carel kept her head down, her eyes on Ian's wound as she stripped off her shirt and packed it. She was wearing another blouse underneath, the straps of the knife sheath stark against her forearm. The silver in the blade would keep the wound from simply closing, and Carel hoped she'd guessed right about how much damage a werewolf could survive.

"Carel?" The Queen's voice had dropped, softened. Carel recognized it: the voice of the woman, not the Queen, unheard in seven years. In another circumstance, she might have found it beautiful.

"It won't kill him," Carel said, hoping she wasn't lying. She flexed her fingers, arched her palm, as if she could scrub away the sensation as of the knife-tip popping plastic wrap. There was almost no blood. "He'll live. Keith—"

"Merlin?"

She smiled at him across the stones, one dragon to another, and saved a tooth for Lucifer. She gestured to the strand across the cobblestones, the space between Àine's galleries, the impassive, waiting angel. "Your battle awaits."

Keith nodded. "Fetch Morgan," he said, and drew his sword from his scabbard. The Queen shied from the sound, the harsh rasp and ring of steel, and Keith let her go, grateful she didn't look at his face. "And, Carel?"

"Dragon Prince?"

He smiled behind his beard before he turned. "I thank you for your betrayal."

"You keep strange company," Whiskey said, as the last swishing horse-tail disappeared under the silver portcullis into the shadow of the gate.

"It's strange to keep company at all, for us." Bunyip hitched himself up the slope, his flukes sliding out of the water. His body rippled with caterpillar muscularity. "I'll be quit of them soon enough; their ambitions are foreign to mine. But we bargain as we must."

Whiskey shifted, ears up, tail bannered to the wind. He had a solid place to stand, and the sea rolled long on either side of him. "Have you come to bargain for your shadow?"

"I've come to take it back," Bunyip replied, and darted forward with a speed impossible to credit.

Quick, but not deft, and the momentum of that slithering, scraping mountain of flesh was not an easy thing to redirect. Whiskey soared into the air, a standing capriole, and let Bunyip's charge carry him underneath. Silver-shod hooves lashed out, but Bunyip rolled and dropped his shoulder, his tusked head twisting to slash. Whiskey's hooves thumped the beach and stones scattered as he whirled.

They faced each other, grinning, each where the other had been. "Whenever you want to start, I'm ready," Whiskey said.

Bunyip thrummed, a deep pleased noise that buzzed the earth against

Whiskey's hooves. He stood up on his tail like a dancing dolphin, tow-ering, awesome, grasping after Whiskey with webbed bear-paws. And Whiskey in turn rose and hurled himself against his enemy, teeth rend-ing, hooves lashing.

They met like storm waves striking, the unyielding impact of moun-tainous waters, and the sea itself rippled with the force. Bunyip's tusks slashed Whiskey's shoulder and glanced away from bone; Whiskey's teeth rent Bunyip's throat where the hide and blubber lay thick. They screamed and hammered each other, red thick blood glossing black hide and staining white, striving chest to chest and eye to eye.

Whiskey fell back and Bunyip humped after him, growling. They cir-cled. Heads slung low, teeth bared, angled to shield throats.

"Cowards fight on land," Whiskey called.

"No one follows *me* into the sea."

"Who said I meant to follow?" Whiskey asked, and hurled himself in Bunyip's face.

Bunyip reared again, clinging, embracing, swaying like a waltzing bear. His claws raked Whiskey's flanks, white skin laid open over red flesh and whiter bone, and Whiskey kicked off, hard, slamming upward under Bunyip's chin, behind his tusks, using his own bony head as a ram. The *crack* of skulls knocked Bunyip's jaw up and Whiskey buried his teeth in the angle of Bunyip's neck, clenched where rending wouldn't help, and *gnawed*.

Bunyip's arms tightened around his chest, squeezing until ribs cracked like green barrel-staves. He grunted at the burrowing pain of Whiskey chewing like a rat. Blood oiled both bodies. Bunyip heaved, his bulk slamming Whiskey's chest. The water-horse trembled under the weight, his hind legs shivering as he shoved, kicked, shoved again. Under the tusks, inside the terrible embrace of those arms.

He did not fail. He pressed up. He fought, each whooping breath a little shallower as Bunyip squeezed him, each exhalation spraying Bun-yip's blood and his own into the air.

Bunyip clutched him tighter, and they toppled into the sea.

Bodies rolled in the shallows, bright and dark, the white foam lath-ered pink among the stones . . . until a wave broke over them, and they slid into the deeps, still striving.

*   *   *

The only brightness in infinite blackness, Lucifer Morningstar bent his head over his folded hands. Angels are not limited in place and time — one presence, one existence. He knew he was approached, but waited for his guest to announce himself.

It was only polite.

Even if it was wasted effort. "Truly, creature," Michael said. "Hast *no* shame?"

:Do the damned not pray?: Lucifer turned to his brother, a monolithic light wrapped in that bony mortal form like a goddess in a paper dress.

"But are they heard? And there's no need for thy thought-games with me, Morningstar. Not when we're alone." As they were: alone indeed. Michael ached with it, in his assumed human heart, in the imagined bones of his human hands.

This is Hell, Marlowe had written. *Nor am I out of it.* And even standing in the courtyard of Faerie, or walking the earth itself, some part of the Devil was never out of Hell.

"Thy pardon," Lucifer answered. His voice was light and sweet, the timbre of violins. It would have driven a man to his knees. "I have not much opportunity."

Michael looked up, the fine lines and hollows of his throat and face shadowed by the light gleaming through his mortal husk. "How dost thou bear it — no, don't answer. I have another question, and better. Dost permit thy servant to challenge me?"

"Tell the truth and shame the Devil," Lucifer said. "Yes."

"It's a kindness."

"How unlike me?" Lucifer smiled.

Michael did not. "Thou'lt not be damned for good works. Always plotting. So tell me; this is thy machination. Why?"

"Why permit Keith to fight thee, angel?"

"Why *arrange* it? *They* may not know. But thou canst hide not the hand behind his choice from an angel. When it was the son, I wasn't certain of thy complicity."

Lucifer shrugged, his wings bellying. "He begged my indulgence. There was no reason to refuse."

"Thou liest."

"I often do."

"What didst thou bargain the Dragon?"

"Her sacrifice the sooner? She's still weak, brother mine. The Prometheans brought her lower than her servants understand. Hast never wondered why she has Merlins and Princes?"

"The stories give her strength," Michael answered. "They give her weight in memory."

"I find," Lucifer said, "that it's always better to master one's own legends. When one can."

"Keith MacNeill still dies damned. Attacking Heaven."

"But he dies alone," the Devil answered. *"He dies alone."*

Michael just stared. Hands in his pockets, glass-green wings folded tight against his shoulders.

"Besides"—Lucifer shrugged—"who's to say the Dragon Prince is a Christian? Surely Valhalla has room for one more—"

"I believe thee not."

"Thou never didst, as I recall." As if by accident, the Devil's wingtip brushed the angel's arm. Michael shivered, but didn't withdraw. Lucifer looked away, up, into the empty blackness then. :Tell me, Michael—as thou knowest mine—tell me, where is His pride? Can He not love those with whom He takes exception? Will He let a Devil love more? Ask Him that, for me.:

Michael curved his wings about him like a shell, like a shroud. "I will ask."

If one must choose, a luxurious prison was preferable to durance vile, if only because it provided room to pace. Autumn watched from the east-facing window until Carel and the rest passed out of sight below, and then she availed herself of that room, stalking back and forth.

No window faced west, into the courtyard, but Autumn heard when the shouting rose, first briefly and then in heartfelt argument. She heard the neighs and the clash of bodies, and *that* battle, she witnessed, her hands tight on the window ledge, her forearm flexing against the warm flat of the knife.

The door lock looked crude, but she couldn't pick it or rattle it open.

There wasn't enough fabric in the bedclothes to braid several stories' worth of rope.

Back and forth, back and forth, until she half thought her best chance of escape was wearing a hole in the floor. An echo reached her: the roar of voices raised together until they no longer sounded like voices at all. She turned, hands spread as if her fingers could grasp her frustration and snap it in half.

The pitcher on the washstand winked at her.

Her palms curved around the smooth, solid weight. She lifted it. Turned it over. Let the water fall, first just a trickle, then a solid stream spattering into the basin. Overflowing the basin. Never ceasing.

The window ledge was midchest height. The hinges were on the outside; the door opened out.

Water weighs more than eight pounds to the gallon.

Autumn left the pitcher overturned, stuffed the crack under the door with the bedclothes, lashed herself to the bed frame with the sheets, and steeled herself to wait.

The Queen and the Merlin sat with two empty chairs between them, in the torch-haunted shadows of a gallery unoccupied except for them and a pensive Morningstar. Carel crouched in her seat, head sunk between hunched shoulders, twisting the tail of her shirt between her hands. Mist had left the Merlin to brood on the scraps of blood on her cuffs and etching half-moons under her nails. The Queen sat chill and proud, her fingers laced and her face still. She stared ahead and did not turn.

On their left and right, the gallery extended, boxes separated from their own by wind-curved tapestries. Below and across, the bleachers teemed with Unseelie, horned and hooved and twisted like tree trunks and harvest dolls, and chipped like ancient flint. Neither woman paid them any heed, even when carelessly managed antlers thumped on the wooden planks below their feet. The Queen's furrowed brow was only for the man and the angel below, and Carel never glanced away from dark and pale Àine, seated opposite, resplendent in queenly violet and green.

She shared *her* box with only one hooded advisor, someone slim and not too tall and wrapped in a red velvet cloak. There were no bleachers beneath her chair. Instead, the Nuckelavee rocked uncomfortably on the beach, brushing sand from its raw limbs with clacking lobster claws.

And Àine's red smile never wavered.

Within the tall wings of the palace, the sea rolled smooth and shining. Ian had been carried within, Gharne hovering beside. The Queen might have been beside him as well, but the Queen had made the Fae choice, not the mortal one, and come to watch her husband die.

The architect of that death sat beside her, and studied the blood under her nails. The babble from the stands drove her mad. She wanted silence, the silence of the graveside, woeful anticipation. Not this festival atmosphere.

It was more than the duel. No matter how Autumn was returned to her—or reclaimed—Àine would not leave this place alive. Carel would leave no stone upon a stone.

There were liberties one did not permit one's enemies, if one wished to walk a free woman again.

The Queen shifted, stern and fair, turning her emerald wedding ring with the nails of her opposite hand. "Carel?"

"Mist demands her sacrifice," Carel said. "My choices aren't mine."

"Ian lives. And what you did will keep me on the throne."

"He does," Carel answered. "It will."

"I have become my mother." The Queen let her hands fall. "She'll rip down a whole world to reclaim me. And I'll—"

Carel leaned across empty chairs and laid her hand on the Queen's thigh. "You'll kill them with your pride."

"Is it pride?"

"Ian's a man," Carel said. It was almost her own voice: someone else spoke through her, but she agreed with the Dragon this time. "He's laid a child of his own in the ground. And you'll sell yourself and cripple those who care for you to bear his burdens for him."

"I gave him back his heart—"

"Then let him use it," Carel said, and squeezed the Queen's leg before she drew back her hand. The Queen's mouth worked, but she never turned.

Down on the sand, Keith MacNeill drew the sword he'd resheathed previously and cut through the torch-bright darkness. Michael watched him, frowning. She seemed very small, wings folded into non-presence, arms folded over her chest. Keith made two of her.

She stood before him, unworried as a swan, and when she unfolded her arms and lifted her hand, it too held a blade. Not the rapier she'd worn in Hell, a frail symbol for a mortal guise, but her *own* sword, a bar of molten light that illuminated the courtyard fiercely, outshining the torches, casting moon-sharp shadows.

She stood unmoving. She did not breathe or blink. But Carel's lips shaped soundless words, though whatever she prayed to did not answer. The Queen seemed not to pray at all, but her hand slipped into her pocket and returned to her lap once more. No marshal took the field. No referee would curb this fight.

As Keith stepped forward, the babble of the crowds hushed for a moment, and then peaked in jeers and shouting. As if she heard nothing, the Queen rose from her chair without unfolding her hands, and stepped to the railing of the gallery. She paused, and did not speak.

The Faerie folk fell silent again, and this time, they stayed silent. And Michael moved, finally, pointing with her chin over Keith's shoulder.

He'd paused when the crowd quieted. Now he turned, slowly, until he faced the gallery. The Queen held out her knotted hands. He came to her, reaching up with his sword, over the heads of the Unseelie on their raked benches. Faeries flinched from his iron gloves, his iron blade.

The Queen leaned down and out, and laid a favor on the flat of the upraised sword. It could have been anything, a scrap of silk, a fresh-cut flower. But what she let fall from her hands, unfurling as it slid down into Keith's hands, was the coiled dark snake of a braid. Keith reached and caught it in a gauntleted hand; it fell over his palm and lay there, limp and soft. "More favor than I deserve, my lady."

"Renounce your challenge," she said. "You're dying for the Devil's honor. I can't think of a stupider thing."

"Elaine," he said. He leaned his sword against his hip, and kissed her braid before knotting it around his arm. "My blood is for buying your freedom. From Prometheus, from Hell, and from the damned Dragon too. It's a gift. Accept it. This is the end of the story now."

"Shove it down my throat, why don't you?" She sat down, lifting her gaze over his head while Àine's creatures hooted in the stands. "Die if you must. But I'll not thank you for it."

"I love you too," he said, and turned away again.

To find himself face-to-face with the archangel, who stood before him having refolded her empty hands. "I will not fight you." She looked away from him, up at the gallery, at Carel and Carel's doubled regard. "Angels do not serve dragons."

Carel fell back against her chair as if something had released her, and let go of a long, sibilant sigh. Keith's fingers gripped his sword. "I'm a danger as long as I live."

"So too is any man."

Keith gestured. "If you don't fight—"

Michael's wings unfolded from her shoulders, fountaining into the night. She turned to the box from which the Queen had remonstrated with Keith, and looked past the Queen and the Merlin to the Devil who folded himself into the shadows behind. He had propped one bootheel on the seat of the chair, and sat with his fingers laced around his knee, beautiful as the failing light of the sun.

"Morningstar, old Snake. Come down."

:I'm quite comfortable, thank you. Do you really mean to refuse my champion?:

"Will you fight me yourself?"

:If *you* won't meet my champion, I don't believe I must. Like Gwenhwyfar's, my innocence is proven in the absence of contenders against it.: Lucifer looked down at his hands, and then, as a motion drew his attention, across the courtyard. Michael followed the flicker of his eyes without physically turning. Àine had risen, her hooded advisor beside her.

Michael sighed. "*He* will not be maneuvered on a technicality. And all you ever had to do was apologize."

"*I'll* fight," Christian said, sliding the red cloak off his shoulders and standing up beside the Unseelie Queen. "But not you, Michael. Or your champion, Morningstar."

:The factions become plain,: Lucifer drawled. He dropped the booted foot to the floor of the gallery and let his hands rest in his lap. When he stood, the incandescence of his wings swept through Carel and the

Queen. He stepped from the lip of the gallery and dropped, landing lightly on the sand. :So it's been your game with Àine all along?:

Christian didn't bother with the theatrics. One moment he stood beside Àine. The next, he stood upon the sand. "I could hardly let you go crawling to Heaven for forgiveness."

:I thought it would be Satan,: Lucifer admitted. He stalked forward, unconcerned. :You've grown more guile than I knew. But I shan't fight you either, Christian. Duels are *boring*. And I am not about to apologize for being what I was made. You may rest in comfort.:

Christian stopped, mouth open, and looked from Lucifer to Michael and back again. For her part, Michael only stared at Lucifer, one eyebrow climbing, and blinked three times before she managed, "You're sincere."

He smiled at her, who would not smile in return. :What did you think?:

"I thought you were Lucifer," she said.

And the castle doors burst off their hinges, swept aside by an unheralded flood.

Matthew dragged himself onto the deck through a mind-altering haze of pain. His left shoulder felt like twisted cable, and the gauze over Fortitude's carved face was soaked, sliding wet and sticky on his skin. He'd broken the scabs, and whatever muscles tore or stretched when he caught at the decking were stiffening now. His right knee bulged against the inside of his jeans. It would be a long time before he ran again.

Halos and flickers of darkness teased his vision. He sprawled on his back, staring up at the rose-colored sky, and watched comets and wreaths of light hurtle through his field of vision like falling angels. Wings, the taste of ink.

The whole undead fleet held its breath. He could touch them all, the ships of war and the ships of commerce, each a shadow imprinting the pained light of his consciousness, bending the membrane of awareness. His power lingered, still unmasterable. Beautiful and useless, unless he wanted to indiscriminately fry the laptops and pacemakers of hapless students and passersby. In a moment of ire, he let it roll out and heard the glass of somebody's wristwatch crack before Jane gasped.

All that strength, and no way to use it to fight. Jane's trick with the decking was like juggling ice when Matthew tried it. The scar across his right hand flared when he tried again. Another hurt. Just one more hurt. You'd hardly think he'd notice.

Don heard Matthew grunt in pain a second after Jane yelped and grabbed her wrist, and the flashlight Felix trained gingerly through the hole in the decking popped like an old-fashioned flashbulb. *Don* hadn't been looking at the light, but listening, eyes on the dark receding sea, hoping Matthew hadn't impaled himself on anything when he fell.

He moved faster than Felix, and definitely faster than Jane. She must have heard it, because she stepped around Felix and headed for the prow, hopping and scrambling over jumbled debris. Don just ran, rust and ruin cracking under his boots, his longer legs an advantage. Matthew was visible as soon as he came around the superstructure, his coat a bloody stain. Don squatted beside him, grabbed his wrist, heard him groan again.

"Shoulder," Matthew said. "Tore my knee."

Don slid under his right arm, which seemed unhurt, and took his weight on that side. Matthew was helping, at least, and seemed clear-headed, though his voice was clipped and sharp with hurt and he slumped against Don, hard, his eyes squinted shut and his head dropped forward, toward his chest.

"Are you all right?" Don asked. "Are you okay?"

Stupid question. All he had.

"When she kills me," Matthew said, picking his chin up, "give her what she wants. She'll take you back. That's the point of this exercise."

"Matthew—"

"The city needs you," Matthew said. "Cop who can talk to Faeries. Cop who's a Mage. Used to be Magi everywhere, keeping things together. If we had that—"

Don swallowed. He could see it. "Jane's crazy. You want—"

Matthew grinned at him, eyes glittering behind glasses that had miraculously stayed stuck to his nose, though they were spattered with muck and rusty water. "Jane's crazy. You're not."

"Matthew," Jane said, drawing up some twenty feet away, beside the battered superstructure, "yield."

"Let's talk," he said. He pushed Don away. Don gave him a look, and went, reluctantly, three steps. Watching Matthew, not watching Jane. "The question is, do you have the guts to do it?"

"Do what?"

Matthew balanced on one leg, not daring to put any weight on the right one. The pain was nauseating. "Felix has a gun. Ask him for it."

She glanced at Felix. The soft light eased her face, made her look startled and a little bit young.

"I always carry one in America," Felix said. "You have to kill him, Jane."

Her gesture swept Matthew aside, and Felix's protestations. "He's finished."

"He didn't yield." Neither did Felix, even when Jane swung her glare around like a torch. She might need coaxing, but this was a ritual. If Matthew didn't surrender and Jane didn't end things, she was not anointed. No one stayed archmage on a draw.

But she stared at him, frowning. "Felix, to think I ever suspected that I might have been wrong about you."

Maybe it was the scorn in her voice, her masks forgotten for a moment. Maybe it was the plain, frustrated necessity. But Felix's hand dropped into his pocket, and came back with a snub-nosed Belgian semiautomatic. He stepped away from Jane, and raised the little gun.

Matthew wobbled. He spread his arms, for balance as much as in surrender. "Oh, for Christ's sake, Felix. You make me tired."

"Wanker," Felix said, and squeezed three times fast.

Matthew didn't expect it to hurt. Perhaps an impact, a blow like a kick in the chest. But Don was there, stepping in front of him, a bulky shadow as the shots echoed like handclaps over the water and slammed into his chest. He was knocked back, staggered—*bang, bang. Bang.* One step. Two.

Felix swore and shifted his aim, the barrel of the little automatic centered between Matthew's eyes. Matthew stepped forward before he remembered he couldn't. The right knee wouldn't hold him. It knuckled over, slid, squished horribly, and failed. He might have caught himself, a wobbling, hopping hitch, but the metal was slick from the snow.

The gun tracked him down.

He fell and hit the deck sliding, crying out, expecting Don to land on top of him. Bleeding. Dying, probably.

The bullets punched through Don's coat and shirt and struck his vest like so many hammerblows. It knocked the wind out of him, but he was a big man and Felix only had a little gun. He lunged for his weapon, hand across his chest. He wouldn't be fast enough, and he couldn't get in the way of Felix's shot again, not with Matthew on the ground.

Something hit Felix from the side, a flurry of black and silver wings, the weight and momentum of the bird knocking the gun off-line, spinning Felix half around, though he kept the weapon and kept his feet. The fourth bullet smoked a hole in Donall's sleeve.

The fifth one missed him cleanly.

Don flinched, leveled his gun, and returned fire as coolly as if he shot men every day. Two bullets, center of mass.

The black bird vanished over the starboard gunwale. Felix went down like somebody had jerked the rug from under his feet. And Don, wincing, turned the weapon on Jane. "Let's just take the end of this as read, okay?"

Silently, she raised her hands.

"Don't shoot her," Matthew said, a gasp between gritted teeth. "It invalidates the forms."

Don nodded. "I don't usually shoot people who aren't shooting back." The semiautomatic wavered, but he nodded toward Felix. "Man, that is going to be *hard* to explain."

"I'll handle it," Jane said. "Now put the gun away, Don. Matthew and I have business to finish."

He would have. The urge to obedience was automatic. But some of what Matthew had told him stuck. *Just oxytocin,* so he steadied his hand on the grips. "Matthew?"

"That's fine, Don," he said. "Did you see what hit Felix?"

"Looked like, I dunno . . . a black swan. Do swans come black?"

"See if he's breathing and call him a chopper, would you?"

"How much you bet I cannot get a cell signal?" But Don pulled his coat open, bruised chest muscles protesting lateral movement, and holstered his gun. "Can you stand on your own?"

Matthew pushed himself to his left knee. He looked at Jane, not Donall. "Do I have to?"

"Matthew. Don't do this."

"Stop me," he said. And stood.

No sorcery to it. One foot down, balanced by his fingertips and then his own tired strength. He stood on one leg, the old ship restless under his boot, the snow frosting his hair. Raw air chapped his cheeks under the grit of silt and rusty moisture. He slid his fingers into his pocket, found wet iron, closed his left hand.

"You can't hurt me," Jane said.

"No," Matthew answered. He smiled, and found the strength, and slipped it around her like a warm fur coat, before she even felt him coming. "Come here, Jane."

And she answered. He could not go to her, and so she came to him. One step, and then two, as if conquering her own fear in the face of temptation. Shaking, she paused in front of him, and reached out to brush one palm down the rusty sleeve of his magic coat. "I always liked that jacket."

"So did Felix."

"Liking isn't the same as coveting. Exactly." She smiled, and leaned on him. It would have been nice to earn that smile. Nice to feel the trust, the partnership, the old friendship they had had. Nice to smile back, reach out and take her hand.

Dammit. He had *liked* Jane Andraste.

The power sang across his nerves like a bow on fiddle strings. He understood it now, the cage she'd hung on him, and in the pain of his knee and the pain of the lion sliced into his shoulder and the numbness of his right hand, he found an answer.

Not the Dragon's answer.

His own.

"Jane," he said, "hold out your hands."

And still grinning at him, still sure she was winning, she did it, and held perfectly still, smiling like a bride, while he slid ten iron rings on her fingers, and bound each one—and all her power—tight.

Wingbeats drew Matthew's and Don's attention. Two more swans sailed overhead, as if following the first one.

And one of these was black, and one was white.

❖   ❖   ❖

Autumn hadn't begun to worry until the water reached her chest. The room filled faster than she'd anticipated, as if the pitcher had a sense of the needful volume.

The open window would keep her own escape attempt from drowning her and she'd lashed herself to the heavy bed. The weight of the tall canopy vanishing into shadows kept it from floating off the floor even when the feather bed she'd clambered onto waterlogged and squished under her feet.

The flaw in her plan was revealed when the door lock creaked under the water's weight, but did not give. The lock was too strong, and the water kept rising beyond the point when it should have been plunging from the window, rolling in a cataract down the tower wall. Water surged against her. Not just rising, swirling—but lapping back and forth, slopping from wall to wall. Waves—they *were* waves—rocked her, slapped her thighs and stomach, rising past the window ledge, climbing her hips and chest. Spray struck her face, and she tasted salt. She spat, clearing her mouth.

Not fresh water for drinking or bathing, but the harsh metal of seawater. She choked on the pungency as it rose across the open window and did not fall.

Every lap of the waves bulged the door against its frame and knocked Autumn against the bedpost. She clutched the thigh-thick column and clung, though now the sea in her mouth tasted of blood and she'd split her cheek and cracked a tooth into pulpy agony.

Wood creaked, cracked, did not shatter. The smack and splinter of spray stung her face, filled her nose, salt in her throat constricting delicate tissues. The weight of the water shifted around her like a living creature, broke over her head. She came up spluttering, deafened by the impact. Something brushed her, moving in the water, a hard knock like a shark bumping its prey.

And then one great undertow hauled and twisted, bruised flesh slammed against the tight-wound sheets until linen threads snapped and her fingers slipped on the wet, swollen wood. The door banged against its frame one more time, and the whole great tower groaned. She imagined fine rock dust worn between the cracks in the mortared stones, and almost felt it sway.

The lock shattered the frame.

Water flooded the spiral stair floor to head height, pouring from the tower room as endlessly as it had from the pitcher. Like a cataract over a spillway, the water slammed around curves, thundering, tumbling. Water without end, yanking Autumn against the sheets, shredding her clothes and tangling her hair and breaking open swollen flesh. Her nails split on wood. The massive bed creaked and shifted under her, scraped across the floor, grinding toward the wall.

The water was gone.

A white horse stood, splotched black on his face and chest, streaked red from terrible wounds on his neck and shoulders and flanks, hung with sea wrack and draggled with salt water, in the center of the tower prison. "Merlin sends her regards," he said in a clear human voice. "May I suggest you flee?"

He spun on his haunches and charged for the broken door before Autumn could answer, leaving her alone to struggle from her improvised ropes.

Whiskey followed the escaped water down the stair, his shoes ringing like an avalanche of silver coins, the beat syncopated by an injured foreleg. He crashed into the courtyard in the midst of the wave that sucked the ankles of the Fae on the bleachers and broke in a great cresting wall over the angels—fallen and otherwise—and the Dragon Prince left standing on the sand.

It could have knocked them aside, driven them into the sea. Instead, Lucifer gestured and it shattered against them as if on pillars of stone. Water swirled over their heads in jadelike colors, green and mauve and violet, netted white with foam.

Whiskey skidded to a halt on cobbles, pearls as big as a woman's fist peeling under his scraping hooves. His mane hung matted across his face, his right foreleg almost dragging. It would support his weight, but little more; the muscle was scored at the shoulder and every movement was like a brand pressed to his flesh. The confined tsunami drained quickly, trickling between cobbles and eroding lightning tracks across the sand.

Whiskey confronted three dripping angels and a Dragon Prince with seaweed in his hair, and managed not to fall. Or fall over laughing. Lucifer, in particular, with the vanes of his feathers soaked and spiked against the shafts and his hair shocked into tight coils dripping across his face, was not the sort of sight one expected to behold twice in a lifetime.

The Devil lifted one hand, and examined the soggy lace at his cuff. :Whiskey,: he said.

Whiskey huffed, ears pricked. "I don't suppose something sort of half elephant seal and half grizzly bear came through here?"

The Bunyip hit him from the left side, a thunderous wave that knocked him onto his bad leg and sent him rolling into the bleachers, scattering and crushing Unseelie courtiers. He let go of the equine form, let it slip into water, and fought current with countercurrent, eddy and whirl, patterns of direction and misdirection and sheer blunt force as they slammed each other this way and that.

As the Bunyip struck, Lucifer took Keith by the shoulder, and relocated them both—dry, and perfectly clean—to the gallery, out of the way of the war underway on the sand. The sea raged below, a black head or a white one every so often emerging from the vortexes and breakers, as Unseelie dragged each other clear. At the top of the courtyard, away from the water, the horses screamed, while Michael rose straight up on slowly beating wings. And Christian relocated himself as easily as before, regaining his place at Àine's side.

She turned to him with a little smile as the slap of hard water shook the box under their feet. "Do you see a reason not to assist our ally?"

"The time for subtlety is past," he said, and shrugged. "By all means, do your worst. They'll bring the walls down in a minute if you let them, anyway."

Àine leaned over the rail of the gallery, a few drops of spray jeweling the sweep of her long dark hair. "Nuckelavee," she said, "kill the Kelpie."

It glared at her from both distorted heads, and stumped forward on its seaweed-shaggy limbs. The sea rose within the confines of the courtyard, and Unseelie continued to teleport, fly, and shamble for higher ground while their Queen watched, unconcerned.

Unlike Whiskey and Bunyip, Nuckelavee did not crash into the waves as part of the water itself. Instead, it waded into the surf and the ocean began to drain away. Nuckelavee lurched through the troughs and caps and wiped them away with sweeps of its chitinous claws, until the castle trembled with the impact of giant bodies striking one another.

Bunyip bled from gaping wounds, runnels of blood soaking the hide, filming the shining claws. Blubber gleamed like wax in the depths of the slashes and cuts, but the injuries were nothing to Whiskey's. The wounded leg was broken now, his muzzle torn from one nostril almost to the opposite eye, showing teeth through the gash in his lip. He limped on three legs, bleeding until the pearly cobblestones gleamed crimson, badly enough hurt that he was reduced to backing away, keeping distance, acquiring new injuries every time the Bunyip lunged. And now Nuckelavee circled from the other direction, penning Whiskey into an ever-smaller range of motion with each dragging step.

The Queen's hands tightened on the gilt arms of her chair. Keith, behind her, squeezed her shoulder just as hard. She lifted her hand as if to brush his off, and grabbed the fingers instead. "Help him," she said.

Not to Keith. To Carel.

And Carel shook her head. "I am not permitted."

"Your damned Dragon," the Queen said. "What good is she?"

In the courtyard below, Nuckelavee grasped after Whiskey. Whiskey avoided the clutch of ragged claws, but not the rake. Another slash marked his hide, parting skin and flesh to bare bone near his spine. He screamed and lashed out, a savage hind hoof spilling putrescence down Nuckelavee's gut. The blow wasn't hard enough; Whiskey could only ground one forehoof to kick. Keith reached for *his* sword, and Carel clutched his wrist.

"He can serve the Queen," Carel said, pitiless, "or he can serve the sea."

The combat became an untrackable whirl, claws and hooves and flashing teeth. Bunyip struck Whiskey a glancing blow with one ponderous claw, knocking the water-horse end over end. Whiskey rolled, sprawled, and heaved himself up without pause. His head hung low on his powerful neck. He wobbled, scrabbled, found his purchase and his balance—and went down again, with no sound but a grunt, breaking his knee open on the stone.

"He'll die for your pride, Elaine."

The Queen's nails parted the skin of Keith's hand. "I take it back," she said. She shoved Keith's hand off and stood. "Whiskey," she called, as the black beast and the red one closed on him from opposite sides, "give me back my name!"

The wide world crystallized. Whiskey heard her through the pain, through the dull distraction of injury. The sea rushed into him, the dam that had held it back for seven years gone in the space of a few words. Savage power filled him, flooded him until he brimmed, salt water pricking from the cobbles under his knee, puddling and coursing down to the ocean below.

A broken arm is less than a broken leg. He folded into another shape and stood, water dripping down the backs of bony hands, over thick nails, water plastering his clothes to his lanky body as he braced his feet and grinned, pulling his split lip wide. Nuckelavee and Bunyip towered over him now, but he'd meet them on his feet.

The blade at his belt came with the human seeming. It was short, eight inches, no more. But it was better than nothing, and comfortable to wield one-handed.

The moon was high. He was himself again; cold joy drenched him in a lucid cataract. And there were only two of them.

He slid the knife free and waited for the enemies to come.

"Want your shadow, Bunyip?" he asked. "What will you give to have it back?"

"I'll take it when I've killed you," the Bunyip answered.

He pounced, a rippling arc of muscle. But Whiskey was no longer where he had been standing when the Bunyip landed. He dove for the Nuckelavee, rolled between its knees when it clacked and hopped after him, and cried out when his broken arm and slashed shoulder struck the cobbles. Still he rolled and kept rolling, the momentum enough to find his feet, and threw himself at the creature's festering back.

The knife bit deep, suck of flesh and scrape of bone, and Nuckelavee gave a thin bubbling scream. Whiplash as it twisted threw Whiskey onto the stones. The knife and his breath were knocked from him; he pushed himself up and fell back, gasping, as a massive shape undulated toward him.

One enemy down.

Bunyip was coming.

One enemy down, and Whiskey down as well.

In the guttering torchlight, he first thought he saw only shadows. But then there were feathers, three swans descending, one white and two black. They came down like a gentling hand, their bodies rising and falling between their wings, their necks stretched, bugling their unpleasing whistle.

The white swan stood, unfolding into a frail human form, her cloak blurring from her hands as she swirled it over her head and cast it like a net across the shoulders of the other two. They did not rise, one huddled inside the embrace of the other, an ash-colored head bent over one whose locks caught unnatural violet accents in the firelight.

Kit shielded Lily against his chest.

She fisted both hands in Fionnghuala's cloak, as the swanmay stood, naked and defiant, behind them, no less stern and wonderful for the marks of age stretching her softened flesh. She reached down and laid her hand on the nape of Kit's neck, and Kit ducked his head, pressed his lips against Lily's ear, and whispered something through her hair.

"Garndukgu-Wurrpbu," Lily said, her voice rasping as if her throat were raw, her pronunciation eerily perfect on the very first try. Better than Kit's, which was just good enough.

Bunyip flinched, and kept coming. Behind him, the Nuckelavee went to its knees, crawling toward the sea, its horse-head leaving streaked, hideous strings of mucus on the cobblestones as it was dragged.

Àine shouted to him to turn back to the attack, hauling with the reins of her power. He tried, as he had no choice, and crashed to his belly on the stones.

"Again!" Kit steadied Lily's shaking shoulders. *"Mean it."*

She gasped and crowded against him. He leaned his forehead against her shoulder, as if willing her to understand. Willing her to read it in her gift, in her bones. "Christian took his magic back," she said, and Bunyip glided closer.

"Use you your own. Garndukgu-Wurrpbu," he chanted. He squeezed her, shook her, the velvet of her borrowed doublet denting under his palms. She jerked again, trying to squirm away from the monster. "Garndukgu-Wurrpbu!"

"Garndukgu-Wurrpbu," she answered. A croak. Kit got his fingers under her arms, lifted, pulled her up. Fionnghuala stood behind them, holding her cloak over their shoulders, shielding them with her wings. "Garndukgu-Wurrpbu!" Lily shouted. She coughed, a hand pressed to her throat. Kit echoed, called again, remembering the Bunyip's mockery of his own small power.

"Shout it, sorceress," he said. *"Push him back."*

His touch was unlike Christian's. Hard, a little painful, each finger indenting her flesh. He wasn't any taller than she was, and he wasn't any stronger. And he was there, right there with her, holding her up, facing the monster anyway.

If he could do it, she could do it too.

"Garndukgu-Wurrpbu!" she yelled, and *pushed*.

And felt something pushing back. Something yielding, but massive, unmovable, implacable. Sliding, as if she buried both hands in a mountainous water balloon and tried to shove it off her face. It slopped over her, slid away when she tried to contain it. She spread her hands out, using the name like a whip, like a plow blade, to sting and shove. She leaned harder. It would roll over her. She would drown. It would crush her, and there was nobody to save her, nobody to charge to the rescue.

But there was Kit, pushing beside her, pushing as hard as he could. She could push harder than Kit. She could push harder than Fionnghuala, than Whiskey who crawled up on her left side and dragged himself to his knees, slipping something black and soft as gauzy silk into her hand.

She was the rescue now.

When it gave, it gave like punching through a wall of glass. A sudden crack, a sensation like sharpness, like shattering. And then she was up to her elbows in cold like ice water and the Bunyip was slumped before her, and Kit had his fingers laced through her hands, dragging them to her head, urging, "Knot your hair, Lily. Lily, knot your hair."

Chapter Twenty-nine
Once Upon a Time in New York City

Christian vanished before Kit even let go of Lily's hands, and Michael drifted to earth beside them a moment later, quietly ridiculous with Matthew borne in her arms as if he weighed nothing at all.

Don had stayed behind to manage Jane and explain the body and the motorboat to the authorities.

Kit shrugged Fionnghuala's cloak off his shoulders, half fearing he'd fall back into a swan's shape as he did. But he stayed a man, and stood savoring free air for a moment before he wrapped the naked swanmay in her feathers.

The feathers shed all around them. He winced and caught a handful before they could fall. They crumbled into shadows in his hand. Fionnghuala tugged the cloak around her shoulders. "Magic well-spent," she said, when Kit frowned.

Lily was stroking the cobweb fabric. "What's this?"

"Bunyip's shadow," Whiskey told her. He sat cross-legged on the stones. "A little bit of insurance, sorceress. He'll try to kill you again now that you've bound him. It'll pay to have the strength to deal with it."

"Bound him?"

"What do you think this was?"

"Like a slave."

"Like a slave," Whiskey said. He shuddered as he pushed himself to his feet. Lily got a grip on his unwounded biceps and hauled, the shadow fluttering between her fingers. When he stood without wobbling, she twined her fingers through the shadow and held it to the light. Torchlight wouldn't shine through it, for all its transparency. "Exactly like."

"I don't want—" She licked her lips. "If I let him go he'll kill me," she said, understanding the ice in Whiskey's pale blue gaze.

"Give me the shadow," he said. "I'll bargain for you."

"Can I trust *you*?"

He stroked her arm with the back of his hand. His wounds were already sealing. "Never."

She held out the bit of cobweb. "Isn't it yours?"

He winked, and turned away. Limping heavily, he walked to where Bunyip lay, heaving, on the stones.

Lily was vaguely aware that, across the courtyard, Carel had broken away from Keith and Elaine and was running from the gallery to the stair, where Autumn—battered and bruise-cheeked—had appeared, holding herself up half by her grip on the doorframe. Lily turned back to Fionnghuala, Kit, and Matthew.

She heard a glad cry. It ached more than it soothed.

Michael had laid the Mage on the stones and stood back, arms folded over her narrow chest.

"Thanks for the help," Matthew said to Kit, and Kit swept a somewhat unsteady bow. Fionnghuala crouched beside the Mage, a knife in her hand, slicing Matthew's filthy jeans open from thigh to ankle along the seam. "This is bad," she said. She dusted more feathers from his leg, from her shoulders, from her hair. "I can't heal it now."

"No," he said. He brushed aside a few feathers himself, rubbing his fingers together, as if bemused. "I see that. But there's always the emergency room."

"She cured Lily," Kit said. "Lily was dying."

"Cured?" Lily looked at them both, then down at her hands. She came to squat beside them.

"Unicorn's horn," Fionnghuala said. "Cures what ails you."

"But I'm—"

Fionnghuala laid her hands on Lily's cheeks and kissed her. "As someone once said, 'I am that I am.' You won't die now. What you make of the rest of it is your own choice."

Kit coughed. Matthew blinked, then winced as Fionnghuala laid a cool palm on his skin. "Ow."

She frowned. "Doctor."

"Morgan," Kit said, and gestured toward the inland end of the courtyard, where the witch stood framed against the darkness of the front gate, her wolfhounds at her side.

Fionnghuala stood. " 'Twill serve, though this shall need surgery. And now excuse me. I have a devil with whom to deal."

Carel led Autumn to the corner by the well, and Autumn let her do it. Shaking, leaning hard on the Merlin as the Merlin curled an arm around her shoulders, she squeezed her over and over again and brushed her fingers across her face.

As for Carel, she sat Autumn down on the bench beside the well cover and touched all of Autumn's wounds, silently, wincing more than Autumn. "I think you'll be okay," she said, finally. "You'll need a dentist. Have you touched food or drink?"

Autumn shook her head, and Carel turned to draw water. "I'll make you some safe." What was the point in being Merlin, otherwise?

"Rumpelstiltskin?" Autumn asked, as Carel brought her the dipper from the bucket.

"I found him," Carel said. "He was under the wine rack. He's safe."

"Gypsy?"

Carel shook her head as Autumn cupped her hands around the dipper to hold it steady, drinking with lowered eyes. "I didn't think so," she said. She sobbed, once, tightly, her hands whitening on the ladle before Carel pulled it back, and bent forward between her knees. "There's a fish in the well."

Carel turned to look: a carp, red-flecked and golden, with black freckles on its back. It hung in the water, fanning slowly, staring up at her with bubble eyes. She knew its expression. "Cairbre?"

It bobbed in the water, up and down. The Merlin dropped to her knees beside the well, and reached down, her brown wrists encompassing the fish as it swam between them. She scooped it up, and drew it out of the water, her fingers slipping into its gills and holding it tight as it twisted.

She hauled it up into the light of the torches. "Give me a reason not to kill you."

Helpless, it flopped, gasping. It had been expecting rescue. Carel stared at it while its struggles grew more frantic. "You won." Scales gritted her fingers, slick with slime. "Ian's King. Elaine is free."

The carp stilled, hanging heavily in her hands, a heavy muscled cylinder. It gaped, glossy eyes darkening, and waited.

"Stay a fish," she said, and dropped it into the water.

Autumn reached out and touched her shoulder. "Carel?"

"I can't promise it won't happen again," Carel said. "I can't keep you safe. I wouldn't blame you."

Autumn's lips thinned. She shook her head. "I'm tired of falling out of love," she said, and slid her hand down the Merlin's arm to squeeze her fingers.

Morgan saw to Ian first, and Carel, Keith, and Elaine left her alone to do it. As for *them*, once Carel had assured herself that Autumn was likely to live, *they* found Àine on the battlements, the wind and the rising sun limning graceful limbs through her robes. Her hair lashed and flew around her, and she waited with folded hands.

"You're not Queen anymore," Àine said. She glanced from Keith to Carel. "The Devil's left me to pay the piper."

"So he has," Elaine said. She glanced at Keith. He folded a hand around the hilt of his sword, and slid it free, frowning.

Àine drew a breath, and closed her eyes. Keith looked from his wife to the Merlin.

"*This* is how the story ends," Carel said.

And so it did, for Àine.

:What is it that you seek, Fionnghuala?:

She paused beside, and a little behind, the Morningstar. He slouched on a stool in the gallery, legs akimbo, wings half extended, fanning on the morning breeze.

"You," she said, and came to stand beside him, holding her cloak closed, one-handed, across her breast.

:He should have loved me first and best, as I loved Him.:

"Are you so sure He didn't?"

:What do you want?:

She smiled without looking to see if he noticed. "To do the Christian thing."

:He won't forgive me. Even should I ask.:

"That's the sin of hubris, you know. And the sin of despair. The same ones that got Judas. *I* forgive everyone who wants forgiveness, and anyway, don't think I didn't notice you pulling threads to free Keith MacNeill from his doom, *Morningstar*."

He had no answer.

"And if I forgive you"—she ran her fingertips along his jaw—"*He* doesn't have to. That's what it is to be a trinity."

:You,: he said, his wings arching up behind his shoulders so the harsh rasp of feathers underscored his words. :But—:

"It never occurred to you that the teind is an echo of martyrdom, and martyrdom an echo of sacrifice? That they're all the same story? Never, Prince of Stories?"

:Prince of Lies,: he corrected.

"Lies are stories."

He closed his eyes. :*Batter my heart, three-person'd God*—:

"Christ," she answered, and folded him in her arms. "Not that damned thing. Come and be forgiven, child."

Whiskey found Elaine alone, finally, when she had left Carel and Autumn together and Keith beside their son's sickbed. She walked along the rocky strand. Whiskey cantered up beside her on three legs. He touched her not, nor spoke her name.

"I am leaving."

She stopped, her hands shoved in her pockets, dressed as Morgan would in blue jeans and a sweater, her cropped hair riffling over her eyes. Her sleeves were pushed up. White scars laced her arms, and the emeralds on her left hand winked when she pulled them into the sun.

Her footprints traced the water's edge, but stopped short of where the waves began. "I know," she answered. "I'm sorry."

He lowered his head, flattened his neck, shook out his white and black streaked raw-silk mane so the sea breeze lifted and tossed it. "Elaine," he said.

She bit her lip. "Uisgebaugh."

Head up, ears pricked. Too much pride to show pain as he pranced — bare-hooved, three-legged — over the stones. His shoulder was barely crusted and other wounds still bled. They'd heal. One more scar, out of Faerie. "One last ride?"

Her lips were wet when she smiled, and the salt wasn't all from the sea. "Will you drown me?"

He tossed his mane, flagged his tail, let the wind stream them wild. "Who knows?"

"Hold still," she said, and grabbed a double fistful of mane, hopping and hauling until she could sling her leg over his naked back.

Lily came to Matthew when Morgan was done with him, and offered her shoulder to lean on. She snugged under his arm, helping take his weight as he balanced on the splinted knee. "Morgan wants me to be her apprentice," she said as she led him out into the sun. "Although I'm going to get my cat first. At least he's black."

Matthew laughed.

She squeezed him. "What are *you* going to do now?"

"I'm going home to Gotham. I can't help it. I belong in that goddamned town." He paused and stole a sidelong, lip-bitten glance. "Prometheus would take you, if you wanted something else. It's just me and Donall now. And Kit. And those kids of Jane's, if they bother to come back."

She squeezed his waist once, quick. "I hope we'll see you in Faerie. *Archmage.* Since you've friends here. And all."

"I don't know. I've got . . . well. Maybe we shouldn't call it Prometheus anymore. Considering — "

"Fionnghuala told you too."

"Fionnghuala told me *first*." He stuck his tongue out.

She laughed, and pointed. "Shall we sit there?"

"It's not too bright for you?"

"I like the sun." She sighed. "I wonder if she's told Kit yet. What will we do for fun without him?"

"Kit?"

"Lucifer."

The stone bench warmed sore muscles. He sank down sighing. "We'll think of something. Hell is full of devils, after all."

"Don't remind me," she said. His leg stuck straight out before him. She took it gently, supporting the knee, and eased it into a more comfortable position. When she looked up into his face, she smiled at him from a distance of a few inches.

He smelled like rust and sweat and blood and dead things. She wrinkled her nose, and kissed him anyway, because she wanted to. Softly, on the mouth, the unicorn-healed scar of the caduceus across her lips rough and tender.

He licked his mouth when she leaned back. "You realize, of course, that I'm far too old for you."

"Please," she said. "What are you, really? Like, twelve? Sticking your tongue out at strange women? Besides, I like boys with glasses. And I'm not like other girls."

Matthew grinned at her. "I'm told I don't know much about them, anyway. Hello, Kit."

"I'll return," Kit said, pausing so his shadow blocked the sun. "If I'm interrupting."

"No," Lily said. "Keep him company. I'm going to find him a drink. And you too."

"And thee," Kit said, and brushed her arm with fingers like trailing feathers when she slid past.

They traded a secretive smile, provoking Matthew to laughter. "Will you flirt with anything?"

"As long as it flirts back." Kit settled beside him, so he wouldn't have to look into the light to talk. "Morgan says Ian will recover. And be King."

"A relief to all concerned, I imagine."

Kit glanced sideways, his mouth pulling down. "Such irony."

"A little." Matthew closed his eyes, the better to appreciate the grace notes in the symphony of throbs and aches echoing through his body. "You know what *really* sucks?"

Kit bumped Matthew with his shoulder, the way, once upon a time, he might have nudged another friend. "What?"

"Felix was right. It's *not* fair. He wanted the talent. It should have been his. Not Geoff's. Not mine."

Kit sighed. "The man who put a knife in my eye was no poet, Matthew Magus, nor ever wanted to be."

Matthew's head rocked in time to a silent, disbelieving laugh. "And you're going to sit there and tell me you didn't earn that bit of double-dealing, Christopher Marlowe?"

"No," Kit said. "But know you this . . ."

"What?"

The poet smiled as he stood. It wasn't pretty. He patted Matthew's uninjured shoulder before he moved away. "When you're moved to count Felix's ambitions forgivable, remember: I never put a knife in *Will's* back."

Kit came up behind her, ran a touch up her spine from the small of her back, laced his fingers through her hair. She leaned into his touch, one hand spread wide on the shattered wooden doorframe of the ruined tower prison. "I forgive thee all thy cruelties," he whispered, through her hair, against her ear, as he had whispered to Lily so very recently.

Morgan shivered, from his breath or from the words, he didn't know. "Thou mean'st it not."

"But I do." He turned her face between his hands, one gentle on her cheek, the other grasping hard, and brushed his lips across her face. "Because I remember now. Things I never remembered before. This story, that story, all of them different. Every one contradicting the others. I used to know history. Now I don't even know my own, who I was, who I loved, how I lived—"

"It's all true."

"It's all lies."

"False things are true," she answered, and tugged restlessly against his grip on her hair. He opened his hand and let her go. "What color is my hair?"

"Black," he said, combing the strawberry locks through his fingers. "Black as sin, black as sorcery, and shot through with silver like moon-lit spiderwebs."

"But it's always been red."

"Yes," he said. "I remember. I could end up like the Devil, all my stories at war."

"You won't. You're one of us now. Among the legends."

"What was it like to change?" he asked. "Do you remember it? When you were just a woman?"

"No," she said. "But I was born a story. You were born a man. You'll manage."

"You sound certain."

She smiled and turned to kiss his palm. "I haven't failed a student yet. Choose your story, Kit."

"Which? The stories choose us, not the other way round."

"Ah," Morgan said. "You know, that's where you're wrong. Still, where there's life there's hope. And I hear these days they're changing stories all the time."

She shook her hair free and stepped back, but she never stopped smiling. Even when he went to seek the Devil.

Who waited for him atop the wall, not far from a sulking angel. "I hoped you would wait," Kit said.

:I hoped you would come. How does it feel to win?:

Kit snorted. He laid his hands on the battlements and rubbed his palms over white stone. He should say something cutting, rough as those sun-warmed rocks. "Win?"

:The long-term goal of the Prometheus Club, in the honest analysis, has been to remake God, whatever lies they have offered over the years. You've lain in wait four hundred years, sweet Christofer. Your opportunity presents.:

"The Devil speaks of truth?" And there was the old Kit, acerbic, mocking. But his heart wasn't in it.

:You remade the Devil in your own image. How much more awful the task of God? You've *your* absolution still to earn.:

"I thought I'd just live forever." Kit looked down at the one iron ring on his hand. "Tell me about Christian."

:What is there to tell?: the Devil asked, and Kit nudged him with an elbow.

:Christian likes his chaos and hates his God. He enjoys playing his brothers against each other. He'd be loath to see Satan unite the Hells and reign, and he'd hate to see me escape them. And then there was the opportunity to cause trouble in the mortal realm, cadge a soul or two. Such things matter to him.:

"And not to you?"

Lucifer laughed.

"Art finished plotting, Morningstar?" Acerbic, the voice of an angel, resonant and true. Michael's face was twisted around the smile she forced, unpracticed. She rustled, and folded her wings. "Art ready to go home?"

:Never done plotting,: Lucifer answered. His wing cupped Kit's shoulder briefly, a fleeting warmth, replaced by the chill draft of the lonely sea below as it flickered away once more. :And never more ready to go home. Never fear, brother — there are stories that end differently. Thou wilt not go unemployed for long.:

"I never liked thee," Michael said, as they ascended.

And they all lived, ever after.

About the Author

Originally from Vermont and Connecticut, **Elizabeth Bear** spent six years in the Mojave Desert and currently lives in southern New England. She attended the University of Connecticut, where she studied anthropology and literature. She was awarded the 2005 Campbell Award for Best New Writer.